# The Marriage Maneuver

ANNELIESE DALABA

# The Marriage Maneuver


Published by Vellichor Publishing, LLC
DeWitt, Michigan 48820
www.vellichorpublishing.com

ISBN: 9781730763922



Cover Design: SelfPubBookCovers.com/RLSathe

Scripture quotations taken from *The Holy Bible*, the King James Version.

William Wilberforce quotes used by permission from
Christian History Magazine Editorial Staff, Galli, Mark, Ed., Olsen, Ted, Ed.
*131 Christians Everyone Should Know*. Nashville: B&H Publishing Group, 2000

# Acknowledgments

Special thanks to my editors, Janet Blakely and Amanda Ghanbarpour. They help make me a better writer. I greatly appreciate all the time they invested in this novel.

I also want to thank Deb Allard, Sherri Alexander, Patricia Brown, Carolyn McElroy, Margo Stiem, Becky Wagner, and Sandy Wolfinbarger for your encouragement, prayers, careful eyes for detail, and helpful input.

I am especially grateful to my husband, Curt Dalaba. He is my partner and listens as I run story details by him. The spiritual truths in this novel were gained by thirty-one years of sitting under his ministry. He is a man who lives at home what he preaches from the pulpit and I am blessed to call him my husband.

I also appreciate my children and their spouses who encourage me in countless ways.

I cannot forget to thank you, my readers, for supporting me in my writing and for taking the time to post a review, a comment on social media, or send a note letting me know you enjoyed my book. You are the ones I think about as I sit down to write. I desire to entertain you in a wholesome manner while encouraging you in your walk of faith. I pray this novel will in some way bless your heart and life.

Most of all, I'm thankful to my Savior, Jesus Christ, who taught me about forgiveness and grace. When I read Revelation 4:10, "The four and twenty elders fall down before him that sat on the throne, and worship him that liveth for ever and ever, and cast their crowns before the throne," I don't marvel at the fact that they cast their crowns before God. What will anything we have accomplished matter considering ALL He did for us?

# Dedication

To my grandmother, Margarethe Flatz, who died in 1999. She loved reading and telling me about the stories she read. Although she loved German indigenous romances, my grandmother especially enjoyed sharing stories of dogs who saved people's lives or poignant stories about children and their mothers. I can still see myself sitting at the kitchen table waiting for Oma "Grandma" to cut a piece of German streusel kuchen for the two of us. As we sat together, we would talk about our day or she would tell me one of her stories. These were precious times I will treasure forever.

It was probably around 1996, while we lived in Germany for a few years and my grandmother came to stay with my husband and me and our two children for a week or two, that I decided I wanted to hear her personal story. She was in her 80s at the time and I wished to have on paper the story of her life. She was happy to comply. While my kids were napping or tucked into bed for the night, I sat with pen and paper as my grandmother told me of her childhood in Germany, which later became Poland, moving to Brazil, and her marriage. The day she and my grandfather surrendered their lives to Jesus, what a difference that made. It was the turning point for generations to come in our family.

The reason I am dedicating this book to my precious grandmother is because a small portion of her life gave me the idea for this novel. When my grandmother was a young girl, she was given to her aunt to raise. My grandmother was one of many children, not the youngest or the oldest, just somewhere in between. She never understood why she had been the one given away. She was later reunited with her family only to be sent off to work as a maid in a wealthy home where she lived in the servants' quarters.

My grandmother's story is quite different from Selina's, the heroine in *The Marriage Maneuver*. But many of the emotions—the questions and the longings—were real in my grandmother's life also.

I will forever cherish the time I had with my Oma and all she taught me. She never knew how much her love of books and storytelling would influence my life to become an author. I felt it was appropriate to dedicate this novel to her memory.

*"And be ye kind one to*
*another, tenderhearted,*
*forgiving one another,*
*even as God for Christ's sake*
*hath forgiven you."*

*Ephesians 4:32*

# *Chapter One*

Hampstead, England, May 1819

Selina's trembling hand smoothed the skirt of the white muslin gown into place while her other hand clutched a bouquet of pink roses mixed with ivy and herbs. Was it only two hours prior, as her abigail carefully pinned the Mechlin lace veil onto the elaborate hairstyle she had created, that Selina still tenaciously clung to hope? Her heart constricted in alarming disappointment as she stood at the front of the chapel. Selina's lovely attire was completely wasted on the bridegroom, who hadn't bothered to cast his eyes upon her even once as she compelled her feet to move down the long aisle while clutching her father's arm. Why she had held tightly to his arm, Selina could not say. Her father had abandoned her long ago and provided no haven of protection. It seemed her soon-to-be husband was cut from the same cloth. As she stood beside Viscount FitzWalter, Selina forced herself to concentrate on the vicar's words, but alas, her mind was too distracted.

She took a deep, shuddering breath, hoping it would cause her hands to stop shaking. Thankfully, few people were in attendance. Only her immediate family, whom she barely knew, as well as Aunt Theo, who was more of a mother to her than her own mother had ever been. A few members of the viscount's family were in attendance. No one else needed to witness this undesired union. Not that the other members of the family didn't desire it. Actually, her parents were ecstatic about the money and connections they would gain. His parents were happy to finally have their heir leg-shackled. Soon everyone would begin watching her closely to see if an heir was on the way. A shiver ran down her spine. Selina could not imagine intimacy with the frowning man who stood beside her.

The clearing of a throat caught her attention and she quickly looked at the vicar, who stared at her expectantly. What had she missed? He must have asked her a question. Her hands became moist. Lord FitzWalter stood stoically beside her making it clear she should expect no help from him. Oh, how she wished she could wake up and find it was a nightmare.

Selina turned pleading eyes to the vicar.

He cleared his throat once more. "Ahem. Do you take this man to be your husband, Lady Selina?"

How she wished she could say, "No, I don't." That wasn't an option. Instead, she whispered, "I do."

The vicar looked toward her groom and repeated the question. Selina forced herself to stop woolgathering and pay attention to what was going on around her. She heard the viscount's clipped response. "I do."

The vicar spoke some words over them and then pronounced them husband and wife. She was now lawfully wed to this stranger—a hardened, scarred, and angry man.

"You may kiss your bride."

Selina lifted startled eyes to her groom. *Oh no! How had it slipped my mind that a kiss was part of the ceremony?* She'd never been kissed by a beau before. What if she did it wrong? Should she close her eyes or leave them open? He turned toward her, slowly lifting her veil. Impassive eyes perused her face. As he slowly leaned closer, she stopped breathing. His breath briefly touched her brow before his lips lightly brushed her forehead for the briefest of moments. He stood straight again and turned to the vicar. So that was it. Selina wasn't certain if she was relieved or disappointed, as this was another demonstration of her groom's disinterest.

As Lord FitzWalter and Selina faced the few attenders, he held his arm out to her. She placed her hand in the crook of his elbow and they made their way out of the church. Selina hadn't been to many weddings, but it seemed peculiar that a bridal couple would hurry down the aisle unsmiling and head straight to the viscount's gleaming carriage. Weren't they supposed to stand and wait outside the church, allowing their guests to congratulate them? Either he forgot or, more likely, didn't care to be congratulated on having acquired her as his bride.

A footman held his hand out to help Selina up the steps and into the carriage. Selina sat on the seat facing forward while the viscount took his place across from her. She lifted timid eyes and caught him staring at her. His somber expression spoke clearly of his unhappiness. Lord FitzWalter discouraged conversation by staring out the window.

Aunt Theo would not be pleased, of that Selina was certain. She knew her aunt loved her and would expect Selina's groom to be proud to have her as his bride. But Aunt Theo had only arrived yesterday. There had been no time for a quiet and comfortable coze, just the two of them. For that reason, Selina had no opportunity to confide in her aunt that her groom had chosen not to see her before the wedding, as her brother, Percival, had cruelly pointed out when he told her, "FitzWalter says, since he doesn't have a choice in his bride, it matters not to him what you look like or if you will suit. He will do his duty."

Oh, how the words had pinched her heart. She had forced herself not to allow Percival to see the hurt his words had inflicted for she knew it would only give him pleasure. Her brother cared nothing for her. It had only been her foolish expectation that had caused her to hope.

If only Kitty Haddington, her closest and dearest friend, could have been at the wedding. It was by watching Kitty's close-knit family interactions that Selina had developed high expectations for her own reunion with her family. She convinced herself her parents must have had a good reason for giving her to Aunt Theo and Uncle Peter to raise. She couldn't imagine what that reason was but certainly they loved her as much as Kitty's family loved Kitty. At eighteen, she should have realized the truth, yet she clung steadfastly to the fantasy that her family loved her.

A quiet sigh escaped her lips as she saw the stern countenance of her groom. Perhaps it was better Kitty wasn't here. There was no reason to make a grand occasion out of this day. Lord FitzWalter obviously wished to be anywhere but in this carriage with her and, if she were perfectly honest, she wished to be far from him also.

When Selina had first been told her groom was Viscount Hugh FitzWalter, she had no idea who the gentleman was since she had never taken part in a London Season. Lydia, her abigail, asked questions of the servants below-stairs and soon discovered he was not so old and, although he bore a scar on his face and had a slight limp due to injuries obtained while serving his country, he was considered to be a handsome gentleman. Lord FitzWalter had been an officer in His Majesty's army before he sold off his commission. He now worked for the Home Office. After Lydia informed Selina of these details, it gave her a measure of hope. Surely such a man must be honorable.

Unfortunately, as much as Selina longed to convince herself Percival had lied, the viscount's continued absence before the wedding gave proof to the truth of her brother's statement. As she sat in the carriage looking at the gentleman sitting across from her, any hope remaining died a sudden death. She knew of a certainty Viscount Fitzwalter had not willingly entered into this marriage and wished her to perdition.

Selina clasped her hands tightly on her lap to keep them from trembling. They were heading to a wedding breakfast at Gracebourne Manor, her parents' home. If only it could be over already, but then she'd be alone with him, and that could be far worse. No, better to stay at the breakfast as long as possible.

Sensing his eyes upon her, she slowly glanced up. Brown eyes stared back at her. What was he thinking? His expression was closed. She couldn't discern his thoughts, but his continued disinterest remained clear in his sober face. Her plain features could not tempt his eyes to linger for he turned his head back to the window without saying a word. Selina slowly let out a breath she didn't realize she'd been holding and looked at her folded hands clenched tightly on her lap.

The landscape drifted past the carriage window. Heavy clouds threatened rain and added bleakness to a day that had frustrated Fitz to no end. He would forever remember the smug grin on his father's face as he nodded in approval while standing beside his sedan chair. *Standing! On healthy legs! It had been a ruse to finally get me to the altar. How could I have been so blind and trusting, not discerning the truth until today?*

With jaw clenched tight, he had stood at the front of the church waiting for his bride to walk down the aisle. He'd briefly glanced at his parents and was shocked to see his father stand to his feet. Only four weeks prior, he'd been on his deathbed and the doctor had informed Fitz his father had but a short time to live. The Earl of Moorbridge's deathbed wish was to see his son wed. As much as he hated the idea of shackling himself to a conniving female, he couldn't deny his father's last wish, so he had acquiesced. Once the marriage contract was signed and the banns were read, his father had gained some strength, being able to get out of bed and sit in a chair. As Fitz stared at his father standing at the end of the aisle near his vacant chair, his shoulders stiffened and his head began to throb. The expression on his father's face told him everything he needed to know. He had been played for a fool. Fitz longed to walk down the aisle and out the doors to spite his father, but pride and obligation to his family's reputation held him in place. A legal contract had been signed and he was a man of his word, doomed to marry the woman the Earl of Moorbridge chose for him.

The doors at the back of the church opened and there stood a lady in a white gown. He couldn't see her face, but her looks were insignificant. He would marry her no matter. The music swelled in the room as she neared, but his eyes remained focused on the open doors beckoning him. If only it were possible.

Sooner than he was ready, she stood before him. He couldn't bring himself to look into her eyes for he was disinclined to allow her to see the battle waging within him. Turning toward the vicar, they stood side by side as the clergy's words rambled on about love and commitment. Fitz pursed his lips and narrowed his eyes. There was very little love to be found in this chapel. He felt no such feelings for his bride, nor she for him. His parents proved their lack of affection for their son when they callously and deceptively forced him into this union. Why speak of love as a necessity in relationships when it was so sparingly found?

The vicar finally began the marriage vows. Forcing himself to pay closer attention, he heard the vicar ask his bride if she would accept him as her husband. There was no answer. Curious, he glanced at her out the corner of his eye and two things became clear to him. She was pretty and she wasn't paying attention. The vicar cleared his throat and repeated the question. Fitz forced his lips into a straight line to hold back his unexpected amusement as she startled back to reality and whispered, "I do." It seemed his bride wished to escape this mousetrap as much as he did.

As if in a daze, he heard the vicar pronounce them husband and wife, and he was expected to kiss his bride. To spite his father, he wanted nothing more than to show his disinterest by refusing to oblige, but he couldn't bring himself to humiliate her. She didn't deserve it. He was fairly certain she had been a pawn in this fiasco. Perhaps a willing pawn, but Fitz doubted it had been her idea. Young innocents seldom had a say where marriage was concerned. He carefully lifted her veil and perused his bride's face for the first time. She was undeniably pretty. Dark hair and smooth, pale skin, along with brown doe-like eyes framed by long, dark lashes, and rosy, full lips made for a breathtaking combination. A slight blush stained her cheeks giving proof of her youth and innocence. Seeing the uncertainty in her eyes, he leaned forward and lightly kissed her forehead.

Fitz offered her his arm as they faced the congregation and then hurried his bride down the aisle, away from their guests, most of them family who had participated in this deception. He had no desire to see their self-satisfied faces congratulating him. Of course, they would have to go to the wedding breakfast. There was no avoiding it, although he longed to do so. As he headed toward the carriage, he knew he would have to put up with their smugness soon enough.

Fitz stared out the window of the carriage. He knew he should try to engage his bride in conversation, but the anger stirring within him toward his family made it impossible to participate in meaningless chatter. His father had been after him to marry for the past two years, ever since he turned six and twenty. "You are the heir and you must fulfill your duty by getting married and providing another heir to inherit after you. You have no remaining brothers and I don't want this estate going to a cousin should anything happen to you. I wish to be certain my son or my grandson will inherit my title." These were the words he heard every time he saw his father. Fitz had avoided going home for Christmas last year so he wouldn't have to hear the speech for the hundredth time. "I'll get to it by the time I'm thirty," he'd promised his father. That obviously wasn't good enough, so the old schemer came up with a farce that would force his son to reconsider and do his father's bidding.

His blood boiled as he processed what had transpired in the past month. How had he not seen the deception played out before his eyes? How could he have been so gullible? His father's plan had worked brilliantly, but he had lost his son's trust in the process. When this day was over, Fitz had no interest in ever stepping onto Moorbridge's estate again. Not after the way he'd been made sport of. His father may have gotten himself a new daughter today, but he lost his son. Nor would he make him a grandfather anytime soon. He would make certain of that. Fitz refused to allow anyone to dictate to him what took place in his bedroom.

Turning his eyes from the window, he looked more

closely at his bride, allowing his eyes to travel over her dark brown tresses, smooth pale skin, and rosy cheeks, probably from the cold spring temperature. Her skin appeared as soft as satin. She lifted her eyes to his and he saw the uncertainty his bride must be feeling. Compassion stirred in his heart, but he moved his gaze back to contemplate the scenery once more. Gracebourne Manor was just coming into view. He would be only too happy when this day finally ended, allowing him to return to Thorncrest.

## *Chapter Two*

As the other carriages rolled up the driveway, Fitz and Selina descended from their conveyance. He held a hand out to her and she placed hers gently in his. "Thank you," she said.

He gave a brief nod, then took her arm above the elbow to guide her into her parents' home, not waiting for the other guests to join them. It seemed her groom wished to prolong the inevitable. They would soon receive congratulations whether he liked it or not. He couldn't avoid them forever.

Selina excused herself and hurried up the stairs to her bedchamber to remove the veil and freshen up. It was a room she had occupied for a brief time. No special memories caused her to want to linger. Once Lydia removed the veil, Selina watched through the mirror as her abigail adjusted her hair to be certain every strand was in place.

"How was the wedding, my lady? I'm certain you outshone everyone there today."

Lydia had been her personal maid for the past two years. Aunt Theo hired her when Selina turned sixteen and began preparing for her first Season in London, which actually never took place. Lydia's quiet, yet friendly manner appealed greatly to Selina and she soon learned to trust and even confide in her.

"It was awful." Selina swallowed hard, attempting to hold back the tears that wished to spill over at the compassion reflected in her maid's eyes. Placing a hand over her mouth, she took another deep breath and soon had control of herself once again. "It was certainly not the type of wedding I'd dreamt of having. But it is done now and . . ." She looked at her maid and shrugged her shoulders helplessly. "I don't know what to expect."

"I'm terribly sorry to hear it. Has your Mama or Aunt Theo not explained to you about your first night with your groom?"

Understanding dawned, and Selina blushed furiously. "That isn't what I meant. Yes, Aunt Theo prepared me and I cannot imagine . . ." She waved her hand dismissively and shook her head. "Never mind. I only meant to say I don't know what we will talk about or how we will go on. He obviously doesn't wish to be married to me."

Lydia nodded slowly. Although older than Selina by ten years, she had never married and was rather plain, but she was all kindness to her mistress and gifted as a lady's maid. Selina treasured her.

"I have no experience where men are concerned, but I know you well, Selina. You will be an asset to him, although I doubt he realizes it as yet. My suggestion is for you to simply be yourself and follow his lead when you're unsure. He will eventually realize he obtained a gem this day."

Selina stood and took Lydia's two hands in her own. She squeezed them gently. "Thank you, Lydia. I hope you know how much I appreciate you."

With eyes shining, Lydia simply curtsied. "Thank you." She extricated her hands and became all business. "Now, you must hurry on down and greet your guests." Looking Selina over once more, she declared her lovely and ushered her out the door.

Selina walked toward the stairs on shaky legs. She hated grand entrances, and it was especially daunting when most of her guests were critical of her. As she stood at the top of the staircase, her eyes searched for Aunt Theo. Selina found her smiling face toward the front of the small crowd. Even as Aunt Theo smiled, concern filled her eyes. Selina was never able to hide any emotions from her aunt. Somehow, the dear lady always knew when her niece was distressed no matter how hard Selina tried to hide it.

Holding the skirt of the gown with one hand, she rested the other on the banister and began her descent. As she raised her eyes once more, her gaze was caught by the woman who stood next to Aunt Theo. Her mother. The expression on her face was in stark contrast to that of her aunt's. Her mother's eyes assessed and judged every movement critically.

Selina found it hard to breathe and quickly averted her gaze back to Aunt Theo's eyes shining with pride. Selina's heart trembled at being the center of attention. She forced herself to smile for her aunt's sake. When she reached the last step, a hand was extended toward her. Her eyes collided with that of her groom. She hadn't noticed him standing there. He must have moved closer at the last moment. FitzWalter's closed expression only added to her fears. She determined to bear through this day with dignity intact.

As she placed her fingers in the palm of his hand, she thought she heard him whisper, "Lovely." Had she heard correctly? Selina wished he would say it again to be certain. Alas, his lips stayed firmly shut as he led her into the dining room to join their guests.

They accepted congratulations while their visitors ate a bountiful breakfast, enjoyed a piece of delicious wedding cake, and chatted with one another as they celebrated this inauspicious occasion. Selina could only force down a bite or two of the fruit on her plate. Her groom held a half-filled glass of champagne in his hand, unable to hide the bored expression on his face.

After two hours, her husband sought her out to say it was time to depart. Nodding, Selina approached Aunt Theo and her mother. "Mama, I must bid you farewell. Thank you for the lovely breakfast."

With a brief regal nod, her mother said, "I wish you well, Selina. Let us know when there is an heir on the way. It would please the Earl greatly."

Selina felt her cheeks grow cold. She'd rather not think about that part of marriage. Bless Aunt Theo for reaching out a hand to pull Selina close for a hug. "Selina, dear, you made me very proud today. A lovelier bride I have yet to see." Pulling back and placing a hand on each cheek, Aunt Theo said, "You will make your husband a wonderful viscountess and friend."

Her mother gave an unladylike snort. "Friend? What man wants his wife for a friend? That's what gentlemen's clubs are for. Selina, you need not concern yourself with such peasant-like expectations. Warm his bed when he wishes it and run his household well. That is all he will require of you. Then enjoy spending his money. You will have earned it."

Her words should not have come as a surprise, yet they did indeed surprise her. Was this cold, emotionless woman really her mother? She felt a greater commonality with Aunt Theo. It was at this moment she realized how blessed she'd been to have been raised by Aunt Theo and Uncle Peter. What kind of person would she have become if her mother and nanny had raised her? Selina's eyes automatically strayed to her older sister, Juliet, who stood resplendently beside her husband, Henry Wildridge, the Viscount of Chesterfield. Was her marriage as cold as her mother described a marriage should be?

Selina was blessedly pulled from her thoughts with Aunt Theo's next words. "My darling girl, you will do well. Of that, I have no doubt. And I will call on you in a couple of weeks."

"Thank you, Aunt Theo. Please do. I will look forward to your visit."

Selina kissed Aunt Theo's proffered cheek. She then felt obligated to kiss her mother as well. Turning toward her, she saw only her mother's back as she had already moved away to speak with another guest. Selina had been dismissed.

Aunt Theo linked her arm with Selina's and drew her a few steps away. A glance around reassured them no one could overhear. Her aunt leaned close to Selina's ear. "Juliet informed me you only met your groom today. I'm terribly sorry for it, Selina. That will complicate things for the two of you, I'm certain. But FitzWalter was a good boy when I knew him years ago. I will admit, he has changed much. Not only the scar on his face and the slight limp. It is the wounds you cannot see that have indubitably affected him. But I believe that kind young man still exists. You must find a way to draw him out, but give him some time and understanding."

Exhaustion from the stress of this day caused Selina's mind to feel muddled. Everything her aunt said seemed as clear as gazing through a window pane in a downpour. Yet Aunt Theo's love and concern penetrated to the recesses of her heart, and that was enough. "Thank you, Aunt Theo, for everything. I love you." She kissed her slightly wrinkled cheek one more time. "I must go now. My groom does not wish to linger."

Aunt Theo squeezed her hand. "I understand. God bless you, my dearest girl."

Selina walked toward her husband, her steps slowing when she saw him standing with his father. Not wanting to interrupt, she noticed her own father standing nearby and, seeing her approach, he said, "Selina, my dear, you did your family proud today." He was a jovial sort, yet always somehow detached.

"Thank you." Glancing at her husband who stood with his jaw clenched tight while his hand fidgeted with a pocket watch, she knew he was impatient to leave. "We must depart now, Father. I bid you farewell."

"Of course, of course! You young people need to be on your way. I wish you well, my dear." His hand awkwardly patted her shoulder and he turned away to speak to another departing guest.

Selina swallowed and straightened her shoulders as she took a few steps toward her husband.

"Don't be a sore loser. Your stubbornness forced me to take matters into my own hands." Selina overheard the words Lord Moorbridge spoke but had no clue what he meant by them.

"I bid you farewell, Father." Fitz grasped Selina's arm, and said, "Come. We must depart now."

She curtsied to her father-in-law as he nodded to her.

"Welcome to the family, Lady FitzWalter. Let me know if you have need of anything."

Her new name sounded strange to her ears. "Thank you, my lord." She curtsied once more.

Fitz grumbled, "She will have need of nothing." He tightened his hold on her arm, as he led her from the room.

Once they were outside, Fitz hurried her across the pavement to the carriage. Selina tried to pull her arm free. "Please, my lord, release my arm. You are holding it too tightly."

He immediately let go. "I beg your pardon. I had no intention of hurting you. It's just . . ." Fitz ran a hand through his hair as he glanced back at the house for a moment, then quickly swung around toward the carriage. "Never mind. Come, let's be on our way." Fitz placed a gentle hand on the middle of her back and the other under her elbow to help her into the waiting conveyance.

Selina could not imagine what had gotten into the viscount. Turning her eyes from the window she'd been staring out of since they'd departed her parents' home, she slanted her gaze in his direction. Once again, he sat across from her. Wouldn't most newlyweds have sat side by side? She stifled a sigh and studied him more closely, glad he was engrossed in the view outside the window. It gave her a moment of undisturbed observation without him being any the wiser.

He was handsome. There would be no dispute about that. The scar on his cheek had healed smoothly, leaving only a silvery line, which didn't detract from his appearance but instead, added an element of mystery. Tall, with an athletic build, blond hair, brown eyes, a long, masculine nose, and a full lower lip made for a potent combination that would have surely rendered him one of the most sought-after bachelors in London, except for the fierce scowl on his face, which would most assuredly send the young debutantes running in the opposite direction. He could certainly have had his pick of marriageable ladies. Why did he agree to marry her?

Selina had no illusion of being a great beauty, but

Viscount FitzWalter couldn't have known that since he hadn't bothered to meet her before the wedding. Obviously, her appearance was inconsequential in his decision to marry her. By all counts, he was certainly wealthy enough and didn't need the dowry her aunt had bestowed upon her, so why had he agreed to the marriage?

Fitz shifted his eyes from the window and caught her watching him. Selina wanted to look away, but her eyes refused to obey. She helplessly shrugged her shoulders as his gaze became probing. What must he think of her gawking at him?

"We will soon be home. I have some business to attend to, but we will have supper together tonight. Afterward, we will discuss our marriage."

Selina wasn't certain what there was to discuss. Perhaps he wished to clarify her responsibilities. Or he planned to explain his reason for marrying her. "Very well, my lord," she said.

He continued to observe her a moment longer, then nodded once and turned back to the window. Selina gazed at the view out the opposite side. They would talk when he declared it was time.

The sun began its descent behind the hills off in the distance as Fitz and Selina sat at opposite ends of the long dining room table. No less than ten chairs sat empty along each side. Selina's eyes were drawn to the lovely view through the floor-to-ceiling windows taking up most of one wall. She glanced at the darkening sky and realized night approached too quickly.

Selina looked down the length of the table and noted her husband quietly eating his meal as though no one else was in the room. The polished wood gleamed in the light of the three candelabras placed along its center. A couple of servants passed dishes between the two occupants so they could fill their plates with the delicacies provided.

Although she'd been ravenous before the meal began, Selina found her appetite diminished. Her husband's cold shoulder was disconcerting. She could barely force herself to eat two bites. Pushing her food around with her fork for most of the meal, she did manage to swallow a bit of her supper for she didn't wish to insult the cook by returning a full plate to the kitchen.

"Are you just going to play with it or actually eat it?"

She lifted wide eyes as warmth infused her face as she stared into her husband's stoic countenance. He'd been watching her. Thankfully, the light remained dim in the room even with all the candles, allowing her to hope he remained unaware of her flushed cheeks.

Why was it she couldn't think of a thing to say? If only she were witty and had the ability to give him a light-hearted rejoinder. Instead, she shifted her gaze to her plate and dutifully placed another bite of food in her mouth. It tasted like cotton. Lifting her goblet to her mouth, she managed to swish it down with some water.

When Selina glanced up, she found his eyes on her still. *Oh, why doesn't he look at his plate?* But he kept right on staring as he slowly chewed his food. She placed another bite in her mouth with a trembling fork and daintily chewed, trying not to choke. After a few more labored bites and swallows, she heard him say, "If you are finished, we can retire to the drawing room."

Selina hurriedly placed the fork on her plate, dabbed her serviette to the corner of her mouth, and placed it on the table. "I'm ready, my lord."

He walked to her side and held out his arm for her to take as he led her out the door being held open by an efficient footman. Soon they were seated on chairs placed near the fireplace in the drawing room. On such a cold evening, the warmth of the flames felt especially comforting.

Sitting on the first half of her chair, not allowing herself to lean back, she folded her hands tightly in her lap, both feet planted firmly on the floor, ankles touching. Aunt Theo had trained her well in what was expected of a lady. She waited silently for the viscount to speak. He leaned back in a comfortable manner, legs stretched out before the fire and crossed at the ankles with his elbows resting on the armrest and his hands comfortably folded over his abdomen. He sat staring into the flames.

After only a moment, Fitz looked up from the fire and into her eyes. She detected turmoil and frustration in his and instinctively knew he was about to give her a glimpse into his thoughts. Her heartbeat accelerated at what might be revealed.

"I think it's best we are honest about our marriage right from the start," Fitz said.

Selina smoothed moist palms over her dress. "Yes, I agree."

Fitz stared into the flames, seemingly to gather his thoughts. He took a deep breath and let it out slowly between stiff lips. "My father has been after me to become leg-shackled for the past two years. I had every intention of waiting for several more years. Of course, I was well aware of the fact that my dawdling frustrated him, but I had no idea of the lengths he was willing to go to see me entrapped." Turning to look into her eyes, he said, "It wasn't until I stood at the front of the church waiting for you to enter that his deception became clear to me."

Her posture stiffened more than it was already and she whispered, "What did he do?"

His mouth quirked in a cynical smile. "My father became ill, to the point of death. His doctor confirmed it to me. He weakened and was confined to bed with only months to live. His greatest wish was to see me wed before he passed away. What could I do? Was I going to be so callous and deny my father his deathbed wish?"

An involuntary gasp escaped her lips. She was afraid she knew where this story was heading. His father had played him false, and she had been the means by which he'd done it. How he must resent her presence in his life!

Fitz slowly nodded. "I can see you've figured it out." He chuckled without humor as he shook his head. "Moorbridge planned the perfect subterfuge. I'm certain he paid the doctor well for his collusion. Imagine my surprise when he stood to his feet at the wedding and smiled smugly in my direction." Gritting his teeth, he spat out, "There was no apology or shame on his face. He stood proudly beside my mother and beamed with satisfaction." The knuckles on his hands were white where they held tightly to the armrest.

Selina squeezed her eyes shut for a brief moment and whispered, "I'm sorry. I had no idea."

"I don't doubt that. You are too young and innocent to be manipulative." His eyes perused her face as he cynically pursed his lips and added, "That will come with time."

Tilting her head, she waited for him to explain himself, but he continued his story instead. "I couldn't do anything about it at the wedding. I was doomed to be married by his chicanery, but I'll not let him have the last laugh. He thinks he won, but he has sadly deceived himself."

"I-I don't understand, my lord? What do you mean?"

His cold gaze rested upon her face. "We are married and there is nothing I can do about it without causing a scandal and bringing shame on my family, and on you, of course. I have too much pride for that. But I will not provide my father with an heir. Not yet. He needs to stew a bit."

She swallowed hard as she waited for what would come next. If he didn't intend to provide an heir, did that mean she would have a reprieve before having to fulfill her marital duty?

"I work for the Home Office and I intend to continue doing so. I'll be living in London and traveling quite a bit, while you will stay here at Thorncrest. Of course, you may come to London for the Season if you wish. However, I will be unavailable to show you around or accompany you to the various balls and events. Perhaps it would be best if your Aunt Theo would join you should you decide to come to Town."

"I see."

"I expect you to remain faithful to me. In the event I hear rumors of your unfaithfulness, I will annul this marriage. If you remain true to the vows we spoke today, we will consummate the marriage at a later date when I am ready—and not when my father demands it of us."

He stared at her obviously waiting for a response. What could she say? She felt uncertain of her own emotions.

"Do you have any questions?" he asked.

Selina looked at the hard and bitter man before her. Aside from his handsome appearance, there was little to draw her to him. She couldn't imagine intimacy with him, so perhaps his plan had merit.

She could enjoy the freedom and lack of societal restrictions as a married lady without the obligation of having to be available to her lord's beck and call. Selina suspected she should feel insulted by his speech, but she couldn't muster any feelings of indignity. That is, not until she began wondering what her neighbors would think if he departed so soon after their wedding. Would she be pitied? Should her family hear of it, they would blame her, of course. Selina could hear them already. "She isn't as beautiful as her sisters, you know. No wonder he left her. The disappointment must have been too great." Doubt seeped into her mind. Perhaps he found her unappealing and only used this situation with his father as an excuse to be away from her.

Selina knew he was waiting for a response. She simply said, "I understand, my lord. I will abide by your wishes."

He raised his brows in surprise. "Is that all? You have no demands of your own?"

She shook her head. "I cannot think of any. I'm certain I will be well provided for here at Thorncrest. If I decide to come to London at a later date, I shall let you know."

He chuckled in disbelief, having expected her to ask what her allowance would be, perhaps demanding carte blanche to redecorate Thorncrest. She could have begged and pleaded to travel to London with him. Instead, she seemed content with her lot.

"You certainly are an innocent, but it won't last. London and time will spoil you. Still, it's refreshing to see, even if it's only for a short period of time." He stared at her young face, naivety evident in her confused expression, and it drew him. Fitz gave his head a quick shake. "It's best I leave before I let my guard down and end up disappointed when you become like all the other ladies in society."

With puckered brow, she gently shook her head, "I don't

understand why you think I'll change."

"It doesn't matter." He stood to his feet and held out a hand to her. She placed her hand in his a bit hesitantly and arose. "Come. We've both had a long day."

He led her up to her bedchamber door. "Goodnight, Selina. I will not see you on the morrow. I plan to leave early. If you have need of anything, you must let my steward know and he will contact me if necessary."

"Very well, my lord. Goodnight." She made to pull her hand away, but he held onto it and lifted it to his lips, placing a soft kiss on the back of it.

"Goodnight, my lady." He bowed and released her hand, turning away to continue down the hallway. Refusing to look back, he shut the door to his bedchamber behind him.

# *Chapter Three*

The sun was high in the sky when Selina finally awoke. After the events of the previous day and her conversation with the viscount, rest did not come easily. It was in the early hours of the morning when the sweet oblivion of sleep finally overcame her thoughts and she drifted off to a few peaceful hours of rest.

Now her curtains were thrown open and sunlight blazed into her room. Selina opened her eyes just enough to see Lydia approaching with a tray. She placed it on the foot of the bed.

"It's time to wake up, my lady."

Selina stretched her arms and mumbled, "What time is it, Lydia?"

"It's after the noon hour."

"What? So late already? Then I suppose I should be glad you woke me."

"I thought you may want to meet with the housekeeper. She has been asking about you. And you will need to explore your new home."

"Must I? I think I'd prefer staying in my room and pretending yesterday never happened."

"No, my lady. You mustn't do that. It's best if you get up and show everyone you are mistress of the house."

Her eyes had finally adjusted to the light, so Selina turned her head toward the window. An unexpectedly sunny day greeted her after days of dreary weather, causing a smile to touch her lips. Looking more closely, she noticed the windows were actually doors that opened to a balcony, for she could see the railing through the glass. *How lovely! I've found two things to feel happy about and I haven't even stepped out of bed yet.* Her smile broadened.

"You're right, Lydia. Please help me get ready."

"Of course, ma'am. Enjoy your chocolate while I prepare your water and choose a dress for you to wear."

Lydia fluffed two pillows and placed them behind her mistress. After Selina adjusted her blankets, Lydia handed her the tray with a cup of chocolate, biscuits, and preserves.

"Breakfast is long passed, but I imagined you could use a little something to start your day."

"Thank you, Lydia. This is splendid."

The maid bobbed a curtsy, then headed toward the dressing room. By the time she returned, Selina had finished her meal and stood beside the bed ready to prepare for her day.

"I imagine the viscount has departed?"

"Yes, my lady. Oh, I just remembered!" She reached into the pocket of her apron and pulled out a sealed envelope. "His valet handed this to me this morning and asked that I give it to you."

Selina took the envelope from her maid. "Thank you," she whispered as she saw her name written on the folded paper in what must be the viscount's scroll. Not in a hurry to see what he'd written, she tossed it on the bed and walked over to the bowl of water to perform her morning ablutions.

Mrs. Godwin was pleased to give Selina a tour of the house. It was much bigger than Aunt Theo's home where she had grown up. Thorncrest boasted at least fifteen bedchambers, not to mention all the other rooms of the house. She had seen glimpses of the gardens through the windows as the housekeeper took her from room to room. Selina looked forward to perusing the grounds and stable yard as soon as she could manage it.

"As you can see, my lady, this is a lovely estate and I feel honored to be housekeeper of such a fine establishment."

Selina smiled at the housekeeper, who stood with her hands folded at her waist. She guessed her age to be in the latter years of her 40s. Although her hair was mostly white, her skin remained smooth, attesting to premature graying rather than aging. Her hair was pulled back in a bun and a white cap rested upon it. While touring the estate, Selina decided she liked Mrs. Godwin, who seemed efficient and knowledgeable of the running of the household.

"It is, indeed, a lovely home," Selina said, "and I appreciate the care you have given it, Mrs. Godwin. When you have a minute, we can go over the menu for this week. Since the master is not at home, I require only simple meals. Nothing too elaborate."

"I have time now if you wish."

"Very well. Let's go to my sitting room."

After Mrs. Godwin departed to speak to Cook about the menu, Selina hurried to change into a pair of walking shoes and a pelisse lined with fur. She couldn't understand why the weather hadn't warmed yet, but she reminded herself it was early spring. She needed to be patient. At least it wasn't raining and, instead, the sun shone brightly. Selina determined not to waste the day indoors. She longed to feel the sun on her face and enjoy the freedom that beckoned to her outside the walls of the house.

Selina picked up the letter she had tossed on the bed, tucked it into the pocket of her pelisse, and tied a bonnet over her dark tresses. Hurried steps took her down the staircase that led to the foyer of the house. Baldwin, the butler, stood at the front door ready to open it. It never ceased to amaze her how the servants seemed to anticipate her every move.

Her eyes sparkled as she thanked him. He nodded but his countenance remained stoic. She had noted yesterday at their arrival that he was a staid sort of man. As long as he did his job well and was loyal, that was all that mattered.

After walking down the front stairs, she stood a moment on the gravel driveway and lifted her face to the sun. Ah, it felt good to be out of doors.

Her gaze swept over the property. A long driveway circled to the front entry and continued to the stables while a vibrant, green lawn surrounded the house. She strolled on the grass, stopping every once in a while to take in the view. A gasp escaped her lips at the rolling hills beyond the back of the house. Thorncrest was situated atop one of those hills, and she could see far and wide. Off in the distance, a pond shimmered in the sunlight, and her feet took her in that direction of their own volition.

As she drew closer to the pond, she saw cat-o'-nine-tails mixed in with the tall grasses growing along the bank. The crystal clear water allowed her to see the fish swimming along the bottom and stones covering the floor of the pond. Lowering herself to the ground on an unshaded part of the lawn, she stretched her legs straight forward and placed her arms on the ground behind her. Closing her eyes, she lifted her face and allowed the sun to warm her on this brisk day. Thankfully, there was no wind. Taking a deep breath through her nose, she let it out slowly through her mouth. All was still, except for the tweeting of birds, the plop of a fish, and the ribbit of a frog.

As relaxing as this moment was, Selina couldn't forget the unopened letter in her pocket. She dreaded its content. Why did he feel the need to write to her? Gathering her courage, she sat up, took the letter into her hands, and broke the seal with cold fingers. Slowly opening the folded sheet of paper, she began to read.

*Selina,*

*By the time you read this letter, I will be on my way to London. I failed to mention one particular last night. As I will be working for the Home Office for our Government in London and possibly further abroad, there may be danger involved. I expect to return safe and sound. In the event that I do not, I want to assure you that you will be well provided for. In such an event, the dower house on Thorncrest would become your place of residence for as long as you live or until you remarry. You will also receive a generous settlement.*

* * *

*I wish you well. As long as you abide by what I stated to you yesterday evening, I will return to you when I deem it necessary and we will begin our married life at that time.*

*Sincerely,*
*Hugh FitzWalter*

Staring at the paper in her hand, she felt unsure of her emotions. He seemed certain he would return to her—that is if she obeyed him, which she would, of course. After all, she was eighteen years of age and had never felt the stirring of love for any man of her acquaintance. If no man touched her heart before she married, why would one do so now? She was certain no one could tempt her to stray from her vows.

Would she be a young widow one day? It seemed beyond the comprehension of the mind that the strong and handsome viscount should be dead in a grave. He seemed too vital, too authoritative to allow himself to be overcome by death. Selina knew she was being ridiculous in thinking such a thing, but he had already lived through a war and, although he'd been severely injured, it could not hold him down. He had a slight limp, that was true, but he moved as well as any man.

Yet the truth was, no person alive was more powerful than death, and everyone could become its victim, including the viscount. In which case, she would be a widow who had never known intimacy with her husband.

Shame washed over her. Unable to tempt her husband to her bed on her wedding night, she must truly be as plain as her brother had predicted she would become the day she was given to Aunt Theo to raise.

Selina knew she must accept her situation and the fact that she would never stand out in a crowded ballroom. Had she been given a Season in London before her wedding, she would most certainly have been designated that most dreaded label of "wallflower." No wonder her husband said he would be unwilling to escort her through a London Season. Such a handsome man would want an equally beautiful woman at his side.

What had her parents done to her by marrying her off to such a man? Had they been aware of Lord Moorbridge's deception and encouraged the wedding regardless? Unanswered questions stirred in her mind. She couldn't wait for the next two weeks to pass so Aunt Theo would arrive and advise her on what needed to be done. In the meantime, she couldn't imagine a lovelier retreat than Thorncrest.

## *Chapter Four*

"What was that imbecile thinking?" Aunt Theo screeched. "Did Moorbridge think he could force his son's hand in this manner and Fitz would do his bidding once the truth was revealed? I almost cannot blame your husband for leaving. Moorbridge will be fuming mad when he hears of it. Yet I do blame Fitz on your behalf. His pride means more to him than your reputation. He is selfish and uncaring. The apple certainly doesn't fall far from the tree in that family."

Aunt Theo sat on the sofa beside Selina, who had just explained about what had transpired before and after the wedding. She grabbed hold of Selina's hands and squeezed them. "There are few men of character like your Uncle Peter. He may have been a merchant and the aristocracy may have looked down their haughty noses at him, calling him a cit, but I tell you few men are as great as he was." Aunt Theo's eyes welled up with tears.

Selina leaned forward to embrace her, placing a kiss on her cheek. "Thank you for being upset on my behalf. I love you more than you can know."

"Aw, dear girl . . ." Lifting a slightly trembling hand, she smiled as she patted her niece's cheek, all the love her heart contained shining forth in her eyes. She took a deep, cleansing breath and let it out in a huff. "We will get through this, Selina. Mark my words, your husband will rue the day he treated you this shabbily. You see, I knew of a kinder Hugh FitzWalter, before the war, and before a self-centered beauty deeply hurt him. I'm certain that kind man still resides within the hardened shell he created to protect himself. His father took advantage of the vulnerable opening that remained—his sense of responsibility toward family. That fool callously hurt him once more by his deception and blatant smugness at the wedding. Moorbridge didn't spare his son's feelings, but publicly humiliated him by revealing his complete health at the nuptials after having been in a wheelchair before the entire ton these past couple of months."

Selina smacked her hand on the sofa cushion. "It was heartless of Lord Moorbridge. I overheard him tell Fitz at the wedding breakfast, 'Don't be a sore loser.' Did he think this was a game? I know Lord FitzWalter didn't see it that way."

Aunt Theo shook her head in frustration and shrugged her shoulders. "Well, the die has been cast, Selina. Now we must decide how you will go on."

Selina had hoped to simply hide away in the country. Thorncrest was a well-run estate and didn't demand too much of her time. She could get involved in the community and pretend she'd never married at all. Unfortunately, Selina suspected Aunt Theo would not see things in the same way, so she hesitantly asked, "What do you suggest?"

Aunt Theo tried to stifle a yawn with her hand. "I don't know. I'd like to rest a bit first and then take some time to pray. Nothing brings clarity and understanding quite like prayer and rest."

"I'm so glad you're here, Aunt Theo."

She patted her niece's hand. "I am, too, for I could not feel at ease after the wedding. I needed to see you for myself." Aunt Theo pulled herself up from the chair. "Now, if you'll excuse me, I'll lay down for a bit."

"Of course. Please let me know if there is anything you have need of."

Aunt Theo nodded. "I will. Until later, my dear."

While Aunt Theo rested, Selina chose to take a walk in the garden. As she strolled on the gravel pathway that meandered through the empty flowerbeds and budding bushes, she contemplated what Aunt Theo might suggest her course of action should be. And who was the self-centered beauty who had broken the viscount's heart? *I'll have to ask Aunt Theo about it later.*

Selina couldn't help feeling history repeating itself. She had been pushed aside once again. The story was the same, only the characters had changed. Her family sent her away last time; her husband walked away this time.

The emotions stirring inside were familiar. She had felt them before. They took her back to a vague memory of living in her parents' home and having a kind nursemaid who cared for her. She had an older sister by a couple of years and a younger sister by one year, both with lovely blonde ringlets and blue eyes. Selina must have been six when she and her sisters were presented to a family member who had come to visit. She couldn't recall who it was, but the lady had a loud and boisterous voice, and went on and on about how beautiful her sisters were with their blue eyes and blonde hair, "Just like their mother." When the melodramatic woman spotted Selina hovering near Nurse and holding tight to her skirt, she gasped in horror. "And what have we here? A brown wren, it seems!"

It wasn't too long after that incident that Nurse told Selina she would be going to Aunt Theo's house. Her aunt had always stopped in the nursery to pay her a visit when she came to Gracebourne. Sometimes she read books to her or brushed her hair, telling her how pretty she was. Aunt Theo smelled nice, too, and always smiled. Selina felt excitement at the thought of visiting her aunt, but why were her sisters' bags not packed? Would she be going alone?

Nurse held Selina's hand as she led her down the stairs where her parents stood waiting. Positioned beside them were her two sisters and her brother.

Father patted Selina on the head, telling her to be a good girl.

Mother said, "Perhaps you may come home when you're older. Be a good girl." She bent forward and offered her cheek to her daughter. Selina gave her a dutiful peck.

Her sisters hugged her goodbye, but when it was her brother's turn, he smirked and said, "If you were blonde and beautiful, you could stay, but you're going to be a useless, plain spinster."

"That's enough out of you," her father gently chided his son. But the hateful words pierced her young heart and remained with her. Her father hadn't denied the truthfulness of Percival's statement. Therefore, from that day on, Selina understood she wasn't beautiful like her sisters, and she couldn't stay.

As it turned out, Selina lacked for nothing while living with Aunt Theo and Uncle Peter, who were both demonstrative in their affection. A governess was hired to instruct her in painting, playing the pianoforte, and dancing. Aunt Theo made certain Selina would one day take her proper place in society. Unfortunately, she could not present her niece herself as she had lost her place of prestige when she married a cit. Uncle Peter wasn't born to a noble family but earned his living as a merchant. His hands were tainted according to people in the highest echelon of society. It didn't matter that he had become successful and enjoyed wealth far greater than most families in the ton.

Although life with her aunt and uncle was pleasant and peaceful, Selina lived for the day her parents would call her home. She imagined many scenarios of how they would embrace her and welcome her back into their fold. As a young teenager, she would stare into the mirror hoping to see her hair had become lighter or her eyes bluer. Rinsing it with lemon juice, she would sit in the sun to bleach the brown out of it. One of the maids had told her the treatment would lighten the color. It had worked a little, but not enough that anyone would consider her a blonde. As the years went by and she became a young lady of sixteen, Selina came to the realization that brown hair does not turn blonde and brown eyes do not turn blue. When her aunt found her crying over this fact, she gently led Selina back to the stool before the mirror in her bedchamber. Selina sat, but her eyes remained downcast.

"Look into the mirror, Selina, and tell me what you see."

Lifting sorrowful eyes, she said, "A brown wren."

"That's not what I see at all," her aunt replied.

Curiously, Selina raised her eyes to view her aunt through the mirror.

"I see satin smooth skin." She gently ran a finger down Selina's cheek. "I see shiny, chocolate-colored hair, so soft to the touch." Her hand gently stroked Selina's tresses. Aunt Theo must have seen the longing in her niece's eyes, for she continued with her praises. "Your eyes are as lovely as your grandmother's, who was quite a beauty in her day. I wish you could have met her. She would have been proud of you, Selina."

"Was my grandmother's hair blonde?"

Aunt Theo shook her head gently. "No, my darling girl. She had the same color of hair as you, and she was greatly sought after by many young gentlemen."

"Mama and Papa sent me to you because I'm ugly. Percival told me so. He said I would be a useless spinster. I'm afraid he's right. I'm useless to them."

"Selina, someday I'll explain it to you. For now, you are still too young. But please believe me when I tell you, your brother did not speak truthfully to you. You are lovely, but more than that, you are intelligent, accomplished, and you have a caring heart. I hope you'll begin to see yourself through my eyes. You aren't inferior to the rest of your family in any way."

Oh how she wanted to believe the words her aunt spoke. Truly she did. But her parents' actions and her brother's hateful comment had left a scar. The only thing that could make her feel worthy would be if she were welcomed home and embraced by her family. That day finally arrived when she turned eighteen years of age.

As Selina now sat in the garden at Thorncrest, she realized it had only been four weeks since she arrived at her parents' home. With all that had transpired, it seemed longer ago.

Selina remembered excitedly packing her luggage after her parents' letter arrived. She embraced and kissed her aunt, thanking her for her love and care, before entering her aunt's traveling coach with Lydia beside her. At last, she was headed home.

Selina hadn't seen anyone in her family the entire time

she'd lived with Aunt Theo, her father's sister. She could well imagine they were as curious about her as she was about them. Father and Mother were not effusive people—that she remembered well—but she was certain her sisters would be happy to see her. And, surely, her brother had matured into a kinder person by now.

When the carriage rolled to a stop in front of her parents' imposing manor, a footman opened the carriage door and helped her out. Selina straightened her traveling suit, then looked to the open front door expecting to be welcomed by her family.

Only the butler stood ready to greet her. As she drew closer, she had a vague recollection of his face.

"Welcome home, Lady Selina."

She tried to smile but wasn't certain she succeeded. Where was her family? "Thank you," she whispered.

"Please, follow me."

He led her to the open doors of the drawing room and announced her arrival. Her father stood by the fireplace with a glass of wine in his hand. He grinned at her, which gave Selina a little courage.

Two beautiful blonde, young ladies sat next to the older woman, whom she immediately recognized as her mother. Selina couldn't say whether she actually remembered the faces of her parents or simply recognized them from a painting her aunt had placed in her sitting room. Gray strands now competed with her mother's blond hair, and tiny wrinkles on her brow and around her eyes marred her once smooth skin. As Selina's eyes glanced around the room, it became evident how much time had passed. They were all strangers.

"Stop gawking, Selina, and come here!" came the strident voice of her mother.

It was then she realized she'd been standing in the doorway, one foot in and one foot out, as though unsure of which way to proceed. She noticed her mother's austere countenance. A snort near the window had her turning her head in that direction, glancing into dark eyes filled with mockery. A derisive smirk caused her to immediately recognize her brother, who had grown into a tall, dark-haired man. Percival was no longer the mean-spirited boy she remembered, but she worried that, as a man, he could do far worse.

Forcing herself out of her musings, she walked obediently toward her mother, who looked her up and down. "I can see your aunt did not spare any expense in providing for you. That dress is lovely."

"Thank you, Mother," she said softly.

Selina continued standing since she hadn't been invited to sit. Mother scrutinized her face more closely. Would she meet her mother's fastidious standards?

"You will never be a diamond of the first water, but you will do well enough." She waved her hand toward the chair across from her. "Sit down. I can't stand having to stretch my neck back to gaze up at you."

Selina's shoulders slumped a bit as she dragged her feet across the small space to do her mother's bidding. She didn't dare lean into the chair, but held her back ramrod straight while folding her hands on her lap, as her mother and sisters were sitting.

"I think it's best if we lay our cards on the table right from the start. The reason your father and I called you home is that it is time for you to marry and help fill the coffers of our estate. We have some rather substantial debts that must be paid and you are of age now."

Selina's heart dropped and she blinked a few times trying to make sense of her mother's words. "I-I don't follow. Am I to have a London Season in the hopes that someone will propose marriage?"

"No, Selina." Her mother frowned and waved her hand dismissively. "We have no money to give you a Season in London."

"Aunt Theo said she would pay for all expenses."

"Stop interrupting!" Mother scolded.

Selina stiffened her shoulders and neck, not daring to open her mouth again.

Her mother looked at Selina's father. "Runswick, please explain to your daughter what is expected of her."

He cleared his throat before speaking. "It's like this, Selina. We have some huge debts to pay off and we need you and Juliet to do your part. You will marry the man your mother and I have chosen for you. Your sister has already married the Earl of Chesterfield."

Stunned, she glanced at Juliet to see if she could discern her sister's feelings on the matter, for it seemed Juliet had been forced to marry also. Her sister's eyes were thoughtful, but Selina couldn't perceive what she was thinking. Surely she couldn't be glad about being forced to marry, yet she seemed . . . serene, which was far from what Selina felt at that moment. She wanted to run out of the room, climb back in the carriage, and return to Aunt Theo's side. Her heart pinched at her parents' betrayal. They had called her home, giving her false hopes, only to be told she must marry for the sake of filling their coffers. How naive she'd been.

As Selina now sat on the stone bench in her husband's dormant garden while Aunt Theo napped, she remembered the countless hours she'd enjoyed stimulating conversation with her aunt and uncle. They had loved her, but she'd been too ignorant to fully appreciate the gift of their devotion.

How wonderful it was to have her aunt at Thorncrest now. Selina needed advice and Aunt Theo's judgment was sound, for she truly had Selina's best interest at heart.

Her aunt was a woman to be admired. She knew how to handle difficulties with dignity. Although Aunt Theo had bitterly grieved the loss of Uncle Peter two years prior, she had forced herself to continue living. She became stronger and more independent, and regained her joie de vivre. Certainly, there were moments when Aunt Theo stared off in the distance or her voice quivered as she shared a memory of her husband, but she soon shook it off and found something to be thankful for. Her aunt didn't need the approval of society to find contentment. She had something Selina desperately longed for, but what was it?

## *Chapter Five*

"Since tomorrow is Sunday, I'd like us to attend church," Aunt Theo announced while partaking of breakfast with her niece the following morning.

"Won't it be awkward? After all, Lord FitzWalter and I were just married, yet I'll be attending service without him." Seeing her aunt's slight frown, she quickly suggested, "Wouldn't it be better if I lived in seclusion for a few weeks before going out? People in town may not be aware my husband has abandoned me. I'd prefer to keep them in ignorance of the fact if I can."

Aunt Theo lifted her serviette to wipe the corner of her mouth. She set it beside her plate, before saying, "I'm afraid they are already aware the viscount has departed."

"How do you know that? He left quite early in the morning. It's possible no one is aware." She desperately hoped this was the case, but Aunt Theo shook her head slowly. Selina's brow furrowed. "How can you be certain?"

"When I arrived in Northbury, we stopped at Three Feathers Inn to ask for directions to Thorncrest. After giving us the information we sought, the proprietor said, 'Such a shame the viscount left his young bride to return to London.' Of course, I said nothing, but merely thanked him for the directions and went on my way."

Selina stared at her plate while biting her lower lip. She'd naively hoped to prevent her marriage from becoming fodder for gossip. Alas, it was already being discussed in the village. What must they think of her?

Aunt Theo noted her niece's crushed appearance and tried to soothe her worries. "Things aren't as bad as they appear. We will simply explain the viscount needed to return to the Home Office immediately, and you will be joining him in London in a fortnight."

Selina lifted her eyes in alarm. "You mean for us to travel to London so soon? I had hoped to stay here for a few weeks." Seeing her aunt's determination, she tried to explain. "Aunt Theo, Lord FitzWalter left because he wanted distance between us. What will he think if I follow after him in such haste?"

Aunt Theo's eyebrows drew together and the corners of her mouth lowered. "His fine opinion is the least of our concerns at the moment. If you stay, you will become an object of pity and scorn. No, we must make haste to join him in London and give the appearance that you and the viscount are living together."

Closing her eyes for a moment, Selina knew swaying her aunt from this course was impossible. She spoke in a voice barely above a whisper. "I don't like this plan in the least."

"Nevertheless, it is a good plan. We can wait to leave for London in a fortnight. I don't believe waiting that long will raise any eyebrows. The townspeople are well aware I just arrived and will need a bit of time to rest and repack. Tomorrow, we will go to church, sit in the viscount's family pew, and greet the villagers confidently. After all, you are now the viscountess."

"I know it's best to do as you say, but I can't help wishing it could be otherwise. I dread forcing myself on my husband." Sighing deeply, Selina said, "Oh, Aunt Theo, will you please tell me what is so unappealing and unattractive about me? I know I'm not beautiful like my mother and sisters, but others who are not their equal in appearance have done quite well. What is it about me that causes my family and now my husband to wish me out of their sight?"

"I will not allow you to wallow in self-pity, my dear girl." Placing two fingers under her niece's chin, she lifted it, forcing Selina to look into her eyes. "I want you to listen closely. There is nothing wrong with you. The problem lies with them." Selina lowered her eyes again. Her aunt let go of her chin and tried again. "I can see you don't believe me, but I'm speaking truthfully to you. Your parents have a history of making unwise financial decisions, which puts them in these precarious situations. The only choice they see is to sacrifice their children or end up in the poor house. As far as FitzWalter, he's been hurt deeply and has built a wall around his heart to guard himself against further pain."

Selina tilted her head and narrowed her eyes. "How do you know this?"

Aunt Theo placed a warm hand over one of her niece's cold ones and gave it a squeeze. "You learn much by observing people, and I believe God sometimes gives us insight into a person's heart and motives—not as a means of gossip, but rather so we will pray and find ways to help them if we can. It takes wisdom to know whether you should pray, speak, or act." Letting go of her niece's hand, she pushed back from the table and faced her fully. "Wisdom comes with age, but it also comes from having a relationship with God. All the years you lived with me, I tried to explain to you about our Heavenly Father who loves you beyond anything imaginable, but during that time all you ever longed for was to return to the bosom of your family. I know God has patiently waited for you to finally recognize you need Him. He's the One who will help you see things more clearly."

Selina's heart squeezed at her aunt's words. She longed for the inner confidence and strength Aunt Theo possessed. For years, her aunt consistently steered her toward God, but He seemed like a fairytale—a nice story she had heard so often it actually became boring.

Selina pushed her chair back to face her aunt. "How do I get this wisdom, Aunt Theo?"

"It's really quite simple, my dear. You begin by acknowledging that you are a sinner and you need a Savior. For too long you have counted on your family to save you—if only your family would call you home, the emptiness and longing within you would finally cease." Aunt Theo took one of her niece's hands between her own and gently squeezed it. "Selina, your parents may not know the treasure they have in you, but God values you to the point he was willing to die for you. He's the only one who can fill the deepest longing inside you. It's time to think about the things I've taught you over the years.

Selina's eyes filled with tears and she pulled her bottom lip between her teeth to keep it from trembling as the truth of her aunt's words penetrated her heart. Yet the battle within her continued. It was hard to imagine the Heavenly Father could love her so much when her own father gave her away to be raised by others. A lone tear rolled down her face, but she quickly wiped it away.

Selina sat quietly for a moment, staring at her wedding ring—a circle that represented a noose around her neck rather than unending love. The ugly dagger of bitterness pricked the surface of her heart and she sensed a wave of hopelessness building. She feared drowning in despair and unforgiveness. "I don't want to be a bitter person." Her voice shook with emotion. "God, help me! I feel utterly abandoned by my family and my husband. They were only interested in me for how they could use me. I was a means to an end. They don't care about me at all!" With heightened color on her face, she said, "I hate them!" Dropping her head into her hands, her shoulders shook as she spoke through her tears. "I know it's wrong of me, but I hate them! I don't want to feel this way. I don't want their actions to destroy me."

Aunt Theo moved her chair closer to place her hands on her niece's trembling shoulders. "Jesus will help you without delay, Selina. Are you ready to invite Him into your heart?"

Selina darted her gaze to Aunt Theo as tears streamed down her face and her heart rate increased. She knew this was a pivotal moment and not something to be taken lightly, but it was her only hope. Selina straightened her shoulders. "Yes, I'm ready."

Breakfast was completely forgotten and the servants had been dismissed long ago. While sitting in the dining room,

Aunt Theo led her niece in a prayer of repentance, letting go of past hurts, and surrendering her life to God.

Selina sobbed on her aunt's shoulder for a time. When the tears finally subsided, she pulled back, wiping the moisture off her cheeks with a sheepish laugh. "I don't know why I'm crying. I'm not sad at all. Quite the opposite really. I-I feel so . . . full. Yes, that's what I'm feeling. Full in my heart." A radiant smile reached her tear-filled eyes. "I feel such joy!"

Aunt Theo's eyes glistened as her face glowed.

"I've never felt such peace as I do at this moment." Selina took in a shuddering breath and gave a decisive nod. "Aunt Theo, we will go to church tomorrow as you said we ought. I must learn all I can, for I know my circumstances remain the same, and I must deal with them. I'm only glad they somehow seem less significant at the moment."

Aunt Theo smiled knowing this was the beginning of a new chapter in Selina's life.

Walking down the aisle of the church to the viscount's family pew, Selina felt the stares and heard the whispers. It didn't surprise her nor was she offended. She had expected as much. Thankfully, the organ began playing and, except for a few surreptitious glances, everyone focused their attention to the front of the sanctuary.

When the vicar stood at the pulpit, Selina was amazed at his youth. She had expected someone quite a bit older. He couldn't have been above eight and twenty, only ten years her senior. And he was a fine looking gentleman. Was he married? If not, he was sure to draw a crowd of single ladies and their parents each Sunday.

The vicar shared the message he'd prepared, but Selina had a hard time following. He spoke much about social efforts and political concerns, but nothing from the Scriptures. She glanced briefly at her aunt, who caught her eye, shrugged her shoulders, and faced forward again. When the lengthy speech ended, they stood to their feet for the benediction. Selina's heart longed for more than what was offered. She determined to study the Scriptures on her own after lunch.

As the congregants shuffled down the aisle toward the exit of the church, Selina and Aunt Theo smiled and conversed with everyone who came to greet them. She felt welcomed.

There had been one sticky moment when an older lady stopped her to inquire about the viscount in a suspicious manner. Selina placed a friendly expression on her face. "He was doing quite well when I last heard from him. Thank you for asking." Quickly changing the subject, she added, "My, that's a lovely broach you're wearing." Sufficiently distracted, the curious lady expounded about the significance of her broach until they were interrupted by the vicar who wanted to meet the newcomers.

All in all, Selina was pleased with their first excursion into Northbury, but Aunt Theo was more reticent. "They believed our story about FitzWalter having to return to the Home Office so soon after the wedding only because they have heard of the fear of another riot in Manchester. If we do not hurry to join him in London, people will become suspicious." Aunt Theo insisted they begin preparing for their trip without delay.

Selina suddenly felt chilled and hugged her arms over her abdomen. What would her husband's reaction be? She had no doubt he would be greatly displeased to see them so soon after having escaped to London.

# *Chapter Six*

"What do you mean, you need five thousand pounds!" Obadiah Kendall, Viscount Runswick, was normally an affable gentleman, who preferred avoiding confrontations. He allowed his wife to run the household and family with minimal bother to himself. Unfortunately, Lady Runswick brought their son into his study where he'd been enjoying a good book and some peace and quiet.

His financial burdens had been lifted with the marriage of both Selina and Juliet. Lord Moorbridge had paid generously for the privilege of Selina marrying his son. He had requested the eldest daughter, of course, who was reputed to be more beautiful than the second. But Juliet had already brought the Earl of Chesterfield up to scratch. Chesterfield had asked for his oldest daughter's hand the day before Moorbridge came to see him. Since both the Earl of Chesterfield and Viscount FitzWalter had deep pockets, he grabbed with both hands at the opportunity to get himself out of Dun territory. Lord knew his estate needed the blunt. So he arranged for his second daughter to marry FitzWalter, explaining to Moorbridge that Selina was an heiress to her uncle's estate and, although not as beautiful as the first, was certainly not hard on the eyes. He didn't actually know if this was true since he hadn't clapped eyes on her for many years. He simply counted on the fact that by the time they were introduced, the marriage contract between the families would be signed and FitzWalter would be obligated to marry the girl.

Without the burden of keeping creditors at bay, Runswick was finally able to sit quietly at home and enjoy his solitude. Unfortunately for him, his wife and son had other ideas. He glared at them across his desk.

Percival stood, shoulders straight, a couple inches taller than his father. He seemed to enjoy looking down his nose at him. "I had a couple nights at a gaming hell. I was on a winning streak for hours when my luck turned. Father, you of all people know how that goes. One doesn't quit on a good night. I knew my luck would reverse again soon."

Letting out a frustrated sigh, Runswick said, "But it didn't, did it?"

"No," was Percival's clipped response.

"I specifically told you not to exceed your allowance with cards. Once again, you didn't heed my advice." Out the corner of his eye, Lord Runswick saw his wife step toward the side of his desk, away from their son.

"Father, I'm not a schoolboy you need to scold. If I need the blunt, it is your responsibility to pay it until I inherit after you're gone."

"If I'm not careful, by the time you inherit, there will be nothing left for you to acquire except the title."

"You do remember you introduced me to gaming, don't you?" Percival sneered. "You've had enough of your own debts to pay off. Why do you stand in judgment of me?"

"Because I'm concerned for your mother, and I have one more daughter to marry off. I will need a dowry for Helena and I must make certain your mother will have enough to live on, as well as keep the estate intact for you." Planting his hands on the desk in front of him, he scowled as he leaned forward. "I cannot afford to keep paying your debts. You must give up cards as I have!"

Percival burst out laughing. When he saw neither of his parents had joined in his laughter, he said, "You are in earnest?"

"I'm certainly not jesting. I want you to stay home during the day so I can teach you about running the estate. In the evening, you may attend balls and parties or concerts and the theater. You would do well to begin searching for a wife and start a family."

"A family?" Percival laughed. "I'm only three and twenty. I will not allow myself to be tied down so soon."

"Do as you please, only desist from visiting another gambling establishment." Runswick pointed a finger at his son. "Listen carefully. If you continue in this way, you had better start seeking for an heiress. Your sisters may take in your mother if you lose your wealth, but no one will help you out if you insist on throwing it all away on cards and entertaining light-skirts. I will not support you ruining our family."

Percival stared daggers at his father. "That will not do! I will go wherever my friends go!"

"Percival . . ." Lady Runswick soothed.

"I'm sorry to hear you feel that way," Runswick interrupted his wife. "Here is what will happen then. I will pay off your five thousand pounds but will spread the word that no one need expect any more payments from me on your behalf. You are on your own. If you create a debt, it will be yours to pay from the generous allowance you receive. If you cannot, you will have to deal with the consequences."

As Runswick spoke, he saw his wife's slight nod of approval. Percival's spending and gaming had been a concern for several years now. It was time to put a stop to it.

Percival's eyes narrowed and his face became red. "How dare you! You are my father and I am your heir." Poking his chest in emphasis, he shouted, "I have a right to live my life as I see fit!"

Runswick took a deep breath and let it out swiftly before speaking in a calm voice. "Yes, you do. And you will face the consequences of your freedom if you live above your means."

"Balderdash! I will not be treated as a pauper. If I fall into Dun territory, you will be forced to help me out."

"No, son. I will not." Runswick spoke with deadly calm. "Now let us be done with this. You know the rules. Would you like to stay for tea?"

Percival walked closer to his father and leaned across the desk. He pointed his finger under Runswick's nose. "You ungrateful old man!" he spoke through clenched teeth. "You won't live forever, and then I will do what I please."

Lady Runswick gasped and quickly moved closer to her husband to stand behind him.

Percival shifted his gaze toward his mother and he sneered. "And don't expect me to take care of you in the future if you refuse to use your influence to help me now!"

Runswick felt an anger rise within him he'd never felt before. How dare his son speak to him with such disrespect and how dare he threaten his mother. "I've changed my mind, you ingrate!" he yelled as Percival stomped to the door of the room.

Percival turned slowly, a smug smile on his face. "Have you?" he drawled.

"Yes, I have. I will not pay your five thousand pounds. You can pay it yourself."

Percival narrowed his eyes as his jaw tightened. "What did you say?"

His son had never looked so evil. Lady Runswick whimpered behind him. He didn't dare take his eyes off Percival. Runswick straightened his shoulders and glared back at his son. "I said, for the disrespect you showed your mother and me, you will pay your own five thousand pounds."

"And how do you suggest I do that?" he sneered.

"You can sell your Arabian horses and your flashy horse carriages. If you continue losing money, you can sell your townhouse."

Percival's eyebrows rose to the ceiling and his eyes bulged. "Never!" he shouted.

"I would also suggest you get rid of the cottage you let for your expensive mistress. Now, leave my house. You may return when you know how to treat us with respect."

Percival walked around the desk and toward his father until they were an arm's length apart. Runswick refused to flinch, which seemed to anger Percival even more. Runswick could feel his wife's shaking hand on his back as she moaned. Percival obviously wished to scare his parents, but Runswick was made of sterner stuff.

Holding a finger under his father's nose, Percival's eyes narrowed as he spoke. "You will regret this, old man." Then he spat in his father's face, spun away, and stomped out of the room, but not before he heard his mother's gasp of horror, which brought an evil smile to his lips.

Both parents stood in shock. Runswick was the first to recover. He pulled out a handkerchief and wiped his beard.

"Percival must have been drinking before coming here. He's awful when he's drunk!" Agnes Kendall said in a breathy voice.

"That boy is unruly, selfish, arrogant, and, when he consumes liquor, I fear he has the potential of being a danger to society. It's time he grows up and takes responsibility."

"I hate to say it of my own son, but he scares me. I don't know what to expect of him," Lady Runswick said. "I desperately hope he will not humiliate us in public, for it would be too much to bear."

## *Chapter Seven*

Fitz carefully disembarked when the carriage stopped in front of Henfort, his London residence. Rubbing his aching leg, he knew the limp would be pronounced after days of travel. His eyes feasted on the familiar two-story townhouse, his home since coming of age and taking on the responsibilities of his title. He sighed. Finally, he was far enough away from the consequences of his father's lies. He felt like a bachelor again, which was exactly what he had been before departing for Moorbridge Manor, his father's estate.

He felt stiff and exhausted after two days of travel from Northbury to London in a closed carriage. It had been impossible to find rest. Fitz was determined to arrive in London as quickly as possible and leave his conscience far behind. They did stop at an inn for part of one night, but Fitz had his servants up and moving before the sun arose. The haste had been worth it. He was finally home.

Fitz leaned heavily on his cane as he made his way to the front door, anticipating a warm bath, a change of clothes, some sustenance, and a brandy to ease the pain. Sitting by a cozy fire while reading a book before falling into bed was his only goal this evening. All else could wait until the morrow.

"It's good to see you, Fitz," Lieutenant Adam Linfield exclaimed as he pounded his friend on the back.

Fitz shook off his great coat and hung it on the coat tree near the door. Rubbing his hands together, he said, "This infernal weather is starting to get through to me. For pity's sake, it's May and we are still shivering from cold."

Adam laughed. "You're certainly in a foul mood today. Can't say I blame you. Why are you even here? Congratulations on your marriage, by the way. I'm surprised you decided to return so soon." Wiggling his eyebrows, he said, "Certainly, you had better ways to occupy your time."

Adam, the second son of the Earl of Summerworth, had fought together with Fitz, also a second son, during the war against Napoleon. By the time Fitz received word that his older brother had passed away and he was now the heir to the title of Earl of Moorbridge, he had already been severely injured. His father, having lost his heir, feared he'd lose his spare son also. Evidently, Fitz was made of sterner stuff. His leg healed fairly well and the scar on his face became less apparent over time, although it had been grotesque when he first arrived home. Actually, it was hideous enough to cause his fiancé to turn her back on him.

Fitz didn't expect Adam to understand his haste to return to work. Until a man got burnt, he refused to believe those sweet-smelling creatures wearing ruffles and lace hid claws under the white gloves society insisted they must wear. Selina was sensitive and innocent now, but she would eventually go the way of all females. He didn't trust himself around her. Although sincere and devoid of artifice at eighteen years of age, which was a potent combination for any man's heart, Fitz knew only too well from personal experience how society could change the weaker sex. They didn't have the strength to withstand the lure of status and the need for the approval from the ton. Since he couldn't keep her tucked away in the country forever, it was inevitable that once his wife developed Town bronze, she would soon break free of the cocoon of naivety and transform into a vixen like the rest.

He hadn't allowed himself to feel any depth of emotion for any woman since Dinah, until now. No, that wasn't quite right. What he felt for his wife was not anything close to love. He wouldn't be foolish enough to give his heart again. But Fitz couldn't deny Selina's innocence drew him.

His heart trembled with longing to care for her. That was precisely why he chose to depart for London post haste. Hopefully, if she decided to come to Town for the Season in a few weeks and he was forced to spend time in her company, London would quickly harden her and cause her to become the avaricious creature he knew to be hidden in every female. At that point, his heart would no longer be at risk.

Fitz mumbled an obligatory "thank you" to his friend for congratulating him on his marriage, which caused Adam to raise his eyebrows. "I'm assuming your disgruntled attitude stems from having to leave your bride so soon, but I mean to inform you that you could have stayed away longer. We have men dispatched to ride to Manchester tomorrow and look more closely at the situation there."

"I'm not disgruntled about being back." Sighing deeply, he decided to be honest with his friend. They had faced a war together. Adam could be trusted to keep his confidence. "My farce of a wedding occurred by my father's manipulation. I have no desire to pretend a happy state of marriage under these circumstances."

A frown slowly replaced the smile Adam had first greeted him with. "He manipulated you? How so?"

Fitz explained what his father had done, and Adam shook his head in amazement. Repeating all that had transpired caused his stomach to tighten in knots. Yet he was helpless to do anything about it, except to thwart his father's wishes in the only way he knew how—by keeping Selina at arm's length. Perhaps it wasn't the honorable thing to do, but others had done far worse to him. At least his bride didn't love him. He could not break a heart that was never entrusted to him. The only emotion he imagined she felt was relief at not having to consummate a marriage to a stranger.

"What about your wife? Was she aware of your father's scheme?"

"No. I'm convinced she was not. Her parents may have

been aware of it. However, I am fairly certain my father needed no accomplices. This was all his doing, of that I have no doubt."

"What will you do now? Whether you like it or not, you have a wife."

Fitz shuffled some papers on his desk and nodded slowly. He let out a frustrated sigh. "You're right. I do have a wife—a young, innocent wife, who must be relieved to see me gone. I've left her at Thorncrest with her aunt. They will be well provided for."

Adam pursed his lips. "You abandoned your new bride in the country? What will your neighbors and tenants think when they realize you left her so soon?"

Fitz rubbed a hand over the back of his neck. "I don't know. I hadn't given it much thought. I suppose she could say I had to return to the Home Office where I was needed on some urgent business."

Adam stared at his friend thoughtfully. "I suppose she could say that, but I doubt anyone would believe her. Gossips love to spread the worst case scenarios and, in your case, it happens to be true."

Fitz waved his hand dismissively. "I'm certain her aunt will know how to handle the situation. Since I didn't create this debacle, this is the best I can do for now."

Adam raised his brow but must have decided it was best not to say anything more on the subject. "You were right about one thing. You are needed here on urgent business. We would have managed without you, but I'm convinced your expertise will make things easier. As you know, we've been dealing with unrest amongst the textile industry laborers." Fitz nodded, so Adam continued. "They feel they are being unjustly treated and are inciting each other to greater discontent. Since the end of the war, famine and chronic unemployment have only exacerbated their fears. Our spies have come back with grave reports about the unrest across England, and especially in Manchester."

Fitz and Adam sat at a table where a map of England was laid out. They began strategizing what needed to be done. They were helpless to do anything about the weather, of course, but they had to find a way to stop the rebels who were most vocal in inciting unrest amongst the people.

One week later, a traveling coach stopped in front of Henfort. Footmen hurriedly opened umbrellas and helped the ladies into the townhouse. The ever-alert butler must have noticed the viscount's crest on the coach and immediately called footmen to be of service to the new arrivals in this miserable weather. Selina shivered as she pulled off her damp cloak and handed it to the waiting servant. Aunt Theo did the same.

Facing the butler, Selina said, "Thank you for your help. It's simply miserable out there. I am Lady Selina FitzWalter and this is my aunt, Mrs. Theodosia Harris."

"My lady, ma'am." The butler bowed to each of the new arrivals. "Welcome to your home. I am Bates, the butler." He extended his arm toward an older lady standing at attention. "This is Mrs. Addams, the housekeeper."

At Selina's nod, Mrs. Adams curtsied and said, "I'm pleased to meet you both."

"If I may show you to the drawing room," Bates motioned with his hand, "there is a fire prepared where you may warm yourselves. We would be happy to serve you refreshments and tea if it would please my lady."

"Yes, thank you. That sounds splendid." The warm bricks placed in the carriage for them had lost their heat hours ago, and Selina was frozen to the bone from the damp weather. She followed the butler while Aunt Theo walked behind at a slightly slower pace, forcing her stiffened joints into action.

After settling into comfortable chairs before the fireplace and partaking of warm scones with butter, preserves, and hot tea, Selina sensed her travel weariness to a greater measure. She asked the maid, who had come to retrieve the tea tray, to please inform Mrs. Addams that they were ready to be shown to their rooms.

The housekeeper promptly answered their summons and led the ladies up the stairs to their respective bedchambers. To Selina's great disappointment, her room contained dark wood furniture and a deep red and gold carpet, while thick red velvet drapery hung on either side of the large window. Thankfully, the curtains were drawn open and allowed the meager light of this gray and rainy day to enter the room. White walls gave the bedchamber some relief from the dreary tones. She preferred the tranquil colors of her rooms at Thorncrest. Trying valiantly not to show her disappointment, Selina met Aunt Theo's understanding eyes.

"If there is anything else my lady needs, please do not hesitate to call." Mrs. Addams curtsied and led Aunt Theo to a guest bedchamber.

The dark colors of the room were the least of Selina's worries. First, she would have to suffer through a reunion with her husband, dreading the moment he discovered her presence in his London townhouse without giving him prior notice of her arrival.

Polly watched as Bates and Mrs. Addams welcomed the two ladies to Henfort. The younger lady claimed to be the new viscountess. That placed a spoke in her plans for the master.

She started working at Henfort a year ago and was well aware of his reputation as a wealthy lord and bachelor not in a hurry to be caught in the parson's mousetrap. The one thing Polly hoped above all else was to be rich and no longer forced into service to keep a roof over her head. She had greater ambition than scrubbing floors, dusting, and emptying chamber pots. Having experienced the fatal results of poverty in her own family, she wanted out.

Her father had fought in the war only to come home without a leg and die of gangrene because he couldn't afford a physician. With the famine in England that began after the war and then the cholera outbreak, Polly had lost her mother to the dreaded disease. While Polly worked at Henfort emptying chamber pots, her mother died . . . alone.

A few months prior, Polly had met a Bird of Paradise, the mistress of a lofty lord. She'd been greatly impressed by the woman. Her clothes were amongst the finest there ever was and her jewelry astonishing. From that time on, the plan began to form in her mind. Well aware her curves could turn the heads of men, she had no intention of wasting her charms on the lower class. Deciding to catch herself a wealthy lord, she set her sights on Lord FitzWalter, who was close at hand. He was fair game.

While the master was away at Thorncrest, she concocted her plan. When he finally returned home, he unfortunately became excessively busy with the Home Office and Parliament and was seldom at Henfort. One evening, Bates sent her to the study to prepare the fire while Lord FitzWalter was upstairs changing out of his travel clothes. Polly purposely dawdled hoping for a moment alone with him. As she waited, she prepared herself for his arrival. Polly unbuttoned the first button of her shirtwaist with trembling fingers. She touched her hand to the neckline and realized she'd have to undo another button for this to work. Taking a calming breath, she opened the button. It was still rather discreet. Hopefully he would understand the invitation.

When the viscount finally entered his study, Polly could hardly breathe as she watched him stroll to his desk and sit down. Her pulse raced. She was uncertain of what to do next. He had obviously not seen her, but this was her opportunity and she would not waste it. Polly slowly stood to her feet and straightened to her full height. Her gaze was fixed upon Lord FitzWalter for signs of interest. She caught his eyes, forcing herself not to look away. With a heavy-lidded smile, she spoke in a raspy whisper, "Welcome home, my lord."

He stared at her a moment. "Thank you," came his clipped response. "You may go."

That was it? He dismissed her? His eyes didn't follow her to the door. She knew it for a fact for she had glanced back twice hoping to catch his interested gaze. He sat at his desk, gawking at flat sheets of paper instead of her bountiful curves.

That had been the only opportunity presented to her, and she had failed miserably. Now it seemed he had a wife. Polly sighed and resumed her duties.

# *Chapter Eight*

Fitz climbed the stairs to the front door of his home just before dawn. The sun would be rising in another hour. Meeting with the spies to hear what they observed had taken longer than he'd anticipated, but the information was enlightening. He would soon leave for Manchester to meet with some textile owners and tour their factories to discern with his own eyes the atmosphere amongst the workers and management, and hopefully determine who the rabble-rousers were. He planned to leave in two days.

Fitz let himself through the front door knowing his staff would be sound asleep. As he closed the door, he was surprised to see Bates rising from a chair in the foyer. Although the staff was told never to wait up for him, his butler had obviously fallen asleep while waiting for the master's return. Since Bates didn't heed his words on this instance, he must have news to share.

"Why are you still up, Bates?"

"I wished to inform my lord of the viscountess' safe arrival this afternoon."

Fitz's eyebrows shot up. "She's here?"

The butler nodded once. "My lady and Mrs. Harris are both in their rooms. We made certain they were comfortably settled. Since you had not mentioned they would be arriving, I felt I should inform you upon your return home."

Indeed, he was grateful to be forewarned but careful not

to let his feelings show. "Thank you, Bates. I will turn in now. Get some sleep."

"Yes, my lord."

Fitz trudged up the stairs to his room. Why didn't Selina inform him she was coming to London? Or perhaps she had. He ran a hand over the back of his neck in frustration as he remembered the stack of letters sitting unopened on his desk. He should have looked through them before now, but the responsibilities of the Home Office had consumed his time of late.

As his valet helped him prepare for what remained of the night, Fitz continued mulling over the fact that his wife had suddenly appeared back in his life and the ramifications thereof. He knew Selina had never partaken of a Season in London. He could understand she would wish to do so, but he dreaded the upheaval her presence would bring to his household. Gone were his quiet evenings after a grueling day at the Home Office.

Fitz remembered he already told Selina while at Thorncrest, in the event she chose to come to London, he would not be available to escort her to the various balls and parties she would be invited to. He would remind her of it if she made demands on his time. Now that she was a viscountess and Theodosia Harris was her companion, her aunt would be welcomed back into society. She could escort his wife hither and yonder. Fitz didn't have the time nor the inclination to traipse about Town unless absolutely necessary. He intended to be away from home as much as possible to avoid time alone in his wife's company. For his peace of mind, it was better to keep distance between them.

Staring at the connecting door between their bedchambers, his brow furrowed. What must she think of the condition of her rooms? Although the entire townhouse had been redecorated, he hadn't bothered making any changes to that bedchamber, dressing room, or sitting room, thinking Dinah would enjoy redecorating her own rooms after they were married. Once their betrothal ended, he had turned his back on the rooms.

Fitz was certain his wife would soon spend his money on

refurbishing. Not that he begrudged her the blunt it would cost. This was just another way for her avaricious nature to develop. It wouldn't surprise him if Selina decided to renovate his entire newly redecorated townhouse.

"Goodnight, my lord," his valet interrupted his thoughts.

"Goodnight, Rawden."

Fitz climbed into bed, determined to stop contemplating his wife's actions and wait until the morrow to hear what she had to say for herself.

Knowing her aunt was an early riser, Selina headed toward the breakfast room early the next morning. She preferred breaking the fast with Aunt Theo rather than eating alone. It wasn't eating in solitude that bothered her, but rather not knowing the viscount's habits. If she waited to eat later and he was a late riser, she might end up having to share breakfast alone with him. Although Selina would have to face him eventually, she simply preferred to have her aunt in attendance when that time came.

As Selina walked along the corridor, she peeked into a room here and there. Each one was well appointed and beautifully decorated. Was her bedchamber the only neglected room in the house?

The footman opened the door to the breakfast room and she saw it was unoccupied. Aunt Theo hadn't arrived yet. Should she turn around and come back later? What would the servants think of such strange behavior? She decided to stay.

Walking over to the sideboard, Selina selected a piece of toast, an egg, and some fruit. It looked scrumptious, but she knew the knot in her stomach wouldn't allow her to do justice to the meal. As she reached for a seat at the table, the door opened.

"Good morning, my dear," came the cheerful voice of her aunt.

Selina's face broke into a smile. "Good morning, Aunt Theo. You look refreshed."

Once both ladies were seated at the table, the servants poured tea for them. They took their serviettes and placed them on their laps. Aunt Theo bowed her head to pray and Selina followed suit.

No sooner had they finished praying, the door opened yet again. Selina stifled a nervous gasp at the sight of her husband. He stood in the doorway and simply stared at her for what felt like ten minutes, but was perhaps only five seconds. Unable to look away, her heart pounded out of her chest. He moved his gaze to Aunt Theo, allowing Selina to breathe again.

"Good morning, Mrs. Harris . . . Selina." He nodded to each as he spoke their names.

"Good morning, my lord," they greeted him in unison.

He moved to the sideboard and prepared his own plate, not speaking another word. What must he be thinking? He didn't seem surprised. One of the servants must have informed him of their arrival yesterday. Of course they had. FitzWalter's servants were well trained and it would be their duty to inform him of anything strange going on. His wife showing up unannounced would certainly fall into the "strange" category.

FitzWalter didn't seem to look upon them with disfavor. Perhaps he didn't mind their presence. After taking his seat, he lifted his fork and began eating. No one talked. The sound of silverware tapping on china was the only sound in the room. Aunt Theo seemed unaware of the loud silence as she continued to eat. FitzWalter lifted his fork to take another bite of the meal he obviously relished.

Selina's eyes strayed from one to the other. This would be a good time for Aunt Theo to explain the reason they had come to London, but she remained stubbornly mute and continued eating. Selina resisted rolling her eyes in frustration. Why was Aunt Theo prolonging this? She should simply explain and have it done with.

Taking another peek in her aunt's direction, they made eye contact. She watched as Aunt Theo lifted her brow in inquiry, then nudged her chin in the direction of the viscount. *What? Does Aunt Theo want me to begin the conversation?* Heart thumping, Selina surreptitiously glanced around the room making sure servants weren't present.

She cleared her throat and the viscount lifted his eyes to focus his gaze upon her.

"I-I need to explain. That is, I wish to..." *Oh, this is all wrong. Why is it so difficult to find words to explain?*

"What is your wish, Selina?" The viscount sounded almost kind.

Selina took a deep breath. "I wish to explain our presence here, my lord. I-I realize I did not send a message to inform you of our arrival, but, you see, Aunt Theo felt it best we depart Thorncrest immediately, and . . . I had to agree—especially after church on Sunday." Selina knew she was babbling, but forced herself to say what needed to be said before she lost her courage.

"What happened in church on Sunday that precipitated such a swift exit from Northbury?" he asked. "Were the people unwelcoming? Did they say something offensive?"

"Well, no . . . everyone welcomed us." At the raising of his eyebrows, she quickly explained. "Many people were curious about your absence." She swallowed hard before continuing. "I explained, of course, you had to return to your post at the Home Office. Although no one seemed overly surprised you were needed in London, it would only be a matter of time before they questioned your motives if I didn't join you. After all, it is rather suspicious that a bridegroom should leave his bride a day after the wedding, which is why Aunt Theo insisted we make haste to join you."

Fitz stared at her with pursed lips. What was he thinking? She breathed a bit easier when he shifted his gaze toward Aunt Theo, who sat silently observing their interaction—almost unemotionally—as though watching a play at Drury Lane. *If only I could hide my feelings in the same way.*

His gaze returned to her and he asked, "What is your plan? Do we pretend to be blissfully married?" Narrowing his eyes a bit, he said, "I will have to be frank with you. I don't have the time nor the inclination to do so."

Selina's eyes widen and her mouth fell open as her heart clenched. "I-I'm not asking you to pretend to love me, but if we are at least under the same roof for the Season, I will be able to depart for Thorncrest without becoming fodder for gossip. Could you tolerate my presence for that length of time?"

Fitz had nothing against Selina except for her unsuspecting part in his father's plan. He didn't know her enough to find her unbearable in any way. It was the situation he found himself in that was intolerable. "You may suit yourself, but don't count on me to escort you around London. I have a responsibility to the Home Office that is currently consuming my time. As a matter of fact, I will be leaving soon on a mission and don't know when I'll be back." *Maybe I can stop somewhere along the way and prolong my journey. Certainly there must be another location that needs inspection.* "If it was your plan to be seen with me, I will not be able to accommodate you."

"We only need you to attend a come-out ball I intend to host for Selina." Aunt Theo finally interjected. "If you will oblige us in this, we will ask nothing more of you except the use of this townhouse to reside in until our departure."

Fitz couldn't refuse to attend a ball honoring his wife. It would be beneath him to insult her in such a manner. She was a pawn in this marriage arrangement as much as he. "Very well. Let me know when, and I will be there."

Fitz and Aunt Theo focused their attention to the plates before them, while Selina gazed helplessly at her own dish. She couldn't bring herself to lift another bite to her mouth. *God, where are you? Please help me. I feel the dark cloud of despair descending.*

"You may address the invitations as coming from me and I will foot the bill for the event," Fitz informed Aunt Theo, "but you will have to do the arrangements and preparations. I will assist as host on the evening of the ball. I can offer no more."

He was willing to do something to acknowledge her as his wife. It was a start. "Thank you, my lord," Selina swallowed her pride at his obvious reluctance to attend. God was beside her and that was enough. "That is most generous. Is there anyone you would like us to invite on your behalf?"

He nodded. "Yes. I'll give a list to Bates before I leave this morning. He will make sure you receive it. Now, if that is all, I must be on my way."

"May I invite your parents?"

Fitz stared at his wife a moment before answering, "No." Bowing to them, he said, "Good day."

Once he was out of earshot, Aunt Theo remarked, "Well, that went rather well."

"Do you think so? I would leave today if I could. My husband treats me only marginally better than my family. At least he didn't send me back to Thorncrest." Seeing the concern in her aunt's eyes, Selina reached over and placed a hand on Aunt Theo's arm. "Forgive my outburst, dear Aunt. With you by my side, I will manage just fine. I know I haven't told you often enough, but I appreciate all you do for me and the love you have shown me all these years."

Aunt Theo blinked away the sudden moisture in her eyes. "It was truly my pleasure."

Blatant love shone on Aunt Theo's face. Selina arose from her chair and embraced her aunt. "I don't know what I would do if I didn't have you." She placed a kiss on her aunt's cheek and hugged her once more.

A servant walked into the room with a fresh pot of tea. Both ladies straightened and continued with their meal. Selina found her appetite returning. They discussed what needed to be done for the ball. As they prepared to leave the breakfast room, Bates came to the door and announced a visitor.

"Miss Kitty Haddington is here to see you, my lady."

Selina gasped. "Kitty! Oh, how lovely!" Turning to her aunt, she said, "Can you believe it? Kitty, here in London! Oh, this is perfect!"

Aunt Theo grinned at her niece. "Yes, indeed, it is."

The butler cleared his throat waiting for further instructions. "Shall I take her to the drawing room, my lady?"

"No. I will follow you to the foyer. And, Bates, in the future, you may receive Kitty Haddington. I will always be home to her."

"Very well, my lady."

* * *

"Kitty!" Selina exclaimed when she saw her friend standing in the foyer still wearing her cloak and bonnet. Selina walked toward her with outstretched arms. "What a wonderful surprise!"

"Selina!" was Kitty's joyful response. The two friends fell into each other's arms. "How I've missed you!"

"No more than I've missed you." Pulling apart, Selina said, "Let Bates take your cloak and bonnet, and we will make ourselves comfortable in my sitting room."

Having spotted Aunt Theo, Kitty smiled. "It's a pleasure to see you, Mrs. Harris."

"The pleasure is mine, Kitty dear."

The younger ladies linked arms and headed up the stairs with Aunt Theo following behind.

"Oh, is this your private sitting room?" Kitty asked.

"Yes, it is." Selina smiled sheepishly. "Dreadful, isn't it? The colors in my bedchamber are the same."

Kitty bit her bottom lip for a moment. "It isn't quite in your style."

Selina chuckled. "Absolutely not. Since I only arrived yesterday and am newly married, I am hardly in a position to make a lot of changes."

Kitty tilted her head. "You must tell me how it happened that you are married."

"And *you* must tell me what has brought you to London."

Kitty and Aunt Theo shared a look of amusement, which caused Selina to become suspicious. "What? Aunt Theo, did you know Kitty was in Town?"

Her aunt laughed. "Actually, Selina, I knew you could use a friend right now and I also felt it was time Kitty was introduced to society. Don't you agree?"

Selina's eyes lit up. "Do you mean Kitty will be presented with me?" Seeing the smiling faces of her aunt and dearest friend, she clasped her hands together and held them over her heart. "Oh! This is truly marvelous! I was terribly nervous to face the ton on my own, but this will be much better!" Turning to her friend, she added, "Kitty, with your lovely blonde hair and smooth skin, your blue eyes and perfect features, you will deflect attention away from me, for which I'm excessively glad."

"That's utter poppycock." Kitty rolled her eyes as she shook her head with a curl of her lip. "You are more lovely than I with your dark, shiny tresses and your big brown eyes. You're the one who will receive the attention."

"Pfft! Now who's talking nonsense? Blondes are all the rage in London, and everywhere else in England, I might add. Besides, you know very well I don't desire the attention nor do I need it since I am no longer in the market for a husband."

"There will be many gentlemen who will wish to dance with you, married or not," Kitty said.

Selina sighed. "That is probably true. Not because they find me pretty, but because I am a viscountess and the ball is in my honor. I dread having to make conversation with total strangers."

"I know you prefer small dinner parties with friends over large events full of strangers, but we will make it fun, won't we?"

Not wanting her fears to put a damper on Kitty's joy, Selina smiled. "Yes, we will." Although returning to Thorncrest would be her preference, she secretly hoped to know her husband better, which would not be possible if she removed to the country. Besides, Aunt Theo would never agree to depart London so soon. She was determined to see her niece enter society this year.

"Where are you staying, Kitty?"

"I'm in Town with my mother and father." Smiling briefly to Aunt Theo, she turned back to Selina. "Your aunt has generously allowed us the use of her townhouse. She magnanimously offered to sponsor my entry into society. I feel unworthy, but she insisted it was for my father's faithful years of service, and that it would benefit you to have me in attendance. Did we presume too much, Selina? I feel a bit like an interloper."

"What? You, an interloper? Never! Aunt Theo had the right of it. Having you with me will be a great comfort and boon to my confidence. You could never be seen as an interloper. Why, your grandfather is an earl. You have every right to partake in the Season."

"Much good having an earl as a grandfather has ever done me. As you very well know, when my uncle inherited, he had no time for my father—his younger brother—and he most definitely would not consider sponsoring his niece. I doubt he would even recognize me if we were to meet."

"It matters not if he recognizes you. You are the granddaughter of an earl and no one can take that away. I'm only glad your parents are here as well. They are respected members of society and will know how to guide us if we need it."

"Unfortunately, father is only here for a fortnight, and then he must return to his parish. Mother will stay with me, but she has little experience in society as she never finished her own Season. You see, my parents fell in love and married in a matter of weeks. After their wedding, they left immediately to settle at the parish where they would serve. Neither of them has a great love for London."

"I see. Well, Aunt Theo will have to guide us. Isn't that right, Aunt Theo? You had two Seasons before you married. I think we can rely upon you to show us the way."

"You may certainly rely on me to know how to assist you. I also have a good friend, Lady Worthington, who has agreed to help me in this endeavor."

"Lady Worthington?" Kitty squealed. "Why, she's the wife of a marquess! How did you become such good friends?"

Selina looked at her aunt for an answer as well. She had no idea Aunt Theo had maintained friendships in the ton after marrying Uncle Peter.

"Beatrice Worthington and I were immediate friends in school. We had our debutante ball the same year and were constantly together. She fell in love with her marquess the same year I fell in love with my handsome merchant. Beatrice understood why I loved him and she encouraged me to follow my heart, promising to remain my friend no matter how society may frown upon it."

"Did she stay true to her word?" Kitty wanted to know.

"She most certainly did. We wrote letters back and forth all these years."

"I never realized," Selina said. "Why did you never tell me of her?"

Aunt Theo shrugged her shoulders. "I'm not certain. It never entered my mind to do so. But I thought of her immediately when I realized your parents were not going to present you to society, and planned to marry you off instead. I am determined to do right by you, my girl. You will have your Season."

All the affection she felt for her aunt shone from Selina's eyes as they glistened with tears. "Thank you, Aunt Theo."

"You're welcome, my dear."

Kitty sat smiling as she looked between aunt and niece.

"Now," Aunt Theo continued, "I need to inform you that Lady Worthington has invited us to join her for tea tomorrow so we may discuss in greater detail what needs to be done." She directed her gaze upon Kitty. "You and your mother will join us, I hope." At Kitty's nod, she continued. "We will pick you up and drive together to the marquess' house. As I mentioned before, you will both be presented at the same time. I will sponsor Kitty, and FitzWalter will sponsor Selina. Are there any questions? If not, I will leave you and proceed with my day."

Selina and Kitty gave each other a searching glance, then shrugged their shoulders. Selina said, "I guess not right now. I'm certain we will have more questions once we've had a chance to talk a bit. Please, don't let us hold you up if there is something else you'd like to do."

"Very well. Shall I meet you at lunch then?"

"That would be splendid."

As soon as Aunt Theo left the room, the young ladies faced each other to discuss all that had transpired since they'd last seen one another. Selina explained of her disappointment in being married off as soon as she arrived back to her parents' home. There was nothing she didn't tell her friend.

"Oh, Selina . . . I'm sorry."

Selina smiled and wiggled her brows. "But I have

wonderful news to share also."

"After all you've told me, I'm glad you have some good news."

Selina took Kitty's hands into her own. Joyful tears glistened in her eyes as she said, "I have wrested free of my independence and have decided to live my life in submission to God by embracing the same faith as you and Aunt Theo."

Kitty's eyes grew wide and she squealed as she threw her arms around her friend. "I am beyond pleased! Then we are truly sisters now!" Pulling back, she asked, "But how did it come about?"

Selina explained and they continued their conversation. Time flew by until a servant came to remind them that Aunt Theo was expecting them for lunch. They hurried to join her.

Fitz never arrived for dinner that evening. Selina didn't lay eyes on him the next day either or the one after that. The only reason she knew he had left Town was that she overheard Bates inform Mrs. Addams of her husband's departure for Manchester. When Mrs. Addams asked if he was aware of when the viscount would return, he told her he did not know. Selina quietly slipped away not wanting the servants to become aware she'd been eavesdropping. It hadn't been her intent to listen in on their conversation. While walking on the carpeted hallway to enter the library and return a book, she overheard her husband's name mentioned. Selina couldn't bring herself to regret having eavesdropped for how else would she know her husband's whereabouts?

Selina longed for a walk, but although the temperatures had warmed slightly, it was raining again. When was the last time the sun broke through the clouds? She had no idea. Maybe it had ceased shining because of the sad state of her marriage. She rolled her eyes at her fanciful thoughts.

Since a walk was out of the question, Selina headed to the music room. Having discovered it while Mrs. Addams took her on a tour of the house, it soon became a place of solace. Sitting at the pianoforte, Selina played a hymn written by

Isaac Watts often sung at her aunt's church.

*My Shepherd, you supply my need; most holy is your name.*

She continued playing and singing the words of the hymn, sensing God's presence surrounding her as she worshipped Him.

*The sure provisions of my God attend me all my days;*
*Oh, may your house be my abode and all my work be praise.*
*Here would I find a settled rest, while others go and come;*
*No more a stranger or a guest, but like a child at home.*

She repeated the last line again, singing it to her Heavenly Father who truly loved and accepted her. He would never abandon one of his children.

"Thank you, Father, for loving me and for keeping me," she prayed. Kneeling by the bench, Selina told God of her disappointment in her marriage and how she longed to be loved by her husband and to be able to love him, too. Soon her prayer changed. She found herself feeling compassion for those who had hurt her. What emptiness her mother must feel to have such a need to seek the approval of society. What had driven her father to the card tables? What must be going on inside her brother to cause him to become cynical and hateful? To what degree had her husband's heart been broken that he felt such a need to protect it? She prayed for each one of them, asking God to reveal Himself to them as He had to her. Her tears were no longer for herself, but for the pain and emptiness of each of her family members.

Aunt Theo had said God would help her see things more clearly. She called it wisdom from God. Now Selina understood, at least in part. When she came to God with her hurts, He didn't allow her to wallow in self-pity. Instead, He helped her to see things from a different perspective.

# *Chapter Nine*

"Will you be attending your sister's ball tonight? Isn't she the plain one who was raised by your aunt?" Tom Hendrick asked.

Percival had told Tom about his homely sister years ago as a way of explaining why she didn't live with the family. Tom was his childhood friend and, at such a young age, Percival searched for a valid reason for Selina's disappearance. It was the conversation he'd overheard while stooped below his father's study window that caused him to assume his middle sister was unappealing to the eyes.

When he was ten years of age, he overheard his parents talking about sending Selina to Aunt Theo and Uncle Peter. While playing in the garden, the ball landed under the open window. He heard them discussing his sister and stayed completely still to listen.

"I hate to admit it, Lady Runswick, but we are in quite deep. The only way I can see clear of coming out of this financial hole we're in is to give one of our children to my sister and her husband. Since they gave us the choice of which child to send to them when they made their generous offer, who should we sacrifice?"

"Sacrifice?" Lady Runswick exclaimed. "What a terrible choice of words! But, alas, we have no other option. I think it best Selina be given to them. Her dark coloring is rather plain and she will never be a diamond of the first water. Next to her sisters, she's bland. Perhaps, with your sister and brother-in-law's wealth, they can make something of the girl."

Quietly, Percival slipped away lest he be discovered. His parents had only considered the girls as dispensable. His name, as the heir, was never brought into question.

Yet look how they treated him now. Percival was honest enough with himself to admit his mind had been fogged by the rum he imbibed before visiting his parents. He cringed when remembering the disrespectful manner in which he'd handled the situation. But his parents knew his weakness and should not have provoked him.

Would he go to the ball in his sister's honor? He had no desire to see his family dressed in expensive finery at the event, yet unwilling to help their son and heir out of a minor debt. It would grate.

On second thought, perhaps he should attend. Although Selina had been the one sent to live outside the family, she landed on her feet, becoming the heiress to Uncle Peter's wealth. It might benefit him in the future to ingratiate himself with his sister. Not only was she an heiress to a large fortune, but married into wealth as well. He rubbed his chin and nodded slowly. Yes, it would be in his best interest to attempt endearing himself to her.

"I suppose I may need to stop in briefly to pay my respects to my sister, but I don't plan on staying long. I'd prefer spending time at one of our clubs," Percival said to Tom. They both enjoyed the seamier side of life. The difference was, Tom had better luck at cards than Percival, and he remained plump in the pockets.

"Did you forget that none of the clubs are admitting you since your father hasn't come up with the blunt to pay your debt?" Tom asked.

"I had a buyer for two of my horses yesterday. The most pressing debts have been paid. I doubt the clubs will deny me entrance."

Tom smacked him on the back. "Good to know. Then I'll join you for a brief stop at the ball before we visit our club.

I'm curious to see what became of the sister your family found necessary to send away."

That evening as Percival prepared for the ball, Selina was on his mind. No doubt, she was a green girl. He was used to the practiced charms of experienced women, and it was glaringly obvious his sister lacked any true knowledge of deceit. His plan to twist her around his little finger should be easily accomplished.

Percival remembered well the eager anticipation in Selina's eyes when she entered their parents' home after years of separation. She'd obviously fantasized a tearful reunion. Hope illuminated her face and he almost felt sorry for her, but he squelched that feeling, remembering she'd grown up in the lap of luxury. Their parents—too consumed with their own needs to notice their daughter's—presented the fait accompli. As the details of the marriage were explained, he watched the light of hope in Selina's eyes flicker out.

One thing he was certain of. Selina was desperate for affection from her family, and Percival was proficient in the art of manipulation to get what he wanted. He determined to provide Selina's heart's desire and, once her trust was bestowed, he would find a way to use it for personal gain. A self-satisfied smile played on his lips as he continued preparing for the evening ahead.

# *Chapter Ten*

After Manchester, Fitz volunteered for additional assignments outside of London, allowing him to remain far removed from domestic obligations. Unfortunately, time passed too quickly. He could no longer delay his return. It was imperative he not miss the ball. Checking out early from the inn that morning, Fitz allotted himself enough time to freshen up at Henfort and arrive at the Worthington residence in a timely manner to greet his guests. Since his townhouse didn't include a ballroom, the Worthingtons kindly offered the use of their home.

"Cold and rain!" Fitz grumbled as he scowled out the window of the carriage. A warm blanket was placed over his lap and lower extremities to keep the cold from worsening his limp so he could dance at the ball this evening. He moved his damaged leg from time to time to hinder it from tightening up as the carriage lumbered along.

CRACK!!!

"What was that?" Before Fitz could open the door to the carriage to see what was going on, the conveyance began to tilt. Fitz stood to his feet to put weight on the side that was lifting in an attempt to provide a counterbalance. He knew his driver was pulling hard on the reins as the horses squealed in fright. Finally, they came to a complete stop.

Hurriedly alighting from the carriage, Fitz asked, "What happened? Did we break an axle?"

The driver examined the conveyance. "Yes, my lord. It's

quite obvious the axle is broken."

Fitz ran a hand of frustration through his hair. With little time to spare, how would he get to London in time for the ball? "We passed a town only a few minutes back. Unleash one of the horses and I'll ride for help." Fitz called out orders as he helped his servant ready a horse for travel. "I want you to stay with the carriage. Keep your gun at the ready, but remember, your life is more important than anything someone may want to steal, so don't try any heroics."

"Yes, my lord."

It would be an insult to his wife if he failed to arrive this evening for the opening dance. Desperately hoping a blacksmith in the nearby town would be willing to accept a bribe for quick service, he nudged his horse into a gallop.

Selina sat before the mirror in the bedchamber provided for her use at the Worthington estate where the night's ball would be held. As Lydia put the finishing touches on the elaborate hairstyle, Selina took a calming breath.

"Close your eyes and I'll lead you to the full-length mirror," Lydia said. Selina did as instructed, shuffling along carefully while her maid held tightly to her arm. She reminded herself not to expect to look like her sisters or her mother. Her appearance could never compare. If she didn't raise her expectations too high, the disappointment would be less severe. "You can open your eyes now."

Slowly raising her eyelids, she gasped, beholding her transformation in wonder. Lydia had outdone herself with the creation of an elegant coiffure like the one Selina had seen on a fashion plate. A few curls were allowed to hang loose near her neck. The dark emerald Indian silk fabric of her dress with short, puffed sleeves hung straight down from just below her chest, as was the current style. Although the dress was open at the neck, it was not cut too low, allowing her to maintain her modesty. A gold ribbon was sewn into the hem of her skirt and sleeves. Lydia's skillful hands wove a thin gold ribbon through her shiny, dark tresses, which pulled the entire ensemble together perfectly. The final touch was the gold dancing slippers. She actually felt pretty this evening. Perhaps even her parents would be proud to claim her as their own.

*Stop it! You no longer need the approval of your family.* The dress was splendid and Lydia had done her best with what the Lord had given her mistress. Selina hoped to display the type of character that would please her Heavenly Father, but she couldn't help hoping Fitz would find her pleasing to the eye. It wasn't wrong to wish to impress one's husband, so she would allow herself to wish for that at least.

Thinking of her husband caused a knot to form in her stomach. He hadn't returned yet from his trip. What would their guests say when they realized her husband could not be bothered attending a ball honoring his wife?

"Selina, do you not like what I did to your hair?" Lydia asked. "Is something amiss? Your face has become quite pale."

"No! Nothing is wrong. Actually, you've performed a miracle tonight. I'm certain I've never looked better."

"Then why the frown?"

"It's just that my mind wandered for a moment to something quite different than my appearance," Selina told her.

"You are concerned the viscount will not arrive in time."

It wasn't a question. The entire staff must be wondering what was going on between the master and his mistress. Perhaps they even discussed their marriage with servants of other households and those servants were passing the information to their masters and mistresses. The knot in Selina's stomach tightened and she felt nauseous.

She took a calming breath. "Lydia, thank you for all you've done. I need some time alone before I go down. You have not had your supper yet. Feel free to do so. I will not need you again until after the ball so enjoy your evening."

"Very well, my lady." She gave a brief curtsy and left the room.

Selina walked the few steps to the window. The sun had set and a full moon cast a dim light on the roadways, making it safer for their guests to travel. Afraid to wrinkle the lovely gown, Selina chose to remain standing as she prayed. "Jesus, please help me tonight. If my husband should let me down, keep my heart from breaking. And make me strong and independent like Aunt Theo. I do not wish to seek the approval of man, but hope to please You always."

As she turned back to the room, she stared at the door. It was almost time to head downstairs. The knot in her stomach squeezed once more. She whispered a prayer for strength, but it remained tight.

Selina clasped her hands together and held them to her chin. "Please, help me! I desperately need You tonight. I'm so scared. I thought I'd be more confident now that You're in my heart, but I feel as helpless and insignificant as ever before. I want you to change me."

A knock at the door caused her to jump. "Oh, Lord. The time has come and I'm not ready." Holding her hands out, she looked at them. "I'm trembling. I won't know what to say to people when they ask me about my husband. Will you allow me to be humiliated tonight?" Selina shook her head in despair. "I'm a terrible Christian. Where is my faith? No wonder You aren't answering."

The knock came again. "Selina, are you in there?"

Hearing Kitty's voice, she hurried to the door and opened it.

"Oh, Selina! You're beautiful!!" But Kitty's smile disappeared as she surveyed her friend's face more closely. "What's wrong? Your eyes are distressed. What has happened?" As she spoke, she moved into the room and closed the door behind her.

"Kitty, I'm scared about this ball. Fitz isn't here yet. What will my guests think of us? My parents will be here, too. They will see how utterly I've failed in this marriage. I've prayed and prayed, but God sees my lack of faith and knows I'm a failure as a Christian, too."

Kitty took hold of Selina's hands and squeezed them gently. "You are *not* a failure." As Selina's eyes lowered in defeat, Kitty said, "No! Don't look away. I'm speaking the truth." She squeezed her friend's hands again. "You are not a failure! If the viscount isn't here, something very important must have detained him. We will simply explain that he is on a mission for the Home Office and wanted to be here in time, but something important must have occurred to prevent him from attending."

Selina rolled her eyes. "They will never believe it."

"It doesn't matter if they believe it. The important thing is that you believe it. It is the truth. The viscount had every intention of being here. He said he would return. And please do not say you are a failure as a Christian. That isn't true either." Squeezing Selina's hands, Kitty said, "You must give yourself time to learn to trust God. People who have been believers much longer than you, still struggle with trust sometimes. Don't be hard on yourself."

Selina gave her friend a self-deprecating smile. "I must admit that your scolding has released the knot in my stomach."

Kitty giggled. "I suppose I was scolding you, but don't you see how God is answering your prayer and helping you? He knew you would need a friend to tell you the truth and arranged it that Aunt Theo would invite me to join you tonight. "

Selina smiled. "I hadn't thought of it that way, but you're right."

"Too many people overlook answers to prayers by seeing things as coincidences, when God is actually at work in their lives. He loves you, Selina. Never forget it."

"I do believe it. Thank you for the encouragement, Kitty."

There was a knock at the door. "Come in," Selina said.

Mrs. Addams entered, holding a slender box in her hands. "I have something for you, my lady. It's from the master."

"He's here!"

"Sadly, not yet. He hoped to arrive in time for the ball, but in case he was delayed, he asked me to give you this."

Selina took the box into her hands and carefully opened the lid. Both Kitty and Selina gasped when they saw the chain of pearls. As Selina lifted it from the box, she found pearl earbobs as well as a pearl bracelet.

"Oh, my! These are exquisite!" Selina said breathlessly.

"They belonged to the master's grandmother. He wanted

you to wear them this evening."

Selina swallowed a lump as she blinked tears away. "I-I'm afraid to put them on. What if I lose them?"

Mrs. Addams gazed kindly upon Selina. "Have no fear. The clasp has been checked and is in good condition. Lydia knows where to store them at the end of the evening. The master specifically said he wanted you to have these for the ball. They are yours now, my lady."

Selina bit her bottom lip as she stared at the exquisite pearls. "Then will you help me put them on?"

"Of course."

When the jewelry was in place, Selina turned toward Kitty, who had a big grin on her face. "My, you truly look like a viscountess now. But we had better hurry or the guests will begin arriving and we will not be there to greet them."

After Mrs. Addams left the room, Kitty peered at her friend once more. "Now your eyes are brighter. Ready?"

"Oh, no! The knot in my stomach is returning."

"Selina, forget the knot! Let's go down and enjoy ourselves, shall we? This is *our* ball." Having said that, she looped her arm through her friend's and they descended the stairs together. They made their way to the foyer as the first guests arrived.

As Selina positioned herself to greet her visitors, she looked down the line to see Lord and Lady Worthington welcoming an impressive-looking elderly couple. Aunt Theo stood next in line followed by Selina, then Kitty, with Kitty's parents at the end of the line of greeters.

*Fitz should be standing next to me.* The knot in Selina's stomach tightened as she realized the guests would soon become aware of his absence. *Help me, Lord!* She took a deep, calming breath and smiled at the elderly couple when Aunt Theo introduced them.

After standing in line for what felt like an hour, but was probably only half that time, Selina's eyes flew to the door when she recognized the voice of her mother. The foyer suddenly became overly warm. Hopefully if anyone noticed her burning cheeks, excitement rather than anxiety would be their guess.

Selina's parents were moments away from discovering her husband's absence. Once again, she would fail to meet their expectations. Lady Worthington greeted them and Selina desperately hoped they would have much to discuss. Aunt Theo stood next in line and then it would be Selina's turn to face them. She made a valiant attempt to maintain a pleasant countenance and listen as guests greeted her, but couldn't stop herself from casting brief glances out the corner of her eye to observe the proximity of her parents.

A sudden warmth behind her caused her to stiffen. Who would dare stand so close? Before she could swing her head around, a hand was gently placed at her waist. With a slight shift of her head, she stared into the sober face of her husband. He winked and the corner of his lips quirked up into a half smile. *He came! He hadn't forgotten after all!*

She heard him whisper, "Sorry, I'm late. I'll explain later."

"Hello, Selina," came her mother's strident voice to her ear. Facing forward again, she greeted her parents, followed by her sisters and oldest sister's husband.

"Chesterfield!" Selina heard Fitz greet Juliet's husband. "It's good to see you."

"And I'm glad to see you, too," he answered. "How are things at the Home Office?"

"Interesting," Fitz said.

"I can well imagine." Gazing at Selina, Lord Chesterfield bowed. "You look lovely, Lady FitzWalter."

Juliet's eyes sparkled. "Yes, Selina, I agree with my husband. You look splendid!"

Selina couldn't help feeling pleased with the complimentary words from members of her family.

After they had moved on to greet Kitty, she sensed her husband stiffen as his hand tightened on her waist. He quietly hissed in her ear, "What are they doing here? I expressly forbade you to invite my parents."

Husband and wife politely greeted the next guests. Once the guests moved on, Selina whispered, "Aunt Theo and Lady Worthington overrode your request."

He mumbled, "It wasn't a request." Before she could respond, the next guest stood before them and they continued with polite greetings until her husband's parents stopped to face them.

"Good evening, Selina, FitzWalter," Lord Moorbridge said. "You are lovely this evening, my dear."

Selina curtsied to her father-in-law. "Thank you, my lord. And thank you for coming to the ball."

"Wouldn't miss it." Moorbridge averted his gaze to his son, who stared back at him. "So you made it back from Manchester in time for the ball. Perhaps you'll stay long enough to start producing that heir."

Fitz spoke through a clenched jaw. "You are only here because Lady Worthington overrode my expressed wish that you not receive an invitation. I may have had no choice in the matter of your attendance, but I will not stand for your interference in my life. Never again."

"Tsk, tsk," Moorbridge shook his head in mock sadness. "You sound as though you are unhappy with your bride."

"The choice of bride was irrelevant, and you know it. This is between the two of us. Leave Selina out of it. Now, please move along. We have other guests to greet."

"He's right, Moorbridge. Please, let's go," Lady Moorbridge pleaded. Since the next guests in line now stood close enough to overhear, Fitz's father chose not to create a scene. They moved on to greet Kitty and her family.

After the greeters curtsied, bowed, and nodded their heads hundreds of times, the line finally came to an end as the last visitors were welcomed. Any latecomers would be greeted by the butler.

Orchestra music filled the air as they made their way to the ballroom. Fitz held out his hand to Selina for the first dance as Kitty's father held out a hand to his daughter. Both couples took their places and began to dance the waltz. When they completed one circle around the room, the other guests joined them on the dance floor.

Although Fitz had a slight limp, he managed quite well throughout the dance. When the waltz ended, he led her to where Aunt Theo sat in conversation with Lady Worthington. His valet surreptitiously handed him a cane, then quickly exited the ballroom.

"FitzWalter, I'm glad you arrived in time for the ball," Aunt Theo said. "We were starting to worry you might not make it."

He glanced at Aunt Theo with his typical sober expression. "I was held up or I would have been here sooner. I apologize for worrying you."

Aunt Theo obviously sensed his reluctance to elaborate on the circumstances that delayed his arrival. She simply said, "You are here now. That is all that matters." She turned to continue her conversation with Lady Worthington.

Fitz and Selina stood side-by-side, watching the dancers. It seemed everyone was enjoying themselves. She heard her husband clear his throat before he spoke in a low voice. "I want to apologize to you, Selina, for having been delayed. The axle on my carriage broke. If it weren't for that, I would have been here sooner."

Fixing concerned eyes upon him, she asked, "Were you hurt?"

Fitz gave his head a slight shake. "No. The driver was able to keep the carriage upright."

"Oh, thank God for that!" Remembering her worries before he made his appearance, she pressed her palm to her heart. "But I will admit I was relieved you arrived when you did."

One side of his mouth lifted in a half smile. He continued staring into her eyes and she couldn't make herself look away.

"Ahem. Please excuse me, FitzWalter, Selina."

They both turned their heads to see her father standing there. "Your mother informs me I must dance with you tonight. Would you do me the honor?" Runswick held out his hand to her.

"Of course, Father." Selina placed a hand on Fitz's arm. "Please, excuse me."

Her husband gave a brief nod.

As she danced the minuet with her father, she realized they had nothing to talk about. They each looked off to the side rather than making eye contact. At one point, he did say she looked pretty, but that was the extent of their conversation.

After her father returned her to where Fitz stood waiting, her dance card filled rapidly. She kept the supper dance open, hoping her husband might sign his name there. Selina had the opportunity to dance with several gentlemen and she especially enjoyed dancing with the Earl of Devonport, a long-time friend of her husband. He told her a couple of stories involving FitzWalter, which delighted her. It also kept her from having to think of what to say. As he continued talking, she could simply listen while enjoying the dance.

Fitz had introduced her to the earl and his wife a half hour prior since they had arrived late. She was surprised when Lady Devonport asked to be on first-name basis soon after meeting them, but Emma informed her she was actually an American and, since their husbands were such good friends, she wanted to do away with the formality between them as quickly as possible. Selina couldn't help liking Emma and looked forward to spending more time with her. She was everything Selina was not: outgoing, confident, and comfortable in her own skin. Selina hoped they would have the opportunity to become better acquainted.

After the dance, Devonport led Selina to where Kitty stood.

"I believe this is my dance?" Lieutenant Adam Linfield held out his hand to Kitty for the next set. She glanced at her dance card and seemed delighted to find the handsome gentleman would be her partner for the supper dance.

Selina didn't need to glance at her card to know that slot remained empty. Fitz had not asked her to dance again. She stepped closer to the palms in the corner of the room, hoping to be inconspicuous, for it wouldn't do for the honored guest to lack a dance partner for the supper dance. As she stepped backward, her heel landed on a shoe. She gasped and spun around to apologize, but stopped when she saw her husband standing there.

"Please forgive me if I don't ask you to dance. My leg isn't up to it. Would you consider sitting this dance out with me, and then I'll take you in to supper?"

Her brow wrinkled in concern. "I'm sorry you're in pain, Fitz. Of course, I'll sit with you. A bit of rest would be welcomed, and I would enjoy having supper with you."

Fitz was pleased with her answer. Placing his hand on her back, he led her to a bench close by.

Once they were seated, Selina looked at her husband as she lifted her hand to the necklace she wore. "I want to thank you for lending me these lovely jewels for the evening, my lord."

"They are not a loan, Selina. They are yours now, and you may hand them down to one of our children one day."

Her cheeks blushed pink. "I'm overwhelmed by your generosity."

He shook his head, "Don't be. You are my wife. My grandmother intended I should pass them to the woman I marry one day."

"I will cherish them always. I only wish I could have met your grandmother."

Fitz surveyed his wife. It touched him that she should wish to have known his grandparent. "She's been gone five years now, but I'll always miss her." Fitz felt uncomfortable sharing his private thoughts with his wife, so he redirected the conversation. "It looks like your ball is a huge success by the number of people in attendance."

As Fitz sat with his wife waiting for the supper dance to come to an end, he sensed her stiffen beside him. Directing his eyes to where she stared, he saw her brother, along with Tom Hendrick, entering the ballroom. Was she bothered by his late arrival?

He leaned a bit closer and spoke quietly for her ears alone. "Most gentlemen don't enjoy balls and such. You must forgive your brother for his lateness. I'm certain he lost track of time."

She turned confused eyes upon him, then shook her head. "I don't trust him." Selina continued watching her brother as he moved around the ballroom with his friend following close behind.

"Why don't you trust him?"

She shrugged her shoulders. "I don't know quite how to explain it. My family is complicated."

Percival stood in conversation with his youngest sister, Helena, who moved her chin in Selina's direction. Her brother shifted his gaze upon Selina. Fitz watched as his wife averted her eyes to her folded hands on her lap. *How strange. Wouldn't a sister wave to her brother?*

"Did you and Percival have a sibling squabble?" Fitz spoke with amusement in his voice, but Selina did not seem to share his humor.

Without giving him an answer, she glanced in her brother's direction. "Oh, no," she whispered as she watched him approach with Tom Hendrick.

Fitz turned a questioning glance at his wife but she didn't notice. Why was she agitated at seeing her brother? Admittedly, the man was a cad, but he certainly wouldn't treat his sister unscrupulously. They must have had a disagreement. He continued watching Selina while she watched her brother. She pulled her bottom lip between her teeth, but quickly released it. Taking a deep breath, she straightened her shoulders.

"Good evening, Selina." Percival bowed. "You have quite a crush here this evening. It seems all of London has come to welcome you."

"Good evening, Percival. I-I'm glad you could make it." She stumbled a bit over her words, giving evidence to her heightened emotions.

After greeting Fitz, Percival said, "I heard you'd travelled north recently. It's good to see you again, Fitz."

Fitz gave a brief nod of his head. "I'm glad to be home."

Percival returned his gaze to Selina. "I'd like to present to you my friend, Mr. Tom Hendrick."

"Good evening, my lady." Tom said with a bow.

"I'm pleased to meet you, Mr. Hendrick." An uncertain smile played on Selina's lips. "I hope you will enjoy yourself this evening."

"I'm certain I shall."

"Besides wanting to greet you," Percival interjected. "I would also like to add my name to your dance card. Please tell me it isn't filled yet."

Fitz couldn't help noticing her slight hesitation before admitting, "I do have a dance open. It's a quadrille."

"Splendid! Please allow me to fill my name in."

Handing the card and pencil to her brother, he scribbled his name before giving it back.

"Now, would you be so kind and direct us to the card room?"

Fitz stopped a passing servant carrying an empty tray. "Please guide these gentlemen to the card room."

The servant bowed. "Of course, my lord." Bowing again to the two waiting men, he said, "Please, follow me."

As Percival and Mr. Hendrick walked away, Fitz heard Selina whisper, "I don't know him at all."

Fitz looked at her quizzically. "I suppose you don't, since you just met him."

She stared at Fitz in confusion. "What? Oh, you thought I spoke of Mr. Hendrick."

"If not Mr. Hendrick, then who were you referring to?"

With a shake of her head, she said, "I didn't realize I'd spoken my thoughts aloud. I was speaking of Percival."

"And you feel you don't know him?"

"It must seem strange not to know one's own brother, but it is nonetheless true in my case."

The final notes of the orchestra music finished playing. It was time to head to the supper room. Fitz led Selina to a table where the Earl and Countess of Devonport were seated.

"May we join you?" Fitz asked.

"Need you ask?" Devonport smirked as he stood to his feet.

Fitz held out a chair for Selina next to the countess.

"I hope you're enjoying yourself, Emma," Selina said.

Emma reached over to pat her hand. "It's a wonderful ball. We're glad to be here."

Selina smiled in appreciation.

"Will you be staying in London for a while or do you plan

to travel again soon?" Devon asked Fitz.

"I haven't received my next assignment yet, so I will be here for at least the next few days."

"Then you and Selina must come to our house for dinner," Emma interjected. "I would love to get to know your wife better." Emma turned to Selina. "And I'd love for you to meet our sons."

He watched Selina's eyes light up. "I would enjoy that very much." She gave him an inquiring look.

Fitz winked at his wife, then looked at Emma. "Let us know when, and we will be there."

"Splendid! How about Wednesday evening?"

Selina again looked toward Fitz.

"Wednesday works for me," he said.

"For me, also," Selina agreed.

Emma beamed, "Then we will look forward to it."

"I see your father is in attendance," Devon said. "Have the two of you made amends?"

Fitz scowled in Aunt Theo's direction, who sat at a table near them, then turned toward Selina. "It seems my wishes were overridden." Selina glanced away, so he shifted his gaze back to Devon. "My father and mother are not worthy of the loyalty I've shown them. They may want to pretend nothing has changed, but I'm no hypocrite."

"Forgiveness is not a choice. It's a command, my friend, for we all need forgiveness from God."

Fitz tightened his jaw and refused to answer. Moorbridge didn't deserve his forgiveness. It was time his father learned there were consequences when manipulating and deceiving others.

Selina turned the subject by asking Emma about her children, a topic that easily distracted both Devon and Emma, which suited Fitz quite nicely. It seemed his wife was a sensitive girl and had her uses.

The dinner hour flew by as the two couples conversed. Before long, they returned to the ballroom where Selina and Emma were swept away by their next dance partners. During a break between dances, Selina found herself beside her sister, Juliet.

"Do you realize that since you left our home as a young girl, I've never had the opportunity to be alone with you?"

Selina was surprised by her sister's comment. "If you had wanted to, you could have come to visit me at our parents' house the weeks before my wedding."

"Mother wouldn't allow it. She was afraid one of us might say something to cause you to balk and not go through with the wedding."

*Was this true? Was I denied the company of my own sisters?* "Is that also why Helena never sought me out? I thought neither of you cared to spend time with me."

Juliet placed a hand on Selina's arm. "Nothing could be further from the truth. Would it be all right if I paid you a call soon? I'd like a chance to become reacquainted."

Juliet seemed sincere, but Selina felt cautious about trusting her. However, she didn't want to deny herself the opportunity of getting to know her sister if, by chance, she was in earnest. "Yes. I would enjoy visiting with you."

"Very well. I will call on you sometime next week." Glancing over Selina's shoulder, Juliet said, "Oh, here comes Percival. Do you realize Mama and Papa threw him out of the house?"

"No! Whatever for?" Selina couldn't imagine such a thing. Percival was their favorite—the heir.

"Gambling debt. I don't have time to tell you more. We will talk next week."

The sisters turned to greet their brother.

"Juliet, I'd always thought your beauty by far surpassed everyone else in any ballroom, but tonight I realize Selina comes very close to matching your looks."

This was almost too much for Selina to take in. First, that her brother would compliment her at all and, second, that any member of her family would say she was a beauty. Instead of believing Percival, it made her more suspicious of him. Her brother obviously expected a response. She curtsied and said, "Thank you, Percival."

"Of course, Selina is beautiful!" Juliet agreed. "When you walked down the aisle on your wedding day, you were a vision! The contrast of your dark hair against the white of your gown was simply stunning. Percival speaks truthfully when he compliments you." Then turning a suspicious look upon her brother, she added, "No matter what his motives may be."

It seemed Juliet didn't trust him, either. Selina noticed Percival briefly narrowed his eyes, but he seemed to quickly get a hold of himself. He smiled at Selina as he held out his hand. "I believe this is our dance."

Percival led his sister to the dance floor and Selina concentrated on the intricate steps of the quadrille. When the dance steps brought them together, Percival said, "You are a hit tonight, Selina. It seems everyone is enjoying themselves. I'm proud of you."

"I'm glad to hear it. Thank you." She couldn't believe the change in her brother. He had never been kind to her. Why was he suddenly so different?

When the dance came to an end, Percival took her arm and they walked slowly to where Juliet now stood in conversation with their parents.

"May I call on you next week?" her brother asked.

"Ah…y-yes. Of course." What else could she say? Percival wished her a good evening, bowed, and departed without acknowledging his parents.

"Selina, your mother and I are proud of you!" her father said.

"Yes, you have done well for yourself," her mother agreed. "It's obvious your father and I guided you in the right direction."

They were finally proud of her. It was what she'd been waiting for, yet it somehow failed to lift her spirits as she had thought it would. Something was missing. "I'm glad you're enjoying yourselves," Selina said.

"The earl expects a grandson soon. Make sure you do not disappoint him," her mother blurted out.

"Mother!" Juliet exclaimed. "These things take time. Certainly, Selina is not expected to produce one on her own. If you are going to make such statements, be sure to include FitzWalter in the conversation."

Lady Runswick gasped. "Juliet, I could never discuss such things with FitzWalter. It would be obscene!"

"My point is, don't put such pressure on Selina alone. Can we please not talk about this tonight? This is Selina's ball and she should be able to enjoy herself."

Selina eyes widened at Juliet's defense. Was it possible they might one day be friends? "I must go and join my other guests. Thank you for your words of encouragement."

"It seems your Aunt Theo has done a good job of raising you. Yet I fear some of her independence may have rubbed off on you," her mother stated. "I simply wanted to remind you to submit to your husband. But I will say no more tonight. Perhaps I will call on you one day next week. Now go and enjoy the rest of your ball."

Selina curtsied to her parents, then wound her way back to where Kitty, Lady Worthington, and Aunt Theo stood in conversation. As they continued talking together, Selina allowed her eyes to wander over the crowded ballroom. She searched for her husband and finally spotted him standing beside Lieutenant Linfield, Devonport, and some other gentleman.

As her gaze continued to roam, she noticed Lady Dinah Blackmore, the Marchioness of Blackmore, standing beside her austere husband, a gentleman approximately twenty years her senior. There was nothing out of the ordinary about them, except that she seemed to be staring toward the group of gentlemen Fitz was in conversation with. Selina remembered listening to Aunt Theo and Lady Worthington discussing whether this couple should be included on the guest list for this evening's ball. Aunt Theo was adamant in not wanting them to attend for a reason that evaded Selina's understanding. Lady Worthington insisted it would be an unforgivable oversight not to invite the Marquess and Marchioness of Blackmore no matter the discomfort it might create.

Selina hadn't understood the significance of their discussion, assuming perhaps this couple or their family had slighted Aunt Theo when she had wed Uncle Peter. Selina watched the lady as she stared at the gentlemen. Could it be there was another reason for Aunt Theo's reticence in inviting them?

Just then Lady Blackmore's eyes lit up as she stared across the room. Selina followed her gaze to the group of gentlemen. Devonport and Lieutenant Linfield continued in conversation, but Fitz stood staring in the lady's direction. They appeared spellbound, and Selina's heart began to race. What did this mean? Who was she to Fitz? His face gave nothing away except a tightening of his jaw. Looking back at Lady Blackmore, her eyes seemed pained. What had passed between the two to cause such emotions? Selina watched as Lord Blackmore leaned down to whisper something in his wife's ear. Lady Blackmore shifted her eyes away to answer her husband, which seemed to finally release Fitz to give his attention to the conversation with his friends. But Selina couldn't help noticing how his gaze kept returning to the now dancing Lord Blackmore and his wife.

Selina observed the couple on the dance floor. Lord Blackmore was handsome and of average height. Neither of them appeared to be enjoying themselves. They did not converse or even make eye contact throughout the dance. If she didn't know they were already married, she would assume they were newly acquainted and uninterested in one another.

It was time Aunt Theo enlightened Selina about the relationship between Fitz and Lady Blackmore. She suspected the reason her aunt preferred not inviting them to the ball had everything to do with the heartless beauty her aunt had mentioned while still at Thorncrest.

## *Chapter Eleven*

Selina stared unseeing into the mirror the following morning as Lydia groomed her hair. The ball had lasted well into the early hours of the morning. It was considered a huge success simply because it was a mad crush. If an event was packed to the gills, the hostess could breathe a sigh of relief for her achievement. Last night's ball was definitely that. Selina couldn't remember inviting quite so many people, but clearly, Lady Worthington and Aunt Theo augmented the list considerably.

After meeting the elite of the ton, it would be expected of her to remember the faces and names and to address them by their correct titles. A daunting task. With so much information thrown at her all at once, the evening was a blur.

Yet there were several people she could easily recall, Devon and Emma being chief amongst them. Lieutenant Linfield, or Adam, as he had asked her to address him, had been an enjoyable dance partner. She didn't think it was proper to call him by his given name when he first suggested it, but he pointed out that she already addressed Devon and Emma informally. He only wished to be considered among her friends. In that case, how could she deny his request knowing he was a good friend of her husband?

Tom Hendrick, Percival's friend, would not be soon forgotten. He was pleasant enough company for the brief moments they spoke, yet there was something very worldly about him. Perhaps because she knew him to be Percival's friend, she had little confidence that Mr. Hendrick deserved her trust.

Lady Dinah Blackmore was certainly unforgettable, for Selina remembered clearly what had passed between Fitz and the lady. Of course, there were others who had cast glances in her husband's direction. After all, he was handsome and mysterious—not a man easily overlooked. That other women found him attractive was not a concern for Selina. What bothered her was that Lady Blackmore had captured her husband's attention. For those brief moments, he had been transfixed, unable to pull his gaze away.

Her toilette complete, she dismissed Lydia and sat at the window in her bedchamber, determined to begin a new habit of spending time alone with God each morning. Her stomach gnawed and she looked forward to breaking her fast but needed some spiritual nourishment first. With an uncertain future before her, Selina opened the Scriptures hoping to gain wisdom.

She soon realized concentrating on the words seemed beyond her ability this morning, for her mind was fixed on the fact her family planned to pay her a visit, which she anticipated with mixed emotions. At the same time, the state of her marriage continued to plague her thoughts. Certainly, she had no desire to consummate her marriage, but couldn't help feeling hurt at her husband's lack of interest. Fitz had been attentive at the ball, of course, for which she'd been greatly relieved, but Selina was well aware he only played the part of a dutiful husband.

Squaring her shoulders, she prayed. "Lord, I cast my cares on You because I know you care for me. Help Fitz to allow you to be Lord of his life. May he desire to lead our family in obedience to Your will. Help him love me, and help me honor him and be the wife he needs. Thank you that you are working in both of us. Amen."

Through the window, she gazed at the cloudy sky. When would the sun shine again? The gardener wore a jacket while preparing the flowerbeds for planting. Selina spun around, picked up her wrap for added warmth, and headed downstairs.

As she approached the breakfast room, a footman opened the door with a brief bow. The room was empty. She walked to the side table and began filling her plate. Having been too nervous to eat much before the ball yesterday, and only nibbling on refreshments during the event, she felt ravenous.

As she sat down to eat, Fitz entered the room. Seeing her, he quickly ran his fingers through his windblown hair obviously trying to bring some order to it. He must have taken his horse out for some exercise.

"Good morning," Selina greeted him.

"G'morning. You're up early. I'm surprised you're not still abed after dancing into the early hours of the morning."

"I couldn't sleep any longer, so I got up to start my day."

"And what are your plans for today?"

Was he asking because he wished to spend time with her? Hope flickered to life and her heart began to beat faster. "I plan to spend some time with Aunt Theo. She worked hard to make the ball the success it was. I would like to do something today that will give her pleasure." Hoping to find something they could participate in together, she added, "I expect we will also receive some callers today. My family indicated they would be stopping by this week, although I'm not certain it will be today."

"Do they visit often now that you're in Town?" Fitz asked.

"No, they have not visited once."

He looked at her curiously. "Perhaps they stayed away knowing how much is involved in planning a ball, and they didn't wish to take up more of your time."

She smiled but shook her head. "That's doubtful."

He tilted his head. "Why do you say that?"

"Has no one mentioned to you that I was not raised in my parents' home?"

His brow lifted. "No. I was unaware."

"My parents gave me to my Aunt Theo and Uncle Peter when I was six years of age. They had no children of their own, so they were happy to take me in. I did not see my family again until I turned eighteen. At that point, they wrote me a letter and said they wished for me to return to them."

"Are you saying your parents simply gave one of their children away?"

"Sad, isn't it?"

"Unbelievable, more like. At six years of age, you must have felt the sting of being sent away. And why you? Why not give away the youngest?"

For some reason, she didn't wish her husband to know how unattractive her family thought her to be. She feared he would begin to see her through their eyes and agree with them, so she shrugged her shoulders and said, "They must have had their reasons, I suppose."

"I cannot fathom it."

"Please do not feel sorry for me. I have accepted it and I was certainly not deprived in my upbringing. Aunt Theo and Uncle Peter loved me like their own. I never lacked for affection."

Fitz searched her face, then slowly shook his head. "I don't pity you, Selina. *They* are to be pitied. I imagine you would have been a source of much joy for them over the years. It's their loss."

Surprised at his kind words, she didn't know what to say, so she simply replied, "Thank you."

They continued with their breakfast, not speaking, each lost in their own thoughts. After a bit, Selina felt she had better engage her husband in conversation. Who knew when he would make the effort to be in her company again?

"What are your plans for today, my lord?"

"Can we dispense with the 'my lord'? I'd prefer you call me Fitz."

Selina nodded. "Very well."

"To answer your question, I will be going to the Home Office. I also have a few errands to run. Don't expect me for supper. I'll be home late."

She lowered her eyes to her plate and lifted her fork to place a bit of egg in her mouth, chewing it, but unable to taste it. *He doesn't wish to spend time with me. Nor does he look at me the way he did Lady Dinah last evening.*

Fitz saw the disappointment in her eyes, which almost

caused him to relent and invite her to join him at the theater that evening. But he hardened his heart, wiped his mouth with the serviette, and got to his feet. "I must be on my way. I wish you a good day." Not waiting for a response, he bowed and departed.

Upon returning from a brisk morning walk, Selina took the stairs to Aunt Theo's sitting room. Certainly, her aunt would be up by now. At her knock, Martha, her aunt's maid, opened the door. "Good morning, my lady." She bobbed her knees in a curtsy.

"Good morning. Is my aunt ready for some company?"

"Come on in, Selina," she heard Aunt Theo call from her seat by the fireplace, a cup of tea in her hand.

Selina entered the room and leaned forward to place a kiss on her aunt's soft cheek. "How are you this morning? I hope you were able to rest well after last night."

Aunt Theo patted the seat beside her. "Come, sit and have some tea." Turning to Martha, she said, "You may go about your duties. I'll call if I need anything."

After the maid left the room, Aunt Theo said, "I slept exceedingly well and feel refreshed. What about you, Selina?"

"Before I tell you how I slept, I want to thank you again for all your hard work for yesterday's ball. I shall never forget it."

Aunt Theo beamed. "You are most welcome. Lady Worthington and I enjoyed organizing the event. The pleasure was definitely ours. And to see you well received into society made it all worth it."

Selina's eyes shone with appreciation and she reached over to give her aunt's hand a squeeze. "Now, to answer your question. I slept well for four hours, but then my mind filled with thoughts and questions, and I couldn't sleep any longer."

"What time did you wake up?"

"Oh, about eight of the morning."

Aunt Theo shook her head. "What's weighing on your mind, Selina?"

She decided to get right to the point. She leaned forward and looked her aunt square in the eyes. "Please tell me who Lady Dinah Blackmore is, and what is the history between her and Fitz?"

Aunt Theo blinked in surprise. "Why do you ask? Has someone filled your ears with gossip?"

"I haven't heard a thing except a while back, you mentioned a heartless beauty who had broken my husband's heart. Is she the one who did so?"

"Something must have occurred to cause you to question the lady's character. Now, out with it."

Taking a deep breath, Selina let it out in a huff. "Very well. I did observe something." She explained to her aunt about the transfixed look she had witnessed between the two. "The look they shared was rife with meaning. Please tell me of their relationship."

Aunt Theo carefully placed the teacup on the table and sat back to face her niece. "I suppose it's best you know the entire story."

"I would appreciate it."

"Very well. Fitz had been engaged to marry Dinah Claremont. Their families were life-long friends and Fitz grew up with Dinah and her siblings. When Fitz came home for a brief furlough from the military, he saw how grown up Dinah had become and they fell in love. During another brief furlough, Dinah became his betrothed and the families signed a marriage agreement. Unfortunately, when Fitz finally came home for good because of his brother's death and his own injuries, I understand Dinah was shocked at the change in him. Not only did he have a pronounced limp and a hideous scar on his face, but he'd become sullen and dejected from all he had seen and endured. Let's not forget he must also have been grieving the loss of his only brother. I was told Dinah tried to pull him out of his dark mood but to no avail. One month after his return from France, she broke the betrothal and married the marquess instead. Blackmore needed an heir. His first wife had been barren. A month after her passing, he married Dinah."

"Oh! I cannot imagine! How did Fitz react to it all?" Selina asked.

"He secluded himself at Thorncrest, which gave him time to heal from his injuries. When he finally returned to London a year later, he was a changed man. His scar and his limp had improved significantly, but he'd become cynical and kept his distance from marriageable females. Whenever Dinah arrived at an event with Lord Blackmore, Fitz would soon disappear. He danced with widows and enjoyed their favors as long as they clearly understood they had no bearing on his future plans."

"Aunt Theo, how can you possibly know this? Is it simply gossip?"

"Lady Worthington is a close friend of FitzWalter's aunt. Please don't think Lady Worthington a gossip. She only broke the confidence that had been entrusted to her because she was concerned Fitz would break your heart."

"When did she tell you this?"

"When she received the invitation to your wedding, she sent me a letter hoping I could influence your situation."

"I see." She felt uncomfortable believing a story secondhand, but it appeared Lady Worthington was a reliable source.

"I don't know what his feelings are toward Lady Blackmore, but your marriage is certainly complicated."

"Yes, it is that." Selina sighed and nodded as she shifted her gaze toward the window. She bit her bottom lip and tried to process all she'd learned. Taking a deep breath, she looked at her aunt. "But I have committed to praying for my husband. As God worked in my heart when you had no idea He was doing so, I believe He will work in Fitz, too. I had hoped my husband was a believer. It seems my parents arranged this marriage without giving any thought to my husband's commitment to God or lack thereof." Lightly placing her hand on her aunt's knee, she said, "Please pray I will have faith, and not lose hope."

"I pray for you always, and I'll continue doing so, my dear child."

"Thank you, Aunt Theo."

## *Chapter Twelve*

The Season was in full swing, and nowhere was it more evident than at Drury Lane as the beau monde flocked the theater for their evening entertainment. Huge chandeliers lit with tallow candles hung over the auditorium and platform. The lights remained bright before, during, and at the conclusion of the play. After all, everyone in attendance was there not so much for the performance of the great actor, Edmund Kean, but rather to see and to be seen. Ladies strolled in wearing fine gowns and hats with ostrich feathers. Pity the person who sat behind such a contraption hoping to see the performance on stage.

Fitz sat in a theater box next to Adam, who sat next to Kitty Haddington, observing the crowd. He hadn't been aware of his friend's interest in Selina's friend. Beside Kitty were Emma and Devon. It was glaringly obvious Selina was missing.

Kitty said to Fitz, "When Adam invited me to the theater tonight and mentioned you would join us, I looked forward to seeing Selina. Is she unwell?"

Before Fitz could think of a reply, Emma said, "I was looking forward to seeing her as well. Is she arriving late with her Aunt Theo?"

He cringed and searched for an answer that would satisfy. The plan had been to go to the theater with Adam, but his friend must have assumed he'd bring Selina, so he invited her friend. They ran into Devon and Emma in the foyer and asked them if they would care to share a box that night. Now it appeared as though he'd purposely banned his wife from an evening with friends. Actually, he had excluded her, but he had no idea her friends would be in attendance. "No, she's not sick and she isn't coming later with Aunt Theo." Feeling defensive, he said, "We don't live in each other's pockets. She had her own plans for the evening." Let them make of that whatever they pleased.

Not giving the ladies a chance to respond, Fitz turned to Adam and engaged him in conversation about an issue at the Home Office. Adam's eyes kept straying to Kitty. Obviously, he preferred spending time with her. Fitz stood and walked to the back of the box where Devon stood stretching his legs a bit before sitting through the performance on stage.

A crooked smiled played on Devon's lips as his eyes surveyed the others sharing their box. "It seems Adam is well on his way to falling in love."

Fitz looked to where his friend sat with an unmistakably rapt expression on his face as he conversed with Kitty. He was smitten, poor fellow. "Hmph. He would be wise to guard his heart. Kitty's a green girl like Dinah was when I went off to war. Her avaricious nature has not had the opportunity to develop yet."

Facing Fitz more fully, Devon said, "From spending only a short amount of time with Selina at the ball, I sensed she is unspoiled and kind-hearted. She will make you a wonderful wife. I pray to God you won't allow your fears to destroy your marriage as I almost did."

Fitz's jaw tightened. He shifted his gaze toward the stage but said nothing. The play was about to begin. He made his way back to the front of the box and took his seat beside Adam.

Instead of listening to the lines the actors recited, his mind wandered back to the night he arrived at Devonport's country seat almost two years ago. Emma had just gone into labor and Fitz stayed to lend support to the soon-to-be father. In the hours of waiting, they had a heart-to-heart conversation about life, death, and eternity.

Fitz had always attended church for Christmas and Easter but never paid much attention to the sermons the vicar delivered. He knew the nativity and resurrection stories having listened to the retelling countless times in his youth, so he made a habit of letting his mind wander. When Devon announced his decision to fully embrace his faith, which he'd only followed nominally for the past years, it explained why his friend seemed . . . changed. Fitz couldn't understand it, but he was unable to deny Devon was happier and more content. Watching him with Emma, and seeing how they loved each other, it could cause a man to long for the same thing for himself.

Knowing Devon would soon be holding his son created a moment of weakness in Fitz. He listened as Devon explained about salvation and how Christ had died for them. The information wasn't new. It simply seemed real when Devon described it, unlike the unemotional sermons he'd endured while listening to his own vicar. Was it possible to find joy again? He still had nightmares about the war and often awoke in a cold sweat. Could he get over his bitterness toward Dinah? Fitz longed to be rid of the darkness encasing his soul.

While Emma continued in labor, Fitz surrendered his life to God. He wept tears he hadn't allowed himself to cry through the entire war. When he got control of his emotions, he felt embarrassed, but Devon assured him it was perfectly normal to cry when God lifted the load of sin that had weighed a person down.

Over the following months, Fitz read his Bible, stopped drinking altogether, and gave up women and gambling. Instead, he threw himself into helping at the Home Office. It was a way he could serve others and a better way of occupying his time. His estate prospered and he tithed diligently to the church. He felt peace.

However, since his marriage, he had used the Home Office as an excuse to take him away from his wife. He knew his anger with Moorbridge embittered him toward God. Since Fitz knew God was well aware of his father's deception but allowed it to happen anyway, he stopped reading his Bible and no longer attended church. A glass of brandy helped him sleep at nights.

Selina had been forced upon him. Every time Fitz looked at her, he sensed his father's laughter and mocking voice sneering, "Don't be a sore loser!" It kept ringing in his ears. If he ever allowed himself to make a real marriage with Selina, his father would win. As long as he kept his distance, Fitz was still in control.

During intermission, Fitz stood to his feet while the others in the box remained seated. Devon sat holding Emma's hand as he explained about a particular scene in the play. Adam leaned as close to Kitty as decorum allowed. They were obviously engrossed in each other. A married man who wished he was still a bachelor didn't fit here. He made his way to the exit without bothering to tell anyone where he was headed.

As he stood in line to order a drink, Fitz greeted the people he was acquainted with, which helped to pass the time. Once he had a glass of wine in his hand, he slowly meandered about the hallway, prolonging his return to the box.

As he wandered, he turned a corner and collided with a female.

"Oh, pardon me! I wasn't paying attention to where I was going," a soft voice said.

Fitz would recognize that voice anywhere. "Dinah . . ."

"Fitz, it's you! It's been an age since you've spoken to me. I've missed you." She quickly placed her fingers over her lips as if wishing the words unsaid.

She was more beautiful than ever. Her thick, dark hair was pulled back from her face in an elaborate hairstyle, drawing his attention to smooth skin, alluring dark blue eyes, and red, full lips. His heart rate increased and he swallowed hard. *Why does she still have this effect on me?*

"How are you, Dinah?" His voice sounded hoarse to his own ears.

"I am . . . content." Her lips lifted in a soft smile. "I have much to be thankful for, especially my son."

"Yes, I heard you had a boy."

Sadness filled her eyes. She looked around and, not seeing anyone, she placed a hand on his arm. "I didn't mean to hurt you. I've longed to explain everything to you countless times. You never gave me the opportunity. I even wrote you a couple of letters, but never had the courage to post them." Removing her hand, she glanced around one more time. They were still alone. She leaned closer, speaking in a low voice, "Would you meet with me once so I can finally unburden myself. Would you do that for me, please?"

His brow furrowed. What was there to explain? He didn't care to hear her excuses then or now, yet, staring into her eyes, he couldn't bring himself to say no. "What would you suggest?"

"Will you meet me in Hyde Park at dawn tomorrow?" She mentioned the exact location. A spot they had chosen for a picnic while he was on a brief furlough from his regiment.

He nodded. "I'll be there."

"Thank you. I must be on my way before I'm missed, but I cannot tell you how much this means to me."

Did her eyes glisten with tears before she lowered her head and turned away? He wasn't certain, but the desire to pull her into his arms was almost overwhelming. Fitz forced himself to stand still as he watched Dinah's hurried steps take her farther and farther away. Angry at himself, he headed in the opposite direction, compelling his feet to move toward his box without looking back. How could he still have feelings for a woman who had treated him so cruelly?

Unfortunately for Fitz, he didn't see the man hiding in the alcove near the spot he'd been standing only moments ago. The man pursed his lips in thought before grinning.

As everyone returned to their seats to view the second half of the entertainment that evening, Fitz's mind was still occupied with thoughts of his recent encounter with Dinah. Had anyone witnessed his conversation with her? It wasn't unusual to speak with a married lady in the hallway of the theater, but it was extremely out of the ordinary for Fitz to be talking to Dinah. He had avoided her like the pox, and he knew the ton was well aware of it. If anyone witnessed their conversation, it would be news for the gossip mill. At least no one had been close enough to hear their plan to meet again.

His conscience pricked him. They were both married now and he knew meeting his former betrothed in a park was unwise. Perhaps he should bring a friend or a servant along to lend some propriety to the meeting, but he knew he wouldn't. Perhaps they should have waited to talk at a ball or house party, which is what he thought she would suggest. To his surprise, Dinah proposed they meet in Hyde Park early in the morning. He doubted anyone from the beau monde would be up at that time of day, making it safe for a rendezvous. Fitz soothed his conscience by telling himself he would only meet with her once to let her explain herself. She seemed desperate to do so and he wouldn't deny her the opportunity.

Staring at the actors on stage, he saw their lips move, but couldn't seem to make sense of what they were saying. His mind was taken up with the memory of glistening tears in the eyes of his lost love. Fitz sensed her regret, causing him to feel weak and vulnerable once more. Where was his anger when it was most needed? How quickly he had succumbed to Dinah's charms. Well, he would guard his heart tomorrow morning.

## *Chapter Thirteen*

Light dew covered the grass the following morning as Fitz made his way to the clandestine meeting. He pulled his scarf higher. Daffodils and crocuses sprang up hither and yonder, but Fitz remained unaware of their efforts. He rounded a stand of bushes and trees in Hyde Park to a clearing by the Serpentine. The surface of the man-made ornamental pond glistened from the weak rays of the first flush of morning. The last time Fitz visited this spot was with Dinah. It had been a warm and sunny day, flowers in full bloom, as they picnicked together a lifetime ago. However, this early in the day, the air felt as cold as their feelings for each other ought to be.

Dinah hadn't arrived yet, but he was early. Having tossed and turned for hours, unable to find rest, he finally turned the wick up in the oil lamp beside the bed and reached for a book lying on top of his Bible. Fitz thought briefly of reading a passage of Scripture but shoved the thought aside, not wishing to read anything that might stir up feelings of guilt. He had finally convinced himself the meeting was to give Dinah an opportunity to explain her actions. Meeting with her was an act of kindness. He should have allowed her to explain long ago. That his heart rate accelerated whenever he remembered the longing in her eyes, giving evidence to her continued affection, was something he didn't wish to contemplate at the moment.

Footsteps approached on the gravel driveway and he pivoted toward her to watch Dinah's elegant gait as she walked closer. A black hooded cloak covered Dinah from the top of her head to the hem of her skirt in an obvious attempt to disguise, but he remembered well her elegant movements and stride.

"Good morning, Fitz." A hesitant smile played on her lips. "Thank you for meeting with me."

"Hello, Dinah. I don't remember you being such an early riser."

"No." Her smiled disappeared. "But this was important. Charles is out of Town, so I was able to slip away without anyone being the wiser."

"You came alone?"

"No. My maid is waiting in the carriage. She's a confidant. I trust her completely. In the little time we have, I'd like to tell you what I should have explained long ago."

Fitz nodded. "Go ahead."

"My father saw me crying one day after I had visited you. I tried everything to get you out of your sullen mood after you returned from the war, but nothing seemed to work. You were completely changed, and I was young and scared."

With furrowed brow, he said, "I was grieving the loss of my brother and healing from severe war injuries. I couldn't get the pictures out of my head of all I had seen."

"I knew you had a valid reason for your depressed state, but you refused to talk. I felt I was losing you. When my father found me in tears, he asked to know the reason. I explained how the war had wreaked havoc on your mind and how different you were." Dinah shut her eyes for a moment and her chin tremble. Taking a fortifying breath, her eyes peered into his, and she continued. "He insisted we should break the betrothal. I pleaded with him, asking for more time, but my father refused. Unbeknownst to me, Charles had confided in my father his wish to remarry to gain an heir. Father decided a marquess was a better prospect for son-in-law than a viscount, even if he was the heir to an earldom."

Fitz looked off into the distance as he ran a hand through his hair. "Why didn't you tell me?" Looking directly at her, he asked, "Why did you send your father to break off the engagement?"

"You know very well my father rules our home. We were never allowed to rebel. It wasn't done. If father said this is how things should be, then that is how things were. We never questioned him. We obeyed. As always, I submitted to his will. As far as why I didn't tell you myself, father wanted to take care of the details. I was forbidden to speak with you again."

His nostrils flared. "Your father told me you couldn't bear marrying a man who was crippled and deformed. That it was heartless of me to expect a gently bred lady like you to marry me. He said, if I had truly wanted to marry you, I should have stayed home instead of fighting in the war."

Dinah placed a hand over her mouth as her eyes filled with tears. "I had no idea he'd been so cruel. No wonder you wanted nothing to do with me." With pleading eyes, she placed a hand on his forearm, "I'm terribly sorry, Fitz. Those were *not* my thoughts. I loved you for so much more than your appearance."

He shook his head in disbelief as he stared at her glistening eyes. Life wasn't fair. She could have been his. She *should* have been his! *You are a married man,* his conscience smote him. But married to a woman his father manipulated him to wed. *It wasn't Selina's fault.* Tears of frustration filled his eyes, but he blinked them away. "I wish I could continue thinking of you as a heartless vixen. It was easier than knowing you were a victim, too."

"My purpose for meeting you was to ask your forgiveness. I should like us to be friends again."

She wanted to be his friend? Was that even possible after all they had been to each other? Dinah should have been his future and his present—not just his past. Knowing she was a pawn in her father's hands confused his emotions. *She seems to still care about me.* How could he bear seeing Blackmore with her? As he stared into her lovely eyes, his heart squeezed. They could never be together.

Fitz cleared his throat but his voice sounded strained. "Please tell me Blackmore treats you well. I need to know you are happy in your marriage."

Dinah moved her eyes toward the Serpentine behind him. "I am content." She spoke slowly, as though choosing her words carefully. "Happiness is not possible when my husband loves another." She shift her gaze back to him. "Charles is still in love with his first wife. Since she never gave him children, he was forced to marry again once she passed away, but he had no intention of giving me his heart. It's all duty and obligation between us. However, he is good to me." Dinah squared her shoulders and lifted her chin. "I promised faithfulness to Blackmore, and I will not break my vow. I asked to meet with you because I needed you to know what really happened. My affections for you were constant, but I couldn't bring myself to disobey my father." Dinah placed a gloved hand on his arm. "I must go now. Thank you for giving me the opportunity to speak in private." Standing on the toes of her boots, she tilted her head back causing the hood to slip off her head as she placed a tender kiss on his unblemished cheek.

Before he could utter a word, Dinah repositioned the hood to cover her hair as she turned and walked away. Fitz stared across the Serpentine instead of watching her walk out of his life once more. *She never stopped loving me.* He imagined he never stopped loving her either. Rubbing his jaw thoughtfully, Fitz realized this meeting would force him to have to change his view of Dinah being a heartless creature. Instead, she was spineless, unable to stand strong in the face of obstacles. Just like Selina, who often lacked for words to defend herself and had bent to the will of her parents. It seemed most women needed to be led by someone stronger.

Percival climbed on his horse with a smirk on his face. "Did you get a good view?"

The cartoonist for the London Gazette chuckled. "I saw enough. Here's your payment." He handed an envelope to

Percival. "This will sell newspapers." Laughter filled the air as he nudged his horse toward his office.

Percival's lips curled into a smirk as he threw his shoulders back. His plan was set in motion. It was time to return to his bachelor suite since he was forced to sell his townhouse last week to get those infernal creditors off his back. Placing the envelope in the inside pocket of his jacket, he patted it in place, grabbed the reins with both hands, and took off at a gallop. The two hundred pounds would get him into another game of cards. He had a feeling his luck would turn tonight and he would finally gain back all he'd lost.

Tomorrow he planned to visit his sister. Without a doubt, she would need some comforting after she laid eyes on the morning news.

"Good morning, Selina!" Fitz greeted his wife as she entered the breakfast room that same morning. He had just arrived back from Hyde Park.

"Good morning," she answered pleasantly as she walked to the sideboard and began filling her plate.

He had yet to see his wife in a foul mood. She was shy, but never unfriendly.

"What are your plans for this morning?" he asked.

"First, I plan to eat breakfast." She smiled mischievously.

He chuckled. "Very well. That's certainly a good start to your day. What's next on the agenda?"

"I plan to take a long walk."

"Do you not enjoy riding?"

"Oh, yes, I do. Very much so."

"Then will you go for a ride with me this morning, to Hyde Park?"

Her eyes lit up. "I'd love to! When do you wish to leave?"

"As soon as we finish eating," Fitz said. "There's a briskness in the air. Be sure to dress warmly."

"I will."

As soon as breakfast was over, Selina hurried upstairs to change into a warm, royal blue riding habit, with a black riding cap perched on top of her head, and black riding boots. Fitz stood waiting for her at the bottom of the front steps to the townhouse when she stepped outside.

"You look lovely, Selina. That color suits you perfectly."

Pleased at his compliment, her eyes lit up. "Thank you, Fitz."

Fitz waved his hand toward the horse standing behind him. "This one is Ruby."

"Oh, you're a beauty, aren't you, pretty girl." She stretched out her hand and allowed the horse to pick up her scent. One hand stroked the horse's face as she ran her other hand down her flank. Ruby snickered and moved closer to Selina.

"I think she likes you. Are you ready to mount up?" Linking the gloved fingers of his hands together, he held them out for her. She placed her boot in them and he carefully gave her a boost. She settled safely into the sidesaddle. Soon they were riding side-by-side down the road toward Hyde Park.

When they reached a clearing inside the park, they gave the horses their heads and raced across the field. Selina laughed as the wind whipped her hair around her face. Since coming to the city, she hadn't had the opportunity for an unrestrained gallop. It felt good. Upon arriving at the Serpentine, they reined the horses in and Fitz suggested a walk. She looked at him curiously, but he didn't see. Why did he wish to prolong their time together?

Once the horses were tethered to a tree, Fitz held out his arm for her to take. Walking beside such a strong and handsome man made her feel small and feminine. Warmth enveloped her limbs and she felt weightless. His masculinity was intoxicating. Hopefully the walk would be long allowing her the opportunity to savor the sensations stirring within her.

"Did you enjoy riding Ruby?"

She looked into his warm gaze. "I did. She's a wonderful horse!"

"She's yours."

Selina's eyes widened. "You're giving her to me?"

"Do you already own a horse?"

"N-no. My uncle only had carriage horses and one horse for riding. We lived in town. There wasn't enough room in our barn for too many animals."

"If Ruby pleases you, I would like to give her to you as a wedding present."

"Oh! That's a wonderful gift!" Selina spontaneously squeezing his arm tighter. "Thank you!"

"You are most welcome." He gave her a wink that sent butterflies fluttering in her stomach.

A frown soon puckered her brow and she said, "I don't have a gift for you."

"You don't need to give me anything."

The sound of a horse hurriedly galloping in their direction caused him to stop talking. The rider came straight to Fitz and dismounted.

"Lord FitzWalter?"

"Yes, I'm Lord FitzWalter."

"I have a message for you from the Home Office."

He handed the missive to Fitz, forcing Selina to drop her hand from his arm. He broke the seal and began reading. After he finished, he looked at the rider. "Thank you. You are dismissed. I will be there as soon as I return my wife safely home."

"My lord, I could escort your wife if you are in a hurry."

He regarded the young man more closely and decided he must be the same age as his wife. He'd never met him and was disinclined to trust him.

"As I said, I will be there soon. You are dismissed."

"Very well, my lord. Good day." The young man bowed before mounting, then prodded his horse into action and rode off.

"I'm sorry, Selina, but I must go. We will have other opportunities to ride together. I will make certain of it."

"Please don't concern yourself about it, Fitz. I understand. I'm proud of the work you do for our country."

As his eyes lingered a moment on her upturned face, he found himself comparing her to Dinah. Both ladies were lovely brunettes, but Selina's hair had more curls. His wife's doe-like eyes were like no other he'd seen. Where Dinah's eyes seemed sad, Selina's had a sparkle of optimism and hope. Where Dinah's were filled with regret, Selina's were filled with . . . admiration? His heart beat faster at the thought. Was she attracted to him? He didn't like comparing the two women, but after having been in the company of both this morning, the comparison came without thought. Each lady was lovely, but one was the past and the other his future. It was time to let go of the past and the love he had lost and make an effort to accept the lady standing before him now.

## *Chapter Fourteen*

"I would like it very much if you would be willing to join me this week," Juliet said.

Her sister came for a morning call, giving them the opportunity to become better acquainted. Selina listened in amazement as her sister explained the conditions of the poor in London. It wasn't that she was completely unaware, but until this moment, she did not realize the depths of the despair many faced. What surprised her most was the fact that Juliet cared about these people. Never did she imagine anyone in her family being particularly benevolent, but it seemed she was wrong.

"A group of ladies has organized to raise funds to help the less fortunate. We try to enlighten our friends and family of the need and ask them to make donations." She explained the weekly meetings took place to exchange ideas and make plans for additional opportunities to raise support for such a worthy cause.

Juliet's eyes glistened with tears as she explained. "People are suffering from famine, unemployment, and disease while our prince indulges in wasteful spending for his own pleasure. Since he chooses to turn a blind eye to the needs around him, we must do something to help the poor in Town. Will you consider being a part of this effort?"

Without hesitation, Selina said, "Yes, of course! I'd love to help if I can."

Juliet squeezed Selina's hand. "I'm so glad, dear sister."

Selina stared at Juliet. A hesitant smile played on her lips. Juliet's warmth was unexpected and seemed . . . surreal. She found herself tongue-tied. Juliet's smile only broadened.

"I want to tell you more about our charitable work, but I think we should speak of personal matters first. Don't you agree?"

Selina bit her bottom lip as she considered her sister. "If you'd like."

"Dearest, I have not been the best of sisters to you in the past. I am determined that must change. You see, when I met Henry, I felt drawn to his depth of character. He was like no other man I had ever met before . . . strong . . . reliable . . . people seemed to respect him and listened to what he had to say."

Selina sat in rapt attention. It seemed her sister had not been forced to marry her husband. She had had the privilege of falling in love. Her ribs squeezed tight. Juliet was beautiful *and* in love. Forcing a smile, she continued listening.

"After dancing with me at my debut last year, Henry asked if I would be interested in going to Holy Trinity Church on Clapham Common with him. Now, wasn't that peculiar? Had he asked me to go for a ride in Hyde Park, I would have readily accepted. But church? I didn't know quite what to make of it. It was extraordinary that he should ask such a thing, and I was inclined to say no. Yet as I looked at his handsome face and into his eyes, I saw warmth, sincerity, and even understanding. I wanted to find out why the church was of such great importance to him."

"You said yes?" Selina asked.

"Indeed, I did. When I told Mama, she laughed and thought him daft in the head. But she encouraged me to go. After all, he is an earl."

Selina chuckled at this. Knowing her Mama, she was not surprised. "What happened at church?" The message Juliet heard that evening must obviously have stirred her heart.

"I had the privilege of hearing William Wilberforce speak. He said, 'The first years in Parliament I did nothing—nothing to any purpose. My own distinction was my darling object.' He pointed out the perils of living only for oneself and one's pleasures. Wilberforce mentioned his concern about the socializing that went along with politicking. He called it 'the temptations at the table,' which consisted of vain and useless conversation. Wilberforce said, 'They disqualify me for every useful purpose in life, waste my time, impair my health, fill my mind with thoughts of resistance before and self-condemnation afterward.'"

"After hearing his message, it grieved me to know my life was, indeed, useless and vain. Henry was obviously a man of greater depth than I had ever encountered before. I felt ashamed of my selfish existence. For me, life was about buying the most fashionable clothes and being admired by polite society. Reading the gossip sheet was a favorite entertainment, and I blush to think that sometimes I even participated in spreading rumors."

"As we sat in the carriage on our ride back to my home, Henry asked what I thought of the message we had heard. I was afraid to tell him the truth, yet I could not bring myself to lie." Shrugging her shoulders, Juliet said, "I told him of my shame at how self-serving my life had become. He wanted to know what I planned to do about it. I didn't have an answer to give him."

Selina listened intently, fascinated by her sister's story. They had missed much of what sisters should have shared.

"He asked if I would be interested in attending another service the following Sunday. Although the message made me uncomfortable, it also drew me. I said that I would like it very much. That Sunday, I fully embraced the faith preached from the pulpit and my life has completely changed."

Selina squeezed her sister's hand. "I'm glad you did."

"Selina, do you believe also?"

Smiling, she said, "I do!"

"Oh, I'm so glad!" Juliet leaned close and lowered her voice. "Would you believe Henry admired me from a distance for quite some time but knew we were far apart in our faith. He finally decided to simply ask me to church. My answer would determine whether there was a future for the two of us." Juliet's eyes sparkled. "Selina, I'm so blessed to be married to him. He is very good to me and together we are able to do ever so much more than either of us could do separately."

Selina's smile wobbled, but she said, "I'm happy for you, Juliet—more than you know." She had to forcefully push back the stab of jealousy that wanted to penetrate her heart.

"I think it was wrong of Mama and Papa to force you to marry FitzWalter," Juliet blurted. "I'm not saying he isn't a good man. But you should have had the opportunity to get to know one another and fall in love. I can't imagine having to marry a stranger. I tried talking to Mama on your behalf before the wedding. She wouldn't listen. She said it was for your good and for the good of the family. I tend to think it was only good for the family."

"Thank you for that, Juliet. However, things are improving between Fitz and me. He invited me to go riding in the park this morning and I think we both enjoyed it until we were interrupted by a messenger. Fitz was needed on urgent business back at the Home Office. Although our time was cut short, he had initiated spending time with me. It gives me hope."

Juliet nodded. "I'm relieved to hear it. You're in my prayers, you know. I couldn't stop the wedding from taking place, but I knew what I could do. And that was to lift you and Fitz up in prayer. Interestingly enough, whenever I pray for you, I feel hopeful for your future. I'm certain God is at work in Fitz's heart also."

"Thank you, Juliet." Selina felt uncomfortable talking about her marriage with her sister. She decided to change the subject. "When is the next meeting with your group? I'd like to join you if there is nothing pressing on my schedule."

"It is in two days at half past ten in the morning."

"I can't think of anything I have planned for that day," Selina said.

"Splendid! Then I will pick you up around ten in the morning in two days. Will that work?"

"Yes. I look forward to it."

After Juliet left, Selina returned to her sitting room to answer some correspondence. Soon Kitty arrived and the two drove off in the carriage to spend a few hours together shopping. They stopped at A.M. Cohen for some accessories. Browsing through Hatchard's Bookshop, each lady selected a novel to purchase. Their final destination was Gunter's Tea Shop where they encountered Emma and made it a threesome. Two hours flew by as the ladies found all sorts of things to discussed. When Emma exclaimed at the time, they gasped in surprise at how late it had gotten. Before departing, promises were made to meet again soon.

That night, Fitz enjoyed a quiet dinner with his wife. Aunt Theo was at a card party at the home of an old friend, so husband and wife had the rare opportunity of dining alone.

"How was your day?" Fitz asked once they were served the first course of their meal.

"Juliet came to visit and we had a lovely chat." Selina pushed her food around on her plate, then raised her eyes to Fitz. "Today, I actually felt close to someone in my family. Of course, Juliet is nothing like my parents. She claims it was Lord Chesterfield's influence on her life that changed her."

"How so?" Fitz asked.

"He invited her to a meeting at Holy Trinity Church."

"To church, you say?"

"Yes."

"Hmm . . . interesting. And this changed her life?"

Selina nodded. "It did. She heard a stirring message and realized how frivolous her life was. When Lord Chesterfield invited her the following week to attend again, she fully embraced the faith they talked about, and that made all the difference."

Fitz gazed at her searchingly. "What do *you* believe, Selina? Is God important in your life?"

"Aunt Theo taught me about God all my life, but I never gave it any serious thought until recently. It was actually while at Thorncrest, I finally understood what Jesus' gift of salvation means to me personally." Selina shrugged her shoulders and added. "I still have a lot to learn, of course."

Fitz pursed his lips for a moment. "I have made the same decision as you, only I did it over two years ago. I will admit, I sometimes struggle to give God control of my life, but I'm working on it."

Selina smiled. "It's a relief to know we share the same faith."

"Yes. I agree." Still feeling uncomfortable talking about God with others, he decided to change the subject.

When dinner was over, they moved to the drawing room for a cup of tea. The flames in the fireplace cast shadows around the room, as they each settled into chairs before the fire.

"Fitz, how was your day after receiving the urgent message this morning?"

"Frustrating."

"I'm sorry to hear it," Selina said.

Fitz lifted his cup for a final sip of the tea, then leaned forward to place it on the tray. He shook his head as he sat back again and explained, "Between the famine, as well as the cholera outbreak, the poor are desperate. They're hungry and need medical attention." Fitz leaned forward and placed his elbows on his knees as he stared into the flames. "Riots and threats of more riots are the acts of people who feel they have little hope. Our country is in a desperate state." Turning this head, he looked at Selina. "If only our prince would spend as much time searching for ways to help our country as he does indulging his own pleasures."

"How can we help these people?" Selina wished to know. "Juliet invited me to join her committee to raise funds, yet our small fundraiser seems insignificant when one considers how huge the problem actually is."

"Don't belittle your efforts, Selina. They may help to feed many of the poor here in London. If everyone did their part, we wouldn't have a problem at all. Perhaps through you, more people will become aware, step forward, and find ways to help."

Selina placed her teacup on the tray.

Fitz watched her and thought how comfortable it felt talking with his wife like this. That she was interested in helping the poor gave him hope for their future. Her mind was obviously occupied by more than parties, balls, and the latest fashion. He would have to keep a careful eye on who influenced her life since women were easily led astray. Juliet seemed a good influence thus far.

"It's getting late," Fitz said. "We'd better turn in for the night. Would you be interested in joining me for a ride in the morning since we were interrupted today?"

"I would like that very much," Selina said.

As Fitz prepared for bed, thoughts of his wife stirred his mind. He couldn't deny the attraction he felt. Her blooming youthfulness was quite appealing. At the moment, his decision to abstain from the marriage bed to spite his father seemed more a punishment to himself. He stood staring at the connecting door, rubbing a hand over the back of his neck. How would she react if he entered her room?

As tempting as it was, he couldn't do it. Uncertainty kept his feet from moving in that direction. If his wife conceived, his father's smugness would be intolerable. That thought alone gave strength to his weakened will. He turned his back on the door and walked to his bed.

# *Chapter Fifteen*

Her chocolate brown hair had appealed to him from the start, but in the early morning sunlight, it shimmered with red highlights, making it more of a chestnut color. There were obviously many facets to his wife's comeliness. Today, her hair hung in a loose, thick braid to just above her narrow waist and bounced with the mare's every step. As they rode along a narrow path, he allowed her to take the lead, giving him ample time to admire her confident posture, which gave clear evidence of her competence on horseback.

When the path widened, she nudged her mount toward the edge of the track and waited for him to come alongside her. Seeing the sweet smile that played on her lips, he had the sudden urge to reach across and pull her to him. Not a good idea while sitting on top of a spirited horse. Instead, he winked, allowing the corners of his mouth to lift in an answering smile.

"Are you up to racing to that stand of trees?" He pointed toward the intended destination.

An impish glint entered her eyes. "Most assuredly." She leaned forward and with a prod of her heels and a flick of the reins, her horse took off in a gallop.

Fitz quickly urged his horse into a run and took off after her.

Selina's laughter filled the air as her hat flew off, hanging by the strings used to tie it. Fitz couldn't resist smiling at her unbridled enjoyment.

His horse was the stronger of the two, but she was much lighter in weight, making the race an even challenge. His horse drew closer bit by bit until they were neck to neck. Their eyes met briefly and he noticed she no longer laughed as she leaned over her horse in full concentration, holding the reins tightly.

He chuckled to himself. She was determined to win, but he knew she would lose this one. Reaching the trees only a moment before she did, they both pulled back on the reins and walked their horses slowly to cool them down.

"Let's stop over there." Fitz pointed to a clearing near the river. Once their horses were tethered to a low branch, he nudged her arm with his elbow and wiggled his eyebrows up and down. "I won."

She looked at his mischievous smile and laughed. "I suppose you did and I'm glad of it."

"And why are you glad?" he asked in astonishment.

"It hurts a man's pride to lose, especially to a woman." She fiddled with her gloves for a moment before glancing at him surreptitiously out the corner of her eyes. "It's best if a woman allows a man to win."

"What?" he almost shouted. "I've never heard anything so ridiculous. Don't tell me you pulled back on the reins to let me win. I saw you leaning over your mount. You were putting your all into the race."

"Do you think so?" She lifted her brows as her eyes were filled with mirth.

"Come now," he said with narrowed eyes. "You wouldn't have laughed uncontrollably at the onset of the race, while you were still ahead, if you were concerned about my tender feelings."

She shrugged her shoulders. "I allowed myself to enjoy a moment of victory before my better sense asserted itself and I heard my aunt's words in my head admonishing me to be careful of a man's sensitive pride. It seems I did the right thing at the end."

With a huff, he exclaimed, "My lady, you are bluffing. Admit it."

"Yes, of course, I am," she said, then bit her bottom lip

and looked away.

He narrowed his eyes as he stared at her. "Do not patronize me. I know what you're doing to. You want me to remain unsure of whether I won fair and square or if you threw the race." He placed his hand on her arm to stop her when they arrived near the river. Facing each other straight on, he said, "Admit it. You did not pull on the reins causing your horse to slow down."

She laughed, "Of course not, my lord."

He began to smirk.

"You are the winner, Fitz," she said with a wink. "All is as it should be." She patted his arm as though soothing a child. She was maddening!

"Selina, you have no idea of the game you're playing. Your teasing is provoking to no end."

He noticed her lips twitch as she valiantly attempted holding back another laugh, but her shoulders shook slightly with the effort. When she had herself under control, she put on a serious mien. "It was as you said. I'm only jesting." She held out her hand. He hesitated a moment before placing his in hers. "Congratulations," she shook his hand. "Perhaps we can race again on our way back. If you win a second time, you will never have to doubt that I'm in earnest when I say you won the race."

Since he still held her hand, he shook it this time. "You're on. We will race to the edge of the park, but first, I plan to claim my prize."

"Prize?" She pulled her hand free, tilting her head with a furrowed brow as her smile disappeared. "I didn't realize there was a prize to be won."

"There is always a prize at the end of a race, Selina."

He stepped closer and placed a hand on her shoulder. The other, he placed on the back of her neck.

"Wh-what are you doing?"

"My prize," he said as he lowered his head.

His lips were warm as they touched hers gently. He smelled of sandalwood and something else. Perhaps his own distinctive scent. It was pleasing to her senses, but all too soon he pulled away. She had to keep herself from groaning in protest.

Swallowing, she spoke with a breathless voice. "We had not agreed on a prize, my lord."

"Hadn't we? My apologies." He held her in a loose embrace and tapped her nose with one finger. "Since I stole a kiss from you, please feel free to steal one back any time you like."

She couldn't hold back a burst of laughter as she shook her head at his ridiculous suggestion and gave him a slight push so he'd release her. "Never mind," she said. Her cheeks felt warm thinking how embarrassing it would be to actually take him up on his suggestion. She couldn't. But, oh . . . she wished she could.

He held his arm out for her to take. "Since you refuse to get even, I think we had better race back."

"Will there be another prize?"

He wiggled his eyebrows up and down. "There is a prize after every race."

Selina's eyes were alight with mirth and she shook her head, but said nothing.

Once they arrived back at Henfort, Selina said, "It seems you won twice today, my lord."

"Yes, I believe I did." His eyes dared her to contradict him, yet there was humor in their depths.

With a brief nod and a smile, she said, "Yes, you did. Congratulations."

He helped her dismount by placing his hands on her narrow waist as she placed her hands on his shoulders to maintain her balance. Once her feet touched the ground, he held on a little longer than necessary. Selina looked into his amused eyes and felt her face become warm. Would he dare kiss her here? In front of the servants? She quickly stepped back, causing him to drop his hands.

"Thank you for inviting me to ride this morning. It was lovely."

"I enjoyed it also." Reaching for her hand, he lifted it to his lips. "We will do it again . . . soon."

When she was halfway up the steps leading into the house, she turned to glance back at Fitz holding the reins of both horses, his eyes still on her. She couldn't resist teasing him one more time. "Imagine winning two races in one day. You must feel very *proud* of yourself. I'm happy for you."

He lost his smile at her emphasis on "proud" and narrowed his eyes when she winked and started turning away. But seeing him hand the reins to a stableboy and take a step toward her, she spun back around and raised a hand to stop him.

"I have no more time, my lord. I must change before my callers arrive." Selina heard him growl, and she giggled as she raced up the stairs at a brisk pace, desperately hoping he wouldn't follow. She hated being chased. Glancing back briefly, she saw Bates join her husband, handing him a missive. Without looking at the message, his eyes returned to her and promised more clearly than words that this conversation wasn't over.

Fitz sat behind his desk staring out the floor to ceiling windows with a view to the small backyard. His intention had been to go over the papers he'd received from his estate manager, but all he'd accomplished so far was to keep rehearsing his morning ride with Selina.

She was a mystery to him that was slowly unfolding before his eyes. He thought her extremely shy and timid at first but was coming to realize his first impression was flawed. Selina was certainly quiet and didn't always seem to know what to say. But quietness did not equal shyness. He'd observed her open friendliness when meeting new people. And when she raced her horse this morning, there was no timidity to be found in her. Her laughter and playfulness made a lie of his earlier estimation of her character. He found himself chuckling and shaking his head as he remembered her teasing about letting him win.

But he would not allow himself to forget his experience with Dinah. He could enjoy his wife. At the same time, it was imperative he restrain his heart from deeper emotions. She responded to his kiss as though her heart was involved, but he knew only too well how female loyalty could change.

* * *

After arriving back from her ride with Fitz, Selina changed quickly into a yellow morning dress before meeting with the housekeeper to go over the menu for the next few days. Once that task was completed, the butler informed her the first caller had arrived and waited in the drawing room.

"Who is it, Bates?"

"It's Mr. Percival Kendall, my lady."

"Thank you." Her voice sounded strained to her own ears. Clearing her throat, she said, "I'll join him directly."

She slowly descended the stairs. Selina was unable to imagine why her brother wanted to see her. Having no fond memories of him, perhaps it would be wise to ask Fitz to join them. No, he would think it strange of her. After a silent prayer for wisdom, she glanced at Bates, who had followed her down the stairs. "Is my aunt at home?"

"No, my lady. She hasn't returned from Lady Worthington's residence as of yet."

"I see." She pulled her bottom lip between her teeth.

"Is something the matter, my lady?"

Selina wished she could ask Bates to stay near the door, but what would he think of her family? It was her own brother, after all. "No, there's nothing the matter. Thank you."

Bates bowed, and she watched as his steps took him farther away, back to the foyer. Selina stood a moment outside the door to the drawing room. It was slightly ajar and she could see Percival standing at the window, his back to the door. She drew in a deep breath, straightened her shoulders attempting to appear confident like her position of viscountess demanded, and entered the room.

"Hello, Percival."

He turned and smiled. It wasn't the cynical smile she was used to seeing on his face. He looked sincere. Why was he being nice to her?

"Selina, you look as lovely as a spring flower." He moved closer and she reluctantly raised her hand for him to take. Closing his strong fingers around her slender ones, he bowed over her hand, placing a gentle kiss upon it. "I think our parents never imagined how pretty you would turn out."

She gently pulled her hand back. "Er…thank you. Please, have a seat." She motioned with her hand to the sofa. Percival walked over to the seating arrangement and waited until she had chosen a chair before sitting on the sofa facing her. Feeling uncomfortable, she didn't know what to say to him, so she waited for him to speak.

He cleared his throat and asked, "How are you adjusting to London?"

"Very well, thank you."

Percival pursed his lips a moment. "I think it's best if I'm honest with you with regards to my visit."

Selina nodded. "Yes, I would prefer that."

He leaned forward, placing his elbows on his knees and steepling his fingers. "I feel abominable about the way I've treated you in the past. I was taking my cues from our parents, you see. Since they looked down on you, I did, too. But observing you since you arrived home, I realize how unfair to you our family has been. How it must have hurt to be treated thus."

She hadn't expected such candid speech nor understanding from her brother of all people. "Aunt Theo and Uncle Peter were wonderful to me, but I will admit, I always longed to return home and be accepted by my family."

"I can well imagine. I know I don't deserve it, but I hope you'll forgive me for my part. I'd like to make amends if I can."

Perhaps Percival was changing for the better. Dare she hope it? Forgiving him was the right thing to do, but forgiveness did not equal trust. That would only come with time. Smiling gently, she said, "Of course, I forgive you."

He placed a hand over his heart. "Thank you."

At that moment, a maid entered the room to deliver their tea. Selina poured a cup for her brother and then one for herself. As she lifted it to her lips to take a sip, she heard Percival say, "Selina, I have something I need to tell you, but it's rather difficult to know quite how to say it."

Oh, no! Had he been buttering her up for some reason? Selina knew better than to allow emotion to rule her heart where her family was concerned.

"What is it you'd like to tell me?"

He cleared his throat. "I saw something that disturbed me earlier this week."

Her brow furrowed. She had no idea what this was leading to. "And what was it you saw?"

"I don't know any easy way to put this, so I will just say it. I saw Fitz at the theater a couple nights ago with Lady Blackmore."

"I-I don't know what you mean. I'm certain he was seen with many people at the theater." Selina didn't bother mentioning she was unaware he had attended the theater. Many husbands and wives lived separate lives. It wasn't what she had hoped for, but it certainly wasn't unusual. But Lady Blackmore? Her heart squeezed a bit.

Percival shook his head. "Unfortunately, it appeared more like an assignation. They met in the hallway of the theater and I happened upon them without either of them realizing it. Out of concern for you, I stayed hidden to see what was going on. I'm certain you must realize by now that she was engaged to your husband only a few short years ago."

"Yes, I'm aware of it." Holding her cup with both hands to keep it from shaking, she gently set it on the table and straightened to clasp her hands on her lap.

His eyes filled with sympathy as he continued. "Lady Blackmore told Fitz how unhappy she is in her marriage and that her feelings for him are unchanged. She begged him to meet her alone."

Percival's eyes were on her, and she tried hard to stay emotionless. How did Fitz respond to Lady Blackmore's comment? She wished she could ask, but felt hesitant to show him the turmoil his comment caused.

"They agreed to meet the following morning," Percival said.

Suddenly, it felt as if a weight fell off her shoulders. "Well, he must have decided against meeting her, for he and I went for a ride early yesterday morning in Hyde Park. He couldn't have been with her if he was with me."

The corners of his mouth lifted as he nodded. "I'm certainly glad to hear it. He would be a fool to risk losing your good opinion. Personally, I think you are far lovelier than Lady Blackmore."

Surprised at his defense of her, she said, "Why, thank you, Percival."

"So you and Fitz like to go riding at early dawn, do you?"

Selina narrowed her eyes and tilted her head. "No . . . we went right after breakfast."

He simply stared at her, and she realized her mistake. The agreed-upon assignation must have been at early dawn. "Where did they plan on meeting?" Selina asked breathlessly. She feared Percival could see her distress, but curiosity got the better of her.

"Hyde Park. It seems he took you to the very place of his earlier rendezvous with Lady Blackmore. I'm sorry, Selina. I can see this upsets you, but you ought to know before it becomes public knowledge."

"There must be a reasonable explanation, Percival. I refuse to jump to conclusions. I-I think you meant well by telling me, but I don't believe Fitz was in any way unfaithful to me." She wasn't convinced of her own words but needed to stop Percival from further speculation. "Thank you for telling me, but I don't wish to discuss it any further."

"Very well. Then we will not speak of it again." He smiled kindly. "So tell me, what sites have you seen since coming to London?"

Her mind was in a whirl, but she tried to gather her thoughts and focus on the conversation. She told him of the various sites she'd seen including Hatchard's Bookstore and Bond Street.

He suggested other sites worth seeing. She'd not been to Vauxhall or Drury Lane. Selina tried to concentrate on the things Percival said, but her mind was preoccupied with what had been revealed to her. As he stood to his feet saying he did not wish to overstay his welcome, the butler came to the door and announced her next visitors.

"Lady Runswick and Miss Helena Kendall are here to see

you."

"Thank you, Bates. Please show them in." He bowed and left the room.

"Thank you for your time, Selina. It was good catching up," Percival said. "I hope I may call on you again soon."

"Yes, of course."

"Selina! I'm glad we were able to find you at home," her mother said as she entered the drawing room followed by Selina's younger sister.

"Mama, thank you for coming, and Helena, too." She smiled at both, although she wished for nothing more than to be alone to think things through.

Selina noticed her mother's face suddenly become pale as she laid eyes on Percival.

"Percival," Mama said, a bit breathless. "I didn't realize you were here."

Selina had noticed Percival's jaw tighten at the arrival of his mother and sister. The corners of his mouth lifted in a cynical smile.

"Selina and I enjoyed a pleasant chat. After all the years she was gone from us and seeing her grown up now—a sister, yet a stranger—I realized the injustice you did us in depriving us of her company."

Lady Runswick glared at her son. "We did it for you, Percival. Uncle Peter and Aunt Theo were unable to have children but had plenty of wealth. We, on the other hand, had plenty of children but were heading to the poor house. When your aunt and uncle offered us an exorbitant amount of money in exchange for one of our children, we saw a way out of the disaster we were heading toward. Your inheritance had to be secured."

Had Aunt Theo and Uncle Peter bought her? Was it true? Selina would ask Aunt Theo about it later. For now, she observed the relationship between her mother and Percival.

Giving her son a sharp look, Lady Runswick said, "It would be incumbent upon you to give up gambling as your father has done. Money doesn't grow on trees. Either you invest it to make a profit or you marry an heiress. Gambling is no longer an option. Helena is too young to marry off, so that leaves only you. It is time you do your duty by us."

"We are certainly doing well now," Percival said. "No need to cut up my peace and rush me to the altar. I'll find myself an heiress soon enough. For now, I've stopped gambling and I've paid off most of my debts."

With raised brows, Lady Runswick stared at her son a moment. Tilting her head and narrowing her eyes, she asked, "You've paid off most of your debt?"

"Yes. I sold off some of my horseflesh and a curricle as father insisted I should, as well as my townhouse."

His mother continued staring in disbelief, hand to her chest. Finally, she straightened her shoulders and raised her chin. "Good. I'm glad to hear it. Perhaps now you can apologize to your father for treating him disrespectfully. Then we can finally move forward."

"Very well, Mama. I'll call on father later today. I must be on my way now. I have a meeting at my club shortly." He gave his mother a peck on the cheek, nodded to Helena, then turned to Selina. "It was a pleasure, Selina. I shall visit again soon."

"Good day, Percival." After he left, Selina gestured toward the sofa and chairs. "Please, make yourselves comfortable."

After they were seated, her mother opened her reticule and pulled out what appeared to be a newspaper clipping. "I didn't want to mention this in front of Percival. This will be difficult enough for you to deal with, without your brother's presence in the room." She handed the newsprint to Selina.

Hesitantly, Selina lowered her eyes and saw a sketch of a man and woman standing near a pond on a misty morning. Her heart sank and she felt numb as she stared at a sketch of Fitz and Lady Blackmore. The couple stood toe-to-toe facing each other, her hand on his forearm, as they looked deeply into each other's eyes. The gentleman leaned down as though about to bestow a kiss to her lips. Selina's eyes alighted on the caption beneath the sketch. "Reunion in Hyde Park at Dawn." Her eyes returned to the picture hoping to see she had mistaken the identity of the two people. One couldn't clearly distinguish the face of the gentleman, so perhaps she was jumping to conclusions. But what of the cane lying discarded on the grass and the man's faded scar on his cheek? The lady's face and dark hair were more distinguishable. There was no denying who the artist had seen.

Before lifting her eyes from the paper, Selina valiantly attempted to bring her emotions under control. She was uncertain as to the reason her mother brought this gossip to her attention. Was she concerned for her daughter or was this another reason to find fault with her?

Slowly lifting her eyes from the newsprint, her mother's calm demeanor gave nothing away of her feelings. Selina felt at a loss for words. What did they expect her to say? She felt numb from shock and desperately longed for some solitude to process what she'd seen, heard, and experienced this day.

"Do you think someone at the newspaper is telling lies about FitzWalter?" Helena, with pretty golden curls artfully arranged atop her head and bright blue eyes, wrung her hands. "Any gifted artist could have sketched such a picture whether it was true or not."

Selina hadn't thought of that. Her younger sister might have the right of it. Before she could grasp onto this lifeline, her mother said, "That would be highly unlikely. It could cost the man his job if it were found out to be a fabrication." She shifted her eyes to Selina. "Someone at the newspaper obviously saw your husband on a rendezvous with a married woman, who happened to be his former fiancé."

Selina squeezed her hands tightly together. She knew her mother was right. They must have been observed at Hyde Park on that particular morning.

"I came directly here after seeing the damaging newspaper clipping to give you sound advice. I know you have your aunt to guide you, but she has been gone from society for quite some time and has some rather independent ways. Unfortunately, such an attitude will not serve you well in London. Will you at least listen to what I have to say?"

Selina couldn't help feeling touched by her mother's concern for her. "Of course, Mama," she said. Selina glanced at her sister and saw she bit her bottom lip. Was she worried for her?

"Very well," her mother said with a nod. "I allowed your sister to join us because I thought it best you both understand that men will be unfaithful. It is the way of all men. Only foolish women get up on the high ropes or become missish."

Seeing Selina's eyes widen in shock, she quickly continued, "Do I need to remind you that your marriage is not a love match and there is no room for such expectations? My advice to you is simply pretend you never saw this article. If anyone questions you, you must claim you have no idea what they are speaking of and then change the subject. Allow FitzWalter his peccadilloes as long as he continues providing well for you. I will ask your father to drop a hint in your husband's ear about using greater discretion in the future, but you must say nothing. Simply go on as though you had never laid eyes on the sketch."

Selina slowly shook her head, but her mother stretched her hand out. "Stop! I don't want any hysterics or denials. Our family's reputation will not be compromised in this. You must heed my words and do as I say. Your husband has the power to shame you with a divorce if you act the shrew. In such cases, it's always the woman who is shunned while the man's reputation is spared and his standing in society remains unchanged."

Selina looked toward her sister who sat with fingers over parted lips, her eyes large in her face. Selina empathized with her younger sister. Had Mama just destroyed Helena's dreams of romance? She seemed more concerned about the family's reputation rather than having any real compassion for her daughter, but Selina chose not to contradict her. Once their visit ended, she would seek Aunt Theo's advice. Certainly, it would be quite different. How should a godly wife respond? Feeling too emotional at the moment for rational thought, she said nothing. Unfortunately, it seemed her mother and sister weren't quite ready to depart yet.

"Now, before we change the subject and never mention it again, I have one more word of advice," her mother said. "I would like for you to attend the theater with your Father and me this evening. Lady Blackmore and her husband always attend on Friday evenings, and I want you to be there as well. You will deliberately not look at their box all evening as though she meant nothing to you. If you, perchance, should cross paths, you will be pleasant to her as though you never saw that sketch. That is how you must go on. We will pick you up so we may arrive together. I'm certain Juliet will join us as well."

It seemed her mother wanted to include her in the family. Selina couldn't deny it warmed her heart. She wasn't blind to the fact her mother's main goal was to preserve the family reputation, yet it did make her feel included after all this time.

"I would like to ask Aunt Theo to attend also, for I know she would enjoy it," Selina said.

"Very well. We will include her in our party. Helena and I must be going now. We have an appointment with the modiste, but we shall see you tonight." Putting up a cautioning finger, her mother added, "Just remember, say nothing to FitzWalter. Even if he were to bring it up, which is unlikely, you must wave it off as something that is of no great consequence."

"Thank you for your advice, Mama," Selina said, although she still intended to ask Aunt Theo.

Lady Runswick dipped her chin once in acknowledgment. "You are wise to heed my advice. Farewell, Selina."

"Good-bye, Mama, Helena."

## *Chapter Sixteen*

"I must speak with you, Aunt Theo. Is this a good time?"

"Yes, of course. What is it, child?"

Fully entering her aunt's sitting room, Selina sat beside her on the sofa. "Mama and Helena visited today. In the course of our conversation, Mama mentioned you and Uncle Peter bought me from them. Is it true?"

The color suddenly drained from Aunt Theo's face. Selina placed a hand on her aunt's slightly wrinkled one. "I'm sure you meant well. Please don't be upset. I only wish to know why you did so?"

Tears gathered in her aunt's eyes and one rolled down her cheek as her lips trembled. Aunt Theo's voice quivered when she spoke. "I dreaded this day for a long time, afraid you would wish us to perdition if you ever found out." She took a deep breath, swiped the tears away, and squared her shoulders. "As you know, Uncle Peter and I were unable to have children of our own, so we decided to offer your parents money if they would give one of their children to us in order to help them in their dire financial dilemma. Your Mama often complained they had too many girls and not enough heirs. When we made the offer, we didn't stipulate it be you, although we were certain they would choose you to give to us."

Selina frowned, trying to understand, but it was a lot to take in. Instead of interrupting with questions, she decided to hear her aunt out.

"We had decided beforehand to help them whether they accepted our offer or not. If they chose to give you to us for the money, we knew you would be better off in our care. If they refused, we would have handed them the money anyway, for we would not have allowed them to go to the poor house."

Of course, Selina already knew of her parents decision to give her away. They were certainly in a desperate situation, but she could not imagine giving away a child of her own. "Did they beg you to consider a different alternative?"

Brow furrowed and eyes filled with sadness, Aunt Theo shook her head. "They chose to give you to us without question. To this day they remain unaware we would have given them the money regardless."

Selina sat staring at nothing for a moment, her mind in a whirl, trying to make sense of it all. On the one hand, her parents must have felt desperate to save their family from scandal. On the other, they chose Selina, of all their children, as the most dispensable child. Her heart pinched, but she refused to give voice to her thoughts for it would only cause her aunt more grief.

"Thank you, Aunt Theo, for explaining it. I understand why you did it and I will not hold it against you. You gave me a good life—I think much better than I could have had with my parents." She leaned over and kissed her aunt's cheek.

"Selina, are you truly not vexed with me? I know it must hurt, but I've seen a change in your family. It's obvious Juliet loves you dearly. You're gaining the respect of your parents. I suspect they regret some of the choices they've made."

Nodding thoughtfully, Selina said, "Thank you, Aunt Theo. I'm fine. Perhaps, like the story of Joseph in the Bible that you shared with me long ago, it was part of God's plan for my life." She folded her hands on her lap and took a deep breath. "I have something else I wish to discuss with you."

"Of course. What is it?"

"Did you see the gossip column this morning?"

"Selina, you know very well I will not waste precious time

on such nonsense," her aunt huffed.

"And I feel the same, but Mama and Helena showed me the column when they came for a morning call as it pertains to Fitz and another woman."

"No! I don't believe it! He may have his faults, but he is not a philanderer. Absolutely not!"

Selina handed the gossip sheet to her aunt, watching for her reaction. After staring at the sketch for a few seconds, Aunt Theo slowly raised sober eyes, not saying anything.

Selina told her of the advice her mother had given. Aunt Theo sat in quiet contemplation, staring off into the distance. She finally began to speak. "Hmm, I'm uncertain how to advise you. Perhaps your Mama is correct in this. It would be best if you did not confront him, but I don't think you should have to hide your feelings once he opens the subject for discussion."

"I'm afraid of what he will say, for I cannot bear thinking my husband will love elsewhere for all of our marriage." She swallowed hard."I think I prefer taking Mama's advice and saying nothing even if he speaks to me, at least for now. As a matter of fact, I don't even want to see him."

Reaching over, Aunt Theo squeezed her niece's hand. "It grieves me to know you must face this gossip. How I wish it were possible to carry you away and protect you from a world which too often is unfair and cruel. Alas, that is not possible. I can only guide, support, and pray for you."

As her eyes filled with tears, Selina's voice shook. "Thank you, Aunt Theo. I don't know what I would do if I didn't have you to talk to. You are my anchor."

"Oh, my darling girl," she said while pulling her niece into her arms and holding her close. They stayed in each other's embrace for a while, gaining strength from the love they shared. Pulling away, Aunt Theo said, "I must caution you to be careful when out in public. If you can pretend nothing of import has occurred and hold your head up in society, the gossip will soon die down. A new scandal will take its place before long and this latest gossip will be forgotten."

Selina nodded. "I will do my best."

* * *

Tonight was Selina's first time to visit a London theater, and Drury Lane in particular. Unfortunately, the scandal on everyone's mind ruined any enjoyment to be gained from the experience.

Shortly after arriving, Mama whispered behind her fan to Selina, "Don't look now, but the Blackmore box is to your left and Lady Blackmore is in attendance tonight as I told you she would be."

Why was it when someone said not to look at something, that was precisely all one wanted to do? Selina stiffened her neck, not daring to give in to temptation.

She felt curious eyes on her all evening, which wasn't surprising. Selina dearly wished she'd stayed home, yet her mother had insisted. Holding her head high, she sat with a straight posture, sweeping a gaze over the audience, yet never allowing herself to make eye contact with anyone.

During intermission, Kitty and her mother visited Selina in her parents' box. They had been invited to attend with Adam Linfield. Kitty whispered when she was certain no one could overhear, "I'm terribly sorry about the newspaper article this morning."

Selina shook her head, "I'd rather not talk about it here. Would you have time to come for a visit tomorrow?"

"Yes, of course. I shall see you late morning, or is that too soon?"

"That will be fine."

They were interrupted when Kitty's mother said it was time they returned to their box. Once her friends departed, Selina moved her attention back to the stage where the performance started once more, but it couldn't hold her attention. Seeing Aunt Theo and her parents occupied with the play or watching the people in the audience below, Selina finally dared glance out the corner of her eye toward the box she had been curious about all evening.

Lady Blackmore stared back. Once caught, Selina was unable to turn away. The depth of sadness in the lady's eyes caused her own heart to squeeze. Finally, Lady Blackmore lifted her nose a bit and shifted her gaze, releasing Selina from an almost hypnotic state. Was the sadness due to the Marchioness's hopeless love for Fitz?

As difficult as this evening had been with the many stares cast in their direction and the whispering behind fans, she'd prefer enduring another such evening to seeing her husband again. Uncertain of her ability to pretend nothing had changed, she determined to avoid him as long as possible.

Her parents' carriage slowed to a stop in front of Henfort, and Selina offered her thanks for the invitation to join them that evening.

"Remember what I said, Selina," her mother cautioned her.

"I will, Mama." She stepped down from the carriage and waited for Aunt Theo. As they neared the front steps, the butler held the door open and then took their cloaks. "Is Lord FitzWalter home?" she asked.

"Yes, my lady. He's in his office."

"Thank you, Bates. I won't disturb him. We will turn in for the night."

"As you wish, my lady."

After Rawden helped Fitz prepare for the day the following morning, the viscount walked toward the door. His servant cleared his throat, holding out a newspaper. "My lord, you may want to look at yesterday's paper."

"I've seen it already, Rawden. You may keep it or pass it along."

As Fitz placed his hand on the doorknob, he heard his valet clear his throat once more. "Pardon me, my lord, but you may want to read the gossip column at your earliest convenience."

Fitz frowned at his servant, but took the paper before leaving his bedchamber. His first inclination was to ignore the paper, but it was unusual for Rawden to make such a request. There must be something that needed his attention. Once seated behind the desk in his study, he opened the paper to yesterday's gossip column.

His head reeled. Had Selina seen the sketch? He banged a closed fist on the desk, then stood to his feet and began pacing.

Should he explain to her about his meeting with Dinah? If she hadn't seen the gossip sheet, certainly her friends had. Selina was bound to hear about it. Wouldn't it be better coming from him? Would she even give him a chance to explain? He had to try, of course. Unfortunately, Parliament was in session this morning and there would be little time for conversation with his wife. He hurried to the breakfast room in case Selina was up already. Finding it empty, he turned toward the foyer.

"How did Lady FitzWalter seem yesterday, Bates?" he asked his butler as he accepted his cane and hat.

Bates was no fool. He must have heard the gossip and knew exactly the information his master sought. "She seemed quieter than usual. After her family left yesterday afternoon, she refused all callers. But she did visit Drury Lane with them in the evening."

So that's how it was. Her family must have stopped by after reading the morning paper. How did they advise her? As he sat in the carriage, his frustration mounted. He should never have met with Dinah. Rubbing the back of his neck, he scolded himself, "Fool!"

Fitz stared out the window without seeing the view. All he could think of was his wife, an innocent bystander, being pulled into this scandal. There were those in the ton who would maliciously malign her, staring and pointing a finger or whispering behind fans loud enough to reach her ears.

He should have told her of the meeting in Hyde Park. There were several things he should have done differently. Shaking his head in self-deprecation, he exclaimed, "Oh, God, I've made a mess of things!" It was the closest he'd come to praying in quite some time.

Fitz leaned forward, placing his elbows on his knees as he dropped his head into his hands, and rubbed his temples. After Parliament today, he had to meet with a couple of lords at his club to hopefully sway them in the right direction for a vote later this week. But he was determined to join his wife for dinner in the evening and clear everything up before the day ended.

Fitz leaned back in his seat and stared out the window. One more thought disturbed him. How would Blackmore react when he saw the gossip sheet? He was a man of good reputation. But who knew what the Marquess might do about a scandal involving his wife? Fitz knew he would have to discreetly find out about Dinah, but how was it possible without causing more gossip?

As he promised himself, Fitz arrived home in time for dinner with his wife. Handing his cloak, hat, and cane to Bates, he asked, "Where might I find Lady FitzWalter?"

"She isn't at home, my lord. She and Mrs. Harris are attending the Mountford Ball."

Fitz had been invited but sent his regrets. Now he almost wished he hadn't done so. If the ton saw him attentive to his wife, it would go a long way toward squelching speculation. Not wanting to show his disappointment to his staff, he only nodded. "I'll take my dinner in my study."

"Very well, my lord."

He reclined in the chair behind his desk, crossed his arms over his chest, and laid his head back, staring at the ceiling, trying to decide if he would stay home and wait for his wife or visit a friend. Devonport might be at home after a long day at Parliament. Talking with his friend would help the time pass before Selina returned home. He leaned forward, placing his elbows on his desk. Picking up a pen, he began tapping it. No, he wouldn't go out. There was no one with whom he wished to speak.

Obviously, the weaker sex was not the only gossipmonger in society. Questioning glances had followed him all day from many of the men at the various meetings Fitz attended.

Unable to sit any longer, he paced to the window. It was dark outside, but the street gaslight shown brightly, and he watched as a horse and carriage lumbered past the row of townhouses.

It was nobody's business what the meeting in Hyde Park was about. If that nosey journalist hadn't seen him, no one would have been any the wiser. It was a harmless meeting—until it was printed in the newspaper. Now it seemed sordid and sinful, which was the furthest thing from the truth. Fitz had not had any intention of being unfaithful when he agreed to join her in Hyde Park. But if he were perfectly honest with himself, his ego did long to hear Dinah say she still loved him and that he wasn't as dispensable as her father had claimed.

Disgust with himself caused him to turn from the window and begin pacing again. If he truly loved Dinah, would he wish for her to continue pining for him? Wouldn't he wish for her happiness? How shallow had his feelings for her become?

Sitting back down at his desk, he pulled out a framed painting of Dinah hidden in the bottom drawer. He studied it closely. The artist had captured her likeness exactly. "Beautiful," he said to himself. Undeniably attractive. Yet there was something missing. She seemed almost a stranger. There was no longer a deep connection between them. Leaning back in his chair, he rubbed a hand over his face and tried making sense of his emotions. After having loved someone so intensely, was it possible to stop loving them?

His eyes gazed at the picture once more. Dinah chose to obey her father and, in the process, rejected him—her fiancé. She had a choice to make three years ago. She didn't choose him.

Evidently, if love is not nurtured, it will die. They hadn't spoken to each other in several years. When he did catch a glimpse of her, she stood beside another man—her husband. Slowly, over time, it seemed his love for Dinah had died, or it at least fell into a deep slumber. Perhaps spending time together even in friendship would reawaken their love.

Fitz stared at the painting once more, then turned it over and laid it flat on his desk. He had no interest in a friendship with Dinah. She had made her choice three years ago. He refused to risk awakening emotions that were better left to die.

There was a brief knock on the door before it slowly opened. "Your dinner, my lord," said a servant girl as she entered and placed the tray on his desk. "Will there be anything else?"

"No, that is all. Thank you."

She bobbed a curtsy and left the room.

Fitz tried occupying himself with paperwork for the next few hours until he heard the front door open. Hoping to intercept his wife before she secluded herself in her bedchamber, he hurried out of his study.

"Selina, I'm glad you're home. Good evening, Aunt Theo."

Both ladies curtsied to him.

"May I have a word with you, Selina, in my study?"

"Please, not tonight, my lord." She placed a hand on her forehead. "I have a dreadful headache and long for my bed."

What could he say? As much as he wished to insist she join him for a few minutes, he could not bring himself to do so. "Very well. Goodnight then."

"Goodnight." Selina gave a brief curtsy and slipped her arm through Aunt Theo's as they ascended the stairs together.

Fitz watched them for a moment, then spun around to his study. He would make a point of seeking her out in the morning.

The following day turned out quite differently than Fitz had hoped. Selina slept in and then received a morning caller, her friend Kitty. Mrs. Addams took Kitty up to Selina's sitting room, where the ladies secluded themselves until past the time Fitz had to leave for his Parliamentary meeting. At the end of the day, he made a point of coming straight home instead of visiting Whites, his gentleman's club, as he normally would. Bates met Fitz at the door and informed him Selina was out with Juliet and Kitty. She wasn't expected home until late.

The next day, Fitz had to go to the Home Office early. He came home in time for supper only to find his wife missing once again. She was attending a ball with Aunt Theo and Kitty. He waited for her, but when he asked if he could speak with her, she once again complained of a dreadful headache.

"Then would you be interested in riding with me in the

morning? Our horses could use some exercise."

Touching her hand to her temple, she said, "I doubt I'll be up early. Perhaps in the afternoon?"

"I cannot in the afternoon. I'll be at the Home Office."

She shrugged her shoulders and smiled apologetically without actually looking into his eyes. "Goodnight then."

His gaze followed her up the stairs. *She's avoiding me.* He'd suspected as much, but now he felt certain it was so. How could he repair things between them if she evaded him at every turn?

After another week of dinners alone at Henfort while his wife flitted about from ball to ball, he decided to resume his normal activities. Sooner or later, their paths would have to cross. He would give her time.

# *Chapter Seventeen*

Selina unlaced and removed her dancing slippers, then fell back onto her bed. "Grrr . . . I'm sick and tired of balls, parties, and late nights!"

Percival had sought Selina out at every event and always secured one dance with her, usually a waltz. He was pleasant enough, complimenting her on her appearance, but she couldn't feel completely at ease. Selina couldn't pinpoint anything specific. Perhaps her past experience with him caused her continued mistrust. *Have I not completely forgiven him?* Selina hoped that wasn't the case. She reminded herself forgiveness and trust were separate issues. She felt no bitterness or animosity toward him but was not confident he had her best interest at heart.

As they danced that evening, Percival hinted Fitz was still in contact with Lady Blackmore. He didn't share specifics but cautioned her about trusting her husband.

"Mama advised I pretend all is well," Selina told Percival. "She was adamant I not confront my husband about any of it."

Percival nodded thoughtfully, "Yes, I suppose that is good advice. It will do you no good to confront him for it will only anger him and, perhaps, thrust him deeper into the arms of his lady love." He walked her off the dance floor, holding her hand on his arm and gently patting it. "I'll call on you tomorrow. All will be well, Selina, if you guard your heart. After all, you are his wife and he is obligated to provide for you. You are the one who will give him an heir. That is something no one else can do."

He was right, of course. But Selina longed for much more than a marriage of convenience. She had seen the love between Uncle Peter and Aunt Theo all those years, as well as Kitty's parents. She witnessed it with Juliet and Henry as well as Emma and Devon, and she desired the same for herself.

Percival handed Selina off to her next dance partner, Lord Devonport.

"You are looking well this evening," Devon said.

"Thank you." Selina tried to push the conversation with Percival out of her head.

"I hoped for a chance to speak with you, Selina." Leaning a bit closer, he spoke in a soft voice, "I want to caution you about believing what you read in a gossip sheet." She lifted her brows but said nothing. "Bear in mind that a sketch is not always reliable. The artist could certainly have embellished it."

The dance steps parted them for a bit. When they met together again, she said, "Do you believe it was embellished?" Her mother told her to pretend ignorance if anyone mentioned the incident, but this was her husband's close friend and a fellow believer.

"I think you should give him a chance to explain."

Selina blinked. "Did he talk to you about it?"

"The subject came up. He only said he thinks you might be avoiding him."

The dance steps parted them again. Her mind was in a whirl and she could not focus on the other dance partners. Percival told her of Fitz's continued unfaithfulness while Devon told her it might all be a lie.

The dance steps brought them together again, and Selina said, "I know you mean well and you want to help your friend, but I have reason to believe he is not worthy of my trust." When Devon started to open his mouth to respond, she shook her head. "Please, no more. I'd rather not discuss my marriage. It is all very confusing. How are your sons doing?"

"Selina, I want to help *both* of you." He saw her chin lift as she gazed over his shoulder refusing to answer. Sighing, he said, "Very well, we won't talk of it. My sons give us pleasure beyond anything we could ever have imagined."

She smiled her thanks as she looked into his eyes. The rest of the dance was filled with stories of his older son's humorous antics. The other was yet an infant.

As Selina lay on her bed, she weighed Percival's words against Devon's. She knew she ought to hear her husband's side of the situation. But was she ready to do so? Aunt Theo often quoted the Scripture that said one must treat others as one would wish to be treated. If the situation were reversed, she would want an opportunity to explain her side of the story. But when she recalled the whispers she had endured night after night, the snide comments members of the ton made certain she'd overhear, as well as the looks of pity, anger stirred once more. Placing both hands over her face, she prayed, "Lord, I know it's wrong of me not to give Fitz the opportunity to explain. But certainly, You understand I cannot bear to look into his face."

Standing up, she walked to the middle of the room and stomped her foot. "He met with his former betrothed in a park at early dawn—the scoundrel! Had he thought of me once as he planned his assignation? Did his conscience never smite him as he rode to his rendezvous?"

Selina marched back to the bed, picked up her pillow, and hugged it close. "What is the sense of talking to Fitz? I'm certain I cannot believe a word he tells me."

Plopping down on the bedcover, she pursed her lips. *How dare he treat me so negligently!* "Selfish, insufferable man! Does he think he's the only one who's ever been hurt? Who's had to sacrifice his dream?"

As she spoke the words, she recognized her own guilt. Had she not done the same to Aunt Theo for years on end? Longing for something that was not to be had? The tears came in earnest and she crumbled to her knees by her bed, pouring her heart out to God. When the tears finally subsided, she prayed, "Forgive me for my stubborn heart. I've been avoiding my husband too long—hoping to punish him. Please, give me the courage to do the right thing."

In the morning, Selina went back to her former habit of eating in the breakfast room. She couldn't help feeling relieved when Bates informed her Fitz had left early for an appointment at the Home Office before heading to Parliament.

Later that day, Aunt Theo and Selina joined Kitty at Juliet's fundraising luncheon. Juliet's speech was inspiring. Selina had the opportunity to meet the matron of the London Foundling Hospital, an orphanage not just for children without parents, but also those forced out of their homes due to overcrowding or abandonment. When Selina asked how she could be of help, the matron told her about the donations that were necessary to adequately run the orphanage. They also needed people to read to the children and simply spend time with them.

Selina's heart ached to show love to these hurting little ones. Having been banished from her own home, she understood to some extent the confusion and hurt these children must feel. The following day she and Aunt Theo visited the orphanage, and Selina knew she would never be the same again. While Fitz remained occupied with parliamentary meetings and Home Office issues, Selina visited the foundling home several times over the next couple weeks. Besides reading to the children, she taught needlework to the older girls and began giving reading lessons. Aunt Theo enjoyed rocking the babies and feeding them.

Life had purpose. She still attended the occasional ball or party that couldn't be avoided, but more often than not, her evenings were spent preparing reading lessons and grading papers.

Since working with the foundling home, Selina thought about the tenants at Thorncrest. Were they well provided for? She had been terribly naive when first arriving at her new home, never giving much thought to her tenants' needs. She was no longer such an innocent about life, having seen, heard, and experienced too much since coming to London.

Fitz had predicted accurately. London had changed her. She did not feel quite as innocent as when she arrived.

At the Gillingham Ball, Selina was met with curious glances once more. Most did not dare to mention her husband to her, but that evening a particular school friend of Lady Blackmore, Lady Belinda Lockhart, stopped to greet Emma as Selina stood beside her.

"It's a pleasure to see you, Lady Devonport."

"Hello, Lady Lockhart. How do you do?"

"I'm well." Looking pointedly at Selina, Lady Lockhart added, "I don't believe we've met."

"Oh, I didn't realize," Emma said. "Please allow me to introduce to you Lady Selina FitzWalter."

"Ah, so you are Fitz's wife. I am a particular friend of his former fiancé and remember well how desperately in love they were." She let her gaze move up and down over Selina. "You are pretty enough, but, alas, you are not her. Do not take too personally the gossip sheet. Many men marry one woman when they prefer another. If you had observed them a few years back, you would realize competing for his affection would be a lost cause. Fitz's heart was completely engaged, and Dinah shall always own it." Shrugging her slender shoulders, she added, "But you will be the mother of his heir and will be well provided for. You must find contentment in that, for that is life, my dear."

Selina stood in silence. She could think of nothing to say.

"You are doing the right thing by attending balls and pretending all is well. That's the best way to handle such awkward situations. Well, it was nice to make your acquaintance." The lady left not waiting for a response.

Selina turned to Emma with widened eyes. "She was rather bold."

"Bold, indeed. And boorish! Give no heed to her words." Selina knew Emma was right, but her heart was not completely untouched.

Devon joined them and put his hand out to lead his wife to the dance floor. Selina watched them walk away arm-in-arm. She sighed. The future that stretched before her seemed lonely and sad.

Forcing her mind away from her pain, she allowed a smile to play on her lips as she glanced around at the many people seemingly enjoying themselves this evening. Soon a gentleman held out a hand and asked her to dance. The evening slipped away as she allowed herself to be swept across the dance floor time and time again. As Selina stood next to Emma between dances, sipping a glass of orgeat lemonade, Mrs. Warwick and Lady Swinton, both notorious gossips, stopped to greet them.

"Oh, my dear Lady FitzWalter," Mrs. Warwick gushed, "my heart simply breaks for you."

Selina felt her cheeks warm. Why did people feel the need to speak false consolations? Everything within her wished to give them the cut direct, but she could not. Doing so would be a terrible insult, and could reflect poorly on Fitz, since Lady Swinton's husband sat with him in Parliament. Selina stiffened her spine and simply stared at them, knowing she would have to endure whatever they chose to say.

"That philanderer does not deserve such a sweet wife," Lady Swinton obviously felt a need to share her wealth of wisdom. She glanced around to be certain no one overheard, then lowered her voice. "If you ask me, Lady Dinah Blackmore is a hussy!"

As much as Selina felt slighted by her husband, she could not stand for such blatant gossip. Normally lacking words to defend herself until hours after an inciting incident, today might turn out differently. Without giving much thought to what she should answer them, Selina simply spoke from her heart. "Lady Swinton. Mrs. Warwick. I do believe you mean well. But my husband is *not* a philanderer. He is a well-respected former officer who fought in the war to protect England. He is an honorable gentleman who manages his estate and investments well. My husband is a man to be admired and not gossiped about. I cannot help what lies are printed on gossip sheets, but I can help what I allow my mind to dwell on and believe."

"Oh, my dear Lady FitzWalter—"

"Please, allow me to finish. I wish to say that I cannot feel comfortable disparaging Lady Blackmore. She does not deserve it. She is the wife of a marquess as well as the mother of their child. I would not wish to call any mother a name that could hurt her children. Please, let's not speak of it anymore."

"But, Lady FitzWalter, surely you know—"

Selina put up a hand, "Please, Mrs. Warwick, no more. I truly do not wish to discuss gossip. Now, isn't this a lovely ball? Did you have a chance to partake of the delicious display of refreshments offered this evening?"

"Well . . . yes . . ." Both ladies seemed uncertain what to say. Forthwith, Lady Swinton said, "I see Swinton waving to me." Taking hold of Mrs. Warwick's arm, she added, "It was a pleasure. Good evening." They turned and walked away.

Emma lifted her fan to wave it before her lips. "Selina, you handled them beautifully!"

"I am ready for this evening to end." Selina took a calming breath. "If you will excuse me, Emma, I see Aunt Theo. Perhaps it's best I return home."

Emma placed a hand on Selina's arm and squeezed it gently. "I understand. Rest well, my dear. You truly comported yourself with excellence tonight. I only wish Fitz were here to see it. He would certainly see the treasure he has in you. One day, he will see it. Of that, I have no doubt."

Selina thanked her friend for her kind words of encouragement, but she refused to allow her heart to hope. Life was less disappointing when one didn't allow false hope to take root in one's heart.

Percival called on her a couple of times over the next two weeks. When Selina mentioned Fitz was representing the Home Office in Manchester regarding the blanketeering, he shook his head sadly. "Do you realize the Blackmores' manor house is in Manchester and that Lady Blackmore has removed herself from London in the wake of the scandal? I heard Lord Blackmore insisted his wife leave Town for the rest of the Season. She returned to their manor a couple of weeks ago."

Selina's heart pinched, yet she hesitated to discuss her marriage with her brother. "Percival, Fitz is my husband and

I'd rather not believe the worst in him. I have chosen to pray for him instead of speculating upon his actions."

"Praying!" Her brother chuckled. "Very well, little sister, you keep right on praying while your husband philanders to his heart's content."

Her shoulders went rigid and she glared at him. "Do not mock me, Percival. I promise you more can be accomplished through prayer than through gossip and disparaging remarks."

Seeing her anger, he changed tactics. "That is admirable, of course. Forgive me, Selina. I don't think I've ever met someone who takes their faith quite so seriously. On second thought, I suppose Juliet and Henry do also. I should not have laughed."

Mollified, Selina nodded once. "I forgive you, Percival."

"I must be on my way," he said as he stood to his feet. "Please feel free to call on me if you should ever need to. If a woman cannot rely on her husband, she may at least rely on her brother." He smiled kindly, but his words hurt.

"Thank you, Percival." What else could she say?

"Would it be all right if I leave through those patio doors? I'd like to stroll in your garden for a bit. After your words about prayer, I desire some time alone."

"Of course. Please take your time."

"You are very kind, Selina." He kissed her hand and exited through the doors.

Percival walked casually around the gardens, pretending to stop and look at flowerbeds. However, he surreptitiously searched for a way back into the house without anyone being the wiser. The door to the servants' entrance stood open as Cook leaned into the back of the wagon belonging to a merchant. They discussed prices as Cook argued over the inferior quality of the produce. As their discussion became heated, they were unaware of Percival's stealthy steps taking him through the entrance and cautiously up the servants' staircase to the floor where the master bedchambers were located. He crept quietly along the hallway.

"May I be of service, sir?"

Stopping in his tracks, he slowly turned to find a maidservant staring at him. Her coquettish smile let him know she was aware of his clandestine intentions. She was a buxom lass and he instinctively knew she would not be adverse to a flirtation. He took a couple steps toward her and saw her eyebrows raise in interest. Reaching his hand out, he twirled a strand of her hair between his fingers.

"It seems I lost my way, but I cannot regret it now that I've discovered you."

Her smile grew.

"What is your name?" he asked.

"Polly," she said breathlessly.

His eyes beamed at the effect he had on the girl. She was obviously an innocent, overwhelmed by the attention of a member of the ton. Of course, he never lacked female attention. He was well aware of his attractiveness to the weaker sex.

"Polly," he said. "Would you honor me by joining me for dinner this evening?" He mentioned a location where few members of polite society would be found, yet it was respectable enough not to be insulting to the girl. "I promise to make it worth your while to join me."

Another flirtatious smile played on her lips and she nodded. "I'd like that."

Holding out his arm to her, he asked, "Now, would you be so kind and show me how to get out of this maze?"

She giggled as she took his arm and guided him toward the main staircase. He stopped her. "Please keep my pride in mind. I don't want anyone to know I lost my way. If you would return me to the servants' entrance, I'd be much obliged."

"Certainly."

As they reached the bottom of the staircase, he held a finger to her lips to silence her. Then he pointed to Cook and shook his head.

Polly seemed to understand. She walked over to Cook and engaged her in a brief conversation as Percival made his way out the door, through the garden, and to the stables.

Things hadn't turned out quite as he expected, but

meeting a servant he could have some influence over suited his plans nicely. He knew immediately upon meeting Polly that she would be putty in his hands.

Polly was both excited and nervous as she made her way to the restaurant where Mr. Percival Kendall waited for her. She had hurried through her chores so she might have a few moments to wash and pretty herself. Although the dress was slightly faded and had seen better days, it was the best she owned. It fit a bit snugly and accentuated her curves. She hoped to please Mr. Kendall, who was the first member of the ton to take an interest in her.

The best she could hope for in her position was to be set up as his mistress. She knew he would never deign to marry a commoner, especially not a servant. But if she played her cards right, she could end up with a cottage instead of a single bed in the servants' quarters at Henfort.

Polly desperately wanted a better life and she finally had her chance. Whatever Mr. Kendall's purpose had been for sneaking up the stairs of Henfort didn't concern her. She saw an opportunity present itself and grasped it with both hands. Mr. Kendall was the heir of a viscountcy and the brother of a viscountess and a countess. Certainly, he was flush in the pockets. If she could please him, she would finally know what it was to be rich. Perhaps this would be her lucky night.

# *Chapter Eighteen*

The carriage rumbled along on its return from Manchester. Rolling through a hole caused the conveyance to jerk back and forth. Fitz's slumbering head fell to the side and woke him. It had been early morning before the sun arose when his trip to London began from the inn they had stopped at the night before. Fitz pushed his drivers, stopping only to change horses when necessary and grab a bite to eat. They had stayed at inns along the way but left again at daybreak each morning. Fitz was determined to make it to Henfort in four days. It wasn't his desire for home that drove him, but rather his sense of responsibility. Now, two hours outside of London, the sun had set long ago. He rubbed a hand over his jaw. How should he go about dismantling the wall his actions had built between his wife and himself?

While Fitz was in Manchester, he heard Dinah was in residence at Blackmore Manor. Anxious to know how she was doing after the scandal in London, he wracked his brain to try and figure out a way to communicate with her without causing another scandal. Why was she in Manchester instead of enjoying the Season in London? Was this Blackmore's doing?

He finally instructed his valet to discreetly ask questions of the other servants. It was imperative no one suspect his interest in the lady. As it turned out, Rawden coincidentally saw Dinah in town and handed her a note Fitz had written in case such an opportunity arose. The note simply asked her to write to him and let him know if she was all right. After glancing at it, she had given his servant a brief nod but said nothing more. Fitz would have to be satisfied with that. He could not risk seeking her out.

Having been gone from London these two weeks, would Selina continue to avoid him or finally give him a chance to explain? He was determined to gain an audience with her, perhaps even force her to listen if he had to.

When the carriage finally stopped in front of Henfort, the townhouse stood in darkness. Fitz let himself in and quietly trudged up the stairs to his room wanting nothing so much as his bed. He would manage without his valet's help for one night, having sent him off to find his own rest. Fitz climbed under the covers and rested his head on the fluffed pillows. "Ahhhh," he groaned in pleasure as his body relaxed, and he soon fell into a deep sleep.

"Good morning, my lord," his valet greeted him.

"Is it morning already?" he grumbled. It didn't seem possible. Hadn't he just laid his head on the pillow?

"You asked me to wake you at this time."

"Yes. Yes. Help me get ready."

After a shave and quick bath, Fitz dressed and left his bedchamber. As he reached his wife's door, it suddenly opened.

"Oh! You're back!"

Selina appeared more horrified than happy to see him. It didn't bode well for the conversation he planned to have. She wore a scarlet riding habit with a white blouse beneath the jacket, the color contrasted well with her dark hair. "Good morning, Selina. It looks as though you plan on riding. May I join you?"

"Good morning. And, uh . . . certainly."

He held his arm out. She placed her hand in its crook and he placed his hand on top of hers. "I hope you slept well," Fitz said.

"Yes, I did. And you?"

"When I finally fell into bed, I slept like a baby. Did you attend an event last evening?"

"Aunt Theo and I attended Almack's. We saw Devon and Emma, as well as Adam and Kitty." Their conversation felt forced, neither seemed ready to discuss what was really on their minds.

"How do you feel about your friend's relationship with Adam? Since you're on a first-name basis with him, I assume you're pleased with the match?"

"I am pleased. Very pleased, actually. He is gentlemanly and kind. Kitty is a wonderful person and deserves someone like him."

They arrived at the stables and soon were mounted on their horses. Fitz surveyed his wife from head to toe as she rode ahead of him on the cobblestone road leading to Hyde Park. Her dark hair hung down her back in a thick braid, tied with a red ribbon. She skillfully guided her horse around a carriage, and he followed closely behind, admiring the smallness of her waist and the gentle curve of her hips. She was lovely. Certainly, if her parents had allowed her to enjoy a Season before arranging a match for her, she would have had many suitors vying for her hand. Instead, she had come to him almost directly from the schoolroom. No experience of life or society had been allowed her. He had married a true innocent. No wonder she'd been avoiding him. In light of her quiet nature and naivety, avoiding a difficulty rather than confronting it head on must have seemed less problematic. If he wanted to explain the situation with Dinah Blackmore to his wife, it would behoove him to bring up the topic himself.

After entering Hyde Park and riding along its paths side by side, each lost in thought, Fitz said, "Selina, let's stop a moment over by that copse of trees. I'd like us to walk a bit if you don't mind."

She glanced at him, before slowly nodding.

Dismounting, he tied his horse to a tree branch. He then turned to give Selina a hand, but she was already on the ground. Once her horse was secured, Fitz held out his arm for her to take.

After only a few steps, he said, "I was hoping to have this conversation weeks ago, but you were extremely difficult to locate."

She looked off to the side as she strolled beside him, biting her lip. As she made to remove her hand from his arm, he placed his hand over hers, holding it in place. She was obviously reticent to discuss the gossip about Town, but he knew they needed to bring things out in the open between them.

"You must have seen the gossip column about me, as well as heard the rumors circulating amongst the ton. I should like to explain to you what actually transpired."

She pulled her hand out from under his grasp and turned her gaze upon him. "Was the sketch not accurate then?"

She had been hurt. He could see it in her eyes. He sighed deeply as he ran a hand over the back of his neck. "Yes, I suppose it was."

Her shoulders stiffened. "I see."

"No, I don't think you do, Selina. A picture can have many meanings. You are young and have little experience of life. I feel ancient next to you sometimes. That sketch was placed with an article that led the readers to believe something that wasn't true."

Selina stared out into the distance, her jaw clenched. She seemed disinclined to say anything.

"Allow me to give you some background information. Dinah and I were engaged to be married before I left for war. When I returned home crippled and scarred, she broke off our engagement, and I became bitter—not only toward her, but toward all women. I even tried sabotaging Devonport's marriage to Emma because I was absolutely certain she would destroy him one day if he gave her his heart."

Selina stared at him in surprise. "You didn't!"

He nodded, "Sadly, it's true. Devon was facing fears of his own, and I took advantage of the situation by trying to help my friend. Fortunately, he came to his senses instead of listening to me. Over time, Emma's persistent faithfulness convinced me Devon had found a rare treasure. There were few women who were worthy of trust, but I was willing to concede Emma was one of them."

"And your poor opinion of women was due to how Lady

Blackmore treated you?"

"Yes, for the most part. I would never have expected it of her. Having known her most of my life, I could have sworn she was incapable of such heartless behavior. I couldn't bring myself to trust another female."

She looked intently at him but said nothing. He was uncertain of her thoughts but decided it was best to continue his story. "My anger at my father caused me to neglect you at first. You stirred emotions in me I wasn't prepared to deal with. Your innocence and lack of artifice drew me, yet I was afraid of what you would become once London society got a hold of you."

"I have met many kind and caring ladies since arriving in London," Selina said. "They are not all as you describe them."

"You may be right, but I was blinded by bitterness. All I could see was the whispering at balls and other events as they spread their lies and called them facts . . . the posturing of debutantes to gain the attention of the wealthiest lord . . . the seductive glances married women generously gave to gentlemen behind their husbands' backs. It made me cynical. I cannot trust easily."

"I understand why you're bitter. But why did you meet with Lady Blackmore after all this time? Please tell me if the newspaper article was incorrect. Mama insisted I pretend I didn't see it. She said men are philanderers and we must accept it. But as a Christian, which you profess to be, certainly you cannot believe such behavior is acceptable?"

Fitz scowled. "Of course I don't think it's acceptable to break a marriage covenant." He ran his hand over the back of his neck again and stared past her, his jaw clenched, trying to calm himself. It wouldn't help matters if he became defensive. Taking a cleansing breath, he forced himself to look her in the eyes. "I went to the theater one night and unexpectedly encountered Dinah in the hallway. We were alone and she asked that I meet with her in private."

"And you thought that was acceptable? To agree to an assignation with another woman?"

He raised his brow. It seemed his wife was learning to

defend herself. "Dinah begged me to give her the opportunity to explain why she broke our engagement. Agreeing to meet her in Hyde Park at dawn the following morning seemed innocent enough. She would explain and we would part ways. And that's what happened."

"Except that she leaned close and gazed adoringly into your eyes. And someone witnessed it and reported it to all of England."

"That was unfortunate and I sincerely apologize to you."

Selina smiled, but it didn't reach her eyes. She shook her head and looked past him. Taking a deep breath, she let it out slowly. "I forgive you."

It seemed she forced herself to speak the words. When he thought of what she must have endured these past weeks, he couldn't blame her.

"I was glad to finally understand the details of what had precipitated Dinah breaking our engagement, but I did not wish to see you hurt in the process. That was never my intention, Selina."

She shrugged her shoulders. "Aunt Theo always says, 'What doesn't break you, makes you stronger.' I must be getting very strong."

He pursed his lips before saying, "You're a bit more outspoken than when I first married you."

"My lord, who will speak for me if I don't speak for myself? When my Uncle Peter passed away, I watched my aunt learn to become independent. She didn't allow herself to fall apart. Instead, she squared her shoulders and learned to become self-sufficient. You have made it clear that you want little to do with me." She saw him stiffen but needed to explain. "This forces me to appear alone, with just my aunt, at every event. I don't believe it's fair to force Aunt Theo into the role of companion. She deserves a life of her own. She *has* a life of her own! You are correct when you say I've become a bit more outspoken. I've had to."

His eyes narrowed. "You knew before you came to London that I have responsibilities at the Home Office as well as Parliament."

"Yes, you made that clear to me. However, as you are

aware, I didn't wish to be gossiped about for having been abandoned by my husband, so I chose to come to London. Ironic, isn't it?"

"I apologized already," came his clipped reply. "Should I do so again?"

Her conscience pricked her. *I said I forgave him but listen to the things I'm saying. God, please help me.* Yet she still felt a need to explain herself. "Your meeting with Lady Blackmore, be it ever so innocent, has placed me in a most uncomfortable position. Society has yet to stop talking about it. When you went to Manchester, someone whispered in my ear that Lord Blackmore owns an estate there and that Lady Blackmore was currently in residence."

His eyes narrowed. "I certainly didn't meet with Dinah, if that was insinuated. I was busy working for the Home Office and returned to London as soon as the job was completed. Selina, there are many spiteful people in this world. You must not give ear to gossip."

How patronizing! He made it sound as though she purposely listened to the talk. She couldn't help overhearing what was being said, especially when that person was her own brother. Again, she heard her mother's words in her head. *Where would you be if you lost your husband by antagonizing him?* She swallowed the words that burned on the tip of her tongue and instead said, "I have accepted your apology." *But trust must be earned.* "May we please return now?"

"Yes, of course."

They arrived back at Henfort and Selina wished him a good day. Fitz watched a moment as she hurried up the stairs away from him. He would have to find a way to regain her trust, but that would take time. As he entered his study, he saw the stack of correspondence that needed his attention. Flipping through the envelopes Bates left on his desk, he immediately recognized the handwriting on a pink envelope. She'd written. He hurriedly broke the seal and began reading.

* * *

*Dear Fitz,*

*I understand you are concerned for my welfare. Please allow me to lay your fears to rest. I explained to Blackmore why we met and that I would not be seeking you out again. I simply needed to explain.*

*He understood but suggested we leave Town for a bit until the gossip died down. I saw your wife at the theater the day the gossip hit the papers. She seemed composed, but when our eyes met, I felt terrible guilt for the sadness I saw there. You and I meant to be discreet, of course, but were obviously seen. I am sorry for any difficulty our meeting may have caused, but I cannot regret having met with you. You will always remain dear to me. If only . . . but, alas, it is what it is.*

*I hope you will find happiness in your marriage.*

*Sincerely,*
*Dinah*

It relieved his mind greatly to know Blackmore had been reasonable about the entire situation and taken measures to protect Dinah from further speculation. *Which was more than I've done for Selina.*

Dinah had always been a biddable girl. She obeyed her parents without question. When Fitz had been betrothed to her, he asked her to write to him each week while he was at war. She did as he requested—without fail. When her father demanded the betrothal be terminated, it seemed she submitted again. Dinah simply obeyed as she'd always done. That she went behind her husband's back to meet with him at Hyde Park, was actually surprising. Perhaps she was finally developing some gumption, but, alas, it was too late for them.

Regardless, Fitz determined to stop thinking about Dinah. He must focus on his own marriage now. He had a lot to make up for, and it was time to begin. On the way to the Home Office, he stopped at a florist shop and ordered a bouquet of roses.

## *Chapter Nineteen*

"Flowers? For me? Who could have sent them?" Selina asked Lydia as she carried a huge bouquet of yellow roses into her sitting room and placed it on a table.

Selina walked over and sniffed the soft petals. "Mmm . . . they are breathtakingly beautiful, aren't they?"

"Lovely, to be sure." Lydia took the card that came with the flowers and handed it to Selina, who quickly opened it.

*"These roses remind me of sunshine and its life-giving warmth. You are a ray of sunshine in my life."* He signed it simply, *Fitz.*

Selina stared at the note, an uncertain smile playing at the corners of her mouth. *Did he mean it?* Unsure of where her husband's true affection lay, her heart filled with doubt.

"My lady?"

Selina glanced up. She'd quite forgotten Lydia was still in the room. Quickly blinking a sheen of tears from her eyes, she said, "These are from my husband. Very sweet of him, wouldn't you say?"

The maid looked at her curiously for a moment, then nodded. "Yes, ma'am."

When she was alone in the room, Selina walked over to her Bible and placed the note inside it before hugging it to her chest. Biting her bottom lip, she stared at nothing, and sighed.

Every summer, before Parliament adjourned, the Templeton

ball was an extravagant affair not to be missed. Ladies in fancy flowing gowns, with ruffles and lace and sequins of every kind, entered the mansion on the arms of gentlemen also dressed in their finest. The room sparkled and glistened creating an atmosphere of celebration. Hundreds of conversations filled the high-ceilinged room with a cacophony of voices as servants in uniform carried trays with long-stemmed wine glasses. The orchestra tuned their instruments and soon a symphony gave competition to the voices. Younger gentlemen chose eligible young ladies to lead to the dance floor, while older gentlemen tapped their feet to the rhythm of the music as they stood debating over politics. Older women sat on chairs lined up along a wall while whispering half-truths behind fans, at times nodding their heads in greeting to passersby or raising a nose in the air when cutting them down to size.

"May I have this dance?" Selina's eyes lifted to piercing brown ones.

"Fitz! You're here! I-I had no idea . . . I mean, yes, of course I'll dance with you." Why had he deigned to join her this evening? To her knowledge, he'd only attended one ball since she arrived in Town—her debutante ball. Earlier, as she stood with Emma, Juliet, and Kitty, she tried her best to avoid curious glances from those who refused to forget the gossip sheet. Evidently, a more interesting rumor had not surfaced as yet. Selina knew it was bad of her, but she almost wished someone in the room would do something scandalous to divert attention from herself. She glanced at her friends who stood smiling at her confusion over her husband's unexpected arrival.

Fitz bowed to them, "My ladies. You certainly all look lovely this evening, as usual."

"It's good of you to notice, Fitz," Emma said in a playfully haughty manner, causing everyone to laugh. "I'm glad you could finally join us for some frivolity. We'd quite given up on you."

Bowing, he said, "You are too kind, Emma."

She chuckled. "I'm truthful, as you very well know."

Fitz laughed. Living in England for several years now had

not changed Emma. "It just so happens that I like the way you are."

Emma placed her hand on his forearm. "Thank you, Fitz. You truly have been missed. I'm glad you could join us tonight."

He dipped his head in acknowledgment of her gracious words, then extended his hand to Selina. "Shall we? The orchestra is about to begin."

Her hand was swallowed up by his as he led her to the dance floor. As the first notes of a waltz filled the room, Fitz swept her into his arms, causing her cheeks to flame as her heartbeat accelerated. Their close proximity reminded her of the kiss they'd shared after their horse race. Longing stirred within her.

Afraid of what he would see in her eyes, she stared at his cravat as he led her around the room to the rhythm of the music.

Finally daring to lift her eyes, she said, "Thank you for the lovely bouquet."

He winked. "I'm glad you liked it."

How could a wink cause such fluttering of her nerves? "Oh, yes. I liked it very much, indeed." Returning her gaze to his cravat, she chastised herself for sounding like a schoolgirl.

He pulled her closer. Although a couple of inches separated them, she felt the warmth radiating from his body and closed her eyes, overwhelmed by the effect of his nearness.

"Selina." His hoarse whisper caused her to raise her eyes in inquiry. He only gazed at her not saying a word, yet searching. What did he see? Afraid her eyes revealed emotions her lips were not ready to speak, she quickly looked down again.

He led her across the floor to the tall glass doors that stood wide open to keep the room from overheating. Sweeping her onto the patio, he took her by the hand, and together they descended a few steps into the garden. Selina followed almost in a daze. What harm could there be in a secluded moment with her husband?

Fitz stopped in a darkened corner of the garden where the light from the house could not reach and pulled her into his arms. "Selina," he whispered before his lips claimed hers and she melted into his embrace, forgetting everything around her. Too soon, he pulled back and stepped away, placing a bit of distance between them. It was too dark to see each other's face. Only his heavier breathing could be heard. It comforted her to know she wasn't the only one affected by their kiss.

He cleared his throat. "We should return to the house."

She nodded but realized he couldn't see it. "Very well." *Was that airy sound her voice?* Clearing her throat, she tried again. "I think it would be best if we did." *There, that was better.*

He placed her hand in the crook of his arm, and they walked the path back to the ball. *What was this effect he had on her? Was she in love? Is that why she felt vulnerable, why her heart ached for his nearness*? Biting her trembling lip, she feared the pain he could cause her. *"Jesus, help me,"* her heart silently cried.

He'd apologized for meeting with Lady Blackmore and not telling her about it. She must let go of the hurt. Holding on to a grudge would only cause bitterness. It had been wrong of her to avoid Fitz for weeks on end. Selina was honest enough with herself to admit she had shunned him out of anger. If they had talked sooner, this could have been cleared up already. She owed him an apology.

As they reached the balcony, Selina pulled his arm back gently. "Fitz, I need to say something to you, please."

He tilted his head. "What is it?"

Selina glanced around to be certain they were alone. "Please, forgive me for distancing myself from you. I should not have done so. And thank you for coming to the ball and asking me to dance. I know what you're doing and I appreciate the effort you made."

Looking into her big brown eyes, he swallowed a lump in his throat. *She* apologized to *him*. His sweet, innocent bride felt *she* needed to ask for *his* forgiveness. He was deeply moved by her sincere humility. If his father were here, he might almost be tempted to thank the manipulative old man. Selina was genuine. At that moment, Fitz determined to win her heart for himself. *Does that mean I would have to give my heart also? Maybe . . . with time.*

"What is it you believe I'm doing by asking you to dance?" Did Selina understand he had begun courting her?

She shrugged her shoulders. "You want to squelch the gossip, of course, by showing your interest in me and being seen together."

He dipped his chin once. "That is one reason I sought you out for a dance. It's not the only reason."

"It's not?"

"No." He reached up and stroked a finger down her cheek. "I longed to take you into my arms again. I wanted to claim you before the ton so that every gentleman in the room would know you belong to me." His smile slipped away as his eyes became intense. "I want you to know how proud I am to have you as my wife."

Her cheeks turned a lovely shade of pink as a gentle, yet uncertain, smile trembled on her lips. "Thank you, Fitz."

He placed his hands on her shoulders and pulled her close, wrapping his arms around her. Fitz breathed in her flowery scent and lowered his head to brush a kiss across her brow. Ever aware someone could intrude upon them, he pulled back as he gazed into sparkling eyes. Grabbing hold of her hand, he swept her back onto the dance floor for the remainder of the waltz the orchestra was playing. Selina filled his arms nicely, and he intended to enjoy the experience more frequently from this day forward. He wouldn't push her but would continue steadily wooing his bride until she walked into his embrace of her own volition.

As they danced, his eyes landed on his mother standing across the room in conversation with Lady Worthington. Their eyes met—his in surprise, for he hadn't realized she was in attendance this evening, while hers seemed pained. He looked away.

*Forgive them,* his conscience smote him, but he hardened his heart. They didn't deserve his forgiveness. *Selina forgave you,* his conscience reminded him. He peered down at his lovely wife, whom he held only because his parents had schemed behind his back. Did he regret having her in his life? No. Not anymore. Dinah was lost to him. It was time to focus on the future. As far as his parents were concerned, they couldn't have known their maneuvering would turn out in his best interest. Their motivation had been an heir to the title and not their son's wellbeing. Fitz danced Selina to the other side of the room, far away from his mother's line of vision.

Fitz stood beside Emma as he watched Selina on the dance floor. She moved with grace, smiling sweetly at her dance partner, but without flirtation. Dinah had been the same. Although many men had sought her out, she only had eyes for him—until he returned injured from war. When her world became complicated and difficult, she crumbled and allowed herself to be redirected. Would Selina do the same? She would. Hadn't the gossip column caused her to avoid him for weeks on end?

"She's become a dear friend to me," Emma interrupted his thoughts. "I know your marriage was arranged for you, but now that I've gotten to know Selina, I can see clearly how God's hand was never removed from your situation. He has blessed you with a sweet wife."

Emma was right. Selina was definitely a sweet wife. Could he trust her to remain constant? Dinah had seemed as perfect, but her momentary weakness caused long-term regret. Was Selina any different? His heart constricted at the thought of having to face such unfaithfulness again.

"You doubt me." It wasn't a question. When he said nothing, but kept his eyes glued to the dance floor, Emma sighed. She moved a step closer and spoke quietly. "Fitz, I know you have a hard time trusting women, but Selina has been tried by fire—the fire of vicious gossip—and has remained loyal to you. You have no idea how many times she has had to listen to sharp tongues slander either one of you. She has been forced to hear insincere sympathy for her plight of being married to you—having to endure your constant love for another."

Fitz looked at Emma in disbelief. His eyes narrowed and he spoke through clenched teeth. "People have dared to say such things to her?"

Emma curled her lip. "I've heard it more than once with my own ears. Yet, Selina stands tall and diverts attention off your marriage as best as she can. I have heard her eloquently defending you, claiming you are an honorable man who has served our country both in war and in the Home Office. She even defended Lady Blackmore when someone dared to call her a hussy. You will be hard-pressed to find a more worthy lady to trust your heart to."

His brows shot up. "She defends me?"

Emma nodded. "I doubt many believe her. She speaks so sweetly though, that they soon walk away and continue their gossip elsewhere." Placing a hand on Fitz's arm, Emma said, "Selina is worthy of your trust. She has comported herself as the countess she will one day become when you inherit. I speak true when I say your reputation is safe with her." Letting go of his arm, Emma whispered, "If it were ever ruined, it would be by your actions, not hers."

Fitz shifted his gaze to Emma and saw fire in her eyes. "I shouldn't have met with Dinah."

"No, you shouldn't have." She seemed to relent a bit when she said, "But I'm glad you're here this evening. Your wife deserves to be doted upon."

"Is my wife ringing a peal over your head?" Devon asked as he joined them and placed his hand on Emma's waist, pulling her closer. "She's been rather vexed with you. I anticipated this moment would come sooner or later."

Peering into Emma's eyes, Fitz's lips lifted in a brief smile, appreciating the true friendship she'd shown him. Not breaking eye contact with her, he answered Devon. "Emma said nothing I didn't deserve."

It was no secret to Polly that the viscount and his wife had a marriage in name only. The evidence stared her in the face as she made their beds each morning. Only one crushed pillow on each bed. A fluffed pillow on the space where no one had laid their head gave evidence to what she suspected already. Lady FitzWalter was left to her own devices while Lord FitzWalter spent most of his time away from home.

Certainly, the viscount had needs that were not being met by his wife. Did he already have a mistress? Is that why he hadn't been tempted to gawk in Polly's direction when she tried gaining his attention? Whatever his reason for neglecting his wife, it boded well for Percival's plan. The viscountess had just arrived back from the ball wearing her expensive heirloom. Tonight would be Polly's opportunity to impress Percival.

Carrying hot water up the stairs with a queue of other servants, Polly entered Lady FitzWalter's bedchamber. She was seated at the dressing table while Lydia removed the necklace, earbobs, and bracelet. She unwound the viscountess's thick brown hair, brushing long strokes through it.

Carefully, Polly poured the hot water into the tub and stepped back to allow the next servant to pour out her container as well. Pretending to stumble, Polly bumped into one of the waiting servants causing hot water to spill on the girl's hand. She yelped and dropped her pail. Water seeped into the carpet as several servants dropped to their knees with towels attempting to soak up the moisture.

Selina jumped. "Oh, no!"

"I'm so sorry, I am." The girl cried, holding her injured hand, while tears streamed down her cheeks.

Lydia and Selina hurried to the girl. "Hold out your hand so I may look at it," the viscountess said.

She uncovered her trembling hand and held it out.

"Oh! That must hurt! A blister is already forming." Her compassion for a simple maid was not lost on the other servants, who seemed to admire her all the more.

"Is anyone holding a container of cold water?" Selina wanted to know.

"Yes, ma'am. I am," said one of the maidservants.

Selina instructed the injured girl to place her hand in the cold water. "Keep your hand in there until you can have it tended." Turning to Polly, who held two empty pails in her hand, Selina directed her to take the injured maid to the housekeeper immediately. "Inform Mrs. Addams this was an accident and the girl is not to be punished. Be sure to nurse her hand in an appropriate manner so it will heal quickly."

Polly bobbed her knees. "Yes, ma'am. Right away."

Unbeknownst to Selina and Lydia, Polly had taken advantage of their distraction with the injured maid and slinked her way over to the dressing table. Surreptitiously slipping the necklace, earbobs, and bracelet into the pocket of her apron, she returned to the injured maid and picked up both buckets without anyone the wiser. Polly felt a twinge of remorse for the pain she had caused the girl, but it was the only distraction she could think of to give herself enough time to achieve her goal. Polly determined to make it up to the maid by helping her with some of her chores. That was until Percival provided the cottage he had promised her. A smile crept into her heart and expanded until it reached her face. Soon, very soon, she would have the wealth she longed for.

Selina finally had enough of her dark, dingy bedchamber. Certainly Fitz would not begrudge her redecorating the room she spent so much time in. Confident he would approve, she knocked on the door to his study. No one answered. She slowly opened the door in case he had not heard the knock, but the room was empty. Not certain when he would return, she decided to leave him a message. While searching the surface of the desk for a piece of paper to write on, her eyes landed on the signature at the bottom of a letter mostly covered by other papers. *Sincerely, Dinah.*

She knew it was wrong to read his correspondence, but how could she resist? The temptation was too great. It would plague her to no end to always wonder what the letter from his former fiancé contained. Did Lady Blackmore wish to see Fitz again? Were they writing love letters to each other? She simply had to know.

Pulling the letter out, she began reading. Her heart sank. Lord Blackmore seemed understanding about the incident at

Hyde Park, but did he realize his wife still harbored feelings for her former fiancé? It was only too evident at the end of the letter. *I cannot regret having met with you. You will always remain dear to me. If only . . . but, alas, it is what it is.*

Selina found it hard to breathe. She felt nauseous and clenched her jaw to keep the tears from spilling over. *I hope you will find happiness in your marriage.* Had Fitz confided he was unhappy? Had he talked about her with another woman—his former betrothed? A woman he still loved? If his heart was still consumed with Dinah Blackmore, there was no hope for their marriage. Were the yellow roses he sent her a guilt offering for the scandal they had caused?

Her hands shook with a longing to tear the letter into tiny pieces and throw it into the fire. She didn't dare. He must never know she had read it. Carefully, she put it back the way it had been.

As Selina straightened, she spied a picture frame placed facedown at the edge of the desk. Papers were strewn upon it, as well as a book. She reached across the desk and slid the frame out trying not to disturb the papers. Selina had a premonition as to whose face would be staring back at her. Turning it over, she stared into the haunting eyes of a beautiful woman with smooth skin, full lips, and dark hair. *How often does my husband sit at his desk staring at the love he lost?*

Breathless, and feeling as though she may suffocate, she hurried to the door, when it suddenly opened. "Oh!"

"Lady FitzWalter! I didn't know . . ."

She had never seen Bates quite so flustered, obviously expecting the room to be empty. Selina mustered a smile but feared it looked forced. "It's quite all right. I-I was searching for my husband." His eyes strayed to the desk and she felt her ears begin to burn as a blush suffused her cheeks. Why did her face have to reveal her embarrassment? Bates would certainly think her guilty of something. Well, she didn't owe him an explanation. She said nothing.

Having regained his composure, Bates said, "My lord is at the Home Office. He left early. Can I help you with anything?" Again, his eyes scanned the desk as though trying to discern what the mistress could possibly have need of in here when the master was out. They stopped briefly on the picture frame. Although Selina knew he could only see the back of it, Bates must have chanced upon it often enough over the years to know whose likeness was captured in the painting.

Selina attempted to act normal as she hid her trembling hands in the skirt of her dress. "No. I was going to leave him a message on his desk but decided against it. I'll speak to him tonight."

"Very well, my lady."

Selina turned and left the room.

# *Chapter Twenty*

The city streets bustled with activity. Hopeful peddlers calling out to potential customers competed with the sounds of carriage wheels and horses' hooves on the cobblestone road, while pedestrians walked along in conversation, dogs barked, and children's voices shouted as they played. Above all the noise, Percival heard the voice of a man standing on a soapbox surrounded by no less than thirty or forty people. "Repent before it's too late!" his voice boomed.

Percival had heard such speeches from street preachers before. Always walking past, he never gave it much thought. He simply reasoned while that man enjoyed preaching, *he* preferred gambling.

Today was different. As he heard those words, something pierced his heart. He stopped at the edge of the crowd and listened a moment longer.

"You may think you have all the time in the world. You're too young to think of dying. Unfortunately, tomorrow is promised to no one. There's not a person alive who can predict their end, yet everyone will die. What if today is your last day? What if this is your final hour? Will you be ready to meet your Maker? Have you repented of your sins?" Raising his hand, he pointed his finger across the crowd. His voice boomed, "No one will enter heaven unless they repent first! What are you waiting for?"

Percival's heart raced like an animal caught in a trap. Desperate to run, his feet felt stuck in cement. To his great consternation, the street preacher peered straight into his eyes. "Stop what you're doing and turn from the wickedness in your heart. Don't you realize God loves you with an everlasting love? He wants to help you. Stop running from Him."

Suddenly his feet were free and he turned his back on the preacher. With hurried steps, almost running, he entered the doors to the gaming hell where Tom Hendrick waited. The preacher's words followed him, but he shut his ears to the sound as he slammed the door behind him. He had money burning a hole in his pocket and hoped Lady Luck would be on his side.

"Miss Kitty Haddington is here to see you, ma'am."

Kitty stood at the sitting room door, a step behind the butler. Selina's face lit up, but quickly became sober when she saw the red rims around her friend's eyes.

"Thank you, Bates." As Kitty entered, Bates bowed and left the room, closing the door behind him.

"Kitty, whatever is the matter?" Selina rushed to embraced her friend. Kitty's shoulders shook as she sobbed. "Kitty, please tell me everything. You're scaring me." Placing her arm around the small of Kitty's back, she led her to the sofa and sat down beside her. "What happened?"

Kitty wiped the tears from her eyes with a handkerchief and took a shuddering breath. "He doesn't wish to see me anymore."

"Who? Not Adam, surely."

Kitty nodded. "Yes, Adam. His f-father made a bad investment and lost a f-fortune. Adam must marry an heiress. It is their only hope."

Selina gasped and pressed a hand over her mouth. "No! He has an older brother. Let him marry to save the family."

Sniffling, Kitty said, "His older brother refuses. Adam was always the dutiful one and his family is depending on him. I have only a meager dowry to offer. It will never suffice to save the estate."

"But he loves you! Anyone with eyes can see it plainly."

"Pfft…Love cannot pay creditors or put food on the

table." Another tear rolled down Kitty's cheek. She swiped it away.

"I cannot grasp this at all. Only yesterday I saw the two of you dancing together, lighting up the dance floor with your smiles."

Kitty burst into tears again as she shook her head. Selina pulled her friend into her arms, allowing the tears to soak the shoulder of the muslin gown she wore. Kitty tried valiantly to compose herself, but tears kept falling.

"It's all right, Kitty, dear. You may cry as long as you like." Kitty's hair hung down her back and Selina brushed her hands over the locks, again and again, speaking in soothing tones, hoping to calm her. "Jesus, please help my Kitty. She needs you so desperately right now."

When the tears finally subsided, Kitty pulled away. Wiping her cheeks with her soaked handkerchief, she took a deep breath once more. Her voice shook as she explained, "As we danced last night, Adam knew it was our last. I had no idea. Although he smiled, I saw the sadness in his eyes and it scared me. He t-took me home after the d-dance and asked if he could have a moment of my time before he had to leave. I dismissed my maid and we went into the drawing room. He proceeded to tell me of his father's poor investment and the consequences thereof."

Kitty paused a moment to stare at her lap where her hands clenched the handkerchief. Slowly shaking her head from side to side, she said, "Please forgive me, Selina, but I cannot stay in London. There is nothing here for me. Everywhere I go and all I see will only remind me of our time together. Adam is best forgotten. I must learn to go on with my life, but it is impossible to do so here."

"Kitty, you mean to give up your Season?"

"I must. I especially could not bear watching him court another lady. And what of the gossip? He quite obviously favored me, and now he will do so no more. People will talk. Yet he must find a wife and cannot ignore the ballrooms. I must make haste to leave for I cannot stay in London a moment longer."

Selina's shoulders slumped and she sighed deeply as she

gazed at her friend with furrowed brow. "As much as it saddens me to see you go, I understand. I'm certain I would wish to do the same."

Kitty's heartbreaking news silenced Selina from speaking of Dinah Blackmore's letter. With the weight of her friend's disappointment, she could not add to her burden. "When we return to Thorncrest, I wish for you to come for a long visit."

"I would be only too happy to do so."

She took Kitty's hands in her own. "You will write to me, won't you, Kitty? I have to know how you are doing. You must not hide the truth of your feelings from me. Please say you will write."

A watery smile played on Kitty's lips. "I promise."

"My lady was reaching for the study door on her way out as I was entering," Bates informed Lord FitzWalter that evening. "She wished to speak with you, but since you were not available, she thought to leave a written note. For some reason, Lady FitzWalter changed her mind and decided to speak with you this evening instead. As you know, that was not possible." Fitz sensed his butler's displeasure of his late nights.

He did not doubt Bates was well aware that the marriage between the viscount and his wife was not all it should be, and he suspected his butler wanted to find a way to bring the two together. He would never have thought of Bates as a matchmaker, but too many slight remarks made him suspicious.

"You have no idea what she wished to discuss with me?"

Bates looked uncomfortable for a moment, then said, "She did not say, but I wonder if perhaps she is ready to redecorate her bedchamber and sitting room and wishes to seek your permission before doing so."

Lifting one eyebrow, Fitz said, "What makes you think that is what she wishes to speak with me about? She is my wife. She can redecorate the entire townhouse if it pleases her to do so."

Bates shrugged his shoulders. "I overheard my lady

asking Mrs. Addams if she knew why her rooms had never been redecorated. Of course, I'm assuming that is the reason for the visit to your study. I could not say for certain."

Fitz doubted Bates was ever wrong about anything pertaining to his household. The man had an uncanny way of knowing everything that went on within these walls. But feeling uncomfortable discussing his wife with one of his servants, he thanked him and entered his study to drop off some papers. His eyes immediately darted to the painting of Dinah. What was it doing in full view on top of his desk?

His eyes narrowed as he walked around to his chair. He peered more closely at the stacks of paper on his desk, the pink letter with Dinah's signature stared back at him. If Selina came this close to his desk, she must have seen it. Was that why she changed her mind about leaving him a note? Was she the one who placed Dinah's picture in plain sight?

He grabbed the painting, stuffed it in a large envelope, and sat behind at his desk. He jotted a few lines on a sheet of paper, folded it, and inserted it before sealing the envelope. Turning it over, he addressed the package to Sir Frances Claremont, Dinah's father, and carried it to the entryway table. Bates would make certain it arrived at its destination.

Fitz continued mulling over the consequences of his wife having read the letter. It was all he could think of as he prepared for bed, and it kept him from falling asleep once his head hit the pillow. *I'll have to be completely honest with her. Secrecy doesn't bode well in a marriage.*

## *Chapter Twenty-One*

"What are your plans for today?" Fitz asked Selina as she sat across from him in the breakfast room.

She shrugged her shoulders. "I don't have any specific plans yet." She took a bite of her strawberry and chewed it slowly. Nothing on her plate truly appealed to her, although she enjoyed the same fare other mornings.

"Are you well?"

Selina slowly moved the eggs around with her fork. "Yes, I am quite well."

"Do you have the dismals then? Has something happened?"

Selina placed her fork on her plate and looked at her husband. *Your letter from Dinah.* Of course, she couldn't say that. He would know she had been snooping. She sat back and folded her hands in her lap. "Kitty left London."

"Did she? I suppose the Season is starting to wind down. Invite her to visit you at Thorncrest if you wish it."

*Does he plan to remain in London when I return to Thorncrest?* "Thank you. I already mentioned it to her."

"Perhaps we should do something to distract you today. The sun is shining and there is only a light breeze. Would you be interested in joining me on a picnic?"

"Truly?" Her eyes widened. "You aren't going to the Home Office?"

"I took the day off to spend some time with my wife. How about it?"

She nodded slowly as she studied his face. "I would like it very much."

"Can you be ready in an hour?"

"Certainly. I shall ask Cook to prepare a basket for us."

"No need," Fitz said. "I've already taken care of the details. You need only to meet me in the foyer."

Selina's heart was lighter as she ascended the staircase to change for her outing with Fitz. Her husband seemed interested in spending time with her. But what of his feelings for Lady Blackmore? *Since I've been praying about my marriage, perhaps I should simply thank God instead of trying to make sense of it all.* "Thank you, Lord," she whispered.

Upon entering her bedchamber, Selina said, "Lydia, make me as pretty as you can."

Lydia looked up from mending and grinned at her mistress. "That will be simple enough to accomplish."

When the carriage stopped at Kensington Gardens, Fitz helped Selina out by offering his hand. From here on, they would have to walk since carriages were not permitted past the gates. After placing her hand on his arm, they walked along the shady alley, nodding their heads in greeting to other strollers taking advantage of the fine weather. Not wanting to run into any acquaintances and thus be forced to stop and visit, Fitz led her onto a path that wound around a large pond in front of Kensington Palace, where a copse of trees made for a secluded picnic spot.

Unobtrusively, their servants followed behind. A blanket was placed on the ground and Fitz held Selina's arm as she carefully sat down, spreading her skirt out to prevent it from wrinkling. After placing the picnic basket on the corner of the blanket, the servants were dismissed to return to the carriage and wait.

Removing his hat, Fitz tossed it on the blanket beside Selina and sat down, stretching his legs out as he leaned back on his arms. There was a particular reason Fitz had asked Selina to join him today. How should he begin?

He heard her sigh of contentment as they sat side by side

facing the pond. Selina's legs were curled to the side as she leaned on one arm, her face lifted to the sun.

"Ah . . . this feels heavenly," she said.

He allowed his eyes to drift over the smooth, satiny skin of her cheeks, longing to touch it, but not daring. It would muddle his thinking. First, they needed to talk.

Fitz cleared his throat. "Bates mentioned you were in my study yesterday."

Selina turned to stare at him before answering, "I was."

"Did you need something?" Wanting to put her at ease, he added, "I'm sorry I wasn't at home."

A blush infused her cheeks. She sat up straight and clasped her hands on her lap. Shrugging her shoulders, she said, "I simply wished to ask if I would be permitted to redecorate my rooms." Searching his eyes, she added, "I didn't know if there was sentimental value attached to the decor. Was it your grandmother's perhaps, and you wished to keep it intact? The entire townhouse has been beautifully redecorated, yet those rooms remain unchanged. I didn't wish to upset you by making changes willy-nilly."

To her great relief, she realized Fitz wasn't upset when a slow smile lifted the corners of his mouth.

"Selina, you may redecorate to your heart's content. I have no sentimental attachment to those rooms."

She tilted her head in question. "Then why didn't you redecorate them at the same time as the rest of the townhouse?"

"I had always intended my viscountess to decide for herself the decor she would find most pleasing. You must do whatever you wish with those rooms, as well as the rest of Henfort, and Thorncrest, too. I apologize for not making that clear from the start."

"Oh," she said. "Well, I will not be changing the rest of Henfort, for I like it as it is."

"That is your decision. I want you to feel at home."

His words warmed her heart. "That is kind of you, Fitz. Thank you."

Knowing he needed to broach the subject of the letter and the painting, he reached over and took one of her hands in his. He stroked his thumb over the back of it. "When you were in my office yesterday, did you notice the letter from Dinah Blackmore sitting on my desk?"

She pulled her hand away as her eyes widened. Fitz watched as the blush on her face reached her ears. A vein throbbed in her neck. Wishing to ease her mind, he quickly added, "If you did, I'm not upset with you." He saw her swallow, but she only bit her bottom lip, saying nothing.

"Selina, you are more important to me than anyone else. I want you to know whatever Dinah wrote, those were her thoughts, not mine."

She seemed to relax the tiniest bit. At that moment, Selina reminded him of an abused mutt he once rescued from the streets. The canine was obviously distrusting even of those who wished to help him. Fitz finally won him over, but it took time and patience. His wife had been hurt also. First by her family, and now by him.

"After the gossip sheet published the sketch of us, I was concerned for Dinah. I wasn't certain how Blackmore would react. While I was in Manchester, my valet passed a note to her in which I asked Dinah to write to me. I needed to know whether it was necessary to approach Blackmore. If you read the letter, then you know he was understanding about the entire incident."

Selina lowered her eyes and plucked a blade of grass. Fitz saw her swallow hard as she wound it around her index finger. "I read the letter." Her breathy voice was so soft, he almost didn't hear her. She looked at him out the corner of her eye.

He smiled and winked. "I would have read the letter, too, if a man had written to you—especially a former beau."

A hesitant smile trembled on her lips for a moment before sadness filled her eyes. "She still loves you." Sighing, she added, "And since you still keep her painting on your desk, I imagine you feel the same."

"Perhaps she still cares for me. Although, I'm not convinced of it." When Selina's brow furrowed and she tilted her head in question, he said, "Dinah has always obeyed her father without question. That is just her way. But

I have to wonder, if she were truly in love, would she not have fought harder to be with me? Especially when I was badly injured, depressed, and at my worst? Tell me, Selina, would you have abandoned someone you loved who found himself in similar circumstances? If the man you loved had recently lost his brother, would you abandon him also?"

Tears glistened in her eyes as she shook her head. "I don't believe I could."

He lifted his hand to catch a curl hanging near her neck and caressed it between his fingers. "I know you couldn't. When you love, you love with your whole heart, don't you? There is no artifice in you." He let go of her hair and shifted to gaze out over the water. "Dinah is loyal. She was loyal to her father and she was loyal to me. Until her loyalty to me conflicted with her loyalty to her father. She had to choose and she chose him. And now she is devoted to her husband. Whether he loves her or not, she will remain faithful to him." Gazing at Selina, he said, "I had stored the painting of Dinah in my desk and forgot about it. It was only recently that I pulled the picture out. I meant to be rid of it, but papers piled on top and I didn't think of it again. Until I saw the painting sitting on my desk yesterday."

She bit her bottom lip for a moment as she studied him. He gave her a chance to process all she'd heard. Did she believe him?

"You had made it perfectly clear after our wedding that you wished me out of sight. Unfortunately, living together in Henfort all these weeks caused my foolish heart to respond like a schoolgirl and hope for something you were unwilling to give. When I saw the painting of your former fiancé, I finally realized what a ninny I've been. I stood the picture frame on your desk as a reminder to myself of how things truly stood between us. Then I turned and left the room."

"I regret how I treated you after the wedding, Selina. I acted like a wounded bear. You deserved better from me. As far as Dinah is concerned, she is my past—a past I cannot change, nor do I feel inclined to change it. You, my dear wife, are my present and my future."

Surveying him closely, she tilted her head. "What does that mean?"

"It means, I'm glad *you're* my wife. Emma told me how you defended me to the gossips. In spite of being hurt by my actions, you behaved in a manner worthy of a queen. No one has ever shown me such loyalty."

With sparkling eyes, she said, "I'm glad you're my husband."

He tilted his head and narrowed his eyes. "Are you? Why?"

She pursed her lips and tilted her head as he had done, her eyes filled with mirth. "Oh, I don't know. I suppose I've gotten used to having you around from time to time." Smiling playfully, she added, "And you are quite handsome to look at."

He threw his head back and laughed out loud. Unable to resist her feisty sweetness any longer, he pulled her to him intending to kiss her gently, but a fire ignited the moment their lips touched. Passion flared as she melted into his embrace. Nothing in his life had ever felt like this moment. But ever aware of their public setting, he pulled away while he still could. It would not do to be found on another gossip sheet, even if it was with his own wife.

The afternoon slipped away as they talked about their interests, hopes, and dreams. Once the servants cleared the picnic away, Fitz took Selina by the hand and led her back to the shady alley. As they strolled, they stopped to chat with friends along the way. Too soon, the sun began to set. Fitz reluctantly suggested they return to their carriage before the gates of Kensington Gardens closed.

Selina heard the knock at the front door of Henfort early the following morning as she stood at the top of the staircase, waiting to see who it might be.

"How may I help you, sir?" she heard Bates ask.

"Good morning. I'm Constable Jones. It's imperative I speak to Lord and Lady FitzWalter."

*A constable?* Selina knew it was never good news when a constable arrived at a home uninvited.

"Very well," Bates said. "Please, follow me." Selina watched as the butler led the man to the drawing room. By the time Bates returned to the foyer, Selina had descended the staircase. At the same time, Fitz closed the door to his study as he prepared to leave for Parliament.

"My lord. My lady." Bates bowed to each. "Constable Jones has arrived and asked to speak with you. He's in the drawing room."

Selina's concerned eyes met her husband's sober ones. He walked toward her and held out his hand. "Come, let's see what he has to say."

As they entered the drawing room, Selina clapped eyes on a burly man with ruddy complexion warming his hands before the fireplace. He turned at the sound of footsteps and bowed.

"I understand you have news for us, Constable," Fitz said.

Selina braced herself for the worst.

The man cleared his throat. "Yes, my lord. I'm sorry to have to inform you. There was a tragic accident last night involving Lord and Lady Runswick."

Selina gasped, touching her hand to her lips. "No . . ." she whispered.

Fitz placed his arm around her waist and led her to the sofa. When she was seated, he sat beside her and took her cold hand into his own. "Please have a seat, Constable, and tell us what happened."

"It seems as Lord and Lady Runswick headed home from an evening at Drury Lane, their driver lost control of the carriage when the axle broke. They must have been going at quite some speed when the carriage overturned, for it was completely broken apart."

"I-I can't believe it. Do my sisters know? What about my brother?"

"Yes, my lady. I informed your sisters before coming here. We have not located your brother as yet."

"I see." Turning to Fitz, her voice seemed breathless to her own ears as she said, "I must go to my sisters. And Aunt Theo needs to know, for she has lost her brother." The men hurried to stand when Selina rose on quivery legs. "Please excuse me. I must find my aunt at once."

Fitz placed a steadying hand on Selina's arm. "Are you all right, Selina? Sit a moment. Aunt Theo is probably enjoying a quiet breakfast or still abed."

She shook her head as tears filled her eyes. "I need to tell her before she hears it from a servant."

Selina hurried from the room, rushing up the stairs and down the hallway to her aunt's door, where she stopped. Longing to throw herself into her aunt's arms as she had always done, Selina hesitated. Her aunt was unaware of the news that awaited her. Her words would break Aunt Theo's heart. "Dear Jesus, help us," she whispered before taking a deep breath and knocking twice.

When the maid opened the door, Selina said, "Martha, I must speak with Aunt Theo."

"Of course, my lady."

Selina saw her aunt sitting before the fire, a Bible open on her lap.

Aunt Theo stretched out a hand in welcome. "My dear girl, how lovely to see you! To what do I owe the pleasure of your company so early this morning?" As she looked more closely at Selina, her brow furrowed. "Whatever is the matter, child?"

Selina knelt at Aunt Theo's feet and took hold of her hands. Her voice shook as she said, "A constable arrived this morning to inform us that Mama and Papa were involved in a fatal accident last night."

"No!" Aunt Theo shook her head in denial. "It cannot be! Did you say fatal?" At Selina's nod, she asked, "How? I cannot comprehend it!"

"I know. I feel the same." Selina rubbed her thumb over the back of Aunt Theo's hand. "The constable said they were returning from Drury Lane when their axle broke and the carriage . . . overturned." Her voice broke as she began to sob.

"Oh, Selina! I'm so sorry." Aunt Theo gathered her close and the two clung to each other. When the tears finally subsided, her aunt said, "I can't believe my brother is gone. Where will he spend eternity? And your mother, too."

Selina swiped at the tears on her cheeks. "I wondered the same. It's so final. Juliet and I hoped for an opportunity to talk to Mama and Papa about our relationship with God. It doesn't seem fair we never had the chance."

Selina moved to sit beside Aunt Theo. They linked arms and she laid her head on her aunt's shoulder as they stared into the flames of the fireplace.

"We must remember God is just," Aunt Theo said. "Even when we don't understand, He is still faithful and deserving of our trust. We must not lose faith simply because we don't have all the answers."

The two spent the next hour together. Aunt Theo shared some of her happy childhood memories of her brother. Sometimes they laughed and sometimes they cried.

"I plan to visit Juliet and Helena today," Selina said.

"I'll go with you if you don't mind."

"Of course you must come. Shall we say, in one hour?"

"I'll be ready," Aunt Theo agreed.

After Selina departed the drawing room, Fitz was left alone with the constable. Assuming the man was anxious to return to his horse, which he must have left standing in front of the townhouse, Fitz thanked him for coming and bid him a good day.

"My lord, I need another moment of your time, if you please."

Raising his brows, Fitz spoke a bit gruffly, "What is it?"

The man swallowed. "It seems Lord Runswick's carriage may have been tampered with. There is concern that this wasn't an accident."

Fitz stared hard at the man as they stood facing each other. "Who do you suspect?"

"We aren't certain. The question is, who had the most to gain from the viscount's death?"

"The obvious answer is Percival Kendall, of course," Fitz said. "He's the heir. But what if it wasn't the person who had the most to gain? It could have been a disgruntled servant or any number of scenarios. Do you have any clue as to where Percival Kendall might be?"

"No, my lord. He left Town yesterday morning, which makes it unlikely he was the killer."

"Unless he hired someone to do the dirty deed for him," Fitz suggested. "But I have a hard time believing he would do such a thing to his own father and mother."

"I understand he has some heavy debts to pay off all over Town."

"From what I've heard, he's paid back most of his vowels. There may still be some promissory notes needing to be repaid, but that isn't cause for killing one's parents. The villain could easily have been some scoundrel on the streets of London. Since they were at Drury Lane when the axle was tampered with, the perpetrator could be anyone. Was anything removed from their bodies? Wallet, purse, that sort of thing?"

The constable shook his head. "It was all there. Lord Runswick's wallet contained fifty-five pounds. Some riff-raff up to no good would certainly have lifted the blunt off of him. And the lady still wore her emerald necklace. I will grant you that it may have been a hired killer, but definitely not a thief looking for easy pickings."

"I see. Well, there is no sense speculating without additional information." Fitz opened the door. "Let me know what you find."

"I will, my lord. Thank you for your time."

Before the constable stepped into the hallway, Fitz said, "I appreciate that you waited until after my wife left the room to discuss your suspicions with me. I'd rather she remain unaware for now."

"As you wish." He bowed and left the room.

Percival arrived back in Town on Friday morning after visiting Newmarket for a horse race. Tom Hendrick insisted this particular horse was a safe bet and would help Percival clear the rest of his debt. It turned out, Tom was right. Percival had enough blunt now to pay off his final promissory note. He had been sober since leaving London, wanting to keep a clear head.

Entering his bachelor quarters, the butler handed him a

message from Juliet. Percival locked himself in his study before opening it.

*Percival,*

*Where are you? I wished to tell you in person, but you weren't here when Henry and I came searching for you, so I'm leaving you this note. Papa and Mama were involved in a tragic accident. Please come see us as soon as you return. The funeral is on Friday afternoon.*

Rubbing his forehead with trembling hands, he tried to grasp the news of his parents' deaths. Why was there a familiar niggling in the back of his mind, as though he had had a nightmare about their death and now it was coming true?

A knock interrupted his cloudy thoughts. As if in a daze, he unlocked the door and opened it. "What is it?"

Before his valet, who doubled as his butler, could announce the visitors, two rough-looking men forced their way into the room and pushed the butler out, shutting the door behind them. Percival stood staring at the two vaguely familiar men.

"We took care of your parents, now pay up!" the burlier one said.

Percival shook his head, his stomach tightening into a knot making him nauseous. He needed a drink badly. His memory was returning, and with it, feelings he longed to squelch. He sat in the chair behind his desk, placing his elbows on it, with his head between his hands.

"I thought it was a nightmare." Shaking his head back and forth, he peered at the two disreputable men. "Tell me you didn't take seriously the ramblings of a man who was drunk as a wheelbarrow."

"It were none of our business if you was jug-bitten or not. You promised the blunt if we snuffed out your sire." He held out his dirty paw and sneered, "Now pay up."

"How much do I owe you?"

They gazed at him strangely.

"Look," he shouted, "I was drunk at the time we talked! You should never have accepted my offer!"

The bigger of the two burst out laughing. "Too late for second thoughts now." Holding out his hand, he yelled, "Pay up the hundred pounds ya promised!"

A hundred pounds for the lives of his parents. *What have I done?* Wanting to be rid of the scoundrels, he took some of the money won at the horse race and handed it to them. "Get out of here! I never want to see you again!"

After counting the money, the big one said, "That's fine by us. We're leavin' Town anyhow."

As soon as the men were ushered out the door, Percival dropped into the chair and covered his face with both hands. "What have I done?" he whispered. Unfortunately, there was no time to waste. The funeral was today. He wiped the tears away with the palm of his hands, then headed to his bedchamber.

His valet helped him change and, in no time, he was on his way to his parents' funeral. Hands shaking, he longed for a drink to help him forget, but he didn't dare. He needed to keep his wits about him.

Percival sat beside his sisters in the church pew, hands clasped tightly on his lap to keep them from shaking. He stared at the two elmwood boxes draped with black velvet. *What have I done?* He lifted a handkerchief to wipe moisture from his brow.

As the vicar spoke, Percival longed to shut his ears, but couldn't. Every word spoken pierced his heart.

"And as it is appointed unto men once to die, but after this the judgment: So Christ was once offered to bear the sins of many; and unto them that look for him shall he appear the second time without sin unto salvation."

A chill ran up his spine and he stiffened his shoulders to keep from shivering. It wouldn't do for anyone to notice his distress. He had to hold himself together until after the funeral.

The men walked toward the gravesite, as the women returned to the house. Aunt Theo chose to join the men and moved alongside her nephew.

"May I hold your arm on this uneven ground, Percival?"

What choice did he have? Holding his bent arm out to her, he said, "Of course."

"I'm praying for you."

His brow furrowed as he stared at her a moment. "You are? Why?" Did she suspect what he was guilty of?

"I simply sense you're distressed about something. In addition, you're taking up the reins of Gracebourne Manor and your father's title. I want you to know God loves you and is willing to help you if you but ask Him."

"Aunt Theo, I know you mean well, but I'm not convinced God exists and, if He does, I doubt He cares about me. I'll manage without His help, thank you." Maybe his lack of faith in a deity would shut her up.

"You are in denial, Percival."

He turned and looked at her with raised brows. "Denial?" he snickered. "What do you think I'm in denial about?"

"I think you're pretending that everything is fine, but inside you long for something more." She ignored his frown and continued. "You try filling the void with things, but nothing satisfies." They had reached the gravesite and people were gathering around, so she whispered, "Your soul longs for its Creator and only God can fill that void in your heart."

Tears filled his eyes. He blinked them away as he peered straight ahead, swallowing hard. "It's too late for me," he whispered.

Aunt Theo placed her hand on her nephew's forearm, but sensing him stiffen, she let go. "As long as you have breath, it's not too late, Percival. God loves you."

Selina sighed as she surveyed her wardrobe. An entire year of grieving lay ahead of her. It wasn't that she didn't want to honor her parents, but black for six months on end seemed daunting. Even her jewelry would have to be matte black. How was she to make herself attractive to her husband while wearing such a drab color?

Since Selina's father was Aunt Theo's brother, she would also be required to wear black, but only for three months.

Her aunt had joined Selina in her room to look through the wardrobe and decide which items could simply be dyed black. Once they finished, they sat together in the sitting room.

"It's difficult to miss someone I didn't actually know. I feel terrible for saying such, but that is the case for me," Selina said. "The loss I feel is for missed opportunities. I would have welcomed them into my life if only they had given me half the chance."

"You certainly need not feel guilty, Selina. It's understandable," Aunt Theo said.

"When I visited with Juliet and Helena, they talked on and on about things they had done with our parents. Papa taught the girls how to ride a horse. Mama told them stories about herself as they embroidered together." Selina shook her head. "While these memories were comforting to Juliet and Helena, they felt like a knife to my chest. My memories of them are only painful—watching them wave goodbye to me when they sent me away, while their favored children stood beside them. And then arriving at their home as a young lady full of joy at the anticipation of a long-awaited reunion, foolishly expecting them to open their arms as you, dear Aunt Theo, would have done. Instead, they looked upon me with hauteur and told me to sit as they presented me with a fait accompli. They didn't want me. My heart feels numb instead of grieved."

"I understand, my dear. This must be very difficult for you." Aunt Theo sympathized.

Selina took a deep breath and smiled sheepishly. "Listen to me feeling sorry for myself. I cannot change the past. But between you and me, this mourning attire I am forced to wear over the next six months does not represent my grief at their loss, but rather my grief at what never was."

Understanding shone from Aunt Theo's eyes. "Be careful not to allow bitterness to enter your heart. It only destroys."

Selina smiled sadly. "I won't. I give you my word. I simply need to spout my anger at the situation." Selina gently placed her hand on Aunt Theo's and gave it a slight squeeze. "If I had lost you, I would have willingly worn this dreadful black color for two years!"

Aunt Theo's eyes filled with tears as she patted her niece's hand. "You must forgive them. I'm not saying it's easy. I'm saying you must do so for your own sake."

"I have forgiven them, over and over." Her eyes glistened with unshed tears. Her voice shook as she said, "Sometimes the hurtful memories creep back in and I find myself having to forgive once again."

"That is the process of healing, my dear. But God understands, and I know He will help you."

"Yes, He does help me."

"And you are correct when you say you must continue forgiving them, for it is an ongoing process. I believe when the hurt is deep enough, the wound takes longer to heal. Every time you feel the pain while in the process of healing, it reminds you once again what had caused it, and you find yourself in the position of having to forgive once more. It may take months or years, but if you keep turning your eyes to the Healer, eventually the wound will heal completely."

Selina gave her aunt's hand a squeeze. "I'm glad I have you to talk to. Thank you, Aunt Theo, for the encouragement."

"As long as God gives me breath, you can always count on me. Now, we had better get ready to join your husband for dinner."

# *Chapter Twenty-Two*

The cottage sat in a hamlet on a quiet road just outside of London. Its white, stucco walls were a perfect backdrop for the rose bushes growing out front. Green shutters hung open at each window and the cross-gabled roof was steeply-pitched. It wasn't as luxurious as Henfort by any means, but it was Polly's home now and she was no longer a servant.

The satin skirt of her red dress swished around her ankles as she walked toward the door, her low-cut dress revealing more than it concealed from the eye. Polly hoped to please the gentleman who paid for all she now enjoyed. By taking the risk of stealing his sister's jewelry, as well as pawning it for him, he rewarded her with this cottage, several lovely dresses, and the privilege of being his mistress.

For two weeks she had been residing in this tucked-away cottage on the outskirts of London. Percival had visited her only a few times since she took up residence. He wasn't terribly demanding of her time, which provided the opportunity to work in the garden and decorate her home. The allowance he furnished afforded few luxuries, but he promised much more if she continued pleasing him.

If her conscience pricked her for the life she had chosen, she quickly squelched its nagging voice. Percival was good to her and treated her kindly. She was a help to him and listened when he needed to talk. They were becoming friends. And she took no other lovers—only him.

There was a knock at the door. Polly hurried to open it.

Feasting her eyes on the dark hair, handsome face, broad shoulders, and slender physique of the man who made her dream come true, she considered herself quite lucky. Polly had every intention of pleasing him in whatever he required of her so she could eventually enjoy gemstones around her neck and on her fingers. Above all else, she hoped one day to be the proud owner of the cottage Percival now rented for her use.

"Hello, Percival. Please come in." She stepped aside, allowing him entrance.

He removed his overcoat and hung it on the coat tree. Turning, he looked her up and down. Not speaking a word, he walked toward her, placed his hand on her back and nudged her toward the bedchamber.

Later, as Percival stood buttoning his waistcoat and smoothing it into place, he gazed at the woman sleeping in the rumpled bed. She had helped him to forget his troubles for a bit, but the emptiness returned with a vengeance.

He walked into the living room of the small cottage and opened a decanter of brandy. After filling it to the rim of a shot glass, he sat in an upholstered chair, staring at its golden color.

Percival had felt a brief twinge of conscience as he held his sister's necklace after Polly had handed it to him. As he stared at the soft pearly stones, he remembered Selina's kindness to him. Should he tell Polly to return it?

But Selina was the heiress to their uncle's fortune. Although Percival had inherited his father's estate, which was now out of debt, it was a far cry from being prosperous. Since Uncle Peter had no sons of his own, shouldn't *he* have been his uncle's heir? If they had given Selina a small portion of the wealth, he could have accepted it. But to give her all of it was too much.

Percival swallowed the brandy in one gulp and savored the burn down his throat and into his heart. Banging the shot glass on the table, he could feel the alcohol flow into his bloodstream. He stood to his feet and stomped around the room. She owed him more than the jewelry. He found some pleasure in knowing the theft would cause her some grief.

Everything had come easy for Selina. She was given to a rich aunt and uncle who bestowed on her everything money could buy. The only thing she lacked was being a part of her own family, but little did she know it wasn't much of a loss.

Selina would never be the beauty her sisters were, but there was something about her—the very essence of her—that drew the eyes. Percival couldn't help noticing she never lacked for dance partners at any assembly. Continuing to pace the confined space, he allowed his anger to simmer.

Not only was Selina an heiress, she married a man who was wealthy in his own right and would become even more so once he inherited his father's title.

Percival refilled his glass with more brandy and stared into the golden brown liquid. "I can barely keep my head above water while my sister landed on her feet." With a humorless laugh, he said, "Let her squirm as she tries to explain to her husband about the loss of his family heirloom." The money he'd received for the jewels would help pay the rent of this cottage for quite some time.

He swallowed another shot of brandy and let it burn away any remaining feelings of guilt. Grabbing his coat and hat, he walked out, shutting the door behind him.

Shortly after the funeral, Aunt Theo pulled her niece aside. "I need a break from London, Selina. My heart longs for my home and I miss my friends dearly."

"You're leaving?" She sensed this was coming. Now that the moment had arrived, Selina had to stop herself from begging her aunt to stay.

"I received a letter that Uncle Peter's sister has taken ill. I would like to check on her to make certain she has all she needs." Stopping outside the morning room, Aunt Theo took hold of Selina's hand and gave it a slight squeeze. "It's time I return home. Things seem to be progressing nicely with you and Fitz. I see the way he looks at you. It is best if I'm not in the way."

"Oh, Aunt Theo, you could never be in the way!" Selina exclaimed. The two ladies sat in the morning room as a maid arrived with their tea.

After the girl left, Aunt Theo reached over to pour the tea. She handed a cup to Selina. "That's very sweet of you, my dear, but I was young once. Accept the wisdom of your old aunt and believe me when I say you and Fitz need some time alone to become better acquainted."

Realizing her aunt's mind was made up, Selina didn't want to make her departure more difficult than it already was. "Thank you, Aunt Theo, for coming to my aid after the wedding and for staying this long. I don't know how I would have managed without you."

She patted her niece's hand. "I was only too happy to help. Lady Worthington and I enjoyed ourselves immensely."

"When do you plan on leaving?"

"Early tomorrow morning."

"So soon?"

"Yes. I'm truly concerned for my sister-in-law and want to see her for myself. But we will write, won't we?"

"Yes, of course we will."

Every day over the next week, Fitz invited Selina to join him for a morning ride, and she accepted. In the evenings, they dined together and, after dinner, they sat in the library, either reading or playing a game of chess. Selina was a worthy opponent.

He fell into the habit of sharing some of his concerns at the Home Office with her. Selina asked intelligent questions, drawing him out to give details he never thought a lady would be interested in. Fitz asked her about the work she did at the Foundling Home. She asked him about their tenants at Thorncrest. He was glad to see his wife was interested in the workings of his estates.

One evening as they drank tea, Selina mentioned how she longed to return to Thorncrest, which greatly pleased Fitz since he preferred his estate in Northbury to being in London. There had been a niggling fear his wife would enjoy the pleasures of the city, with all its entertainments, to the extent he would be forced to spend most of his time in

London. Once again, she surprised him by saying she preferred the country.

"Parliament will adjourn this week. I was hoping we could travel to Thorncrest in a fortnight. Unfortunately, an investigation is underway with regards to the death of your parents, and we must stay in London for now."

"An investigation? Whatever for?"

As they sat side by side on the sofa before the fire, Fitz took Selina's slender hand into his larger one. If only he could spare her this news. But, alas, it was better she heard it from him than someone else. Clasping her cold hand between his warm ones, Fitz said, "There are some suspicious circumstances surrounding the deaths of your parents. The constable believes foul play was involved."

Selina's eyes widened. "It wasn't an accident?"

Fitz shook his head. "The axle had apparently been tampered with."

With furrowed brow, she tilted her head. "Who would want to do such a thing?"

"They don't know yet." He thought it best not to mention her brother was a suspect. "I'm sure they will come to the bottom of it soon enough, and we will finally be free to return to Thorncrest."

## *Chapter Twenty-Three*

Two weeks after the funeral, Bates led the constable into Fitz's study. Fitz walked around his desk to greet the man. "Please, take a seat. I assume you have news for me."

"I do," was the constable's clipped reply. After each man sat on one of the upholstered chairs before the fireplace, the constable got right to the point. "After further investigation, it has become abundantly clear that Lord Runswick's carriage had, indeed, been tampered with. This is now a murder investigation." He cleared his throat . "Unfortunately, our prime suspect is your wife."

"What?" Fitz chuckled in disbelief. "This is hardly a time for jesting, man!"

Shaking his head, the constable said, "I'm not jesting, sir. All the evidence points toward your wife."

"Impossible!" Fitz waved his hand dismissively. "What evidence? My wife would never do such a thing!" Standing slowly to his feet, Fitz narrowed his eyes, placed fists on his hips, and scowled at the man. "What kind of investigation are you undertaking? It certainly can't be thorough if you've drawn such a ridiculous conclusion."

The constable stood to his feet and jutted out his chin. "I'm not saying she actually carried out the murder herself, but it seems she paid someone to do it for her."

Fitz laughed abruptly and shook his head. "Never! Give me clear evidence and I still won't believe it of her. It isn't in her nature to do such a thing."

The constable spoke in calming tones. "My lord, please, allow me to explain what we've found. Perhaps we made a mistake. I only said she is the prime suspect. She's certainly not the only suspect. We will continue the investigation until we have enough evidence to convict someone."

Taking a calming breath, Fitz waved the constable to his seat again and sat also. He stared hard at the man. "Now tell me, what is this evidence you think you've found?"

"Does your wife own a pearl necklace with matching earbobs and bracelet?"

"Yes. I gave her my grandmother's jewelry. She's worn it on special occasions. We keep it locked in the safe, of course. What does that have to do with anything?"

"Since Percival Kendall is also a suspect and is notorious for his debts, we searched to see if he recently acquired a large sum of money. In our investigation, we found something unexpected. A pawn shop dealer recently acquired a pearl jewelry set from a patron by the name of Selina Kendall."

Staring at the constable in disbelief, he slowly shook his head. "No. That can't be right." Fitz stood to his feet again and walked to the bell pull. "I will prove to you how unlikely your story is. Obviously, someone posed as my wife, using her maiden name to implicate her in the theft."

Bates knocked before entering the study. "My lord?"

"Bates, please retrieve my wife's pearls, but do it in such a way as not to alert her. I'd like to keep her in the dark about the constable's visit."

"It shouldn't be a problem. She went to the park with her sisters."

"Very well. Please bring it here. We will wait."

"Yes, my lord."

The constable sat silently watching Fitz pace to the window and stare out at the dreary day as they waited for the butler's return. Neither man uttered a word, the silence thick in the room. In less than fifteen minutes, the doors opened and Bates entered carrying a locked box. Everything moved in slow motion as Fitz watched Bates place the box on the desk, push a key into the lock, and turn it. The click echo in the room as the lock sprang open. Bates raised the lid. Fitz and the constable leaned forward to gaze inside. Fitz's eyes looked past emerald, opal, and topaz gemstones in search of pearls. There were diamonds, amethyst, and aquamarine, as well as several others, but no pearls could be found.

"Perhaps Selina or her maid forgot to put it back. It could be laying in a drawer in her room. Bates, please ask Lydia about the pearls and have her search my wife's bedchamber thoroughly. Mrs. Addams can help in the search."

"Yes, my lord. Right away." He left the room once again, forgetting to bow in his agitation. Fitz knew Bates was loyal to his mistress. Selina had won over the staff completely with her ability to run his household well, yet rewarding the staff with praise for work well done. Bates couldn't know what was going on, but Fitz imagined he instinctively knew the jewelry needed to be found for more than the possession of it. He was confident Bates would seek for it thoroughly.

Meanwhile, the constable must have felt more firm in his belief that Lady FitzWalter was involved in the murder for he said, "Certainly, you have to admit this does not bode well for your wife. What are we to believe?"

"What you ought to believe is that I know my wife's character. Someone has done a thorough job of framing her. She is innocent. I'm willing to stake my life on it."

"My lord, please allow me to explain my reason for doubting Lady FitzWalter."

Fitz sat with a bored expression on his face and raised his brow as he peered at the constable. "I'm listening."

Lifting one finger, the constable said, "First, we found out your wife was raised by her aunt and uncle, and she did not see her family until just before her wedding day. That can only mean she never had the opportunity to develop any great depth of affection for her parents or her siblings." Lifting the second finger, he continued. "Second, she finally returns home and is immediately married off to a stranger who leaves for London the day after the wedding, leaving her to rusticate in the country." Fitz pulled his lips into a straight line but said nothing. "Third, she becomes bitter toward her parents and her thoughtless husband, and plots revenge."

When Fitz attempted to interrupt, the constable raised his hand to stop him. "Please allow me to finish."

Fitz shrugged his shoulder and continued to look bored. "Your third point is not evidence. It's an assumption."

"Yes, perhaps. But it's a good assumption according to the evidence before us. When one has allowed anger and bitterness to fester for years on end, one is likely to have it destroy rational thinking. I will admit it wasn't smart of her to use her maiden name. It could easily be traced. But when rational thought is compromised, unwise decisions occur. We see this all the time in our line of work. After looking in that jewelry box, I realize she could have pawned far more valuable gemstones. But I believe she pawned your grandmother's jewelry as vengeance for the way you had treated her after the wedding as well as that damning article in the gossip sheet. The murder plot was vengeance against her parents. I believe she was killing two flies with one swat."

Fitz rubbed his chin in a thoughtful manner. "I understand your reasoning, but an important piece of the puzzle is missing."

"And what is that?"

He leaned forward with his elbows on his knees and pierced the constable with a direct gaze. "You don't know Lady Selina FitzWalter. She is incapable of such behavior."

"I understand you want to protect your wife, my lord. Even more importantly, you wish to protect the reputation of your family. But if the jewelry is not found, I will have to question your wife . . . today."

There was a knock at the door and both men stood to their feet. Bates entered, followed by Lydia and Mrs. Addams. "I'm sorry, my lord. We were unable to find the pearls."

"Lydia, when was the last time you remember seeing them?"

"As we looked for it in the bedchamber, I kept searching my mind trying to remember the details of when I last saw the jewelry. Lady FitzWalter wore the pearls the night of the

Templeton ball."

Fitz nodded. "Yes, I remember seeing them as we waltzed together."

"I placed them on the dressing room table. Servants arrived with a tub and hot water. There was a commotion when one of the servants spilled most of the water she carried onto the floor and on herself. Lady FitzWalter and I hurried over, concerned the hot water had scalded the maid. After everything settled down and once my lady was ready for bed, I went about the task of cleaning up, but I didn't see the jewelry. I thought the mistress had put it away herself since she had done so the first time she wore it. Lady FitzWalter had said she'd rather see to its safekeeping herself for she'd sleep better knowing such a precious family heirloom was locked away. I assumed Lady FitzWalter did so that night also and I gave it no further thought."

Fitz knew this didn't help his wife's case. He wanted the servants out of the room before the constable gave voice to his thoughts. "Thank you. That will be all. Please return to your duties. And ask Lady FitzWalter to come to my study as soon as she arrives home."

"Yes, my lord," Bates said as he left the room.

Fitz fixed his gaze on the constable and narrowed his eyes. "I know what you're thinking, but you are dead wrong. I plan to start my own investigation. However, I will allow you to speak to my wife. You are welcome to stay here until she returns, whenever that may be."

"I'll wait."

"Very well. You may wait in the drawing room. I have work to finish in the interim."

After a carriage ride in the park, Selina felt refreshed. The weather had finally warmed in August, but now that fall approached, there was a slight briskness in the air. Still, the exercise and lively conversation helped the three sisters refocus. Two weeks had passed since the funeral. Juliet recently learned she was in the family way, which was cause for some delightful squealing. They talked of plans for the future and possibly meeting together at Christmas.

After dropping her sisters off at Juliet's house, Selina returned and entered the foyer of Henfort. She handed pelisse, gloves, and bonnet to the waiting butler. Facing to the mirror near the door, she smoothed her hair in place.

Bates cleared his throat. "My lady, Lord FitzWalter requested you join him and the constable in his study as soon as you arrived home."

Selina swallowed a sudden lump in her throat. "Very well. I'll go there directly. Thank you, Bates."

Fitz stood behind the desk when she entered, his expression serious. The constable, who had been watching out the drawing room window for her return, had quickly rejoined Fitz in the study and now stood in front of the desk, hands behind his back. Both men faced her.

"Selina," Fitz was the first to speak as he walked toward her. "You remember the constable, of course."

"Yes, I remember."

"My lord, I must ask you to allow me to take over from here. I need to ask some pertinent questions I want only your wife to answer."

Fitz narrowed his eyes at the man, then reluctantly nodded once. "You may begin."

"Please, let us sit." He motioned to the chairs before the fireplace.

Selina chose the seat closest to the fire as she felt chilled. Fitz sat on the chair next to her and the constable sat across from them.

"When was the last time you saw the pearl necklace, earbobs, and bracelet belonging to your husband's grandmother?"

Selina's eyebrows shot up as her eyes opened wide. She glanced at Fitz trying to gauge what was going on. She thought the constable would ask her questions about her parents' murder. What did the jewelry have to do with any of this? Selina shivered slightly and returned her gaze to the constable. "I wore them to the Templeton ball. I haven't seen them since. Why do you ask?"

"I will answer your questions shortly. I must know what happened to the jewelry once you returned home."

Her brow puckered. "I don't understand. Is it missing? Why are you asking me these questions?" She shifted her gaze to Fitz and asked, "Would you like me to retrieve the jewelry?"

He gave her a pained look, but shook his head, saying nothing.

"The jewelry is missing," the constable said. "I need you to tell me when you saw it last."

Looking to her husband again, she asked, "You think I stole it? Is that why the constable is here?"

Fitz shook his head, but the constable spoke before he could open his mouth to utter a word. "My lady, you must answer me and stop asking questions of your husband. It will all become clear once you answer truthfully. If you don't, I will assume you are attempting a delay tactic to come up with a lie."

"What? No! I'll answer your question, of course. I need a moment to think." She sat in silence trying to gather her thoughts. "I wore it to the Templeton Ball. I don't recall what happened when we returned home. I-I'm having trouble remembering what occurred. No, wait! I do remember. I asked Lydia to have a bath prepared. As we waited for the servants to arrive, Lydia removed my jewelry and laid it on the table in my bedchamber. When the servants arrived, there was a commotion. As soon as it was all cleared up, Lydia cleaned the room while I sat and read for a few minutes. Since I was exhausted from the ball, I soon climbed into bed and fell asleep."

"And where were your pearls at that point?"

"I assumed Lydia returned them to the box in the safe. I'm certain she did."

"I beg your pardon. You cannot be certain. As a matter of fact, you didn't trust Lydia enough the first time you wore the pearls, choosing to return them to safekeeping yourself. Why did you suddenly trust her that evening?"

"It wasn't that I didn't trust her the first time. I simply needed to see them locked into the box myself. I don't know why I didn't worry about it after the Templeton Ball. I simply believed Lydia had put them away since I knew I had not."

"How do you think the jewelry disappeared? Could Lydia have taken it?"

"No! Lydia would never do such a thing." Swallowing hard, Selina said, "If you will allow me to search my room, I'm certain we will find it."

"As a matter of fact, my lady, you will not find it. The pearls have already made their way to a pawn shop and were sold for enough money to hire someone to murder your parents."

Selina stared at the constable. Her breathing became shallow. "W-what are you saying?"

"The person who was hired did a fine job of sabotaging the axle so it would break at just the right moment when the horses were moving at a good clip. Fast enough to overturn the carriage and kill the passengers and the driver. It was done by skillful hands. I suspect you had a motive for wanting to hurt your parents, as well as your husband, by using his grandmother's pearls to pay the killers."

Selina stared at the constable in amazement. She realized her mouth must have been hanging open, so she quickly shut it. "What motive?"

"Revenge. Inheritance."

*Jesus, help me.* She straightened her shoulders and lifted her chin a notch. "Constable, you are far off on your suspicions. I will inherit nothing from my parents and I have no reason for revenge."

"You may not have inherited anything from your parents, but you have plenty of reason for revenge. With this one act, you took vengeance on both your husband and your parents."

Selina tilted her head and narrowed her eyes. "Please explain yourself."

"I know your parents gave you to your aunt and uncle to raise. They considered you the least attractive of their children and the easiest one to dispense with."

"Constable, this is mere speculation!" Fitz protested. "How can you possibly know what Lord and Lady Runswick's motives were?"

"I have my sources." Turning to Selina, he asked, "Is what I'm saying incorrect?"

Selina felt the wound in her heart reopening. She shut her eyes a moment and silently asked God for strength to walk in forgiveness and to know how to answer. *I need you now, dear Lord.* Opening her eyes, she peered at the constable and said, "You are not incorrect. My parents did exactly as you said."

He gentled his voice into one of sympathy. "And wouldn't that type of wound inflicted on a child fester over the years? Tell me, my lady, when your parents called you home only a few months ago, were you hoping to be welcomed into the bosom of your family?"

Selina nodded her head slowly. "I did hope to be welcomed back."

"But that didn't happen, did it? Instead, they informed you they had arranged a marriage for you. To a complete stranger, nonetheless. Did the wound reopen and continue to fester? And when your husband left you in the country the day after your wedding, while he returned to London, how did that make you feel? What about the recent scandal with his former fiancée?"

Seeing it from his perspective, she certainly had a motive for revenge, but Selina had chosen to forgive. She squared her shoulders and gazed intently into the constable's eyes. "Sir, I will speak plainly to you." He leaned forward, obviously expecting a full confession. "Yes, I was hurt by my parents' rejection, both as a child and again when they informed me of my upcoming marriage. However, I was not upset with my husband when he left for London. Instead, I felt relief. He was a stranger to me. Everything happened so fast that I was glad for some time alone."

Disbelief was clear in the constable's eyes. Selina glanced at Fitz. He wore a stoic face. It was impossible to read his thoughts. Looking the constable in the eyes, she continued. "I have been blessed with a wonderful aunt. Not only did she raise me not to feel sorry for myself. She also taught me to trust God. I realized my parents would never live up to my expectations. They were victims of their own weaknesses and couldn't see how their actions had hurt me. But my aunt helped me see that God understands my pain. Although it still hurts sometimes, I am allowing God to heal my heart, and I've chosen to forgive my parents." A supernatural calm settled into her being as she spoke. "I have no need for revenge. God is able to turn everything around for my good if I will trust Him."

The constable wore a cynical smile. "Your religious words do not impress me, my lady. You speak with confidence, but I see it for the mask that it is. I was willing to believe that perhaps you were framed. But once you began spouting your religious nonsense, it became clear to me you are trying to cover your deeds of darkness by talk of God and faith. You see, religion is for the weak. Your disturbed mind may have reached for the church for help, but it cannot help you now. You took matters into your own hands, didn't you?"

Selina shook her head in denial. Before she could answer, Fitz stood to his feet. "Constable, if anyone is spouting nonsense, it is you. I'm sorry for whatever negative experience you have had with the church or religion, but don't allow it to darken your understanding in seeking the truth. A person is not automatically guilty of a crime simply because they speak about their faith. Look at the facts."

The constable shot to his feet. "The facts don't look good for your wife. I'm inclined to arrest her right now, but since she is a lady, I will do some further investigating." Pointing a finger at Selina, he said, "Don't leave the city. If you do, you will immediately face arrest."

Selina gazed calmly at him and asked, "Who was your source that gave you inside information about my family?"

"I cannot disclose it to you. Time is on the side of truth, my lady. If what you say is true, it will reveal itself. Good day."

When the door closed behind the constable, she turned to face her husband. He defended her, but did he believe she was innocent or was he protecting his family reputation?

"You must be tired, Selina. Why don't you rest a bit and we can discuss this later."

"Do you believe me, Fitz?" she asked. Tears filled her eyes

and she tried blinking them away.

He pulled her into his embrace and held her close. "We will get to the bottom of this. Have no fear."

It wasn't until she was alone in her room that she realized he never said he believed her.

## *Chapter Twenty-Four*

Upon entering the drawing room, Fitz saw he was the first to arrive. He picked up the poker and absently nudged the burning logs.

"Good evening, Fitz."

He straightened at his wife's greeting. "Selina, you look lovely as always. Did you rest well?" Fitz placed the poker back in the stand.

"Yes, thank you." Walking to the sofa, she sat and straightened the skirt of her dress.

Just then, Bates stepped into the room to inform them supper was ready to be served. Fitz held out his arm for Selina and led her to the dining room. Instead of sitting at either end of the long table, he pulled out the chair situated to the right of the seat at the head of the table. Selina glanced up in surprise. He winked and said, "This will allow us some quiet conversation without the need to shout across the table."

A smile played on Selina's lips. "Have we been shouting across the table at our meals?"

He chuckled. "Perhaps 'shouting' is a slight exaggeration, but this is cozier, don't you agree?"

"Yes, quite."

After they were seated, servants carried in platters one by one. They busied themselves with tasting the delicacies presented, neither saying a word. It pleased Fitz to see his wife's appetite unaffected by the accusations thrown at her earlier in the day. "I have to say, you no longer seem overly concerned about the constable's accusations."

Picking up the serviette on her lap, she wiped the corners of her mouth before speaking. "I cannot say I am unconcerned, but I'm convinced God is well aware of my circumstances. I've presented my worries to Him." She smiled sheepishly. "That is not to say I won't worry again, but I pray God will help me to continue trusting Him."

His warm hand rested briefly on hers and squeezed it before letting go. "I won't let anything happen to you."

Fitz was a gentleman and would do all he could to protect his wife, even if he suspected her guilty of a heinous crime. Summoning her courage, for she was curious to know his thoughts, she asked, "Do you believe me innocent then?"

"Selina, what I believe to be true is unimportant. We need to prove you are innocent. I hired a private investigator this afternoon. I don't trust the constable to be unbiased. We will get to the bottom of this."

"Thank you," she whispered.

"You don't need to thank me. You're my wife—my responsibility—and I *will* protect you."

Her shoulders slumped. She was his responsibility. Again, he didn't say he believed her innocent of the crime.

After dinner, they sat together in the drawing room. Fitz casually mentioned, "Mr. Green, the investigator I hired, will be joining us this evening. He needs you to answer some questions for him."

Raising her eyes from her cup, Selina looked at her husband. Why had he waited until now to inform her? Perhaps he knew she would lose her appetite anticipating the interview. "Yes, of course," she said.

Selina watched as Fitz stood and walked to the fireplace to stare into the flames. Lowering her head, she briefly closed her eyes, silently asking God to guide her as He promised to do. Selina desperately clung to the peace she'd found earlier.

"Mr. William Green," the butler announced.

"Thank you, Bates. Please show him in."

After the introductions were made and everyone was seated, Mr. Green said, "I don't want to take a lot of your time, so I'll get straight to the point."

"Yes, please do," Fitz said, as he sat back comfortably and crossed his legs.

Mr. Green turned to Selina. "I want to assure you, I will do all I can to get to the bottom of what is going on and discover what truly happened. If you would be so good and answer some questions for me, my lady, I might get a better understanding of where to begin."

"Of course, Mr. Green. What is it you wish to know?"

He asked her to explain what occurred in her bedchamber following the Templeton Ball the night the jewelry disappeared. Selina explained it in detail to the best of her recollection, watching him jot notes in a black notebook.

"Have you had any servants leave your employ recently?"

Selina thought for a moment. "Yes. One of our maids, but she did not have access to the safe."

"Was she by any chance in your bedchamber after the Templeton Ball?"

"Yes, she was there. One of her duties was to care for the bedchambers."

"So it is possible she may have snuck over to the dressing table and plucked a valuable unobserved during the commotion?"

"I-I don't want to accuse her of any wrong-doing simply because she was in the room and then left our employ. She said she had a new position, something too good to turn down, but I don't know where she's working now."

"My lady, I beg your pardon. No one is accusing her of anything, but we must not pretend it isn't a possibility. Now, what is this maid's name?"

"We called her Polly. I know little about her, but perhaps our butler or housekeeper could give you more information."

Mr. Green turned to Fitz and asked, "Would you allow me to interview the butler and housekeeper, my lord?"

"Yes, of course."

"I will get them," Selina quickly stood to her feet. The

men stood also. "If there are no further questions, I'd like to retire for the evening."

"That will be all for now. Thank you for your time, Lady FitzWalter."

Nodding, she said, "Good night," then turned and left the room.

After Bates and Mrs. Addams were questioned, Fitz realized they still had very little information. No one knew much about Polly, except that she had no family and she was a good worker.

"Will you search for the maid?" Fitz asked.

"I will. I have little to go on, but there are some stones yet to be turned over." Mr. Green cleared his throat before saying, "I must ask you if you have any reason to suspect your wife?"

Fitz's brows puckered. "I don't like this line of questioning. If I suspected my wife, I wouldn't need you. The constable is already investigating her."

"I understand, but I must rule everything out, my lord." At Fitz's reluctant nod, Mr. Green asked, "Did your wife show any resentment toward her family?"

"No, she did not." Fitz shifted his gaze to the door and swallowed hard. Had Selina deceived him? There was much he didn't know about her, but he squelched the thought. Fixing his gaze intently upon Mr. Green, Fitz spoke decisively. "I have no reason to suspect my wife. She isn't capable of such deceit."

"Very well. I will search out this Polly and get back to you as soon as I have more information."

Selina knelt by her chair before the fire once again and sought help from God. What if Polly had taken the pearls, but she was never found? They would never be able to prove that Polly had done it. Would Fitz always wonder if Selina had deceived him? Instead of praying, her mind wandered and worried.

Finally, reining in her thoughts, she prayed, "God, is there any hope for my marriage? Why are there so many obstacles in the way of us finding happiness together? Please allow the truth to be revealed."

Getting up from her knees, she climbed under her feather blanket and turned to look toward the connecting door to her husband's bedchamber. Never once had that door opened since she took up residence in Henfort.

"Jesus, we need your help," she whispered. "I desire more than a marriage of convenience."

Her mind wandered back to the Templeton Ball when she had waltzed with her husband and he had said, *"I longed to take you into my arms again. I wanted to claim you before the ton so every gentleman in the room would know you belong to me."* If only she could have made time stand still at that moment. Selina sighed as she rolled onto her back. It was inconceivable that, since the evening of the ball, she had lost her parents and become a suspect in their murder and theft against her own husband.

*How can anyone believe me capable of such a crime? If Fitz suspects me of such abominable behavior, he doesn't know me at all.*

Selina sat up, knowing sleep was impossible. Throwing her legs over the side of the bed, she placed a wrap over her shoulders and grabbed the pewter candlestick from the nightstand. Carefully, she made her way to the library while holding her hand in front of the candle to keep the flame from blowing out. Once in the library, she held the candle up near the spines of the books, hoping to find something to hold her interest enough to distract her from her worries.

"Can I help you find something?"

Selina gasped and turned suddenly, the momentum causing the candle to fly out of the holder and extinguish the flame before landing on the carpeted floor. In complete darkness, except for a bit of moonlight coming through the windows, Selina could see the shape of her husband as he stood up from his chair and took careful steps toward her.

"I'm sorry, Selina. I didn't mean to startle you."

"I-I didn't see you sitting there. Why didn't you say something?"

He chuckled. "I did. That was the problem, I believe."

She sensed him standing before her now. "You're right, of course," she said with a smile in her voice, although it was too dark for him to actually see her face. "I had no idea you were in the room. Forgive me for disturbing you."

His voice sounded low and husky as he said, "It was a delightful disturbance and one I hope you will repeat."

Her heart rate accelerated and she jumped when he placed a hand on her shoulder but she didn't shrink away. His other hand touched the back of her neck. Strong fingers moved upward to weave into her loose hair. "Selina." His hand moved from her shoulder to the middle of her back and drew her closer. His warm breath caressed her face. Slowly, as though giving her time to resist if she should choose to, he lowered his head. Warm lips lightly touched her own. *How could he kiss me like this if he suspects me of stealing and murder? He must believe I didn't do it!* As he pulled her more fully into his embrace, she stopped thinking altogether.

Too soon he lifted his head and she longed to pull him close again, but didn't dare. Fitz moved away to relight the candle and held it near the shelf.

"Go ahead and choose a book," he said. "Then I will escort you back to your room."

Her mind was in a fog. None of the titles made sense to her. She simply reached up and pulled a book off the shelf.

Fitz offered her his arm and held the candle in his other hand as he led her back to her bedchamber door. He handed Selina the candle before wishing her a good night and walking away.

Once she was settled on her bed again, Selina stared at the title of the book. Her eyes grew wide and she placed a hand over her mouth, desperately hoping Fitz was unaware of the book she'd chosen. Quietly laughing, she clutched to her chest a book on horse breeding. It occurred to her that kissing was more effective at helping to forget one's concerns than reading could ever be. Smiling softly, she lifted her fingers to her lips.

## *Chapter Twenty-Five*

"I want you to leave, Polly."

"Leave?" She suddenly felt lightheaded. "But where will I go?" Tears filled her eyes as she stared at the man who had promised so much. "What have I done to displease you?"

Percival ran a trembling hand through his hair. "It isn't what *you've* done. It's what *I've* done."

What did he mean? Had he found someone else to take her place?

"Polly, I've enjoyed my time with you. It isn't that." His jaw clenched tight and she watched a muscle jump in his cheek. Letting his breath out in a huff, he said, "I did a terrible thing, and now I want nothing more than to drink myself into oblivion."

"I'll stay and take care of you. I'll clean up after you. Please, don't ask me to leave."

He shook his head. "You don't understand. I'm a vicious drunk. You have no idea what I'm capable of when I'm jug-bitten." Running a hand through his hair, he shook his head again. "I'm carrying enough guilt as it is. You have to go. NOW!" he shouted. Taking a calming breath, he spoke more gently. "Be a good girl and pack your bags."

She fell to her knees before him and begged. "Percival, I have nowhere to go! I can only afford a hotel for perhaps two nights, maybe three. What will become of me? You must know you were my first. I don't want to stand on street corners. Please, don't do this to me!" Tears streamed down her face.

He exhaled an exacerbated breath. "Go to my sister. She's a do-gooder. Tell her about the theft. Tell her I coerced you into helping me."

"But that isn't true! I was a willing accomplice."

"She doesn't know that. Tell Selina whatever you wish to tell her. It matters not. I know my sister. She will forgive you of anything and take you in again." Standing up, Percival walked to the decanter and poured himself a glass of brandy. He lifted it and stared into the amber liquid. "I regret having to give you up. You may very well be one of the best things that happened to me recently. I like you a lot, Polly. Go to Selina. She will help you."

Polly took the few steps separating them and lifted her hand to touch the arm that held the glass. She gazed into his eyes and her heart squeezed at the despair she saw in their depths. "Percival, something is terribly wrong. I can feel it. Please allow me to help you."

He shook her hand off his arm. "You can't help me. No one can." Looking away, his brow creased. "If only I had been in that carriage instead of my parents . . ."

"Please, don't talk like that. There's always hope as long as you're still breathing."

He shook his head and lifted the glass to sniff it. "There is no hope for me." Setting the glass on the side table, he turned and gently grabbed her arm as he led her toward the bedchamber. "Start packing."

"Percival . . ." she tried once more.

"NOW!" he shouted.

As she hurried to do his bidding, her tears continued to flow. Polly packed as much as would fit into the valise. Shutting it, she grabbed the handle and carried it out to the living room where Percival sat staring at the glass of brandy, not having taken a sip yet for it was filled to the rim.

"Will you reconsider?"

"No!" came his cold response. "Go before it gets dark. Lady FitzWalter will help you. Of that, I have no doubt."

Polly's feet felt heavy as she walked to the door and shut it behind her. As she stood on the pavement, her eyes caressed the flowers she'd lovingly planted around the front of the cottage. Polly's hopes of one day owning all this were dashed. She'd heard mistresses of lords could expect large parting gifts, and she had secretly hoped Percival would give her the cottage when that day finally came. What an imbecile she'd been. Polly shuddered as a heart-wrenching sob pressed through her lips. How foolish to have such lofty dreams. How naive.

She had not expected Percival's gentleness toward her all these weeks and found it hard to make sense of what had just transpired. Instead of Percival walking away and leaving her the cottage, she walked out of his life leaving her heart behind as tears rolled down her face.

On the long trek into London, Polly became increasingly concerned for Percival. He sounded dreadfully hopeless. What had he done to cause himself such despair? Had he gambled beyond the ability to redeem his finances? Was he desperate enough to consider ending his life? That thought caused her to increase her pace.

"I must speak with Lady FitzWalter," Selina heard the words as she reached the bottom of the staircase, but couldn't see who was at the front door.

"Absolutely not! You have no business coming to the front door! Go around to the servants' entrance and I might listen to what you have to say," Bates scolded.

"Please! It's urgent! The mistress will want to see me, Bates."

"No. Begone!"

"Who is it, Bates?"

As Bates turned to answer, Selina saw Polly take advantage of his distraction and push her way through the door.

"My lady, I must speak with you. Please!"

"Polly? Whatever is the matter?"

Bates grabbed Polly's arm, holding her in place, and turned to Selina. "My lady, there is no need for you to bother yourself with this. I'll see to her myself."

Selina walked closer and gently placed a hand on Polly's

shoulder. Looking more closely, she saw her former maid's anguished state and felt the slight tremble beneath her hand. "Bates, please send for tea. Polly and I will be in the drawing room."

Bates hesitated but must have sensed his mistress's resolve. "Yes, of course, my lady."

"Come, Polly. You need to sit." Selina led the way to the drawing room, seated herself on the sofa, and patted the seat beside her.

Polly sat down and swallowed hard before speaking. "My lady, I did a terrible thing." Her voice quivered as she spoke. "I'm certain it's too much to ask for your forgiveness, but will you please hear me out?"

"Of course. What is it?"

After a brief knock, the door to the drawing room opened and a maid brought in the tea tray. Once the servant left, Selina lifted the teapot to serve them. Before she could hand the cup to Polly, the door swung open once more.

"Bates mentioned Polly had come to see you," Fitz spoke without preamble as he walked in and took a seat across from them, never removing his eyes from the former maid. "Perhaps you'd like to tell us about the missing jewelry?"

Hearing Polly's gasp, Selina couldn't help feeling sorry for her. She seemed nervous enough already. If only Fitz wouldn't make it harder for the poor girl. Selina held out the cup of tea to Polly. "Here you go. Drink this, and try to relax. We are willing to listen to whatever you have to say."

Polly's teacup shook in her hand as she raised it to her lips. After taking a tiny sip, she leaned forward and placed it on the table. Clasping her hands on her lap, she lowered her eyes.

"Polly," Selina gently spoke her name. "It is quite obvious something has greatly vexed you. Please, tell us how we can be of help."

Polly lifted fearful eyes. "I stole your jewelry." She bit her bottom lip, waiting for their reaction.

Selina glanced at Fitz, but since he said nothing, she assumed he would let her deal with her former maid. "Why did you do it, Polly? Were you in desperate need of funds?"

Polly took a deep breath. "I don't know where to begin, but I'm worried about Lord Runswick."

It took her only a moment to realize Polly was talking about her brother. Selina wasn't yet accustomed to hearing her brother referred to by her father's title. "Percival? What does my brother have to do with this?"

Selina saw her visibly swallow before continuing. "I was cleaning the bedchambers when I ran into him in the hallway."

"My brother has never stayed the night at Henfort. What was he doing in that hallway?"

"I'm not certain. Whatever it was, he must have changed his mind. Instead, he asked me to meet him after work and he left soon after. He's quite handsome, you know? Not that I had any marital expectations." She lowered her eyes to her hands as she said, "I'd hoped he might set me up in a cottage somewhere."

For a moment, Selina didn't understand what Polly meant by that statement, but it soon dawned on her. *Why would a young maid as pretty as Polly wish to be set up as someone's light o' love?* Before she could stop herself, Selina asked, "Why would you wish for that, Polly?"

Polly's eyes flew briefly to Fitz and she colored up. "I-I didn't want to end up in poverty like my parents. I wanted more. I thought if I became someone's . . ." Shaking her head miserably, she shut her eyes. "I was such a fool." She wiped a tear off her cheek and lifted her eyes to Selina. "I met a woman once who wore fancy clothes and fine jewelry. She owned a cottage. I saw it from the outside and it was lovely. My mother, on the other hand, died from lack of a physician in a cold, rat-infested building, a faithful wife and mother. I didn't want to end up like her."

Selina knew only too well the conditions of poverty in London. She had heard plenty of stories since helping Juliet with her charitable work. Most of them lived in muck and filth.

"I'm sorry about your mother." Her words seemed inadequate to her own ears. Tears filled Selina's eyes as she thought about the injustices in life.

Polly only shrugged her shoulders.

"What did Percival want from you?" Fitz asked. "Was he involved in the theft of my wife's jewelry?"

Polly nodded. "He told me to confess everything to you when he sent me here. Percival said I should place the blame on him. But I cannot. I was a willing accomplice."

Fitz stared at her a moment. "Why did you decide to be honest with us and not blame everything on Percival?"

"Percival told me to leave the cottage. He wanted to drink himself to oblivion but didn't want me around. He warned me that he could be vicious when drunk and that I had no idea what he was capable of." Polly turned to Selina. "I am hoping you care enough for your brother to help him. I have never seen such despair in anyone's eyes as I did this evening in Percival's."

"Why was he in such despair? Did he say? Was it grief over the loss of our parents?"

"I don't believe so. He seemed . . . I don't know . . ." Polly shook her head and search for the right words to explain. "His grief seemed desperate. He said no one could help him. My lady, I'm concerned Percival may attempt ending his life."

"No! Where is he now? Why do you think he may do himself harm?"

"I left him at the cottage holding a glass of brandy. He hadn't placed it on his lips yet but sat staring at it. And he said he wished to have been in the carriage the night his parents died instead of them."

"Where is this cottage?" Fitz asked.

After Polly gave them directions, Selina asked, "Fitz, would you please—"

"Yes, of course," Fitz said before she could finish her thought. "I'll depart immediately." He pierced Polly with his gaze. "You will have more questions to answer when I return. Do not leave until I've had the chance to ask them."

"Yes, my lord. I will stay."

Selina arranged with Mrs. Addams to place Polly in a room in the servants' quarters. In the meantime, Fitz ordered Bates to make certain Polly did not leave the premises.

## *Chapter Twenty-Six*

Selina delayed dinner for an hour past the usual time, hoping Fitz would return, but finally gave up and entered the dining room alone. What was taking so long? Had Percival been found? She played with her food more than eating it, unable to relax enough to enjoy the meal.

When the footman entered the room, she smiled apologetically. "Please tell Cook the meal was delicious as always, but I simply could not eat tonight. It's no reflection on her skill."

He bowed briefly. "Yes, my lady. I will tell her."

Perhaps reading would distract her. She headed toward the library. A commotion at the front door stopped her in her tracks.

"My lord!" she heard Bates say. "What have we here?"

Fitz was home! Selina took a step toward the foyer but stood still when two servants carrying a man between them came into her line of vision. Her heart almost stopped. Was it Fitz? But it couldn't be. Although the man's head was slumped forward, she saw his dark hair, unlike her husband's blond locks. Before relief could settle over her, the man lifted his head, crying out in pain as one of the servants adjusted his hold. Selina saw a swollen and bruised face with blood oozing out of several cuts. Lifting a trembling hand to her lips, she could only stare. It was impossible to recognize him, but she instinctively knew it was her brother.

"Take him to a guest room," Fitz instructed the men.

"And be careful."

Fitz shifted his gaze to the butler. "I want a physician here immediately."

"Yes, my lord. Right away."

As Fitz turned toward the stairs, his eyes caught Selina's. She realized she still held a hand pressed to her lips as tears blurred her vision. She watched him approach.

"What happened to Percival?"

"From all we could gather from eyewitnesses, your brother entered a pub drunk as a wheelbarrow, calling out to two ruffians. Someone said he called them murderers and demanded they leave London. They were somewhat disguised themselves. In no time, they pulled him into a back alley. Those scoundrels obviously meted out their own brand of justice. When we came upon them, they ran off." Seeing her shiver, he placed a hand on her back. "Come. Let's go to the library. You've had a shock. We need to get you warmed up." He instructed the footman standing at attention to bring tea.

Fitz led her to a chair before the fireplace and placed a warm blanket over her lap. He sat in the chair facing her.

"I should go to him," Selina said, but couldn't bring herself to move.

"Not yet, my love. Mrs. Addams will see him settled as comfortably as can be. The physician will see to his injuries. After that, we will go and check in on him together."

Selina nodded. "I suppose we will need to inform Juliet and Helena."

"Chesterfield was with me when we found Percival. I'm certain he's already filled them in on everything."

A servant carrying the tea tray entered the room. Fitz poured a cup and handed it to his wife.

"Thank you." She held the cup between her hands and closed her eyes for a moment. A vision of her brother's injured face swam before her once more. "Why are people so cruel to each other?"

Her husband's eyes glistened with unshed tears. He shrugged, but she knew there was nothing he could say.

Selina was deeply moved by his empathy and swallowed

hard before asking, "Was Percival able to tell you anything? Why did he seek those men out at the pub?"

"He was in too much pain to answer questions. I suspect your brother has suffered broken ribs and a broken arm."

Selina shook her head. "Self-indulgence and greed cause people to behave in despicable ways. They think they don't need God because He's only necessary when one is weak." Clenching her fists, she said, "They don't even realize how pathetically weak and enslaved to sin they are. My parents ruined their family and estate with uncontrolled gaming and spending, and my brother is no better. They were desperately trying to fill a void. Why else would they have behaved so excessively?"

"I think you may be right," he answered calmly.

"If they had only understood their need of a Savior." She shook her head helplessly. "Except for the grace of God, I could be like Percival. My heart could be consumed with bitterness, desperately seeking for something to fill the void in my life."

One side of Fitz's mouth lifted in a half smile. "Selina, in my most wild imagination, I cannot see you behaving like Percival. You don't have it in you."

She shrugged her shoulders. "I'm not a violent person, but who knows what someone might be capable of when their heart is given over to bitterness and greed?" She placed the cup back on the tray then lifted the blanket up over her shoulders. "I think an unfulfilled longing that turns to greed can cause a person to become self-destructive. Yet it cannot satisfy the craving deep within. It only increases desperation."

Fitz sat leaning forward with his elbows on his knees, while clasping his hands out in front of him. "You're right, of course." He fixed his gazed upon her. "Considering how your parents treated you as a child, I'm amazed at the sweet and caring person you've become."

A tear rolled down her cheek. Fitz reached into his jacket pocket, pulled out a handkerchief, and handed it to her.

"Thank you." She smiled through her tears. Her husband was a true gentleman. In spite of their rough beginning, he had always treated her kindly. As he returned her smile, she saw something in his eyes. Something . . . more. She felt herself drowning in his gaze, surrendering to the inevitable. The blanket fell from her shoulders and crumpled on her lap.

Fitz moved forward and took hold of her hands. Standing, he drew her up with him and into his embrace, never breaking eye contact. Neither seemed concerned that the blanket laid puddled at their feet. Fitz pulled her closer and Selina rested her head in the crook of his neck. Fitz's warm breath touched her cheek. "Selina."

So much emotion in one word. The breathtaking tenderness when he spoke her name caused the dam inside to break. Every emotion she held in check over the past days suddenly poured forth and sobs shook her whole frame as Fitz held her close. He ran a soothing hand up and down her back. The loss of her parents, Kitty's heartbreak, Aunt Theo's departure, and the false accusations of theft and murder. It all collided at once. She couldn't stop the tears from flowing.

"I-I'm s-sorry," she said.

"Shhhh . . . You have nothing to be sorry about," Fitz soothed. "I will hold you as long as you need me."

Selina wished she could tell him there would never come a time she wouldn't need him, but she didn't dare give voice to her feelings. He tenderly placed a kiss on her forehead and she settled fully into his warm embrace. If only Fitz would hold her like this forever.

But what was she thinking to cry in his arms like this? He must think she'd become an absolute watering pot. Reluctantly, Selina pulled way, but he didn't let go. She tried keeping her head down, for her face would certainly be red and blotchy. Her husband had other ideas. Two fingers lifted her chin. Having no option but to look into his eyes, the depth of concern she saw there caused her chin to quiver. Selina's heart leaped in her chest as she watched him lean closer. His head moved slowly toward her until his lips touched her own in the lightest of kisses, like the brush of a feather. She held still, afraid he'd pull away.

A knock at the door tore her from a dream-like state.

Selina jumped back, but Fitz kept his arm firmly around her waist as Bates entered the room.

The butler's eyes briefly glanced at the forgotten blanket on the floor, but he quickly averted them.

"Pardon me, my lord, my lady. The physician is ready to see you."

"Besides the bruises and lacerations, Lord Runswick has at least three broken ribs, a broken arm, and a concussion. What is most concerning is the internal bleeding. One cannot be certain as to what kind of internal damage has occurred. I have done all I can. The rest only time will tell."

Selina sighed heavily. So little hope for such a lost soul. If he died, there was no doubt where he would spend eternity. "Is there nothing we can do to possibly assist toward a good outcome for my brother?"

"Of course, it is important he rests comfortably. I've left instructions with your housekeeper how best to care for him. In his weakened state, I hope he doesn't develop a high fever. If he does, please contact me immediately."

"Yes, of course," Selina said.

"Your housekeeper has designated a maid to sit with Lord Runswick tonight. I will check on him tomorrow afternoon."

"Thank you for coming out at such a late hour."

"I was glad to be of service. Goodnight."

After the doctor left the room, Selina turned to her husband. "I need a bit of time to myself. Will you please excuse me?"

He looked searchingly into her face for a moment. "Would you like to talk a bit longer?"

Shaking her head, she said, "I simply need some solitude."

"Very well. I'll check on Percival to make certain he is in good hands before I turn in for the night."

"Thank you."

Selina wore a dressing gown over her night-rail as she sat with the Bible on her lap, staring into the low-burning flames. She should have checked on Percival, yet couldn't seem to make herself rise and take the few steps in that direction at the moment. She felt queasy thinking of the almost unrecognizable man the servants carried into the house only a few hours ago.

She dreaded the sight of blood, yet what kind of selfish creature would think of her own comfort at a moment like this? Selina massaged her temples and admitted to the reason for her hesitation. *He feels nothing like a brother to me. He stole from me and implicated me in the theft!*

Selina shook her head as she picked up her Bible and hugged it to her chest. *And yet he is, indeed, my brother.* She knew she should go and care for him. Fitz said he would check on Percival to be certain he had everything he needed, but what if Percival needed a friend? Could she be a friend to him? Did she want to be?

*No, I don't. I don't trust him.*

"God, please help me love the unlovable—to love Percival —for surely You do."

*Why didn't he take the rubies or the emeralds or even the diamonds? Why the less expensive pearls?* Banging her fist on the armrest, she answered herself out loud. "There is only one reason! He chose the ones with the most sentimental value. My husband's grandmother's jewelry. He wanted to hurt me!"

She stood and paced across the room. "What have I done to make him dislike me so? I have no idea." Pacing to her bed, she fell on her knees. "God, please give me the ability to see him through Your eyes."

She waited, but nothing changed. Her heart was not suddenly overcome with depths of feelings for her brother. Selina slowly walked back to her chair and lifted her Bible off the table. Maybe reading some passages of Scripture might help. After several minutes of reading each sentence over and over again, her mind still refused to grasp the words. She gave up. It was no use.

Setting the Bible aside, Selina stood and squared her shoulders. She already knew what the right thing to do was. She would love her brother whether she felt like it or not.

As she walked toward her brother's room, her feet felt like

they were stuck in molasses. Selina cringed inside at the memory of Percival's badly beaten face. What would she have to face once she walked through those doors? She silently turned the knob. A candle next to the bed cast a low glow over his sleeping form.

On soundless feet, Selina slowly approached the bed. Blood oozed a bit at the corner of his mouth. The fireplace kept the room warm enough that a white sheet was sufficient to keep him comfortable. Pity welled up in her heart for a brother who had everything but was bent on destroying it all.

"Why?" she whispered.

"Did you need me to do something, my lady?"

"Oh!" She'd completely forgotten about the maid. "What did the doctor say we should do for him?"

The maid pointed to the nightstand. "He left laudanum for the pain and to help Lord Runswick sleep. Aside from that, we are to watch for signs of infection, such as fever. The doctor will return tomorrow to check on him."

"Please show me the dosage we are to give him," Selina said. "I want to stay with him. You may go to your room and get some rest."

After the maid left, Selina pulled the chair closer to the bed and laid her hand on her brother's forearm. She prayed for healing so Percival would have time to repent. She prayed God would have mercy on his soul. From what Selina had been told, hell must be a dark, smelly, lonely place of excruciating pain without hope of escape—a place prepared for the devil and demons.

She imagined her brother in such a place—no hope, only screams of agony, loneliness, and deepest darkness . . . forever. She squeezed his hand as though trying to hold him in the room so he could not slip away. Her shoulders began to shake as compassion for her brother filled her. "God, please help Percival while there is time. Save him!" Tears coursed down her face as she wept. "Please, save him before it's too late."

Feeling the exhaustion of the day, Selina leaned forward and placed folded arms on the bed, resting her forehead on top of them. Slumber soon overcame her desire to keep watch.

## *Chapter Twenty-Seven*

He could hear her voice but was too tired to lift his eyelids. *That sounds like Selina. Am I at Henfort? But how? Ah, yes . . . Polly.* It was coming back to him in bits and pieces. Polly must have done as he suggested. Even though Selina knew by now he had stolen her jewelry, she had forgiven him—even prayed for him.

He felt something tickle his arm but heard no sound. Curious, he forced his eyes open a sliver and looked down. Her hair brushed his skin as her head rested on her folded arms.

So trusting. After all that had been done to her, how could she still care? Taking a deep breath, he shut his eyes tight as a searing pain almost suffocated him. *Don't panic. Take shallow breaths.* As the pain slowly subsided, darkness approached but he clung to the feel of her hair on his arm as a lifeline keeping him on this side of eternity. An intense longing gripped his soul.

Selina awoke when the bed shifted. She lifted her head at her brother's moan. Jumping to her feet, she rushed to the medicine bottle and poured the recommended amount of laudanum onto a spoon. She retraced her steps to the bed and faced the dilemma of how to get him to swallow. If she attempted to lift his head, it would surely spill. Gently placing a finger between his lips, she slowly poured the liquid into the opening, watching it seep between his teeth and disappear. She placed her fingers on the front of his neck with the slightest pressure, rubbed up and down, and watched as he swallowed.

Percival hadn't awakened but seemed restless. How could she calm him? Selina recited softly the twenty-third psalm. "The Lord is my Shepherd; I shall not want. He maketh me to lie down in green pastures: he leadeth me beside the still waters." By the time she reached the end of the psalm, the medicine began to take effect. Or perhaps it was the psalm that soothed him. His body relaxed and his breathing became less labored.

"I'm sorry, my lady. With the internal bleeding and now the fever, there isn't much hope for him. Only a miracle can save Lord Runswick now."

Selina sat beside Fitz in the morning room as he clasped her hand in his own. The doctor imparted the grim prognosis, but she wouldn't give up hope. There was nothing too difficult for her heavenly Father.

"Thank you, Doctor. Did Bates ask you to check on Polly, one of our servants? She hasn't been feeling well."

"Yes." He cleared his throat. "I think you should know, she is in the family way."

Selina sensed the slight tightening of Fitz's hand on her own. Although a cacophony of emotions played in her head, she made a valiant effort to show none of it on her face.

"Thank you for your time," Fitz said as he rose from the sofa.

The doctor grabbed his black leather medical bag and stood up. "Yes. Yes, of course. Glad to be of service. Let me know if anything changes with the viscount."

Nodding to Selina, he headed to the door Fitz already held open. Once he departed the room, Fitz closed the door and sat beside Selina once more. "It seems your brother has fathered a child on the wrong side of the blanket."

"We must help her, Fitz. I don't know how, but the child's best interest must be carefully taken into consideration."

* * *

Mrs. Addams stopped at the grocer to pick up a few items on her way home to Henfort after visiting her sister. Since the items were too heavy, she instructed they be delivered as quickly as possible. The grocer was only too happy to comply since Lord FitzWalter was never in arrears for paying his bill.

As the Henfort housekeeper strolled home enjoying the warmth of the sun, she noticed a carriage moving slowly beside her and coming to a stop. She turned her head to see who it might be. The door opened and Lord Moorbridge stuck his head out.

"Mrs. Addams, I'd like a word with you."

Shocked at being addressed by such a lofty lord, she stared at the man. What could such an esteemed person have to say to her? Her tongue seemed unable to move. She simply said, "Yes?"

"Step into the carriage and I will explain myself."

How could she refuse the father of her employer? Had something happened to Lord FitzWalter? Of course, she did as instructed. After seating herself opposite Lord Moorbridge, the door was shut, and the carriage began moving.

"We will take a little ride, shall we? I believe you are in possession of information that will be helpful to me."

## *Chapter Twenty-Eight*

Percival's skin almost burned her hand when she touched it. Selina had to find a way to bring the fever down. Wringing out a cloth after dipping it in cold water, she placed it on his forehead. She then dabbed his lips with another cloth drenched in cold water, allowing some moisture to seep between his parched lips. If she could get him to swallow the liquid, it might help.

"Jesus, we need a miracle," she prayed for what must have been the hundredth time over the past two days.

"S'lena," came the slurred sound from his swollen, chapped lips.

She stared at him for a moment, then leaned closer. "Percival, can you hear me?"

"Wa-ter."

Selina grabbed a glass of water and carefully lifted his head, attempting to spill a bit into his mouth. More fell on the bed, but she saw him swallow before gently placing his head back on the pillow.

"I-I'm sssso…"

What was he trying to say? "It's all right, Percival."

He shook his head and tried again. "I-I'm ssso-rry."

He was sorry? For stealing her necklace? For how he'd treated her all these years? Uncertain what his regret was, she wished to reassure him to keep him still. "I forgive you, Percival." She watched in amazement as a tear squeezed out the corner of his eye, rolling down the side of his face.

Eyes widening, she stared at her brother. What tortured him? He was obviously delirious. She felt helpless in the face of his discomfort and did the only thing left to do. Gently taking Percival's hand, she prayed, "God, have mercy. Please, forgive him and heal him."

"Selina."

She startled awake and lifted her head from her arms that were folded on top of Percival's bed. "Percival?"

"Sshh . . . it's me."

"Oh!" Turning, she saw her husband. "I thought Percival had called out to me."

His lips lifted in a half smile as he shook his head, "You need to rest in your bed. I brought a maid to relieve you for a few hours."

"No, Fitz. I can't leave him. What if he wakes and needs me?"

"You'll become ill and be of no use to him if you don't rest." Holding out his hand to her, she stared at it a moment. "Do as I say, Selina. You will collapse from exhaustion if you continue in this way."

Her limbs felt heavy. She knew Fitz was right. Lifting her hand, she allowed him to pull her out of the chair.

She glanced toward the maid. "Please wake me if he calls for me or worsens in any way."

"Yes, my lady. I will."

"You know the dosage of medication to give him. His last dose was three hours ago."

The maid nodded. "I will take good care of him."

Selina placed a hand over a yawn that tried to escape and mumbled, "Thank you."

Fitz escorted his wife to her bedchamber. Opening the door, he followed her in. "Would you like me to call your maid?"

Selina gently bit her bottom lip. This was the first time her husband stood in her private room since she took possession of it. It felt strange. "No, I can manage. I don't want to wake her."

"And how do you intend to unbutton your dress?"

A blush warmed her cheeks as she looked down at her gown knowing buttons ran down the length of her back. "I-I'm going to leave it on. I'm too tired to move." Hoping to encourage his departure, she quickly added, "Goodnight."

He chuckled softly as he shook his head. "I don't think so, wife. I will play lady's maid for you tonight."

Eyes wide, she yelped, "No!" Selina ignored the amusement on his face and raised her chin. "That's not necessary. Perhaps we should call Lydia after all."

He took the three steps separating them and gently turned her around. Selina jumped when his hand touched her first button.

"My lord! Lydia won't mind."

"Shhh . . . It will only take a minute."

She swallowed hard, stiffening her shoulders.

"Relax, Selina. Don't you trust me?"

"Yes," she squeaked. Closing her eyes in embarrassment, she heard his low chuckle. The brute was enjoying her discomfort!

Her dress began to slip from her shoulders and she quickly crossed her arms over her chest to keep it in place. Feeling a further tug in the middle of her back, she realized he intended to untie her corset. Shocked, she pulled away and turned to face him.

His lips twitched with mirth, "You certainly can't sleep in your corset. Allow me to untie it for you."

"No!" She took a calming breath and lifted her chin. "I can do it myself. You may go now."

His smile broadened and his eyes narrowed. "Don't I get a goodnight kiss?"

"Oh . . ."

Hands behind his back, he leaned close to kiss her cheek. "Goodnight, wife."

Selina could only stare as he walked to the connecting door while whistling a tune. Once it closed behind him, she kept her eyes on the door in case it opened again. It didn't.

"Goodnight," she whispered, as she lifted a hand to touch the cheek his lips had rested upon for the briefest of moments.

* * *

Selina awoke after a surprisingly restful slumber to find a fire gently burning on the grate of the fireplace. After her husband's antics the night before, she'd been certain sleep would evade her. But it seemed exhaustion was more powerful than daydreams, for once her head hit the pillow, she was out.

Lydia handed her a cup of chocolate then left in search of a dress for her mistress to wear. Selina lifted the warm drink and tasted its sweet flavor, licking the froth from her lips. When Lydia returned, Selina asked, "Have you heard anything about my brother this morning?"

"The maid said his skin feels less hot to the touch than before."

"Oh, thank God!" She placed her cup on the nightstand and climbed out of bed. "Please help me prepare, Lydia. I want to see him right away."

"Yes, of course."

After washing, and donning a morning gown, Lydia pulled Selina's hair back in a simple chignon. Once finished, Selina hurried to Percival's room, quietly opened the door, and entered on silent feet. His complexion was pale, but he breathed more easily.

Selina glanced at the maid who rose from her chair in the corner of the room. "Have you given him more medicine recently?"

"Almost two hours ago," the maid answered.

"Then he will sleep a while. Thank you for caring for him through the night. Please go and rest now. We may need you again tonight."

"Very well, my lady." She curtsied and left the room.

Selina drew near her brother's bedside and placed a hand on his forehead. His skin felt cool to the touch. Eyes closing in quiet relief, she whispered, "Thank you, Lord." Not wishing to disturb him further, Selina turned and walked to the window. She pulled the curtain open only slightly to allow a bit of light to enter the room, and gazed at the cloudy sky. "Thank you, Father, for helping him. Your grace and mercy are astounding. There is no one like You."

Selina didn't know how it happened, but she realized while taking care of Percival despite her ambivalent feelings for him, God healed her heart. She loved her brother. It wasn't a love that required reciprocation, but rather an unconditional love. "Lord, fill the emptiness in his heart—that gnawing dissatisfaction that has driven him toward destruction. Please, help my brother."

## *Chapter Twenty-Nine*

Polly sat in a chair in her room when Selina entered after a brief knock. A basket filled with clothes that needed mending sat at her feet, as her nimble fingers worked on a hem.

"Has Mrs. Addams put you to work, Polly? I was unaware you had been re-hired."

Surprised eyes met Selina's. "Oh, my lady!" Polly pushed to her feet.

"Please don't." Selina put out her hand, hoping to stop her. "I will simply sit here on the edge of your bed."

"Oh, no! I will give you the chair."

"That isn't necessary. Please, sit."

Reclaiming her chair somewhat hesitantly, Polly picked up needle and thread once more. "I couldn't stay here without working. After all, I am being fed and have a roof over my head. I begged Mrs. Addams to allow me some work to keep my hands busy."

Selina nodded in understanding. "Since Lord FitzWalter and the detective have already questioned you, you're no longer forced to remain here. What is it you would like to do?"

The maid sighed as she shrugged her shoulders and lowered her eyes to stare down at her hands. "I must have a job, but how can I ask you to rehire me? You certainly cannot trust me after all I've done." Her eyes glistened with tears when she looked up.

"Dr. Herbert informed us you are increasing." Seeing the panic in Polly's eyes, she quickly reassured her. "I want to help you, Polly."

Gawking at Selina, she asked, "Why would you want to help me? I stole from you. I flirted with one of your guests. And now . . ." She placed her hand protectively over her abdomen.

"Is it correct to assume my brother is your baby's father?"

Pink infused her cheeks. "Yes, he is the father. I don't blame you if you don't believe me, but he's the only man I've ever known intimately."

"I would help you even if your child was not Percival's. Since you are carrying my nephew or niece, I would like to get to know your child and provide for it. Do you intend to keep the baby?"

Polly's mouth gaped open. She opened and closed it a few times before finding her voice."Oh, if only it were possible. But I must have employment. How can I raise a child if I have no income? Who will hire a woman in my condition?"

"Do you have any family?"

"No. My father died from war injuries and my mother died last year during the cholera outbreak. There is no one else."

Selina's heart broke for her servant. "I'm sorry for your loss, Polly."

She spoke in a thickened voice. "I saw how my parents suffered without proper medical care. I wanted more for myself. Look where that's gotten me." Polly stared down at her clenched hands as she shook her head and spoke through clenched teeth. "What a fool I was to hope for more. This is my lot and I must learn to accept it."

"You must stay here then. I will talk to Bates and Mrs. Addams."

Eyes wide, Polly stared in disbelief. "Do you mean it? You will allow me to continue working here?" At Selina's nod, Polly placed a hand over her heart. "You have no idea how much you have relieved my mind." Tilting her head, she asked, "What about the baby?"

"Your baby will also stay, but I will have to talk to my

husband about it first. Please give me your word you will stay faithful to our family. Can I trust you, Polly?"

"I know I've given you little reason to trust me, but I give you my word that I will be loyal to you from here on out. If you will allow me to be near my child, I will do anything you ask of me."

Selina arose. "Take good care of yourself. I will have the doctor check on you regularly as your pregnancy progresses."

"You are too kind, my lady." When Selina got up to leave, Polly hurriedly stood to her feet and asked, "How is Lord Runswick? Please excuse my impertinence, but I heard from the servants he was hurt badly and might not . . . survive." She hugged her arms close and rubbed her hands up and down.

Selina gently placed her hand on Polly's forearm. "I must apologize for not informing you sooner."

"Oh, no, ma'am! You owe me nothing."

"But I do. You obviously care for my brother." Polly's eyes dropped to the floor as pink suffused her cheeks. "Please, don't be embarrassed about your feelings. The doctor gave us a grim prognosis about Percival's condition, but God has given him a second chance. His fever broke and he is showing signs of improvement."

A smile lit the maid's face. "I'm glad to hear it. I prayed he would recover."

"You did?"

Her shoulders slumped in defeat as she said, "I doubt God heard my prayers. I haven't spoken to him since Mama died, but I was so scared for Percival."

"God heard you, Polly."

She shook her head in denial, "I doubt God listens to a lightskirt."

"God's love is everlasting and reaches higher, deeper, and wider than any one of us can comprehend. I have no doubt God loves you and heard your prayer."

A tear rolled down Polly's cheek. She wiped it away with the back of her hand. "My mama told me about God all my growing up years, and I believed her. But when He let her die, my faith died, too." Polly took a deep breath and let it out in a huff. "Trying to do things my own way didn't work. I still don't understand why He allowed Mama to die, but I know I can't make it on my own." She placed a hand on her abdomen. "I wonder if God sometimes allows us to come to the end of ourselves, so we will learn we cannot do it without Him."

"I believe you're right. At least, that is how it was with me also." Selina's smile broadened. "I'm so happy to know you believe. Do you realize we are now sisters in Christ?"

"Oh, ma'am . . . I would never presume . . ."

"Nevertheless, it is true. I do not want you to fret about your future. We will both pray about it. Who knows what God has in store for you?"

For some time now, Fitz contemplated resigning his position at the Home Office. He desired to give more time to his wife and other obligations. This morning, as he looked forward to seeing Selina at breakfast, a note from the Home Office put a spoke in his plan. He was forced to leave before anyone awoke.

After another trying day of ironing out governmental difficulties, Fitz presented his letter of resignation. He felt no regret. He could finally focus on his estate. But that wasn't the cause for the lightness in his step and the outrageous desire to grin at everyone he passed on his way home.

Fitz bit down on a smile that wanted to burst forth as he remembered his visit to his wife's bedchamber the previous evening. Helping her unbutton her gown and attempting to loosen her corset had nearly undone him. He wasn't surprised when she pushed him away, but he couldn't resist teasing her.

As much as he longed for a real marriage, the timing was all wrong. Her brother lay at death's door and she was exhausted. Walking away last night expended every bit of self-control he could muster. It also made clear to him the depth of his affection. He realized he cared more about her well-being than his own.

Fitz replayed Emma's words to him at the Templeton Ball

over and over again. Selina had remained loyal to him, defending him in spite of the evidence staring her in the face from the gossip sheet. When the constable made his ridiculous accusations, instead of causing him to doubt her, they had quite the opposite effect. Fitz knew he finally found a woman he could trust. His wife was incapable of such unfaithfulness. Her word could be trusted—always.

He was determined to woo Selina and slowly win her heart as she had already won his. Eventually, his patience would pay off. He wanted Selina to come to him because she longed to do so, and not because she felt it her duty.

Whistling while walking along the dim road lit only by moonlight, he anticipated seeing his wife. Hopefully, she was still awake.

The bedchamber lay in complete darkness except for the flicker of a low-burning candle next to the bed. A quilt covered Percival as he rested peacefully.

Fitz had not returned from the Home Office in time for dinner, so Selina dined alone. Although she enjoyed solitude for reading and writing, and relished walking alone or working in the garden by herself, the one thing she could not bear doing in solitude was eating a meal at the long dining room table intended for a crowd. She should have asked for a tray to be sent to her room.

As soon as the meal was over, Selina made her way to her brother's bedchamber to see if there was any change in his condition. She dismissed the maid and sat in the chair next to his bed.

Why hadn't he awakened yet? The fever broke hours ago.

"Percival, can you hear me?" She gasped when his eyes fluttered, but they remained shut.

Stroking his arm, Selina said, "It's all right if you cannot bring yourself to wake up yet. Perhaps, you need more time to regain strength." She picked up the Bible on his nightstand and turned to the Book of Psalms. "I'll just read a psalm aloud."

As she read, she became lost in the words on the page, so poetic and lovely. Reading David's words of praise and seeing his complete trust in God lifted her spirit. "There is nothing too difficult for you, Father. Please, help Percival."

With eyes shut, she sat in quiet meditation for a few moments. Slowly, she opened them again to find her brother's brown ones staring back at her. "Percival! You're awake!"

"Selina?" His voice was raspy from disuse, but she could understand him.

Leaning closer, she placed a hand on his arm. "I'll get you some water."

She poured a glass, then placed an arm under his head to help support it as he drank a bit.

Percival watched her closely, his brow puckered in puzzlement. "Am I at Henfort?"

"Yes."

"How did I get here? I can't believe I survived."

"It seems God, in His mercy, gave you another chance."

He nodded as he narrowed his eyes. "Are you aware of what I've done?"

"Yes, Polly told us of the stolen jewelry."

His eyes shut tightly for a moment. When he looked at her again, the agony in his eyes chilled her.

"I've forgiven you, Percival. I don't know why you chose to steal the pearls except to hurt me, but I have chosen to forgive you."

"Of course you forgive me," he huffed. "You even forgave our parents for selling you and you forgave your husband for meeting with his old love." Smiling unkindly, he said, "Does nothing hurt you enough to become bitter? Must you always remain amiable?"

"You have certainly tried to test my limit." She frowned at her brother. "When they brought you here, I wanted to leave you to the care of the maids, whether they did a good job or not. I didn't want to be bothered with your care. You purposely tried to hurt me, and I was not unaware of it." Swallowing hard, she gazed at him with tear-filled eyes. "I felt bitter, Percival, but I hated the feeling. I went to the only One who could help me. I had no idea how He would do it, but I trusted God could help me. Do you know how He did it?"

Percival peered at her, frowning, but didn't say anything, so she continued. "It was when I came to your room and sent the maid away. When I wiped your brow and moistened your chapped lips with a wet cloth. It was while I was caring for you, that the bitterness fled."

Selina sat still as her brother stared at her with his jaw clenched tight. She could see a battle raging in his eyes to his very soul. At the knock on the door, he blinked and his eyes became devoid of emotion once more.

"Come in," he said.

Mrs. Addams opened the door and ushered the constable into the room.

"Excuse me, my lady, but Constable Jones is here to see Lord Runswick." The man pushed his way into the room.

Selina stood up and stared at the man. "At this hour? My brother has been gravely ill and is still quite weak. This is not a good time, Constable. Surely, whatever you wish to ask can wait a few more days."

"I find it interesting that you, Lady FitzWalter, wish to protect the man who framed you for a theft," he sneered. "You are both suspects in the murder of your parents. Do you need time to devise a plan?"

Percival watched as Selina narrowed her eyes. He couldn't believe this fool suspected his sister of murder. "What evidence do you have against my sister, Constable? It must be solid for you to dare point a finger at the daughter-in-law of the Earl of Moorbridge."

"Oh, it's solid. This little witch has fooled most of you. She is sweetness on the outside, spouting her religious nonsense, but has a bitter and vengeful heart."

The man seemed only too happy to accuse Selina. "Tell me of your proof. That is, *if* you have any."

"Lord Runswick, I know *you* weren't taken in by Lady FitzWalter's schemes since you obviously hated her enough to steal from her. I'm glad she was unable to deceive *someone* in this family. You want proof? I'll give it to you." Raising a finger, the constable said, "Your sister was so embittered by your parents' actions, she decided to kill them." He lifted his second finger and added. "She hired two ruffians to do the job for her. We caught the men. They admitted she hired them to kill her parents."

"What?" Selina's brow furrowed as she stared in disbelief. "No. That's not true."

"The truth has been revealed," sneered the constable. "I am about to seal your coffin. I only came to ask your brother a couple of questions to wrap up my case."

Constable Jones definitely had it in for his sister. He probably offered those killers a lesser sentence if they would confess to being hired by her. Of course, those two would say anything to save their skin. Percival realized he could actually go free, but at what cost?

He knew the truth. She was innocent. Her faith was real. Even with such accusations thrown at her, she was not in despair. Certainly, distressed, but seemingly not lacking hope.

"What are your questions, Constable Jones?" Percival asked.

"Where were you the night your parents were killed?"

"I was in Newmarket, at a horse race."

"And why is it you never trusted your sister? Why did you frame her for stealing and pawning her husband's family heirlooms?"

Percival looked into Selina's hurting eyes. He had spoken cruel words to her often enough that it seemed she braced herself for the worst. Instead of answering the constable, he addressed his sister. "You said you found healing by caring for me while I was sick." She hesitantly nodded just once, obviously uncertain of what he would say next. "I want to be healed of my bitterness also."

Percival pierced Constable Jones with his eyes. "It was never an issue of trust. My sister is the most trustworthy person I know. I framed her because of my greed. She had everything I longed for. I was jealous of her wealth!"

"That's certainly disappointing," the constable frowned. "I will admit, I'd hoped you had additional evidence to offer. Doesn't matter though. I have enough proof to bring this witch to trial."

"No, you don't," Percival said with deadly calm. He saw Selina's eyes widen. "I happen to know those two killers lied. Did you promise them a lesser sentence if they named Lady FitzWalter as the murderer?"

"Are you insinuating I interfered with justice? That I bribed those villains?"

"I'm saying, for some reason you have something against Lady FitzWalter. I don't know why, but this case is personal to you. I wonder if you mishandled the questioning of the scoundrels you bargained with." Shifting his gaze to the housekeeper, he said, "I would also like to know, Mrs. Addams, how the constable got past Bates tonight? Why are you helping him?"

"I-I'm not!" The flustered housekeeper seemed unable to make eye contact. "He's an official! Bates was occupied, so I answered the door. I-I thought I must do as he said."

"It's quite all right," Selina soothed. "What's done is done. You may show the constable out, as he will be leaving now."

"*I* will say when I am ready to depart."

"It seems you have no real proof, Constable. My husband will be home shortly. Would you care to wait for him in the drawing room? I'm certain he would like to hear this evidence you've found. Mrs. Addams will show you out."

"I'm not waitin' around for Lord FitzWalter. You will hear from me again soon."

"Thank you for defending me," Selina said when they were alone again.

"I couldn't bring myself to cause you more hurt. When he called you a witch, I felt deeply the injustice of such an accusation against someone who has only shown me kindness. Instead of treating me as the enemy, you nursed me back to health and prayed for me. I couldn't let him accuse you." Smiling self-deprecatingly, he said, "It actually felt good being the nice guy for a change. I may very well have done something unselfish for the first time in my life. Sad, isn't it?"

Selina saw clearly the agony of his soul. Before her sat a

man who had looked death in the face and, as his life flashed before him, felt only deep sorrow and regret. "Percival, you can be free of all guilt and bitterness. God will forgive you and set you free. He will even give you a brand new start."

He shook his head. "How can I be forgiven? How is it even possible? Selina, you have no idea what I've done."

A chill went up her spine. She had a premonition what he was about to reveal. It was what she had suspected, but was pleased to remain in denial. Frozen in place, she couldn't stop his words.

He squeezed his eyes shut as he clenched the bedsheet in his hands. When he looked at her again, his face contorted in anguish. "In a drunken stupor, I planned the death of my own parents."

"No!" Selina cried, as she placed a hand over her mouth.

Carefully lifting a hand, he rubbed it over his forehead. "How I wish it weren't true." His voice shook. "When the ruffians I hired approached me for the reward I'd promised them, I realized what I'd done. To my horror, it was too late. There was no turning back." Tears rolled down his face and he squeezed his lips together, trying to stop them from quivering. "I felt sick. I was in a nightmare from which it was impossible to awaken. How could I live with myself?" He shook his head. "I couldn't, so I reached for another bottle wanting to slack the pain." His tears fell in earnest and his sobs filled the room. Percival spoke through his tears. "I can't live with myself! How did I survive the beating? I should have died!"

Selina sat in shock. Her brother murdered their parents. *God, help me. I don't know what to say. Should I call the constable back?* As her brother's shoulders shook and sobs wracked his body, compassion stirred her heart. Jesus died for the worst of sinners. She felt terribly inadequate at the moment. How she wished there was a preacher in the room to help her brother.

"Percival, please listen to me." She spoke calmly, although inside she was screaming. "Did you know Jesus hung on the cross between two criminals? One of them repented and Jesus saved him from his sins. He will do the same for you."

"I killed my parents, Selina! How can I ever be forgiven? I don't deserve to be forgiven!"

"No one deserves forgiveness. Jesus didn't die for our sins because we deserved it. He did it because He loves us. He knew you would one day need forgiveness, and that's why He died for you. It has nothing to do with deserving, but everything to do with the depth of love He has for those He created. Jesus wants to save you."

He took a shuddering breath and lifted his hands to wipe the tears away.

Selina handed him a handkerchief.

"Thank you." After wiping his eyes and cheeks, he lowered his arms to his side and stared at her. "I cannot fathom how this is possible. But I'm desperate, Selina! I can't live with the guilt, but I'm afraid of dying. I heard a street preacher talk about what hell will be like. I don't want to go there! If Jesus has already paid the price for my sins, then I want what He paid for."

"All you need to do is ask for forgiveness. Pray to Jesus and repent of your sins. Ask Him to come into your life. When he has set you free, then obey Him so you will not fall back into your old habits again."

Percival nodded and shut his eyes. He began praying. "Jesus, I certainly don't know how You can love me. Why You would die for someone like me. But Selina says it is so. You know what I've done. It pains me to list my sins to you. There are many. I regret them all, but mostly," his voice broke and his sobs kept him from continuing. Through his tears, he cried, "I killed my parents. Mama and Papa! Oh, God, I can't believe I killed my parents!" He covered his eyes with his arm and the sobs wracked his entire body. "Forgive me. Pl-please f-forgive me!"

Selina placed a hand on his shoulders, praying silently with him. She could only imagine the depths of despair and regret when one was guilty of such depravity. *Please take the broken pieces of my brother's ruined life, and create something beautiful in its place.*

When the tears finally slowed, he lowered his arm, folded his hands, and finished his prayer. "God, I'm astonished to hear Selina say you're giving away forgiveness for free. But if it is so, I want my part. Please, forgive me. Come into my heart and be the Lord of my life. I desire to be Your humble servant. Amen."

"Amen," he heard his sister whisper.

Percival lay completely still. Something had changed. He couldn't remember his heart ever feeling so light. Holding his breath a moment he anticipated the heaviness to return, but it didn't. *I'm free!* Looking at his sister, his eyes filled with wonder. Overwhelmed, his face crumbled and he threw an arm over his eyes as sobs wracked his frame.

"Percival, what's wrong?"

He heard her concern and tried valiantly to stop the tears. He took a deep, shuddering breath and finally pulled himself together. Turning toward his sister, he gave her a shaky smile.

Selina's eyes opened wide. "Percival?"

He nodded. "I'm a new person, Selina. I don't know how it's possible, but I'm free! Come what may, I am free! If I hang, I am still free! I've been forgiven!" He laughed as more tears gathered in his eyes. "I don't know whether to laugh or cry."

Selina leaned forward and carefully embraced her brother ever mindful of his wounds. His one good arm held her close as her tears soaked his shirt.

When they finally pulled apart, they both smiled in complete abandonment. Percival suddenly yawned.

"You're tired," Selina said. "Get some rest. I'll return later to check on you."

"I won't argue there. I'm exhausted, but can't remember ever having such peace before. Thank you, Selina. I love you."

Her lips quivered with emotion. "I love you, too, Percival."

Too stirred up to sleep, Selina headed to the library in search of a book. Fitz sat in one of the upholstered chairs, his feet propped up on a low table, as he browsed through the newspaper he hadn't had time to read that morning.

"Fitz, you're home!"

Looking up in surprise, he dropped his feet to the floor and stood. "Selina! I thought you were asleep already."

Remembering the night before, her cheeks grew warm and she felt shy. "I-I wanted a book to read, but I don't wish to disturb you."

Quickly walking toward her before she could turn and leave the room, Fitz said, "You can never disturb me. Come. I would love some company." Placing a warm hand on her back, he led her to a chair. Fitz sat in the armchair facing her.

When he asked about her day, she told him all that had transpired in her brother's room.

"What was Mrs. Addams thinking to allow the man above stairs without first receiving approval from one of us? She is too well trained for such a mistake."

"I know, Fitz, but she seemed overwhelmed by the man's authority. Let's overlook it this time, shall we?"

"You are too kind sometimes, Selina."

"Please, Fitz."

"Very well. Although I find her behavior unacceptable, I will do as you say, this time."

"Thank you. Now, let me tell you the rest."

"There's more? You've had quite an evening."

"I most certainly have," she said, smiling broadly. At the rise of his brows, she told him of her brother's conversion. Fitz's face became more stoic as she spoke. "He was completely transformed, Fitz. I've never seen anything quite like it. All the evil in him just left! Darkness fled and only light remained."

Fitz nodded with a tight expression on his face.

"You don't believe me?"

"I'm not skeptical of you, Selina. It's Percival I cannot trust. He's a manipulator. Could he be playing on your emotions? What if this is a scheme he concocted to try to escape his punishment?"

Her shoulders slumped. She'd been excited and animated about what had just taken place in her brother, but Fitz's words tossed cold water on her enthusiasm. Reaching across, he placed a hand on hers, giving it a slight squeeze.

"It's not that I don't want to believe you, but your brother has had much practice in manipulating people. I need to see him for myself."

She nodded. "Yes, you should pay him a visit. I know you will agree that he's changed."

"You do realize, don't you, that even if it's true and he has truly become a believer, he must still face his punishment?"

"Yes, of course." She pulled her hand out from under his. "And he knows it, too. He told me, even if he hangs, he is still free. God has forgiven him and he won't have to face eternal damnation. That's what seemed to plague Percival the most. His eternal destiny." Her eyes glistened with unshed tears. "Fitz, it was truly wonderful!"

He nodded thoughtfully. "I'll check on him in the morning. Now, I have some news for you also."

Tilting her head, she asked, "What is it?"

"I've resigned my position at the Home Office."

"You did? Why?"

"For a few reasons."

When he said nothing further, she asked, "Will you not share them with me?"

"This wasn't an easy decision to make since I've been in the Home Office for quite some time now." His elbows rested on the arms of the chair as he steepled his index fingers and touched them to his chin. "One of my reasons for resigning was that I wanted to invest more time in my estate. I've left it all to my steward, but look forward to more closely overseeing the running of it." He lowered his hands. "As a matter of fact, as soon as this whole mess with Percival is cleared up, I'd like us to move back to Thorncrest until spring."

She inwardly cringed, knowing her family was the reason Fitz was stuck in Town longer than he wished to be. But she didn't want him to know how his words affected her. The Kendall family was a mess. He wasn't wrong in saying so.

"I'd like that, too," Selina said.

"Would you? Are you certain you won't miss the balls and entertainments in the city?"

"I enjoyed the entertainments, of course, but the newness

of it has worn off. Certainly, you are not unaware that I'm somewhat of an introvert. The country suits me better than the city ever could."

A smile lurked on his lips as he gazed into her warm brown eyes. "I like you just the way you are."

Selina's cheeks warmed and she felt breathless as his eyes lowered to her lips. Nervous suddenly, she gazed down at her folded hands. Unable to look into his face, she asked, "What are your other reasons for resigning?"

"Actually, they concern you."

Her eyes shot to his face. "Me? What do you mean?"

"It just so happens I've become quite fascinated by a certain brunette who sways her hips when she sashays around my home."

Her mouth must have hung open. "I do *not* walk in such a manner, my lord!"

He grinned and waggled his eyebrows.

Choosing to ignore his provocation, she rolled her eyes. "Surely you jest. Let's get back to the subject at hand. How was I one of the reasons for your resignation?"

His lips twitched at the corners as his eyes filled with mirth. "I have come to realize the Home Office has taken too much of the time I'd prefer spending with my wife. I'd like to attend balls and entertainments with you rather than having you accompanied by others." Fitz leaned across and took her hand once more. "Selina, I desire to know you better and I want you to get to know me as well."

Inhaling a swift breath, she stared at her husband. Could it be he was falling in love with her? No, he said "desire." He was letting her know he was ready to consummate the marriage. That must be it. Deeper feelings were not involved. She knew he waited for a response from her, but what should she say? "I-I'm glad."

"You are?"

Forcing shyness aside, she lifted her face to gaze fully into his eyes. "I look forward to spending time with you, too." There. She said it. Now he must know she would not deny him access to her bedchamber.

His smile broadened. "Then I must tell you my third

reason for resigning."

Her brows raised in question. "Oh?"

"I think it's time I provide my estate with an heir and, thereby, help my father become less anxious about the future of his title."

So she had been correct. This was not about love, but about obtaining an heir and fulfilling an obligation. Blushing to the roots of her hair, she looked down at her hands but heard him chuckle softly.

"Selina, you are delightful! I certainly enjoy teasing you."

Lifting her eyes again, she tilted her head as her brow furrowed. "You're only teasing? You don't want an heir?"

"Of course I want us to have children, but first I want to get to know you. I want to enjoy our marriage, just the two of us, before we add children. Nevertheless, they will be most welcome when they decide to make an appearance."

She smiled uncertainly and nodded her head in agreement.

Fitz stood to his feet and pulled her up with him. Drawing her close, he said, "I've thought of doing this all day today." Slowly, he lowered his head to place firm lips on her upraised ones. When they pulled apart, she laid her head on his shoulder and he leaned his cheek on the top of her head. A sigh of contentment escaped her lips. It felt wonderful to be held thus.

## *Chapter Thirty*

Juliet and Helena arrived for tea the following afternoon. Fitz had already explained to Juliet's husband about Percival's confession and conversion, so her sisters were aware of it.

"This morning, he asked for a Bible."

"Is he sincere or looking for a way to manipulate you?" Juliet asked.

The corner of Selina's mouth lifted as she rolled her eyes and shook her head. "You and Fitz have both responded alike, but I assure you, he is sincere."

"I'll have to see the change for myself," Juliet said. "Forgive me, Selina, but I've known Percival many years longer than you. I feel justified in being skeptical."

Selina saw Helena nodding in agreement.

She couldn't blame them for doubting their brother. " Very well. You will see he is sincere, eventually."

Juliet had a pained look on her face as she said, "If it's true, then it's not fair that a cold-blooded killer, even if he is our brother, should so easily be pardoned."

"Percival said the same thing. But don't think for a moment he will not have to face his punishment here on earth."

"Yes, you're right. And he will deserve it. I've struggled half the night trying to forgive him as I know I ought. And I thought I had, but the anger surfaces at unexpected moments." Juliet glared. "Whenever I see Mama and Papa's faces in my mind, I long to tear out Percival's hair strand by strand!"

Selina's eyes welled up with tears. "Sometimes you have to forgive more than once. When the hurt re-enters your thoughts, causing emotions to stir up once more, you have to forgive again. You keep choosing to forgive."

Helena's shoulders shook as tears rolled down her cheek, but she didn't share her thoughts.

Juliet dabbed a handkerchief to her red-rimmed eyes and sighed. "Like you had to forgive Mama and Papa for sending you away while keeping the rest of us."

Selina visibly swallowed before answering. The sadness in her heart spilled into her eyes and caused her lip to quiver. "Yes. Just like that."

"Selina, this isn't the same," Helena protested. "I understand how difficult it must have been for you to forgive Mama and Papa, but our brother murdered our parents."

Selina reached over to rest a gentle hand on Helena's knee. "You're right. It's not the same. But knowing Percival was drunk when he arranged their deaths and not in his right mind has helped me to some degree." Helena's jaw tightened, so Selina moved her hand away. "I saw the agony our parents' death has caused him and I cannot help feeling sorry for him."

"What about Mama and Papa?" Juliet asked. "We don't even know if they were ready to face eternity. It isn't right, Selina."

"No, it isn't right and it isn't fair. I only know from Scripture that God is just. I'm clinging to that."

"Stupid Percival! Why did he drink again?" Juliet scowled. "He was *not* unaware of how it affected him."

Not wishing to tell her sisters of the theft of her jewelry and heap more condemnation on their brother, Selina said, "Probably the same reason others gossip and overspend simply to fit into society." Seeing her sister wince, Selina added, "And the same reason I was obsessed with returning to my family and could think of nothing else until I received what I longed for. We desperately tried to fill the emptiness in our souls, and couldn't."

Helena's lovely face was marred by frown lines between her eyebrows as she stared toward the window with her jaw clenched tight.

Juliet sat staring at her hands, her brow furrowed. When she lifted her gaze to Selina, she said, "If God truly has forgiven him, I can only stand in wonder at God's amazing grace."

Selina nodded. "Yes. I wish you could have been in the room. He sobbed as he told me all he'd done. He was a broken man with no hope in sight. But after he prayed, what a difference!"

"I must see him for myself!" Juliet said.

"But what about Gracebourne Manor?" Helena wanted to know. "Percival will have to face his punishment, which will certainly mean he will have to leave England. Who will inherit Papa's title and estate?"

"I'm not certain, Helena." Juliet sighed. "I believe there is a distant cousin next in line to inherit, but must we speak of it now? Can it not wait?"

Helena shrugged her shoulder. "I suppose."

"Percival," Juliet's voice caught on her brother's name causing her to swallow as she dabbed the corners of her eyes. "You seem changed—in every way. Your countenance—it's as though a hard outer shell has crumbled away."

Tears glistened in his eyes as he smiled. "I'm glad you are able to see what I feel on the inside. I never want to be the man I was before."

Helena stood to the side, watching her brother closely, apparently unwilling to move near.

"Do you realize how many people are as miserable as I was? They live life with a gnawing emptiness inside, not understanding that God can fill that void. They don't know about the free gift, having never heard." Percival's face looked pained as he described the hopelessness of so many. "If I had my days to live over, I would be happiest telling people about God."

"Let's not lose hope yet," Juliet said, as she reached over

to squeeze Percival's hand. "Perhaps a judge will listen to your full story and offer a lesser sentence."

"If they choose to transport me, it would not be a hardship. I am determined to share the good news of salvation wherever I go as long as I have breath. But first . . ." He turned to Selina. "Do you know where Polly is? I must apologize to her."

"She's in the servants' quarters here at Henfort."

"Is she?" His face lit up. "I must see her. Would you ask her if she will come to my room? You must stay with us for propriety's sake, of course. I only wish to apologize."

"I think she will be relieved to see you. She was quite worried. Fearing you might end your life gave her the courage to return to Henfort and ask for our help."

Percival nodded. "She wasn't far off. By searching for those villains, I was hoping they would do the deed for me. How grateful I am that Fitz found me." Looking each of his sisters in the face, he sighed heavily. "I deeply regret what I did to Mama and Papa." His lips trembled and he took a deep breath to compose himself. "If only I could reverse time and know what I know now, I would make quite different choices." He swiped a tear away with the back of his hand. "I will forever regret ripping your parents away from you." Peering into Helena's eyes, although addressing all of them, Percival said, "I only pray you will one day be able to truly forgive me."

Helena lifted her chin and turned her back, walking the few steps to the window. She moved the curtain aside and stared out, seemingly wishing to be anywhere but in this room.

Juliet stood and leaned over to hug her brother. "I forgive you already, Percival. My heart grieves their loss, but it grieves for you, also."

"Thank you, Juliet."

Selina walked over and placed a kiss on his cheek, whispering in his ear, "Give Helena time. She needs to heal." His eyes looked pained, but he nodded.

Polly was overjoyed to hear Percival was improving. When

Selina told her he wished to see her, she couldn't imagine why. What a very peculiar family. They should have sent her packing for several reasons. She had stolen from them and allowed herself to be set up as a courtesan. She had lied to them. And now she was carrying Lord Runswick's by-blow.

Instead of the family behaving as expected, Polly was astonished to find herself continuing to reside under the roof of Henfort, and now being invited above stairs to visit with Lord Runswick, Lady FitzWalter herself chaperoning them. A most peculiar family, indeed.

But Polly consistently prayed. And wasn't it just like her mother had told her? God cared deeply for her and would walk beside her if she would only trust in Him. Her mother also said God would take the broken pieces of their lives and fashion them into something beautiful. If only she had believed her mother's words, she could have been spared much heartache. Whatever the outcome of this meeting, Polly was determined to walk in faith and trust God for her future and the future of her child.

Polly entered the room on hesitant feet, uncertain of what might transpire. She stared at the man sitting in bed in a nightshirt and robe, recognizable but much changed. The bruising was still rather pronounced, but the swelling was almost gone. It was the smile reaching into his eyes that changed his appearance the most. She tilted her head in question.

"Good evening, Polly. Thank you for coming to see me."

It was early evening. The servants hadn't partaken of supper yet. She would join them later.

Polly nodded and responded simply, "My lord."

His smile dimmed as he winced. He took a deep breath. "I'm terribly ashamed and sorry for the way I treated you, Polly. I was an imbecile, consumed with myself and my needs." Running a hand through his hair, he looked toward the corner of the room as he said, "I used you like I used everyone around me—to acquire happiness or wealth—and I failed miserably." He peered into her eyes. "I'm sorry I involved you in stealing Selina's jewelry, and I'm sorry for taking advantage of your vulnerability."

He clenched his jaw tight, and Polly was astounded to find tears filling his eyes.

"I was a miserable excuse for a man and behaved quite ungentlemanly toward you."

She couldn't believe this was the same person. Her brow furrowed as she studied him. "You seem so changed. What happened?"

As Percival explained to her what he had done and how he was responsible for his parents' death, Polly finally understood the depths of his despair and the deep agony she had seen in his eyes the evening she departed from the cottage. He also told her about how God had changed him.

"I would like to make it up to you for how I misused you, but I don't know how at the moment. I have some money I can give you, but it isn't nearly enough."

She placed a hand over her abdomen, and shrugged her shoulders. "How can you help me when you will most likely be stripped of your title and possibly deported to some faraway land? But don't let it worry you. Your sister has generously offered to assist me, for which I am deeply grateful."

Percival's eyes went to Polly's hand placed protectively over her belly, then up to her face. "Polly?" He knew he was staring. Was it possible? Of course, it was. Unable to ask her outright, she seemed to understand.

Polly raised her chin and said, "Yes."

He squeezed his eyes shut and took another deep, calming breath. "That is a surprise." He gazed at her again and saw before him a young, helpless maid. What would become of her and their child? "It never occurred to me you might become in the family way. Foolish of me, I know. But there you have it." Staring into her eyes, he said, "This is quite a shock. If you will give me a day to think about it, I will find a way to help you."

"I don't see how you can, Percival. But rest assured that I have embraced the same faith as you since our goodbye. God has provided for me through your sister's compassionate heart." Her eyes shone as she glanced at

Selina. Polly shifted her gaze back to Percival. "I will pray for you. I know you were unaware of what you were doing where your parents were concerned, but you must still face the consequences. I pray it will go well for you." She curtsied and made to turn away.

"Wait, Polly! Please."

She spun back with raised brows.

"Will you visit me again? Tomorrow?"

She shrugged her shoulders. "If you wish it and if Lady FitzWalter allows it."

"I do wish it, Polly. Thank you."

Smiling gently, Selina said, "And I will allow it."

After Polly left the room, Percival asked Selina. "Did you know?"

She didn't pretend to misunderstand. "Yes, but I didn't think it was my place to inform you."

"Would you please bid Fitz to see me when he has the chance? I have an idea. But I will need to talk it through with your husband."

"Yes, of course, I will. Now, if you will excuse me, I need to prepare for supper." There was a brief knock at the door before a maid entered carrying a tray. "Ah, here is your supper now. Goodnight, Percival."

"Goodnight, Selina."

## *Chapter Thirty-One*

"Percival has improved. He said his ribs only hurt a little now," Selina informed Fitz as they partook of breakfast.

"It's five weeks since we found him. The physician said it would take up to six weeks to heal. It seems your brother is recovering nicely."

"When I think of how he looked when you brought him home and how he looks today, I am amazed at the transformation."

"I think the greatest healing took place in his heart. Your brother is fairly unrecognizable from before."

Smiling, Selina nodded in agreement. "How wonderful that you were able to locate the Reverend Geoffrey Brown, the street preacher Percival kept talking about. They study the Scriptures three times a week. I believe my brother has a better understanding of the Bible than I do at this point." She placed her silverware on her plate and folded her hands. "I've been afraid to ask, but do you know what is to become of Percival?"

"Not yet. I believe we will hear something soon." Fitz placed his hand on top of hers. "Please don't fret. I think it will all work out as it should. I'll let you know as soon as I hear something definite."

She sighed and nodded. "Very well. I will continue waiting." She picked up her fork to resume eating.

"And while you're waiting, would you care to join me for a constitutional this morning?"

Her eyes lit up. "Yes, I'd like that."

Taking her free hand, he raised it to his lips and placed a kiss on the back of it. "Have I mentioned I find you enormously pretty, my dear?"

That evening, Percival insisted he was well enough to join them for dinner in the dining room. "It feels good to finally leave my room," Percival said as he slowly lowered himself on the chair.

Fitz sat at the head of the long dining room table while Percival sat to his right and Selina to his left. "I'm glad you've recovered well," Fitz said.

They spoke about mundane things over dinner. Afterward, as they sat before the fire in the drawing room, Percival announced, "Selina, I have some astonishing news I must share with you. It's something the Reverend Brown told me about our parents."

Selina's brows shot up. "Our parents? I can't imagine he was in any way connected to them."

He nodded in agreement. "I was as surprised as you. It turns out that Father heard Reverend Brown preaching only a week before the accident. He sent a message to the reverend inviting him to their home where he shared the message of salvation in greater detail." Percival's eyes filled with tears and he visibly swallowed.

Selina's heart beat faster. Could it be that her parents were saved? Watching her brother fight back his emotions caused her own eyes to glisten.

Percival's voice shook. "Father knelt with the reverend and asked Jesus into his life that very day. He asked the reverend to stay and explain it to Mother, also." Swallowing hard, he continued sharing what he'd heard. "Mother said she had seen such a change in Juliet since she began attending church with her husband. She longed for the same peace and contentment both you and Juliet seemed to have. And then . . ." Percival looked away as he pinched his lips together for a moment.

Fitz and Selina stayed quiet, allowing him time to compose himself. She fought back her own tears, amazed at what she was hearing.

Percival spoke through his tears. "They asked the reverend to pray with them . . . for me." At this, he began to sob into his hands.

Selina hurried over, knelt before him, and pulled him into her arms. Brother and sister cried on each other's shoulders. How it must pain Percival to know he had caused their death. The death of the parents who cared enough to pray for him. At the same time, it must thrill his heart to know they loved him that much in spite of the way he had treated them. Bittersweet tears wet her shoulder as she hugged him close.

Pulling away, he wiped the moisture with the palms of his hands. "I know I'm forgiven, but I will forever regret what I did to them."

Selina took her brother's moist hands into her own and bowed to kiss the back of each one. "I love you, Percival." She gazed into his eyes. "God gave us the gift of knowing our parents are in a better place. Let's not look back. I'm certain God has a plan for your life and there is much to look forward to now."

His eyes glistened as he sniffed and nodded. "You're right. I will resist living in the past."

When Fitz entered his study the following morning, his eyes immediately landed on the envelope in the middle of the desk. There was no need to open it. He knew who had sent it. This was the sixth letter since the day of his wedding and it would remain unopened like the rest.

His father was unrelenting. The man was not to be trusted and Fitz was certain this letter would be filled with continued lies and manipulations.

He had made it plain to his father that he wanted nothing more to do with him. Of course, it didn't surprise him that Moorbridge gave no heed to his request. Everything must always be as his father wished it. No exceptions. Not even his choice of a bride.

He was honest enough with himself to admit his father had chosen well. Fitz's fist pounded the envelope still sitting on the desk. "That's beside the point!" he said to himself. It could just as easily have gone all wrong. His father had no way of knowing Selina would make him a good wife. The only thing that mattered to the high and mighty Lord Moorbridge was his title and estate.

*Forgive him,* the words whispered in his ears.

"I can't!" Fitz said. Yet immediately a verse from the Bible entered his thoughts. *"If ye forgive not men their trespasses, neither will your Father forgive your trespasses."*

Fitz placed his elbows on the desk and held his head in his hands. Tears stung his eyes. "I hate him for deceiving, manipulating, and humiliating me. I can't stand the sight of his arrogant face."

Pushing his chair back, he marched to the window, and stared outside. His arms hung at his sides with clenched fists and his nostrils flared. "I hate my father! I know it's wrong of me, but he deserves my anger." A sob escaped as Fitz lifted his eyes to the sky and cried, "Help me, God!" He reached for the knob of the floor-to-ceiling window, twisted it, swung the window open, and stepped into the garden. The air was cold, but he didn't care. Brisk steps took him along the gravel pathway as he poured out his heart to God. He didn't know how long he walked, but by the time he returned and shut the window behind him, he no longer felt alone in this battle.

Fitz stared at the envelope on his desk. Should he open it? Would reading his father's words bring healing or would it harden his heart? Slow steps toward the desk brought him closer to the moment of decision. His hand shook slightly as he reached for the envelope, staring at his father's handwriting. Fitz picked up the knife, broke the seal, and pulled out the letter. Unfolding it, he forced himself to begin reading.

*FitzWalter,*

He could almost hear his father's voice. It was always his title, FitzWalter. Not the shortened Fitz and most definitely not his given name, Hugh. His father lived and dreamed his heritage, and he raised his son to think like him.

However, he and his father parted ways in their thinking when it came to marriage. Fitz would never have agreed to an arranged marriage. Unlike his father, within him beat a romantic heart hoping for that elusive emotion—love. Even after Dinah's betrayal, he still couldn't bring himself to agree to a loveless marriage. But his father knew of his son's Achilles heel. Fitz loved his family. Lord Moorbridge used his son's vulnerability against him for the sake of his greatest treasure—his estate. Always his estate.

Fitz scowled at the letter again. The words blurred for a moment, but he blinked the moisture away. He didn't need his father's love. Not anymore. Not since he opened his heart to his Heavenly Father. "God, please guide me. Help me forgive my father." Looking down, he began reading.

*You haven't answered any of my letters. I imagine you tossed them into the fire before opening them. You see, I know how stubborn you can be at times. The apple doesn't fall far from the tree, I suppose.*

*I'm not apologizing for what I did in forcing your hand. You needed to get married and you were taking no steps in doing your duty to the estate. My one regret is that your mother was hurt in the process. She misses you. She tried to talk me out of it, but I knew what needed to be done and she was never one to gainsay me. Your mother cried the day of your wedding for she felt certain she'd lost her son that day. It seems she was right.*

*For her sake, I keep writing to you. Let's stop wasting time and put this behind us. If it makes you feel any better, I regret the agreement I made on your behalf with the Kendall family. Had I known the scandal that would attach itself to them, I never would have arranged for you to marry Selina Kendall. For that, I am deeply sorry. We must do all we can to separate ourselves from this mess. I will help in any way possible.*

*If I do not receive an answer to this letter, I will come for a visit. This silent treatment needs to end. There is much we need to discuss.*

Of course, he signed it "Moorbridge." Nothing less formal would do for his father.

Fitz laid the letter on his desk, leaned back in his chair, and closed his eyes. How should he respond?

He would write to his mother, but he wasn't ready to compose an answer to his father. He hadn't thought of it until now, but it pleased him a bit that his father regretted being attached to Selina's family. He certainly wasn't glad about all his wife was facing. Quite the opposite. His heart grieved for her. Yet it served his father right for trying to arrange everything in his son's life and seeing it fall apart—at least to his father's way of thinking.

God had used the machinations of his earthly father to give Fitz the gift of a godly wife, and one he loved like no other. Selina had become his life. Suddenly he could see things more clearly. *God, you were in control the whole time. You gave me a present and I was too blind to recognize it because of the circumstances.*

Fitz placed his elbows on the desk, folded his hands, and rested his forehead on them. "I forgive him, Lord. I choose to forgive my father and my mother. If Selina had not been your daughter, I believe you would have stopped me from marrying her. Instead, she believes in You and loves You like I do. Thank you for giving me such a treasure." He chuckled as he added, "And thank you that she's beautiful! That's a wonderful bonus!"

He picked up a fresh sheet of paper and quill. Dipping it in the inkwell, he wrote.

*"Dear Mother and Father,"*

Fitz smiled knowing his father would cringe when he read the salutation of "father" instead of Moorbridge. With a smirk on his face, he continued writing, inviting them to come to dinner in two days' time.

"Two days? Why, that's wonderful, Fitz! I've been hoping to

have them in our home for quite some time now."

"My father is a curmudgeon, Selina. He can be pleasant if he cares to make the effort, but he is more often than not quite toplofty. Don't put your expectations too high."

Selina smiled. "That's quite all right. I'm only glad we will finally have them in our home. I look forward to getting to know your mother especially."

"You will like her, of that I have no doubt. She has often lamented never having a daughter, and wished me to marry so she could at least have a daughter-in-law."

"I like her already."

"But remember, with her, my father's wishes are always first and foremost."

They discussed what foods his parents preferred. Selina was determined to make them feel welcome.

# *Chapter Thirty-Two*

Selina sat before a low-burning fire while reading her Bible the morning of the dinner with her in-laws. Wrapped in a warm robe, the only sound in the room was the crackling of the wood in the fireplace. The words of Scripture helped to prepare her for whatever the day might bring.

A soft knock preceded the door opening and Lydia entered bearing Selina's morning cup of chocolate on a tray along with a biscuit and marmalade. A slender vase containing a rose sat next to the plate.

"Thank you, Lydia. This is perfect! And thank you for the pretty flower."

"Lord FitzWalter sent it along with the note."

"Oh, yes. I see it." She lifted it off the tray, unfolded it, and read silently.

*Good Morning, my dear.*

*I have errands to run this morning. Will you partake of lunch with me this afternoon? I have some things to discuss with you.*

*Yours faithfully,*
*Fitz*

Selina made her way to the breakfast room to join her husband for lunch. She preferred it to the large dining room. It was more conducive to intimate conversation.

She had been both anxiously awaiting this moment and dreading it since reading the note. Would she finally hear what Percival's punishment would be?

When she entered the room, Fitz stood to his feet and walked to her side. Leaning forward, he placed a kiss on her cheek. "You look lovely, my dear."

She smiled her thanks.

"How was your morning?" he wanted to know.

"I've been feeling anxious since receiving your note, wishing the time would move faster."

"I'm sorry, Selina. Perhaps I should have worded it differently. It was not my intention to cause you to worry."

"It's quite all right, Fitz. Must I wait until after the meal before you tell me what this meeting is about?"

Chuckling at her impatience, he led her to a chair near his own. "We will eat and talk at the same time. I'm ravenous and don't wish to delay partaking of the wonderful meal I'm certain Cook has prepared for us." He winked at her.

She rolled her eyes. "Very well. We wouldn't want you to faint away from hunger. I couldn't be so cruel."

"Thank you, my dear," he said in mock humility.

The cold dishes were laid out on the table, which consisted of meat, cheese, bread, and fruit. They helped themselves, although Selina took precious little. Apprehension robbed most of her appetite.

Taking his first bite of meat, he closed his eyes in appreciation. "I missed breakfast this morning because of my meeting with Prinny."

"You met with the Prince Regent? Why?"

"Percival has renounced his title. That is why he wanted to meet with me a few weeks ago."

"Oh . . ." she gasped, then pulled her bottom lip between her teeth. "I expected he would have to do so, but it seems surreal. My father's title was always intended to go to my brother. It doesn't seem possible that it won't be his."

"Fortunately, I was allowed audience with Prinny and discussed Percival's situation with our monarch. He approved of my plan, which was actually Percival's plan, but I didn't enlighten the prince for I doubt he would believe or understand about Percival's conversion."

Selina could hardly wrap her mind around all Fitz was sharing. She knew the Prince Regent would have to be involved in a case pertaining to a lord, but she assumed her brother would stand trial.

"Prinny agreed to allow the title to pass to a distant cousin of yours, who is next in line to the title."

Clasping her hands tightly on her lap, she asked, "What will happen to Percival?"

"He will be sent to America."

"And this is his wish?"

"Yes. He said he spent much time praying about it and feels certain this is the right path to take."

She shook her head, "I can't imagine my brother living in such a primitive land. What will become of him?"

Taking her hand in his, he lifted it to his lips and placed a soft kiss upon the back of it. "Selina, I understand your confusion, but I think it would be best if Percival explains it to you. And do bear in mind that America is not as primitive as it used to be."

She nodded slowly. "Yes. I suppose you're right. I'll go see him after lunch."

After a brief knock, Selina opened the door to her brother's sitting room attached to his bedchamber. Her eyes widened as she stepped through the doorway. Polly and Percival sat side by side on the sofa, their fingers intertwined, both smiling from ear to ear.

"I'm sorry to interrupt. I can come back later."

"No, Selina. Please stay," Percival said. "Fitz informed us, before meeting you for lunch, about Prinny's decision."

"Oh, Lady FitzWalter!" Polly exclaimed. "God has been so good to us! Imagine, we have been given a second chance!"

"We?"

Percival chuckled as he proudly stated, "Polly has agreed to go with me—as my wife."

A smile slowly grew on Selina's face until it reached her eyes, and she beamed. Clapping her hands, she exclaimed, "That's wonderful! Oh, I'm so happy!"

"Truly? But I am only a maid. I was afraid you would think it presumptuous of me to assume such a role."

"Pfft! Society has a lot of prejudices, but it matters not to me. I am happy my brother will have a helpmate. And I'm especially pleased to know my niece or nephew will have both parents to love and care for him or her." Wincing a bit, she said, "But America? I cannot imagine you living in such a wilderness."

Percival chuckled. "I've always been interested in that part of the world. Over the years, I have read quite a bit about the colonies and the expansion west and secretly hoped one day to visit there. Of course, it never occurred to me I'd be transported as an act of punishment." All humor was gone when he said, "I'm certain it is only God's grace that has given me the opportunity to tell others about Him. Reverend Brown and I have talked about this possibly being the outcome, and what my future might look like."

"What do you mean?"

"I first heard Reverend Brown talk about the missionary work he's involved in in America when he was preaching on the streets of London. He was only visiting England for a brief time and will be returning soon to Virginia. It's strange, but I remembered his name. I have no idea why the man's name stuck in my mind. It seems God has been guiding me all along. Not that it was His will for me to sin, but rather He knew I would eventually submit and believe in Him. God already had a plan in mind of how this could be turned around for good, bringing honor and glory to Him."

"Do you plan to work with Reverend Brown?"

"Yes. At least for a while. He will continue training and teaching me. I want to learn all I can from him."

Brother and sister smiled at each other. Staring pointedly at Percival and Polly's interlocked hands, she raised her brows. "Should I be planning a wedding?"

"We were simply going to have the Reverend Brown marry us here in my sitting room."

Selina's eyes widened. "I think we can do better than that. Obviously, an elaborate wedding is out of the question, but let's plan to use the drawing room and invite Juliet and her husband, and Helena, too." She gazed at Polly and asked, "Would you like the servants to be invited also?"

She dropped her eyes to the bedspread, her face becoming red. "I think I have stooped beneath their notice by becoming a woman of easy virtue."

"Oh, Polly. I'm so sorry! Have you been treated cruelly?"

Looking up, her eyes widened. "Oh, no! They wouldn't dare. Not with you taking such interest in me. But they do not speak to me unless absolutely necessary. I would rather they not be invited."

Percival's jaw was clenched tight when Selina glanced at him. Life was certainly unfair. As a man, he was pardoned and accepted in spite of a promiscuous lifestyle, but the woman was shunned. "Polly, now that you are almost a part of our family, I will instruct Mrs. Addams to move you to a bedchamber near my own rooms. I will also provide you with a personal maid while you are under my roof."

"Oh! Truly, that isn't necessary!"

"Yes, it is. The servants will soon understand how I expect them to treat you. Please tell me if there is one maid who has accepted you. I will make her your personal maid. Otherwise, I will hire someone."

"Lizzy. She had a sister who served as a maid and was raped by the lord of the manor. When his wife found out the maid was increasing, she made her leave, without a reference, of course. Lizzy's sister died in childbirth, and the baby, too. Lizzy has treated me the same as always."

"I will tell Mrs. Addams. Lizzy will join you above stairs."

"Thank you, Selina," Percival said. "Your kindness never ceases to amaze me."

"Thank you, my lady."

"Polly, you may thank me by calling me Selina. We will be sisters soon."

Polly bobbed a curtsy. "Thank you, Selina."

Selina had taken great pains to be certain everything was perfect that evening. She wore an emerald green satin gown with a lower neckline, yet discreet. An emerald and diamond necklace with matching earbobs were the perfect finishing touch to her ensemble. Lydia had tied a matching ribbon around the loose bun, with curls framing her face.

As Selina glanced into the mirror, she felt pretty. "Thank you, Lydia. You did a splendid job."

"You're welcome, ma'am. I wish you a wonderful evening."

Selina took a deep breath, opened the door, and headed to the staircase.

Fitz entered the drawing room to welcome his parents, his mother's bright smile warming his heart. He leaned down to kissed her cheek.

Placing her hands on his cheeks, she said, "How I've missed you, my son!"

He straightened and said, "It's good to see you, too, Mother. You're as lovely as ever."

"Thank you, my dear boy, but the looking glass tells me otherwise."

"I believe you need a new looking glass. Yours must be damaged."

Lady Moorbridge laughed. "You are too kind."

Greeting his father wasn't as easy. Awkward, actually. Fitz put out his hand. "Moorbridge."

His father shook it, and said, "FitzWalter."

Before he had time to decide what to say next to his father, Selina entered the room, her beauty almost taking his breath away.

"Ah, there you are, my dear!" Walking toward her, Fitz leaned close, kissed her cheek, and whispered in her ear. "Lovely." She smiled at him and placed her hand on his arm. He led her further into the room. "You remember my parents, of course."

She curtsied to them. "I'm pleased to have you in our home this evening. Thank you for coming."

His mother slipped her arm through Selina's other arm and said, "I've longed to get to know you better, my dear. Thank you for the invitation."

Selina's eyes filled with joy. "It's my pleasure, ma'am."

* * *

Bates soon appeared at the door informing them dinner was ready to be served. The conversation around the table was pleasant enough, although certainly not relaxing. Selina often sensed her father-in-law's eyes studying her as he sat across the table. Her heart sank when she remembered he had hoped for Juliet to become his daughter-in-law. She knew she couldn't measure up to her sister in appearance. Moorbridge must realize it, too. Selina held her shoulders firmly in place, not allowing them to slump. What did it matter if her father-in-law found her wanting? Fitz's opinion was the only one that mattered.

Once the last dish was served and enough time had passed, Selina stood to her feet. "We will leave you gentlemen now." Turning to the countess, she said, "Would you like to join me in the drawing room?"

"Of course, my dear."

After the ladies left the room, the earl asked his son, "What is being done about Selina's brother?"

"How did you hear about it?

"You know very well nothing passes my notice. I want to be certain it doesn't become public knowledge. We must keep it out of the press. What do you have planned to protect our family reputation?"

"Percival has renounced his title and will be transported to America."

Moorbridge shook his head in disgust. "I can't believe I allowed such bad blood into our family!"

Fitz's back stiffen. "Be careful what you say. You are speaking of my wife's family."

"Pfft . . . I should have chosen better for you."

"What's done is done." What he wanted to say was how perfect Selina was for him, but he couldn't bare his heart to his father. "Why did you choose Selina for my bride?"

"I knew Runswick played too deep and was desperate to repair his losses. I wanted his eldest daughter for you since she was a diamond of the first water. With your scarred cheek and limp, what were the chances you could obtain such a girl on your own? My intention was to present you with a bride you would find difficult to resist. Although

Runswick was deep in debt, he had impressive blood lines. When Runswick told me his eldest was already betrothed, I felt momentarily defeated, but he quickly informed me of his second daughter's wealth and beauty. Since Selina was an heiress, I found it an acceptable alternative even if she did not turn out to be as beautiful as her sister."

Fitz's jaw clenched tight. Was there ever a schemer like his father?

Moorbridge continued explaining, "Runswick knew you were unaware of my plans for you but agreed to stay quiet. That's why I chose him. I knew he wouldn't balk at a bit of underhanded measures to achieve my goal of seeing you married. He had the bloodlines, beautiful daughters, and a desperate need for wealth. It was perfect." Banging a fist on the table, Moorbridge exclaimed, "Unfortunately, his son ruined it all. If this gossip is bandied about Town, even our impeccable reputation cannot survive such a scandal attaching itself to our family. We will do all we can to make certain that doesn't happen."

Fitz agreed with his father on that point. If news of Percival's crime hit the gossip mill, such a defamation would haunt their children and future generations.

Thankfully, Moorbridge changed the topic away from the Kendall family. They discussed their estates instead, then joined the ladies in the drawing room.

After a few minutes together, his mother asked, "Fitz, would you show me your conservatory?"

Fitz looked at Selina and asked, "Would you like to join us, my dear?"

Moorbridge spoke before his daughter-in-law could answer. "Fitz, your mother has not had you to herself in quite some time." Piercing his gaze upon Selina, Moorbridge asked," Would you mind granting me the pleasure of your company? I would enjoy the opportunity to get to know you better."

"But, Selina, please feel free to join us if you'd rather." Lady Moorbridge said.

Again, Moorbridge spoke before Selina could respond. "I insist you have your son to yourself for a few minutes and not deprive me of my daughter-in-law's company." Turning to Selina, Moorbridge smiled in a manner intended to be charming, but made her feel ill at ease. Unaware of her thoughts, he continued smiling. "We haven't had a chance to chat since the two of you spoke your vows. You don't mind a few minutes alone with your father-in-law, do you?"

What could she say? *Yes, I mind. You scare me.* That would never do, of course. Instead, she attempted a smile as she said, "I don't mind."

Once Fitz and his mother left the room, the earl got up and shut the door to the drawing room, surprising Selina. He returned to his chair, leaned back, and comfortably rested one leg on his knee. "I understand your brother instigated the murder of your parents."

So this was why he wanted time alone with her. *How did he even know about Percival? Fitz must have told him.* "He was drunk at the time and not in the right frame of mind, but he accepted responsibility for his actions and will be punished."

"Thankfully, he won't be hung from a tree and humiliate our family further, although he deserves it."

He was goading her, and she refused to give him the pleasure of a response. It seemed her husband's opinion of his father was correct. His estate took precedence over everything.

"If you ask me, he's getting off easy," Moorbridge said. "Your father and mother didn't deserve to be so ill-treated."

The knot that started forming in her stomach at dinner suddenly grew tighter. Of course Percival deserved a worse punishment than he had gotten. God had been merciful. Unlike her father-in-law. Did he expect her to argue and defend her brother? She simply answered, "Yes, he is. And no, my parents did not deserve to die."

Moorbridge narrowed his eyes. "When I arranged this marriage between you and my son, I assumed you came from good bloodlines. Unfortunately, I was mistaken. I detest this blemish on our family tree."

He looked at her as though she were a street peddler standing at his front door. Her cheeks grew warm. Why did she have to blush now? He would think her embarrassed—

and she wasn't that. She was angry. If anyone were to take the time to search deep enough into the precious Moorbridge history, there were bound to be some skeletons in the closet there also. Yet, how could she blame him for feeling vexed with her family?

"I understand you and my son have not consummated your marriage."

Selina gasped as her eyes widened and her cheeks became hotter still.

"You do realize my son is free to seek an annulment and be released from this marriage. Your father is no longer here to protect you, so I am making you an offer. I will give you twenty thousand pounds and a pretty cottage near your aunt, as well as servants of your choosing, if you will agree to quietly leave my son to seek an annulment."

Her eyes narrowed as she asked, "Is he aware you are making me such an offer?"

"No, but when I mentioned my concern about bad blood in our family, he resignedly said, 'what's done is done.' He doesn't see a way out. I wanted to talk to you first and give you the opportunity to do the honorable thing. I know my son. He will be glad to be free of this marriage that reminds him he had to bend to my will. That alone will always stand between the two of you."

"My lord, I would like . . ."

"I can well imagine it's the reason he didn't seek your bed on your wedding night or the months thereafter. No man can resist an available woman in his house, especially when she is his wife. Yet your husband hasn't come to your bed, has he? That must prove to you how undesirable this marriage is to him."

She sat staring incredulously at Moorbridge. How did he know? Who had betrayed them? Had Fitz confessed the state of their marriage to his father? Was this planned between the three of them? Fitz leaving the room with his mother so Moorbridge could make his despicable offer? She lowered her eyes realizing her father-in-law spoke all her fears aloud. She was undesirable. She didn't deserve to be FitzWalter's wife. He didn't want her.

Moorbridge's voice was quiet but firm as he spoke. "I understand your brother is leaving on Sunday morning. In the afternoon, I will ask FitzWalter to join me at my club. While he is gone, pack your trunk into the carriage I will provide. It will be best if you take your maid with you. In the meantime, I will share with my son the good news that he is free of his obligation to you. I will also allow him to choose his own bride. You and I both know that will please him."

Still uncertain of her husband's involvement, Selina asked, "Why don't you tell him tonight? Shouldn't we discuss this together with him?"

"Absolutely not! He will feel it's his Christian duty to continue with his vows, but you and I both know he has resisted long enough. FitzWalter has clearly shown his repulsion for this arrangement. It's time to stop the charade. I would have kept him to his promise if your brother hadn't been such a scoundrel. Now I have to agree with my son that you are not the wife for him."

Selina forced herself to stand on shaky legs. She feared they would not hold her. Standing straight and forcing courage into her limbs, she raised her chin and said, "Please excuse me. I am certain you will know what to say to your wife and son if my absence is questioned."

Head held high, Selina left the room and hurried up the stairs. Mrs. Addams made certain Selina didn't see her entering the drawing room to speak with the earl.

"You did very well, Mrs. Addams. She didn't deny our suspicions that the marriage hasn't been consummated. Very observant of you." He handed her a thick envelope.

"Thank you, my lord." She curtsied and left the room with her head down and shoulders slumped, quite different from her normal erect posture.

## *Chapter Thirty-Three*

Fitz waited in the breakfast room hoping Selina would join him. After an hour of reading the paper, he finally gave up.

Entering the foyer, he saw Mrs. Addams. "When you see Lady FitzWalter, please inform her I wish to speak with her."

"Yes, my lord."

He sat at his desk and worked through the piles of papers that needed his attention. An hour later, a knock at the door interrupted his thought process. "Come in."

"Lord Runswick would like to know if you still plan on joining him today when he goes to his apartment?" Bates asked.

Fitz jumped up from his chair. "Yes! I completely forgot. What time is it?" He glanced at his pocket watch and saw it was well past the noon hour. "Have you seen Lady FitzWalter this morning?"

"She and Polly left for the cottage an hour ago."

His brow furrowed. "Did she not get my message that I wished to speak with her?"

"I cannot say, Sir. I was unaware you had left instructions."

Taking a calming breath, he let it out swiftly. *It seemed Mrs. Addams was slacking off on her job again. What was going on?* "I mentioned it to Mrs. Addams."

"She said nothing to me, Sir."

"Tell Lord Runswick I will join him shortly. He can meet

me in the foyer in fifteen minutes."

After only ten minutes, Bates returned. "Constable Jones is here to see you, sir."

"Very well. Show him in, and let Lord Runswick know I will need a few additional minutes before we can depart."

The burly constable entered the study holding his hat in his hand. "Good morning, my lord."

"Constable, what can I do for you?" Fitz knew he sounded impatient. He had no use for the narrow-minded man.

He cleared his throat and looked rather sheepish. "It seems I was wrong about Lady FitzWalter."

Fitz nodded. "And you were wrong to enter my home without my prior knowledge to interrogate my wife and her brother."

Shoulders slumped, the constable gazed at the floor. "Yes, it was wrong of me. My superiors took me off the case last week after I handed in my findings."

"I'm curious, Constable Jones. Why was this case personal to you?"

Peering into Fitz's eyes, the constable swallowed hard. "My younger brother was the driver of the carriage that took Lord and Lady Runswick's lives."

Fitz's eyes widened. "I'm terribly sorry for your loss, Constable. You should never have been placed on this case."

"No, I shouldn't have, but we were short-staffed."

"I see. And why did your temper become inflamed when my wife spoke of her faith?"

The Constable spoke through a clenched jaw. "My little brother got religion when he heard a street preacher this summer. God was all he could talk about. He called Him a loving God." He narrowed his eyes and sneered. "How much love did God show my brother when He allowed him to die at five and twenty? He had his whole life ahead of him."

"It could be your brother would have died whether he received salvation or not. It was a loving God who helped him believe before the accident took his life and, in this way, spared him an eternity in hell."

"Hmm . . . I hadn't thought of that." The constable stretched out his hand which held a piece of paper.

"What's this?"

"The name and location of the man who has your grandmother's jewelry. I'll warn you, he's asking a steep price for it."

"I'm sure he is. Thank you for the information."

"It's the least I can do. I bid you a good day, sir."

"Before you go, Constable, will you at least tell me who your informant was?"

"Tom Hendricks."

"Tom Hendricks? Percival's friend?"

"Yes, my lord."

"Well, that explains how he knew such personal details about the family. Percival must have confided in him."

"Mr. Hendricks was approached by an undercover agent. He didn't realize he was being used in an investigation." The constable shrugged his shoulders. "Probably shouldn't have gossiped, but, alas, that is human nature. It often works in our favor."

"Yes, when the information is reliable. *Your* information was filled with supposition. As I said before, you don't know my wife. My word you could have relied upon."

A nerve jumped in the constable's cheek as he spoke through gritted teeth. "I apologize, my lord. I was wrong."

"Well, thank you for the information about the pearls."

"You're welcome and good day, my lord." After a brief bow, he turned and left the room.

More than half the night had been spent tossing or drenching her pillow with tears. Exhaustion finally overpowered Selina's unceasing deliberation and she fell asleep only to awaken a couple hours later when Lydia brought in her chocolate. Selina soon remembered Polly needed her to help empty the cottage of her personal belongings. She bound out of bed, determined to occupy her time with constant activity the next few days. She would make certain there would be no time to feel sorry for herself.

Selina was happy to leave Henfort that morning to help

Polly pack her belongings. When the packing was completed, Polly moved to the kitchen and started cleaning. Selina did the unthinkable. She picked up a dust cloth and began polishing the furniture.

"Oh, no, my lady!" Polly gasped.

Selina raised her brows. "I thought we had dispensed of my title."

"Selina, you must not dust. What will the servants say?"

She looked outside at the two maids working in the garden, watering the neglected flowers and rose bushes. She shrugged her shoulders. "Let them say whatever they please. I need to stay busy."

As Selina dusted, she felt Polly's eyes on her from time to time. She knew it was very odd of her to do household chores. After all, a lady had maids for such tasks. Unfortunately, she soon realized working with one's hands did not stop the mind from thinking.

As her hand moved in a circular motion over the surface of the table, she forced her thoughts to the upcoming wedding for Percival and Polly tomorrow morning. The bouquet of flowers for the bride had been ordered, as well as flowers to decorate the drawing room. Selina intended to make the wedding as festive as possible under the circumstances. She had already discussed the menu for the wedding breakfast with Cook.

Polly asked her to stand up with her at the wedding and Selina was happy to do so. Percival asked Fitz if he would do him the honor of standing up with him also. *Fitz . . .* She sighed as her heart squeezed tight.

Glancing around to see what else needed to be polished, Selina saw the servants who had entered the cottage quickly turn away pretending they hadn't been staring at her curiously. Looking down at the rag in her hand, she smiled.

"Polly, what else needs to be done?"

"I believe we are finished here."

Selina sighed. "Very well . . ." There was no more avoiding returning to Henfort.

By the time everyone arrived back at Henfort, two hours

remained before dinner. Selina entered her bedchamber, plopped down on her bed. What could she do to pass the time. The last thing she wished to do was sit and rehearse the conversation she'd had with her father-in-law once more. No matter how many times she thought about it, nothing changed.

She didn't for a moment believe her husband wished her out of his life due to Percival's actions. That didn't ring true with his character. But her father-in-law did have the right of it nonetheless. Fitz hadn't been able to bring himself to consummate the marriage all these months. Having been devastated by his father's manipulation, he could not allow Moorbridge to win. If he were to share her bed and she became with child, in her husband's mind, his father would win. That was the crux of it. Fitz could not bear to see Moorbridge gloat.

Selina could tell him of Moorbridge's plan for her, of course, but if she did so, Fitz would realize he was at checkmate. If she stayed, Moorbridge would win by gaining an heir for his estate. If she left, Moorbridge would win by having the Kendalls out of his son's life. Either way, Moorbridge wins.

If she didn't tell him of his father's demands and simply did as her father-in-law commanded, she would no longer be around to remind him of what he would consider his gullibility. Selina doubted Fitz would ever ask her to leave. He was too much the gentleman for that. Yet each time he looked at her, he would have at least a little regret for how things had turned out. She was a bride forced upon him.

The one dilemma that continued plaguing her the previous night was in regards to the vows they had spoken. How did God view their marriage? After tossing and turning until early dawn, Selina finally realized there never was a marriage. Even the church would allow an annulment of a marriage never consummated. With a heavy heart, she knew her decision had been made.

This was their last meal together before Percival and Polly's wedding the next day. In two days, Fitz and Selina would travel the short distance with the newlyweds to the wharves on the River Thames so they could board a ship set to voyage to Virginia.

When dinner was over, Percival asked to be excused. He had overdone it that day and needed rest. Polly retired to her room also. When Selina made to leave, Fitz asked her to join him for a few minutes in the drawing room.

Unable to think of an excuse not to do as her husband requested, she straightened her shoulders and followed him. As she sat in the same chair she had occupied when facing his father, she felt the humiliation of that moment once again.

"What happened last night, Selina? Why did you retire early?"

Selina didn't know what excuse his father had given for her early departure. Unsure of how to answer, she asked, "Didn't your father tell you why I left early?"

Fitz stared at her, his eyes searching. What was he looking for? What did he see? Slowly, he leaned forward with his elbows on his knees and clasped his hands out in front of him, bringing him a bit closer to where she sat before him. She wished to sink back into the chair to keep the distance between them but forced her back ramrod straight.

"I'd like to hear your reason," came his soft reply.

Pulling her bottom lip between her teeth, she stared at her hands, unable to make eye contact. Without lifting her eyes, she said, "Fitz, are you so distrustful of your father that you don't believe the excuse he gave you as to why I retired early?"

"Selina, look at me . . . please."

Heart beating faster, she slowly lifted her eyes. Her heart squeezed and she couldn't breathe. She loved this man who sat before her, but she could never have him. As she gazed into the eyes she would never forget for as long as she lived, Selina silently prayed she'd have the courage to do what was best for Fitz.

"I know you well enough, Selina, to know when you're avoiding giving me a direct answer."

As she stared at him, he waited. Oh, how she longed to

feel his arms holding her close once more. But she reminded herself that after months of marriage, he remained unwilling to truly make her his wife. His pride meant more to him than she did. It was time to let him go.

"I developed a headache," she said. It wasn't exactly a lie. After she had cried her eyes out in her bedchamber, she had developed a terrible headache indeed.

"Moorbridge said your brother had called for you. He needed some assistance with regards to the wedding. Tell me, Selina, did you visit your brother's room before going to bed?"

She sighed, refusing to lie. There was no blessing in disobeying God's commands. She tried to do things as her father-in-law had stated, but not if it conflicted with obedience to God. "I did not."

"Did you tell my father you were going to check on your brother?"

She stared down at her clasped hands again. "No."

"So he lied to me."

She shrugged her shoulders but said nothing.

"What excuse did you give him for leaving early?"

Swallowing, she stared at him a moment before saying, "I didn't give him an excuse."

"So you simply got up and walked out?"

She nodded.

"And said nothing?"

She wished he would stop asking her questions. Scowling, she asked, "What does it matter why I left the room? Perhaps your father assumed I had gone to visit my brother. I didn't owe him an explanation."

Fitz rested his chin on steepled fingers as he looked closely at her. "I want to get to the bottom of what my father said to make you rush off to your room."

Selina crossed her arms. "It was between Moorbridge and me. You need not concern yourself about it, Fitz." For his sake, she would hold her ground.

"You, my dear, are not a liar." He lowered his clasped hands and straightened. "But you will withhold information. I'm trying to ask questions that your conscience will require you to answer honestly so I can figure out what happened last night."

"Nothing happened. We talked. Mostly Moorbridge talked and I listened."

"What did he talk about? Your family?"

Her eyes widened, which she feared gave her away, so she quickly looked down.

"My father told you how your family has brought bad blood into the pure, aristocratic, Moorbridge line?" His words dripped with sarcasm.

Selina pursed her lips as she watched him through her lashes.

"I'm getting warm, aren't I?" A smile played on the corners of his mouth. "Let's see, he told you your brother is a scoundrel and deserves far worse than the punishment he's getting."

Selina gave a brief nod.

"Ah, so at least you admit to that. Let's see . . . Moorbridge told you he regrets arranging our marriage."

Selina quickly lowered her eyes, biting her bottom lip to keep it from trembling.

Fitz fell to one knee on the floor in front of her and took her hands in his. "Selina, I don't care what his opinion is. I don't regret marrying you."

A tear rolled down her cheek followed by another. She didn't try hiding her pain. Her glistening eyes stared into the warm depths of his tender gaze.

Fitz cupped her cheeks with both hands and gently wiped the tears away with his thumbs.

Swallowing hard, she said, "He forced you. You left me at Thorncrest. You didn't want me. I know you're trying to do right by me by taking me as your wife, b-but I am not as lovely as Juliet." All her fears began to spill out. "I know I'm a disappointment. More importantly, your father will be the winner if I bear you a child. Fitz, I want to set you free of this marriage. You deserve to choose your own bride."

Pulling away a little, but taking hold of her hands, he squeezed them slightly. "Is that what you want? You want me to choose?"

"For myself, I shall never marry again. But you should have the right to choose your own bride."

"Very well," he said, letting go of her hands.

She watched as he stood, her heart pounding in her ears. This was the moment she had dreaded. He was going to let her go. His father had spoken true. Fitz didn't want her.

Fitz held out the palm of one hand to her. "Stand up, Selina."

She placed her hand in his and stood before him. Only a few inches separated them. She could smell the musky scent of his cologne as well as a scent that was all his own. She breathed in deeply hoping to remember it always.

Fitz gave her hand a slight squeeze. Her eyes shot to his face as she braced herself for what would come next.

"I realized something the other day that I wish to share with you. On the day my father planned his scheme to arrange a marriage between us, God was still in control."

As he spoke, his thumb caressed the back of her hand. Why did he have to be tender while asking her to leave? *It would be less painful if we were to fight.* Anger would make leaving a bit easier. Unable to maintain eye contact, her eyes rested on the knot of his cravat.

"I believe with all my heart that if the woman Moorbridge chose had not been a believer, God would somehow have stopped the marriage from taking place. Instead, what my earthly father intended as a manipulation to impose his will on me, our Heavenly Father used to give me a gift more precious than I could ever have imagined."

Selina's eyes widened and her lips parted. Had she heard correctly?

"For the record, I have never wanted you to look like Juliet. When I compare the two of you, I find you far lovelier."

She gazed at their clasped hands. He was lying. No one could find her lovelier than her sister.

"Please, look at me, Selina." When she did so reluctantly, he said, "I can see you don't believe me. I wish you could see yourself through my eyes. Your brown locks shine in the sunshine and in candlelight. Your doe-like eyes speak to my heart." Letting go of her hand, he lifted his to take hold of one of the curls that escaped her chignon. He stared at it a moment, rubbing it between his fingers.

She could hardly breathe. Was this a dream? He began speaking again and she longed to hear every word.

"I find you lovely beyond description. There is a depth of character in you that draws me like a thirsty man to a glass of water. I'm a better person since you've come into my life. Seeing how you care for people and search for ways to show kindness to them, sincerely forgiving those who have hurt you, challenges me to do the same. Your intelligence during our quiet conversations stimulates my mind." He chuckled before adding, "And your animated conversation as we each discuss opposing views on a topic makes me want to kiss you."

His voice became raspy as he said, "I'm so sorry for all the times I've caused you pain. Please forgive my selfishness."

"I forgive you."

"Of course, you do," Fitz chuckled as his finger traced a line from her cheek to her bottom lip. Pulling away, his eyes narrowed. "As far as you thinking I have to force myself to make you my wife—if you only knew how many nights I couldn't sleep for thoughts of you keeping me awake. These past several weeks, it was only my love for you that made me strong. I didn't want you to come to me out of duty. I wanted to woo you and allow you to feel more comfortable in our marriage." Cupping her cheek, he said, "When we finally consummate this marriage, I want you to want me as much as I want you."

"You love me?" It was the one thing she heard above all else.

"With my whole heart." He tapped the tip of her nose. "I choose you, Selina. If I were not already married to you and the room was filled with beautiful, eligible, young ladies, I would still choose you without hesitation. There is no one else for me."

"I love you, too," she whispered.

He must have read the truth in her eyes, for his face beamed as he declared, "You love me!" He placed his hands on her waist and pulled her closer. She wrapped her arms around his neck and closed her eyes as he lowered his head. Selina felt warm lips touch hers, and she breathed in his scent. Liquid heat rushed through her limbs and her body melted into his embrace. As he pulled away, she moaned.

Fitz chuckled deep in his throat as he held his arm out to her. "Come, my lady. You won't need Lydia's assistance tonight."

Light flickered on her closed eyelids as she slowly awoke in the warm cocoon of her husband's embrace. As memory edged in, a smile began at the corners of Selina's mouth and grew until it filled her heart to bursting. She opened her eyes longing to see her husband, but she faced the wrong way. Carefully, hoping not to disturb him, she turned bit by bit until she faced him. He rolled onto his back but kept on sleeping. His disheveled hair caused her to chuckle soundlessly. No one else would ever see him like this, warm from sleep and completely relaxed. She bit her bottom lip. An annulment was out of the question now.

"If you don't stop staring at me, I won't be able to sleep."

She smiled at his raspy mumble. "I can't help myself. You're so handsome."

"Woman, you are staring at the side of my face that bears a scar. I'm certainly not handsome."

"That's where you're wrong, husband. Your scar makes you mysterious and brave." She ran a finger along the silvery line. "How fortunate I am to be your wife."

He growled and rolled toward her. It was much later before they arose.

On Sunday, after Percival and Polly's tearful departure, Fitz and Selina returned to Henfort. A missive awaited Fitz's attention. It was from Moorbridge.

"What does it say?" Selina asked.

"He wants me to join him at his club this afternoon."

Selina gasped. She had completely forgotten the earl's plan for her. In the midst of their wedded bliss and her brother and sister-in-law's imminent departure, she never told her husband the rest of Moorbridge's plan.

"May I have a word with you, please?" Selina asked. Fitz looked at her curiously. "In private."

"Of course." Taking her by the hand, he took her into the drawing room. "What is it?"

"While you're at the club with your father, Moorbridge will be sending a carriage for me. His plan is that I pack my trunks and be gone before you return."

"What?" Fitz scowled. "When did he tell you that?"

"The night they were here. That's why I left and ran up to my room. He said you'd be glad to be free of me. Your father also said that when he mentioned his regret about our marriage, you told him, 'what's done is done.' I realize he must have lied about that, too."

Rubbing a hand over his face, Fitz shook his head. "It wasn't a lie. I did say that." At her look of alarm, he quickly placed his hands on her shoulders and gazed intently into her eyes. "I only said that because I couldn't bare my heart to him." Fitz lifted his hand to stroke her cheek with his thumb. "I wanted to tell him that you are a treasure and I can't imagine my life without you, but can you imagine me saying such a thing to Moorbridge? One doesn't talk of one's feelings with him."

"I see. Well, are you going to the club?"

Fitz pulled her into his embrace and held her close. "Yes." She stiffened. He placed a quick kiss on her brow. "But I will first take you to visit your sisters. On the way home, I'll pick you up again. How does that sound?"

Selina's eyes sparkled as she gazed at her husband before standing on her toes to place a kiss on his lips. "That sounds splendid."

Moorbridge sat at a table in the corner where they wouldn't be overheard. That worked well for Fitz's plan.

"Good afternoon, Moorbridge."

"FitzWalter, I'm glad you could make it."

"I apologize for being a bit late, but I dropped Selina off at her sister's home on my way here."

Moorbridge's eyes narrowed. "What?"

Fitz raised his brows as he asked, "Is there a problem?"

"Ah, no. No. I was surprised you were late, that's all."

Fitz had never seen his father quite so flustered before. It gave him a secret pleasure to see him discomfited.

"Father, it might interest you to know Selina and I will be departing for Thorncrest soon. I will inform you as soon as we are certain she is with child, which could be in the next few weeks. I imagine you and Mother would like to be at the birth or shortly thereafter."

"Yesss . . . Yes, of course."

"I don't think we have much else to say to each other, so I will leave you." Fitz stood but stopped to lean one arm on the table as he looked his father in the eyes. "Don't try coming between my wife and me ever again. What God has joined together, let no man put asunder. God used your manipulation to give me a treasure. I love her." Straightening, Fitz said, "Let me know if you wish to come for a visit. If so, you might want to consider apologizing to your daughter-in-law."

Moorbridge raised his chin but didn't utter a word. So be it then.

When Selina and Fitz arrived home, a pale Mrs. Addams asked if she could meet with them. Fitz nodded and said, "This way." After they entered the study, Selina watched the housekeeper shut the study door behind her before turning to face the master and mistress.

"I did a terrible thing!" Mrs. Addams's voice sounded breathless.

Selina glanced briefly at Fitz. His jaw was clenched tightly. What could Mrs. Addams possibly have done? Trying to ease the poor woman's obvious discomfort, Selina asked, "Would you like to sit?"

Mrs. Addams looked quickly to the viscount and, seeing his stoic face, shook her head. She shifted her gaze to Selina. "I'd rather stand, my lady. But thank you." She cleared her throat while clutching her hands. "As I was walking home from errands several weeks ago, Lord Moorbridge stopped his carriage alongside the road and bid me to enter. It was right after Polly and Lord Runswick arrived. He told me how unhappy both of you were in your marriage and about the scandal with the Kendall family. He said it was imperative to save the Moorbridge name and he needed my assistance." Twisting her hands together, she continued. "Your father told me he had created this mess and he needed to clean it up again. He offered me one thousand pounds if I would give him information about the state of your marriage."

Selina turned wide eyes to Fitz and saw him stare hard at the housekeeper. "Why would my father approach you? He must have been certain you would be disloyal to my household."

"He did his homework well, my lord, before seeking me out. He knew my sister retired a few months ago and was left with little to live on. After the years of service she gave to the Langdons, all they gave her for her retirement was ten pounds! If it wasn't for the extra money she saved over the years, she would be penniless. I-I feared for my future. How could I possibly support both of us? The temptation was strong and I was weak. I reasoned that I was helping the two of you. It seemed obvious you were not close." Mrs. Addams dabbed her nose with a handkerchief. "The money Lord Moorbridge offered would keep both my sister and me comfortable for quite some time if we lived frugally. To my shame, I informed Lord Moorbridge your marriage did not appear to be consummated. I wasn't certain, but I suspected it."

Fitz's jaw tightened, and Selina felt the need to smooth things over. "Mrs. Addams, I wish you would have come and told me about your sister. Surely we could have worked something out."

The housekeeper's eyes filled with tears as she looked at Selina. "Oh, how I wish I had done so. Instead, I conspired with the devil." She gasped and spun her gaze toward Fitz. "I beg your pardon, my lord. I should not have said such a thing."

"No, probably not. But at times I have felt much the same

about the man."

"On the night Lord and Lady Moorbridge came to dinner, Lady FitzWalter retired early. Once she left the drawing room, I entered to collect the money he promised me. From the time he handed the envelope to me until now, I have hardly slept a wink. My conscience wouldn't leave me be. Both you and Lady FitzWalter have been good to me. And then I have witnessed the joy between the two of you these last couple days. Oh, if you could only forgive me. I will understand if you feel you must dismiss me from my position. But if you choose to keep me on, I tell you truly, you will not find a more loyal servant." She held out an envelope.

"What's this?" Fitz asked.

"It's the money your father gave me. I cannot keep it. It's tainted."

Fitz took the envelope from her and said, "Please step outside of the room, but stay close. Lady FitzWalter and I need to discuss this alone."

"Of course, my lord, my lady." She curtsied and left the room, shutting the door behind her.

Turning to his wife, he asked, "How often must we forgive, Selina? And should she be punished?"

"Mrs. Addams came to us of her own free will. She didn't have to confess."

"True. But perhaps she was aware a carriage was sent for you today and you did not leave with it. There is the possibility that seeing Moorbridge's plans falling apart made her fear for her own part in them. Maybe she confessed in an effort to manipulate our feelings."

"Fitz, after what happened with her sister, I can understand her moment of weakness. And we both know how convincing Moorbridge can be. I think she is sincere in her regret."

"You may be right, my dear, but I want to question her a bit further."

Fitz called Mrs. Addams back to the drawing room and asked, "Was there a carriage here this afternoon for my wife?"

"Not that I'm aware of. I was above stairs helping the maids put the bedchambers back in order. After that, I went to the grocer. Cook wanted a specific cut of lamb and I offered to purchase it for her. Bates was here all afternoon, but he mentioned nothing about a carriage to me."

"Please ask Bates to join us."

When Mrs. Addams returned to the room with Bates, he informed them a carriage had arrived. "The driver said it was for Lady FitzWalter, but he refused to tell me who had ordered the conveyance. I told him the mistress wasn't at home. He refused to believe me and insisted on entrance. I shut the door in his face, and he left."

"Were any of the other servants nearby?"

"Not that I was aware of, my lord."

"Thank you, Bates. You were right to handle it as you did. That is all. You may return to your duties."

He bowed and left, shutting the door behind him.

Fitz peered at the housekeeper. "Mrs. Addams, Lady FitzWalter and I have chosen to forgive you. You will not be dismissed since you came and confessed of your own accord."

"Oh, my lord, my lady! Thank you!" she said as tears filled her eyes and spilled down her face. "God bless you both!"

"Where is your sister now?" Fitz asked.

Mrs. Addams wiped her cheeks and dabbed her nose. Pulling herself together, she answered, "My sister has a small room in her daughter's house."

"Is this where she wishes to be?"

Mrs. Addams's shook her head. "No. They have two bedrooms and four children. She sleeps with her grandchildren."

"If she would be interested in moving to Thorncrest, I have a small cottage she may reside in. It will be yours when you retire, but she is welcome to live in it in the meantime."

Clasping folded hands to her chest, Mrs. Addams exclaimed, "Oh, my lord! You are too good!" She shifted her gaze to Selina. "Blessed was this house the day you came to live in it."

"Thank you, Mrs. Addams," Selina spoke kindly. "I hope you will sleep well tonight."

"Oh, ma'am, I'm certain I shall!" She curtsied and turned to leave the room.

"One more thing, Mrs. Addams," Fitz said.

With her hand on the door, she faced her employer again. "Yes, my lord?"

Fitz walked the few steps separating them and handed her the envelope. "Give this to your sister."

Eyes wide, Mrs. Addams stared at the envelope uncomprehendingly. Tilting her head, she asked, "Why would you give her this, my lord?"

"Because she should have gotten this from her own employer. Since he failed her, I wish to bless her instead. I would appreciate it if you didn't tell her where the money came from. I want no thanks."

"Then how will I explain it to her?"

"Tell her God wanted to bless her. It is the truth."

"Thank you, my lord. It is far beyond what I deserve." She lifted a handkerchief and wiped away the tears as she curtsied again and departed the room.

Once Mrs. Addams was gone, Selina turned to her husband. "You're a good man, my lord."

Fitz moved closer until she was in his arms. "No one said that about me until you entered my life, Selina."

"I don't believe it."

"Ask Emma. She will tell you how I tried to come between her and Devon."

Selina looked doubtfully at him. "I can't imagine you doing so. You'll have to tell me that story one day."

"Oh, believe me. It's true."

"I cannot fathom it."

"God got a hold of my life and changed me. When He gave you to me, all my defenses crumbled, one by one. He knew who I needed." Lifting a hand to play with a curl near her neck, he gazed into her eyes. "It was you and only you, my beautiful love."

He thought she was beautiful, and she believed him.

Nothing had changed in her appearance. But Fitz's desire for her and the way he cared for her convinced Selina he spoke the truth. Her eyes sparkled as she gazed at his handsome face. "I love you, Fitz. My heart will always belong to you."

# *Epilogue*

London, England, May 1820

Selina moved the fork around on her plate, but couldn't force herself to eat a bite. She set the utensil down and lifted her cup of tea to her mouth.

"Are you not feeling well this morning?" Fitz asked. "I hope you're not coming down with something. Maybe you should rest today."

"I'm fine."

"I forgot to ask you about the letter you received from Juliet two days ago. How are your sisters faring?"

"Juliet and Henry are doing well, but my sister is concerned about Helena. She spends much time secluded in the library to improve her mind and shuts herself away in her room for hours on end. I fear my sister is becoming a bluestocking." Seeing her husband's smile, she said, "Please, don't misunderstand. I am all for improving the mind, as you well know, but I fear it will make Helena less marriageable. There are few men in the ton who wish for a wife who is perhaps more intelligent than they are."

"Is she attending balls and mingling in society?"

"Yes, Helena attends various events with Juliet and Henry, and she doesn't lack for dance partners. But Juliet begs her not to show in public the depths of knowledge she's gained in private." Selina shook her head. "She should be spending hours looking at fashion plates and browsing through shops, but Helena would sooner be found in a bookstore or library. I admire her interest in learning, but I fear she is too obvious about it."

Baldwin entered the room with the post. Fitz ruffled through the envelopes, lifting a crumpled one out of the pile.

Selina's eyes widened. "Is it from Percival?"

Smiling at his wife, he handed her the letter.

She slit the envelope with her knife, unfolded the letter, and began to read aloud.

*Dear Selina and Fitz,*

*Rose Agnes Kendall was born two days ago, named after both her grandmothers. By the time you receive this letter, she may already be two or three months old. Polly is doing well and adjusting to our new life. She's a huge blessing to me.*

*We currently live in a cabin in a small town in Indiana. Instead of ministering to Indians, God opened the door for us to work amongst the brave souls who have journeyed here to start a new life. Too many of them see this new land as the answer to their needs instead of seeking God. We also minister to slaves whenever we can. It saddens me to realize how little they have to look forward to in this life. Hopefully, that will change in the near future, for there are many in Indiana who oppose slavery. Unfortunately, there are also many who are for it.*

*I've had the privilege of leading a young man to the Lord. He's become a fine assistant in our work here. With the generous gift you and Fitz gave us before we left, I opened a mercantile. We sell everything imaginable, except alcohol. My competitor can provide that if he likes. I was told I could get wealthy in this town if I were to sell liquor, and I'm certain it's true. Unfortunately, I see too many lost souls—as I used to be—hiding behind a bottle because life is too disappointing to face.*

*I trust you are both in good health. Will I be an uncle soon? I don't know if it will ever be possible to see each other again, but if not here on this earth, then definitely in heaven.*

* * *

*May God bless, protect, and guide you always.*

*With deepest affection,*
*Percival*

Selina wiped a tear from her eye. Folding the letter, she placed it in the pocket of her skirt. "Fitz, if you'll excuse me, I want to start a letter for Percival and Polly. I wish to inform them they will be an aunt and an uncle within the next six months.

Before he could respond, Selina stood and swept out of the room. She had taken only a few steps up the staircase to her sitting room when she heard him shout her name. She smiled to herself and continued up the stairs.

"Wait a minute! Wait just a minute!"

She stifled a giggle as she heard his footsteps approaching from behind. Selina was halfway up the stairs when she suddenly felt herself swept up into strong arms that held her close. His heart beat hard against her arm as he carried her to their bedchamber. They hadn't slept in separate rooms since he made her his wife in earnest several months ago.

Kicking the door shut with his foot, he gently set her down on the bed. Fitz stood before her, hands on his hips. "Now, tell me what you meant by your offhand comment."

Keeping a straight face, she said, "You are going to be a papa in about six months."

A chuckle began to rumble deep in his chest until it burst from his lips. "I'm going to be a papa!" Grabbing a hold of one of her hands, he lifted her to her feet and moved his other arm behind her back. He waltzed her around the room singing, "You are going to be a mama!" to the tune of a familiar waltz. "And I'm going to be a papa!"

His enthusiasm was contagious. They laughed as they danced together. Suddenly, he stopped and pulled her into his embrace. Fitz whispered softly, "Thank you, Lord. You have blessed me beyond anything I could ever have imagined!"

Selina snuggled close and added, "Me, too."

# *Glossary*

**Abigail** — A lady's personal maid

**Beau monde** — The world of high society and fashion

**Bird of Paradise** — A woman of easy virtue

**Blunt** — Money

**Bluestocking** — An academic female

**By-blow** — Illegitimate child

**Cit** — A contemptuous term for a member of the merchant class

**Coiffure** — Elaborate hairstyle

**Coming out** — A young lady's first entry into society; usually between 16 to 18 years of age; her parents determine if she is old enough and has enough accomplishments

**Constitutional** — A walk

**Courtesan** — A prostitute, especially one with wealthy or upper class clients

* * *

**Cut direct** — A deliberate and public snub

**Cut up my peace** — Disturb me

**Debutante** — An upper-class young woman making her first appearance in fashionable society

**Diamond of the first water** — An exceptionally beautiful young woman

**Disguised** — Vintage slang for drunk

**Deep pockets** — To have a lot of money or wealth

**Dun Territory** — Heavily in debt

**Fait accompli** — A thing that has already happened

**Flush in the pockets** — To be rich

**Gaming hell** — A gambling den

**Green girl** — Young, inexperienced girl

**Half-sprung** — Drunk

**Hauteur** — Haughtiness of manner; disdainful pride

**High ropes** — To be in a passion

**Joie de vivre** — Joy of living

**Jug-bitten** — Drunk

**Let** — Rent

**Light o' love** — Mistress

**Light-skirt** — A woman of easy virtue

* * *

**Missish** — Affectedly demure, squeamish, or sentimental

**Night-rail** — Night garment; a loose robe worn as a nightgown

**Parson's mousetrap** — To be married

**Peccadilloes** — Small, relatively unimportant offenses or sins

**Pelisse** — A coat with armholes or sleeves worn by ladies over their dresses

**Poppycock** — Nonsense

**Prinny** — King George IV; the Prince Regent

**Promissory note** — A signed document containing a written promise to pay a stated sum to a specified person or the bearer at a specified date or on demand

**Season** — The London Social Season in which the fashionable, social elite, and nobility dominate the city

**Ton** (pronounced tone) — High society; the elite

**Toplofty** — Haughty and arrogant

**Town** (always capitalize) — London

**Town bronze** — Polish or style

**Up to scratch** — Up to the mark; reaching an acceptable standard

**Valise** — A small traveling bag

**Vowels** — An IOU

* * *

**Wrong side of the blanket** — A child born out of wedlock

If you haven't read the first book in the
Arranged Marriage series,
turn the page for a sneak peek into the first two chapters.

ANNELIESE DALABA

## *Chapter One*

Sitting in her grandfather's traveling coach, Emma suddenly felt the impact of her decision. She watched the unfamiliar scenery through drops of rain slowly trickling down the window like the tears on her mother's cheeks as she waved good-bye. Was it only a little over a week ago? It seemed much longer. Emma's heart squeezed at the memory and she grieved the distance that was placed between herself and all that was familiar to her.

It wasn't that she hadn't considered the consequences of her choice before embarking on this journey, but once the decision was made, she'd been swept up in a whirlwind of preparations that gave her little time for contemplation. The voyage had been exciting at first. Emma had met several people and was fascinated by their stories. Her Uncle Gus, who was her mother's only brother, had traveled from England to accompany her on the voyage back to his homeland. He shared many stories of her mother's childhood, things Emma had never heard before.

They encountered a storm one night, which made for a turbulent few hours and caused her to miss the safety of her home. But the sun broke through the clouds at dawn and took with it the vestige of loneliness, soon replacing it with apprehension at seeing another ship off in the distance. Everyone speculated as to who might be aboard, from pirates to prisoners to soldiers to slaves. Fortunately, the ship never came near. They finally docked in London, and

Emma's eyes darted here and there trying to take in everything there was to see. Another ship must have docked before them as Emma observed people joyfully greeting each other. She saw rough-looking sailors unloading cargo off the ship. Over all the many voices, she heard the crashing of waves and seagulls flying overhead squawking and searching for food.

Her grandfather's traveling coach sat waiting for them at the dock, along with a horse for her uncle since he preferred riding even in drizzly rain to sitting for hours in an enclosed carriage. Emma sat alone, and she found herself facing the questions she'd pushed out of her mind for the past few days: What had she gotten herself into? Had she made the right decision? Would her grandfather be a kind man or a curmudgeon? She didn't even want to think about her soon-to-be husband. It was just too much to take in all at once.

Even the coach she traveled in gave clear evidence to the changes her decision had wrought. Emma hadn't known such luxury in all of her eighteen years. This was the life her father had turned his back on when he left all that was familiar to him in England and set sail for America more than twenty years ago. Forsaking his life of luxury, he chose to live in a cabin on a farm in Somerset, Pennsylvania. And now Emma, who'd been raised on that same farm, had chosen to live at Wooten House, in Fenbridge, England, the home of Baron Houlton, her grandfather, and the home where her father had grown up. Having finally completed her voyage over the Atlantic, she arrived in England that morning and, as she sat in her grandfather's coach, she knew she would now be privileged to enjoy the wealthy lifestyle her father had left behind. Would she come to regret the choice she made?

Her father had left England as a young man after marrying the local vicar's daughter, Mary, Emma's mother. Unfortunately, he died, leaving behind his wife and daughter to manage on their own. That was why her mother chose to marry again soon after losing her first husband. What had started as a marriage of convenience soon became a second chance to love and be loved. This gave Emma hope for the path she had now chosen for herself.

Her mother had made certain Emma clearly understood what had precipitated her father's departure from England. She didn't want her daughter having unrealistic expectations of what her reunion with her grandfather might entail. Emma's mother recalled the baron having a pleasing demeanor, but warned her he was a proud and unbending man who would not listen to reason if it was contrary to his plans. Emma understood her grandfather had clear plans laid out for her, but since she had agreed to do his bidding, she imagined he would welcome her with open arms in order to see his plans set in motion.

Now that she had convinced herself of her grandfather's warm, if not effusive, welcome, she lay her head on the cushion of the seat. The gentle rocking of the well-sprung carriage lulled her into slumber.

When she awoke to near darkness, the sun had set and the rain had ceased. Looking out the window, Emma saw lights flickering in the distance, soon realizing they were approaching a large estate. She bit her lower lip as her heart began to beat faster. Was her grandfather watching from one of the windows of the house?

As the horses drew near, she saw the front door of the house open and a man in uniform step out. Not her grandfather, obviously. She kept looking toward the door in case he appeared to greet her. The horses came to a complete stop in front of the house, but only the man in uniform stood there waiting. The door to the coach opened and Uncle Gus held his hand out ready to assist her.

"Are you ready to get out of that trap yet?" he asked with a twinkle in his eye. Although she had only met her uncle three months prior, in Pennsylvania, he was now familiar and dear to her. She would forever be grateful that Grandfather had sent Augustus Harrison, his solicitor and her uncle, to accompany her on the journey.

She gave him her hand as she smiled. "Oh, yes, indeed, Uncle. But at least I remained dry and slept a bit. How miserable it must have been for you sitting on the back of a horse in the drizzle. You should have joined me inside the carriage."

"I'm glad you were able to rest, my dear, but you need not concern yourself about me. Believe me when I tell you, I am much happier on the back of a horse, even in rain, than in a closed-in carriage for hours on end." He tucked her hand in the crook of his arm. "It's time for you to meet your grandfather. I imagine he is quite anxious to know you have arrived safely."

Emma took a deep breath for courage and nodded her head that she was ready. Together they walked up the stairs of the grand house.

The butler greeted them and Uncle Gus introduced him as Higgins. Higgins bowed politely and asked them to follow him to her grandfather's library where he was awaiting her arrival. Emma repeated the butler's name a few times in her mind, not wanting to forget it. When they arrived at the door, they were announced, and Higgins held the door for them to enter.

The first thing Emma's eyes landed on were the floor to ceiling shelves of books. She stared in wonder. She'd never seen so many books in one location, and they apparently all belonged to one man, her grandfather. Her jaw must have dropped a bit as she stood there in wide-eyed wonder. She absolutely loved reading and had read all the books at home over and over again. She couldn't imagine having such a vast selection in her own home. Emma sighed.

She heard a man clear his throat and quickly turned her head. Oh! Had he seen her gawking at all his books? Of course he had. He must think her quite simple-minded and backward. What a terrible first impression she must have just made.

There stood an elegantly dressed, older gentleman sporting a full head of white hair with a bit of a receding hairline. He stood tall and straight in suit coat, crisp white shirt, vest, neckcloth, and pantaloons, with a gold watch on a chain in his hand. His eyes were not quite stern, but neither were they smiling. He looked her over from head to foot and Emma was afraid he didn't like what he saw. She couldn't blame him. She felt travel worn and knew her attire must be wrinkled. But as she looked into his eyes, they seemed to brighten a bit and he almost smiled. "I see your face is quite lovely."

Emma didn't know what to say. She didn't really think he was complimenting her as much as looking her over as she often saw her stepfather do when looking over one of his farm animals. She saw him nod his head a couple of times. "Yes, with a little polish, you will do nicely."

No warm embrace was offered. She watched as this stranger, her grandfather, walked closer. He stopped about five feet in front of Emma and looked at her intently. She felt like fidgeting, but forced herself to hold still.

"So you are my son's daughter."

Emma swallowed and nodded her head. "Yes, sir."

"I hope your journey was uneventful and you didn't suffer any ill effects?"

"I enjoyed the voyage, sir, except for the storm we encountered, but I remained in excellent health throughout. Thank you for asking."

"Well, I'm glad you arrived safely."

"Thank you for sending my uncle to accompany me on this trip. It was really quite thoughtful of you. And my mother enjoyed seeing her brother after all these years."

At the mention of her uncle, her grandfather looked at the man as though he had quite forgotten his presence. He looked back at Emma, cleared his throat and huffed, "Well, now, no need to thank me. It was the right thing to do. Cannot have my granddaughter accompanied by just anyone."

Having said that, he turned to Uncle Gus, "I appreciate how well you handled everything. We can talk further tomorrow, but right now I'd like to spend some time with my granddaughter. I'm sure you desire to return home after so many weeks away."

Uncle Gus gave a slight nod, but looked at Emma with concern.

Was Uncle Gus reluctant to leave her alone with her grandfather? Wanting to reassure him, she walked to her uncle's side and placed a hand on his arm as she raised her heels off the floor to place a kiss on his rough cheek. "Thank you, Uncle, for all you did for me. I cannot imagine having faired as well or enjoyed myself as much without you by my side."

He patted her arm and smiled gently. "I'll see you tomorrow, my dear."

"Yes, but get some rest first," her grandfather cut in gruffly. "I'll see you tomorrow afternoon. That will be early enough to resume our business." Then he walked to the door and held it open.

Emma watched as Uncle Gus walked toward the door, suddenly feeling as though her one remaining friend in the world was walking away. He looked back one more time when he reached the door, bid her and the baron goodnight, then turned and walked out.

Emma swallowed the lump in her throat. Reminding herself she had agreed to her grandfather's plan, now it was time to follow through with her commitment. She took a deep breath and pulled her shoulders back. Lifting her chin, she turned away from the door and looked at her grandfather who had walked back into the room shutting the door behind him. He smiled a bit haughtily and held out his hand. She placed her hand in his and he led her to a chair in front of the fireplace. "Sit here, Emma, and I will order tea and some refreshments. You must be famished after such a long trip in the carriage. We can talk while you enjoy some sustenance."

Emma was actually quite hungry. They had stopped at an inn to change horses about four hours ago. The food had been only passably good, so she hadn't eaten much. Wanting to avoid long travel in the dark, they had pressed on without stopping again in order to finally end their journey. Now she felt almost ravenous, but with her formidable grandfather watching her, she wasn't sure she could swallow a bite.

Emma sat back in her chair and felt the warmth of the fireplace seep into her body. It reminded her of home and the many evenings her family sat around the fireplace after all their chores were done.

In the meantime, her grandfather walked over to the bell

pull, then returned to his chair opposite her. He surprised her when he asked, "How is your mother doing?" She hadn't expected him to mention the woman his son had loved and eloped with, turning his back on his family.

"My mother is doing well. Thank you for asking. She and papa had been concerned about losing the farm, of course, but your generous gift helped to relieve them of that burden."

"I'm glad it helped," was his clipped answer. Placing his elbow on the armrest of the chair and cupping his chin with his hand, he looked into the flames. For a moment he seemed far away. Perhaps wondering what could have been if he had welcomed Emma's mother into his family instead of insisting on having everything his way. Or perhaps he was thinking how different things would have turned out if only his son had obeyed his wishes and married the woman he had chosen for him.

At that moment, the doors opened and a maid entered the room carrying a tea tray. She placed it on the table. Grandfather looked at Emma expectantly. It took Emma only a moment to realize he wanted her to serve them. "I'll pour the tea," she announced, and quickly stood to her feet and walked over to the tea table.

"Would you like a sandwich, too, Grandfather?"

"No, thank you. The tea will do for me."

After pouring tea into a cup, Emma placed a cube of sugar on the saucer along with a spoon and handed it to her grandfather. He nodded his head. She returned to the table and poured tea for herself. She chose a sandwich, then walked back to her chair and sat down.

Grandfather cleared his throat and began to speak. "Emma, I want to begin setting my plans in motion, but first I will need to make a lady out of you."

Emma almost choked on the bite she'd taken. She looked at the baron in confusion and quickly took a sip from her tea to help swallow the food. "What do you mean, Grandfather?"

"You are quite lovely, so don't take offense, but you will now enter a very different world than you were accustomed to in the past. You no longer live on a farm out in the middle of nowhere. There are things that are expected of a lady in the peerage of England. You will need to learn how to walk, talk, and dress in a proper manner."

Emma knew what her grandfather was saying was true, but somehow it hurt that in their brief acquaintance her grandfather had decided she didn't quite measure up. Uncle Gus hadn't treated her as though there was anything wrong with her appearance. He hadn't seemed embarrassed traveling with her. On the other hand, she hadn't been in London very long before being swept into her grandfather's coach. Perhaps he, too, didn't care to be seen with her in her current state of dress. Emma knew her hackles were up, and she felt defensive. She had to be fair to her uncle. They had been in a hurry to leave London, because they were expected to arrive in Fenbridge by evening.

It didn't really matter how she felt about her grandfather's opinion of her. She had agreed to his plan to help her parents, so she must now be willing to swallow her pride and accept the consequences.

She heard her grandfather continue, "We will start with the maid I have provided for you. Her name is Bessie and she will attend to your wardrobe. She is also well-versed in a lady's toilet, how a lady must comport herself, and how she must dress for every occasion. She's older than you by a few years and more experienced, but young enough that, I think, you will get along quite well together. But, Emma, although I want you to learn from her, you must remember that she is your servant and she must follow your instructions. Never confide too much to your servants unless you care to be the topic of conversation below stairs and have that information passed along to the neighboring estate."

"Yes, Grandfather," was her obligatory response, but her mind had wrapped itself around one fact only. She, Emma, from a small farm in Somerset, Pennsylvania, would now have her own personal maid? She couldn't imagine needing a servant to help her with the things she'd done for herself all her life. Would her maid make her bed for her? That wouldn't take all day. What could her maid possibly find to do to occupy her time?

Grandfather had gotten up and walked to his desk, returning with an envelope in his hand. Before he could say anything, she quickly asked, "Grandfather, what does a lady's maid do?" At his look of confusion, she clarified. "How does she occupy herself?"

"Why, she does a number of things. She straightens your room, prepares your bath, washes your hair, chooses your clothes, helps you dress, mends your clothes, and makes certain they are clean. She styles your hair. She does countless things most ladies take for granted. When you leave the house, she will accompany you so you are chaperoned."

"I don't think my maid will have much to do, for I do most of those things for myself."

Grandfather slowly shook his head back and forth, "No more, Emma. You are now a lady and you will not be able to do the things you were used to doing. I see your look of confusion, but you will see what I mean. I have hired a woman to teach you about all these things. You will learn about the peerage and how to address each person in the nobility correctly."

He handed her the envelope he'd been holding and explained, "You will also receive a small allowance each month. You must try not to spend beyond this amount. If you need more, please come and see me, but this will hopefully suffice."

"Grandfather, I don't feel right receiving an allowance from you. Perhaps I can do some chores and earn the money instead.

"Earn the money? Do chores?" He chuckled disbelievingly and shook his head. "Absolutely not! That's unheard of! My girl, you will accept this allowance and that's the end of it. When you are married, your husband will also give you an allowance. I will make certain it is generous, and he will expect you to budget well. Although, of course, there are times you will need more and must not hesitate to ask for it."

Emma listened intently, trying to understand what was

expected of her. Apparently, doing chores was unheard of. At her grandfather's shocked reaction, one would think she had offered to do something immoral.

Her grandfather was still talking, so she pulled her thoughts back to attend his words. "I realize you may always sound like you were born in America. There may not be much help for that, but we must help you learn the proper way of addressing people in various stations of life. You will understand better what I mean when Mrs. Stanley arrives in two days. We must teach you to behave in such a manner that no one will suspect you lived on a farm in the middle of nowhere."

Emma couldn't contain the words. They were out before she could stop herself. "I'm actually quite proud of my farm out in the middle of nowhere, Grandfather. It was a wonderful place to grow up, and I hope I will not be forbidden to talk about the place that is most dear to my heart."

"Calm yourself, Emma," her grandfather commanded. "You may still love that place if you so please, but you agreed to this plan. You accepted the money I gave your parents to save their farm and, in the process, you committed yourself to helping in the future of my estate. You must now trust me, abide by my rules, and allow me to lead you in this."

"Are you saying I cannot tell anyone where I come from?"

"Of course that's not what I'm saying. As soon as you open your mouth to speak, it will be quite apparent you're not from here. However, you must not speak about it as though you wish you were still there. Everyone in the ton knows that England is a far superior country, so there is no use pining about your home as though you had left something precious behind." He held up his hand when Emma opened her mouth to retort. "Yes, yes, your family will always be precious to you, but you don't have to dwell on this when becoming acquainted with people in the ton. You will soon have a new wardrobe and the most illustrious entertainments to attend. And before long, you will even become a countess! How can anything you left behind even compare to that?"

Emma realized wealth and prestige meant more to her grandfather than family. She sighed sadly, "Yes, grandfather. I will do as you say."

"Good girl!" He leaned over and patted her knee. "With that attitude, you will do quite well, my dear."

Emma simply gave a small nod of her head. She had agreed to this plan and had even prayed about it. She felt certain this was the path she needed to take to help her parents and to help her grandfather. She would allow herself to be led by him.

They talked of her voyage and the rest of her travels as she finished her meal. As she suspected, she wasn't able to eat much. Not because she felt nervous, but rather because she felt upset about all the changes she would have to make. It wasn't that she was set in her ways. She actually enjoyed experiencing new things. It was just the more her grandfather belittled her past, the more her heart longed to cling to it.

Grandfather got to his feet and Emma quickly followed suit. "I'll ring for Bessie now. She will show you to your room and provide what you need."

## *Chapter Two*

Wiping sweat from his brow with the sleeve of his shirt, Colin Beauford, the Earl of Devonport, or Devon to his friends, was enjoying his afternoon at Gentleman Jackson's. He looked over at his fencing opponent and long-time friend, Viscount Hugh FitzWalter, who was panting as hard as he was. They were equally matched and enjoyed fencing whenever they found the time.

"Fitz, I'm worn out." Devon said. "We need to end it here. I have an appointment with Lord Houlton's solicitor in two hours, and I must make haste."

"Don't tell me you're going through with marrying this buck-toothed, frizzy-haired, mannerless provincial from the colonies!"

Devon laughed out loud. "Surely she can't be all that bad."

"Why else do you think she would leave her family and all that's familiar to her? Trust me, she was unable to make a match of it back home."

"My guess is her family needs the money. Either that or she's looking for prestige."

"I thought Americans don't lay much value on class distinctions. I doubt prestige will matter much to your wife. Mark my words, she will be a mannerless hoyden."

"It's most probable her family is in desperate straits and they are selling her off to Lord Houlton. Regardless, my father's will has removed all options. I will marry the girl and be done with it. If she's impossible, I'll leave her in the country and not bring her to Town until she learns to conduct herself properly."

"For your sake, I hope she'll be willing to learn."

Devon had the same fears, but tried to squelch such thoughts. He was obligated to follow through with his father's agreement with Lord Houlton. It wasn't as though he had another choice.

Seeing the concern on his friend's face, Fitz said, "You know very well it was your father's intention you marry the baron's older granddaughter, the lovely Catherine. When she eloped, you should've been free of all obligation."

"For whatever reason, my father didn't name Lady Catherine specifically in his will as my promised bride. The will only stated I must marry Lord Houlton's granddaughter if I wish to inherit the unentailed properties of my father's estate. I must do so, for I have much to lose if I don't fulfill the requirement of the will, and I have much to gain if I do. However, there's more to it than that. I could afford to let that property go, but I cannot allow my father's honor to come into question. He didn't push me to marry Lady Catherine when she turned 18. He allowed me to wait and enjoy being a bachelor a couple years more. I cannot let him down now."

Fitz breathed in deeply through his nose, and exhaled with a huff. "I guess that's it then. You'll marry this stranger and be tied to her for the rest of your days. I don't envy you, my friend, but I will give you my word here and now. I will stand by your side and help distract you and ease your burden to the best of my ability."

Smiling at his friend, Devon placed his hand on Fitz's shoulder and said, "I'll hold you to it."

They continued walking to their horses. Devon mounted his stallion, Sampson.

"Will you join me at White's tonight?" Devon asked.

"I'll be there. I'm anxious to hear how your meeting with the solicitor went and how long before you have a harridan of a wife to contend with."

"Perhaps I will be one of the lucky ones," Devon

countered. "There is the possibility she will be sweet and unspoiled, and even beautiful."

Fitz snorted a laugh. "A very small possibility, I'm sure. After all, why would such a perfect female be willing to travel across the ocean to marry a stranger?" Quirking the corner of his mouth, Fitz continued. "It's best you prepare yourself for the worst. Hopefully, she will at least be tolerable to some degree. Doubtful, but you can hope."

Dismissing Fitz's comment with a wave of his hand, Devon stated, "Be that as it may, I have a duty to my father and my estate. No matter how distasteful, I must comply." With a quick wave to Fitz, he turned in the opposite direction toward his home on Shaftesbury Avenue. Stopping in front of his residence, he dismounted. He handed the reins to his groom and hurried up the steps and into the house where his butler, Barkley, stood holding the door open. Tossing his hat to Barkley, he raced up the stairs to his room to prepare for his appointment.

Devon managed to complete his toilette with time to spare, so he decided to sit at his desk and look through his mail. Once seated, instead of looking at the stack of envelopes, he leaned back in his chair, folded his hands over his abdomen, and continued to ponder the conversation he'd had with Fitz that afternoon.

Devon shook his head slightly thinking of Fitz's prediction. Certainly he was wrong. He desperately hoped the baron's granddaughter from America wasn't a harridan or mannerless with buck teeth and frizzy hair.

These thoughts drove Devon to his feet as he began pacing around his office. He'd observed how beleaguered his acquaintances were who had already been caught in the parson's mousetrap. Those poor fellows left early from their clubs most evenings, saying "Yes, dear" to their wives in that tolerant manner. They gave them generous allowances so the women could spend money mostly on frivolous items, never considering the needs of their estates. To his way of thinking, a wife was simply necessary to breed a son and provide an heir.

Devon stopped his pacing in front of the fireplace. He

looked up at the portrait of his father and mother. The portrait had been painted when Devon was still a small lad. His parents' arranged marriage had never been a happy one, and had only deteriorated further as the years dragged on. His mother had been 34 years younger than his father, who had married at the age of 55. His father had never felt the necessity to marry since he was a second son and not the heir, but when his older brother died while racing his carriage, leaving no progeny, the title went to Devon's father. He knew he must do his duty since his brother had failed in this matter, so he allowed a friend of the family to arrange a match for him. Once he married the 21-year-old daughter of a viscount, his father soon realized they had nothing in common. Looking at the portrait, Devon's heart despaired for his future.

Devon checked his watch and saw he must make haste or he would be late. He rang for a footman to send word to the stable to have his horse brought around. Having informed Barkley of his intention to stay out late and not to bother with supper for him, he departed the house.

For information about when my next novel will be released as well as recommendations about other good books to read and so much more, visit my website at www.anneliesedalaba.com and sign up for my newsletter.

Check out my blog. I'd love to interact with you, so feel free to leave comments.

CPSIA information can be obtained
at www.ICGtesting.com
Printed in the USA
LVHW011949300820
664591LV00008B/1231

9 781730 763922